Heirs

Of

Darkness

E.J. LINDELL

E.J. is a Metis indie author, living in the bush in Eastern Manitoba, Canada with her partner and children, a couple dozen chickens and 4 fur babies. She adores escaping into a book and creating her own adventures.

She is the author of *The Soulbinding Chronicles*, a five-book bestselling dark fantasy romance series set years before *Heirs of Darkness*.

Want to be a part of the adventures? Follow EJ's book group; *EJ's Fantasy Darlings* on Facebook to talk all things books and more.

Follow her socials! She can be found under the handle **EJ Lindell Author** on FB, Instagram, threads and Tik Tok. EJ always has time for readers. Send her a message; she'd love to hear from you!

E.J.'s Fantasy Darlings club

Paperback: ISBN 978-1-0690509-1-5

eBook ISBN 978-1-0690509-2-2

Cover by E.J. Lindell created in Canva

Illustration by Gabriela Birchal

Map created by Inkarnate

Interior formatting by WritersEmporiumCo Etsy Shop

Published by Mossy Birch Publishing

For anyone who has ever been made to feel like they weren't enough, like
their voice didn't matter, or their dreams were too big for their reach...
this is for you.

Remember the fire that flickers within you. It's wild, untamed, and no
one has the power to extinguish it but you.

You were made from the stars.

Be a supernova.

THIS BOOK HAS DIFFERENT ASPECTS OF FOLKLORE AND TRADITIONS INTERTWINED INTO IT.

You will see references to some of them which I have detailed below.

BAOBHAN SITH

The Baobhan Sith are shapeshifters who can glamour, take the form of a wolf, and even take the form of a raven or hooded crow. It is rare to see a lone Baobhan Sith as they prefer to hunt in packs. They love to dance and use this to seduce men, their main prey.

They tend only to appear when the men hunting make a wish for female company, tying into the Scottish superstition that if you make a wish at night without asking God's protection it will be granted in some horrifying way.

Should you ever encounter a Baobhan Sith then you simply need to find iron to ward them off because, like most fairies, they are vulnerable to it. Interestingly, this means they also tend to not be fond of horses as they are often shod in iron. In this book, the Baobhan Sith Queen is accustomed to light for the purpose of the storyline.

STIKINI

The Stikini is a creature with origins in the Native American mythology, legend and folklore. In particular, accounts of its existence first arise within the mythology, legend and folklore of the North American Seminole tribes.

A Stikini resembles an avian humanoid; in particular, it resembles a strigiform humanoid (a humanoid owl), not unlike legends of the creature called the Owl Man. Some even claim the creature is impossible to tell apart from a regular owl.

Though, it should be known, neither the owl form nor the humanoid owl is the entirety of the Stikini's being. Rather, this is simply a supernatural manifestation of the Stikini's spiritual nature, when its powers are in effect. Before it makes use of its supernatural abilities to manifest an owl exterior, the Stikini is otherwise indistinguishable from an ordinary human. In this book, they are not evil; they are protectors of their covens and protectors of the woods.

LAYING DOWN OFFERINGS FOR THE USE OF MAGICK

In many Indigenous cultures, when taking from the land, offerings like tobacco, prayers, or a small portion of the harvested item are commonly given as a way to show respect and gratitude to the land and its spirits, demonstrating a principle of reciprocity where people acknowledge the land as a giver and not just a resource to be exploited; this practice often includes verbal expressions of thanks and requests for continued provision. In this book, you will see many instances of the users of magick laying down bundles and saying a prayer.

SIGN LANGUAGE

As a severely hard of hearing author, we use some sign language in our home; adding in an elite army of deaf elves was a way to include my disability in the book.

THIS BOOK CONTAINS DEPICTIONS OF:

Graphic battles
Scenes of conversation of not being able to conceive/barren
Pregnancy & childbirth (no miscarriages)
Graphic consensual sexual scenes
Domestic abuse
Flashbacks of various forms of abuse (alluded rape, forced confinement
etc.)
Kidnapping
Graphic death scenes
And some other darker themes.

Please check your triggers and take care of your mental health.
xo

RÉIMSE AN TSOLAS
TÍR AN UISCE
LOCRYA
ISTSHORE

Clan of
Clan of Mystics
The Night Realm
Estia
The Silver Lands
Clan Empereal
Willowgreen
Blackwood
Vascar
Docren
Clan Aether
The Whisperwoods
Asthemar
Clan Tempestus
Tir Siorghlas
Clan Bayle
Efrana
Oblor
Prathuro
Riverstone Keep
Bloodrose
Castle

LOCATIONS

Réimse an Tsolas- The Realm of Light
Tir Siorghlas- The Evergreen Land
The Silver Lands- Where the Clan of Mystics resides
Castle Dewmire, located in Asthemar- Clan Tempestus
Castle Greywood, located in Estia- Clan Empereal
Castle Leyebourne, located in Oblor- Clan Bayle
Castle Stowerling, located in Ochor- Clan Basalt
Castle Elden, located in Vascar- Clan Aether
Docren- city in Blackwood Lands
Efrana- city in Bloodrose Lands
Prautho- city in Stonecastle Lands
Whisperwoods- Where the Silverbark Coven resided years ago
Tenebris, The Night Realm- under the mountains in the Silver Lands
Tír an Uisce- Land of Water
Locrya- Island to the cast of Tir Siorghlas
Mistshore- city in Locrya

Family Tree
Clan Tempestus

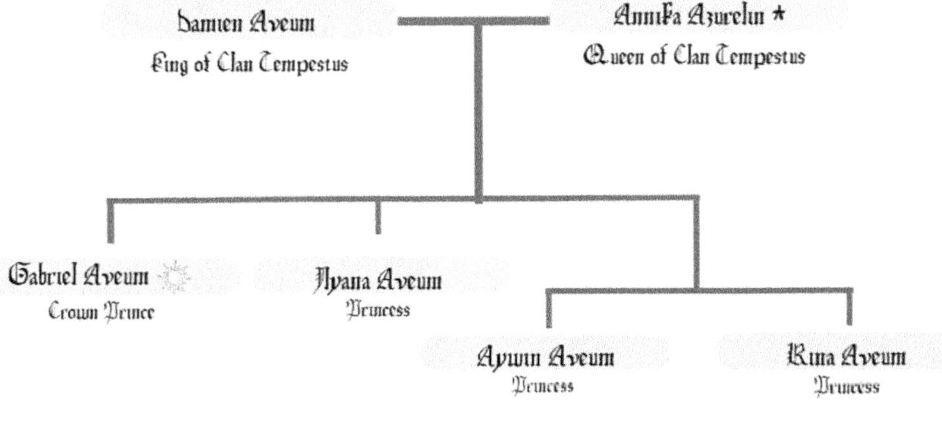

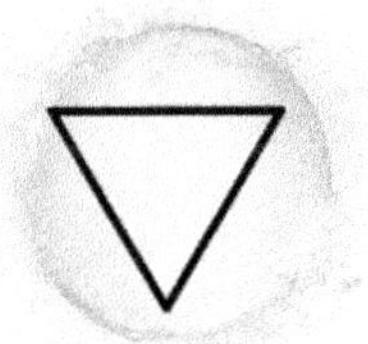

Family Tree
Clan Bayle

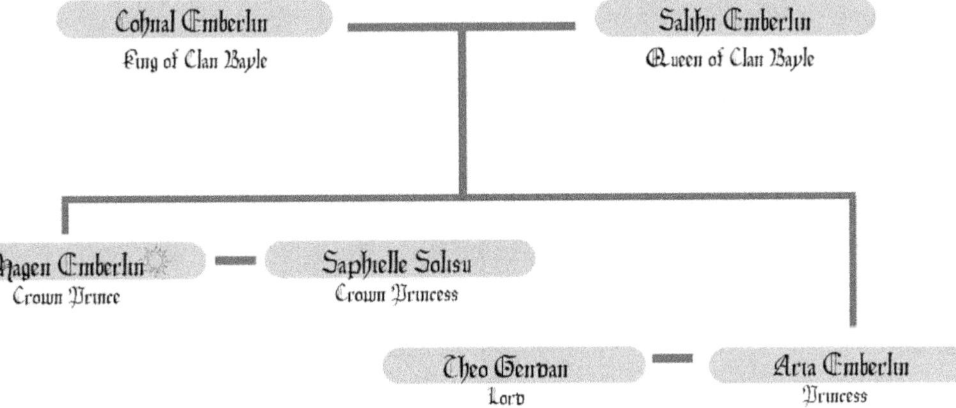

Family Tree
Clan Basalt

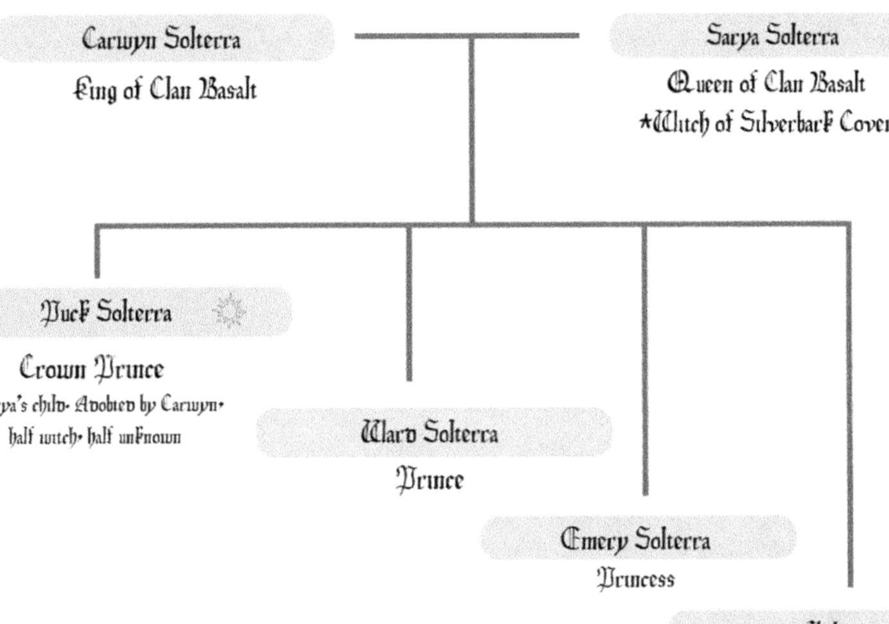

Family Tree
Clan Aether

Ostan Aveum
King of Clan Aether

Damien Aveum
*Brother; see clan Tempestus

Amodra
Queen of Clan Basalt
*of Baobhan Sith Blood

Orin Aveum
Crown Prince
*half elf - half unknown

The Night Realm

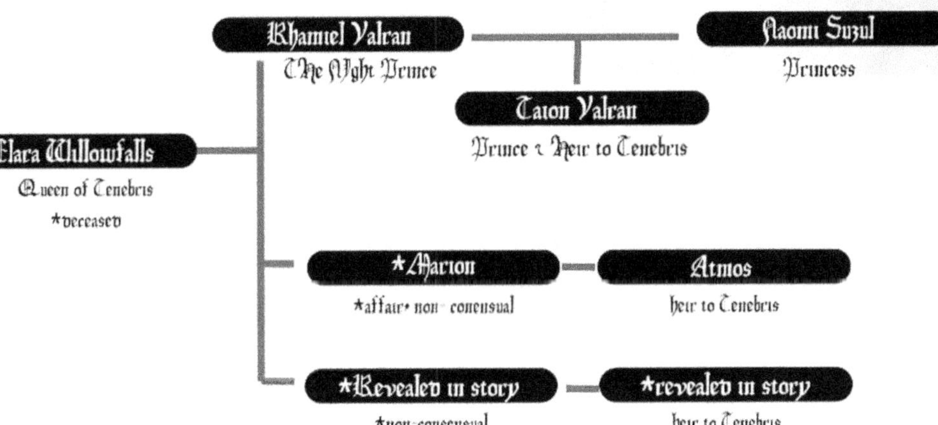

CHARACTERS

Clan Tempestus
Annika Aveum (Azurelin)- Queen
Damien Aveum- King
Ilyana Aveum- Princess
Gabriel Aveum- Crown Prince
Aywin Aveum- Princess
Rina Aveum- Princess
Maelyrra- General

Clan Aether
Osian Aveum- King
Amodra Aveum- Queen
Orin Aveum- Crown Prince
Solana- Osian's General

Clan Empereal
Silvan Galestrum- King of Clan Empearal
Alyndria Báistí- Queen of Clan Empereal
Ashryn- General

Clan Basalt
Carwyn Solterra- King
Sarya Solterra- Queen
Puck Solterra- Crown Prince
Ward Solterra- Prince
Emery Solterra- Princess

Clan Bayle
Hagen Emberlin- Prince of Clan Bayle
Saphielle Solisu- Princess of Clan Bayle
King Cohnal + Queen Salihn Emberlin- Hagen's parents
Aira Emberlin- Princess and sister to Hagen
Theo- Aira's husband

Riverstone
Prince Callum Azurelin- Annika's younger brother, Lord of Riverstone
Morena- Wife to Callum Azurelin, Lady of Riverstone

The Mid-lands of Tir Siorghlas
Lera- wood elf
Aurae- wood elf, Lera's friend

The Silver Lands
Gaeleath Solterra- Carwyn's brother
Magnolia- wife of Gaeleath, witch of the Circle of Mystics
Piper- daughter of Gaeleath + Magnolia

Tir an Uisce
Kilyn Báistí- Alyndria's brother
Taeral + Tawny Báistí- Parents to Alyndria + Kilyn

Locrya
Nyana- half elf, half merfolk. Daughter of a rich merchant

The Night Realm; Tenebris
Lady Elara Willowfalls- (deceased, was the Queen of Tenebris)
Rhamiel Valran- The Night Prince, dark Nephilim
Naomi Valran- The Night Princess, light Nephilim
Atmos –Nephilim warrior, spy for Tir Siorghlas
Ephyra- spy for Tir Siorghlas
Miriam- Atmos' mother

TERMS:

Gaelic:

A mhuirnin: my darling (uh WUR neen)
Mo Chuisle mo Chroí: my pulse, my heart (Moh cooish-lah moh kree)
A stor: my dear (A-stoR)
A rúnsearc: secret love, beloved/soulmate (uh ROON-shark)
Faugh a ballagh- Clear the way (faw-khuh-BAL-uhkh)
mo ghràidh (moh grah)- my dear
Mo ghaol (mo gale)- my love

Elvish:

lá caritas, navin, alasaila ná: not doing this would be (I think) unwise (la
car-E-tas na-VIN, ALA-sail-a na)
Euchia (u chIA) Open
Avalyta (ava-lita) Close
Amil- (A-mil) Father
Amille- (A-mill-ie) Mother
Seldo- (sel-DO) son
Selye- (sel-YE) daughter
Selda- (sel-da) children
Hina- (hE-na) child
Melda- (m-eld-a) dear
Elentári- (Elen-t-A-ri) Queen
Eldatár- (Eld-A-tar) King
Hano- (ha-NO) brother
nésa-(nE-sa) sister
wembë- (wem-b) worm
quendë- (ken-d) elf
Melethel- (mel-ET-hel) darling, sweetheart

Prologue

Years before the start of our story....

Rhamiel, the newly crowned Night Prince, paced the hallway, his footsteps echoing with a heavy thud, almost creating a rut in the polished stone floor, his black wings flexing behind him. Inside the Queen's birthing chambers, the sounds of hushed conversation, soft moans, and the occasional muffled cry reached his ears.

He'd stop pacing at each sound, his heart hammering against his ribs, waiting for the door to swing open, for a glimpse of Naomi, for the first cry of his child.

Hours had passed since Naomi had been taken to the birthing chambers. Hours of agonizing anticipation, of pacing, of whispering prayers to the old gods and goddesses. This child, their child, was the culmination of years of longing, of duty.

Naomi had been an arranged marriage, a political alliance forged between his family, the House of Twilight, and the powerful White Nephilim dynasty across the Silver Lands. Their kind of Nephilim were coveted, sought after for their flawless lineage, their wings a dazzling, pristine white. His parents, eager to secure their family line, had pushed this union, viewing Naomi as a prize, a trophy wife to solidify their power.

But Rhamiel had seen beyond the political maneuvering, beyond the expectations that the crown held. He had met Naomi, with her soft pale hair and iridescent eyes of blues and purples that held the depths of a thousand stars, and fallen utterly head over heels in love. Their marriage, though initially a contract, had blossomed into a genuine, passionate love. And now, the culmination of that love, their child, was being born.

Rhamiel stopped pacing, his ears straining for any sound. Then, it came. A soft, mewling cry, followed by a gentle cooing sound. A wave of relief washed over him, so intense it almost brought him to his knees.

The door to the birthing chambers creaked open, and a midwife emerged, her face beaming. "My Prince," she said, her voice filled with joy, "it's a boy. A strong, healthy boy."

Rhamiel felt a surge of overwhelming love. He wanted to rush in, to see his son, to hold him in his arms. But then, the midwife's smile faltered slightly. "There is... a peculiarity, my Lord," she said hesitantly.

Rhamiel's heart plummeted. "What is it?" he demanded, his voice tight with apprehension.

The midwife hesitated, then said, "The child... his wings... they are not white, my Lord. They are grey."

Rhamiel felt a small wave of sadness. Grey wings. In their society, grey wings were considered an aberration, a sign of weakness, a blemish on an otherwise perfect lineage.

The midwife, sensing his unease, quickly added, "But he is strong, my Lord. And his mother, oh, she is overjoyed."

Rhamiel closed his eyes, trying to reconcile the news. Grey wings. It was unexpected, certainly, but it didn't change the fact that he was a father. He had a son. His son.

He took a deep breath, a shaky exhale. "Let me go to them," he said, his voice firm. He would protect him, cherish him, and show the world that he was the heir to the throne of Tenebris, of the Night Court and a Night Prince.

As he held his son in his arms, his heart overflowing with a love he never knew existed, he knew this child, with his unexpected grey wings, would be the greatest joy of his life.

He cradled his son close. The baby, still drowsy from the ordeal of birth, stirred slightly, his tiny hand reaching out and grasping Rhamiel's finger.

Tears welled up in Rhamiel's eyes. He had never imagined a love this profound, this all-consuming. He looked at Naomi, who was gazing at their son with a mixture of awe and tenderness. Her face, pale from childbirth, was radiant with joy.

He leaned over and kissed her forehead, his lips lingering on her skin. "He's perfect," he whispered, his voice thick with emotion.

Naomi smiled, a tear escaping her eye. "He's ours," she murmured, her voice soft as a sigh.

Rhamiel gently slid into the bed beside her, pulling the covers over them. He carefully nestled their son between them, his tiny body warm against their skin. As he held his son, he thought about how complete his life was now.

All that mattered was this moment, this precious connection between them, this tiny miracle cradled in their arms. He closed his eyes, the sound of their son's soft breathing a lullaby.

In this moment, surrounded by the love of his wife and the warmth of his child, Rhamiel knew that he couldn't ask for more from the gods. He fell asleep, a contented sigh escaping his lips, the world fading away.

5 years later

His footsteps echoed through the grand halls of the Night Castle. Rhamiel, his broad shoulders swaying as they moved with the weight of his wings on his back, strolled along, his five-year-old son perched on his hip. Their son, a whirlwind of energy, giggled with delight as his father swung him around, his tiny legs kicking out with glee.

Finally, Rhamiel sat him down, the boy immediately launching himself towards a nearby tapestry, his small hands reaching out to touch the vibrant threads. Rhamiel chuckled, his hand finding his son's, their fingers intertwining. He looked up at the tapestry, a depiction of his parents sitting on the Night throne.

They walked towards the sitting room, the sound of their footsteps a gentle rhythm in the otherwise quiet castle. As they approached, Naomi was sitting on the window seat, her gaze drawn to the sprawling city of Tenebris below. A serene smile played on her lips, her pale hair catching the light streaming through the window.

Their son, upon spotting his mother, let out a joyful squeal and broke free from Rhamiel's grasp, running towards her as his wings flapped behind him. Naomi scooped him up, her laughter mingling with his.

"Look, little one," she said, pointing towards the city which was bustling with light, merchants setting up tables and a band warming up next to a dancing space. The decorations could be seen from the castle, "Melethel! See all those lights? Oh!" she gasped, "Is it not beautiful, all the decorations and music? They are celebrating the goddesses Aine and Macha today."

The boy, captivated by the twinkling lights, pointed excitedly towards the ceiling of the mountain, their sky. "Stars!" he exclaimed, his voice filled with wonder.

Naomi chuckled. "Yes, my little stargazer," she said, "Those are the lights that shine for us, millions of light bugs that the goddesses have blessed us with."

Rhamiel stood in the doorway, watching the two of them, his heart overflowing with a warmth he never thought possible. This was his life now, filled with the laughter of his son, the love of his wife, and the quiet contentment of a life well-lived.

He had never envisioned himself as a father, never imagined settling down in the castle, fulfilling the expectations of his family. But looking at them, his heart felt full. He had found happiness not in the pursuit of power or glory, but in the simple joys of family, in the quiet moments of love and laughter.

He smiled, a genuine, heartfelt smile, and stepped into the room. "Shall we join the festivities, mo ghaol? It's the Summer Solstice, we should pay respect to the goddesses for their gifts." he asked, his voice gentle.

Naomi turned to him, her eyes sparkling. "We shall," she replied, a mischievous glint in her eyes. "But first," she added, holding their son out to him, "I believe it's time for a little story."

Rhamiel took his son from Naomi's arms, his heart light as a feather. As he settled into a chair beside his wife, he looked over at the sidebar where their last dragon egg sat, nestled in a bed of straw inside a crate. Its blue-gold scales capturing the flickering light in the room. One day, that egg would pass down to his son and perhaps hatch.

He turned back to his family as Naomi handed him a small storybook that their son loved, "The Littlest Dragon and the Lost Star."

Their son squealed with delight, his iridescent purple and blue eyes dancing as he hugged himself with excitement as Rhamiel chucked, turning the page, "There once was a small green dragon named Swiftfly who lived under the mountain with his amil and amille…"

Later that evening, the city of Tenebris under the mountain erupted in a vibrant celebration of the Summer Solstice. The streets were ablaze with lights, the air thick with the scent of roasting meats and sweet summer wine. Music filled the air; fiddles, lutes and harpsichords played along as the partygoers danced.

Rhamiel, Naomi, and their son joined the revelry, their laughter mingling with the joyous din of the crowd, their guard detail not far behind, ensuring the safety of the Royal family. The young child, mesmerized by the fire dancers and the acrobats, tugged at his father's hand, his eyes wide with wonder. They stopped and talked to the merchants selling their wares, Rhamiel finding Naomi a beautiful necklace and their son a small wooden dragon.

Their people smiled and bowed as they walked through Tenebris; welcomed and loved. Naomi and Rhamiel took a moment to dance to the music while their son was held by one of their guards, his eyes filled with wonder as he watched his mother and father move to the music.

As the night wore on, exhaustion finally caught up with the little family. Rhamiel and Naomi stopped at the statues of Aine and Macha, laying their offering of flowers and honey amongst the others. Rhamiel carried their son back to the castle, the boy already fast asleep in his arms, his wings flopping by his sides.

They walked down the hall, Naomi's arm threaded through his. As they walked towards the royal chambers, Naomi whispered, "Let him sleep with us tonight, he will only be this little for such a short time."

Rhamiel smiled and turned towards their rooms, "Perhaps we should give him siblings, mo ghaol?" Naomi smiled back at him and gently cupped his face in her hands, "I would never say no, not when we made the most perfect one."

She turned and walked over to her armoire, her maid quietly appearing to help her undress. She tucked her white wings in as the maid helped her into her nightgown, and she thanked her. The maid bowed and left the room. Rhamiel pulled off their son's shoes and unbuttoned his shirt, carefully pulling his arms and wings around the fabric.

The little boy sighed and fussed as Rhamiel laid him in the bed, Naomi crawling in to pull their son close to her. He tucked them in, watching as Naomi gently stroked their child's dark hair. A profound sense of peace washed over him at the sight of them nestled together. He wanted to give her more children to fill their bed and their home with laughter and love.

Leaving them to sleep, Rhamiel walked along the wide corridors, his footsteps echoing in time to the distant music drifting up from the city. He walked along the hallway, passing by the throne room and the front doors towards the east of the castle. The open air of the hallway with its multiple terraces created a feeling of being outside, which was essential for his kind.

He paused and looked down at his city; he carried full responsibility for this beautiful place. His latest discussions with the Kings of Tir Siorghlas would hopefully create more trade opportunities for his people; the mountain produced more than enough precious gems to trade with.

He turned and continued walking, two guards quietly following now as he stepped down the stairs into the dungeon; he always checked to ensure he was kept abreast of the prisoners once his family was asleep. As he walked the dungeon, a chilling sound pierced the night – the raucous laughter of the siren, a creature of ancient evil imprisoned deep within its depths.

"Silence!" Rhamiel growled, his voice echoing through the stone corridor. The siren was an irritating reminder of his father's transgressions. It had come from beyond their borders; a 'gift' he had told Rhamiel. After it had killed a dozen soldiers with its glamour, they had caged it with a magickal binding seal, protecting anyone who had to go near the cell.

The laughter subsided, replaced by a low, pleading whine. "Release me, Rhamiel, oh Night Prince," the siren hissed, its voice a venomous caress. "I can offer you power, unimaginable power."

Rhamiel scoffed. "You offer only destruction and despair. You have taken too many lives. You will remain here, forgotten, until the end of your days."

He continued his walk, the siren's pleas fading behind him and the footsteps of his guards following him to the deeper level. As his feet stepped off the last stair, reaching the last level of the dungeon, he paused in front of a particular cell, a nagging doubt prickling at his mind. He couldn't place that cell being occupied or being told a new prisoner had been brought to the castle.

"Who brought this prisoner in? Why was I not notified?" He turned to the two guards who both shrugged as they looked towards the cell.

"Our apologies sire, we do not know why that cell has an occupant." The one guard bowed as he spoke. Rhamiel cleared his throat and frowned at them as he crossed his arms, his wings flexing behind his back. His irritation was showing; he mentally reminded himself to keep his temper at bay. He rolled his shoulders and relaxed his wings.

"Go and find out where this prisoner came from, NOW," he instructed as he turned to the cell. The guards quickly bowed and one of them walked away to find the master of the dungeons, while the other stood back, watching.

As Rhamiel peered through the thick iron bars, his breath caught in his throat. Inside, a woman sat on the floor, her long raven hair cascading around her like a dark cloak. Her eyes, the color of bruised plums, met his with a chilling intensity.

"My apologies," Rhamiel said, his voice cautious. "What... what crime brought you to this place?"

The woman smiled, a slow, predatory smile that sent shivers down his spine. "Crime?" she echoed, her voice a silken whisper. "Oh, I believe I was merely... misplaced."

Rhamiel frowned. "Misplaced? By whom?"

She shrugged, a careless gesture that seemed to ripple through the air. "A... misunderstanding," she explained, her voice laced with a dangerous amusement. "A rogue guard, you see. Overzealous. And... rather... forceful."

Rhamiel's temper flared. His guards should not be harming anyone, let alone imprisoning innocent women without his knowledge. "This is unacceptable," he declared, his voice firm. He fumbled with the lock, his hands trembling slightly.

As the door swung open, he felt a sharp pinch on his hand and watched as a drop of blood splashed on the floor inside the cell. The snap of a magickal binding broke across his fingers holding the door.

He looked up as he heard a low chuckle, a sound that seemed to slither from the very depths of the dungeon. He turned to the woman, a look of concern etched on his face; why was there a magickal blood binding on this cell?

The woman was no longer the same. Her eyes had turned inky black, swirling with a malevolent energy. Tendrils of darkness, like living shadows, began to seep from her fingers, reaching out towards him.

"I've been waiting for you and your blood, Night Prince. You seek power, Rhamiel," she hissed, her voice a venomous caress. "Power to command, to rule. But you are weak. Easily swayed, easily manipulated. The Kings of Tir Siorghlas... they do not fear you."

Rhamiel recoiled, fear gripping him; he knew belatedly what he had released. The darkness had consumed one of his ancestors, causing destruction and chaos until they had figured out how to remove the cursed being.

"Sire, step back!" the guard yelled as he stood in front of Rhamiel, his sword drawn, fear radiating off of him.

The Nightsinger's dark tendrils drifted around Rhamiel, reaching around the guard's neck as she pulled him to her in the cell. She clamped down on his artery, draining him quickly before he could scream. As the body slumped, she grinned and swirled around Rhamiel.

Why had he not been warned that all this time, the darkness had been lying in wait? The Kings of Tir Siorghlas had worked with his great grandfather to vanquish the darkness; he had been told by his father that the darkness had been sent across the realm, dissolved to dust, never to be again.

He couldn't understand why his father had lied to him- to not let him know of the blood magick binding the darkness to the cell all this time. His blood, for only the blood that was used for the spell to be created would be able to break it.

He tried to step back, to escape the encroaching darkness, but it was too late. The darkness, swirling and twisting, enveloped him, slithering down his throat, consuming him from within.

The woman watched him with a triumphant smile, her eyes gleaming with an unholy light as she faded. "Welcome," she whispered, her voice a chilling echo in the depths of the dungeon. "Welcome to the darkness, sweet puppet. You may call me the Nightsinger. I'm going to enjoy the fun we will have together. This time though, I'm not going to be vanquished so easily."

Rhamiel's eyes snapped open, the inky black swirling to take over the soft brown as he looked across the dungeon towards the steps, towards the castle.

You see, I have plans, Prince of the Night. And you're going to make sure they're accomplished. We have time before a new vessel will be needed. When she's born, the real war begins."

The darkness controlled his body, making him stand and walk up the stairs, out of the dungeon and down the hallway, towards his family. Inside his mind, Rhamiel screamed with all his might, struggling to take back control before it was too late. The guards came running to warn him of what was in the cell after having woken the dungeon master. The dungeon master was scrambling behind the guard, his robe haphazardly tied around his waist.

Before they could open their mouths, Rhamiel felt his arm raise, tendrils of darkness streaming out and enveloping their bodies. He watched in horror as it pulled back, their bodies nothing but husks inside their armour and clothes.

He struggled again to push the darkness out and heard her purr inside his brain, "Oh but you are strong, Rhamiel. This will be fun."

His body continued walking down the hallway towards his chamber; Rhamiel tried with all of his might to push the evil out, to save his family before it was too late.

Naomi woke to Rhamiel standing over them, his chest heaving as the darkness swirled around them. With a pained cry, Rhamiel was able to push it back just enough to scream, "Run, Naomi!" as he fell to his knees, the insidious blackness squeezing his heart.

Naomi flung herself out of the bed, holding little Taion tightly to her chest as she ran down the hallway screaming for help, her wings helping push her forward. She looked down at their son, his eyes open with fear, his little hand clinging onto her nightgown.

She looked behind her to see Rhamiel; his eyes dark, a feral grin on his face as he followed her. His steps were slow and measured, his arms hanging by his side as inky tendrils slowly swirled out of them.

Naomi turned and ran down a side corridor, praying they'd make it. She quickly stepped down the curling stairs, going deeper into the castle. As the stairs ended, they opened up into the grand library, the torches flickering softly, lighting the large space up with warm light.

She stopped as she scanned the library, trying to remember what the royal scribe had told her about Rhamiel's family. She turned down one of the rows, quickly grabbing a book as she ran through the room towards the back. She pushed a chair aside and with her free hand, ran her fingers across the stones, whispering as she felt a click.

She felt her body drop with sheer relief as the small door opened. She shoved the book into the room ahead of her, watching as it slid across the stone floor. With Taion firmly pulled to her, she crawled forward into the small room, her wings brushing the doorway.

As she entered the room, she quickly pushed the stone door shut behind her. She leaned up against it, her breathing uneven, sweat glistening on her forehead as she rested her head back for a moment, her eyes closed.

The room had been shown to her when she had first arrived, the old scribe had cryptically pointed it out. He had muttered something about 'the darkness that will befall Tenebris', instructing her to go there if she was in danger. The room had everything they would need to stay safe for a small period of time.

She listened quietly to see if she could hear Rhamiel through the wall, praying that he hadn't succumbed to it. The book sat beside her, waiting. She ran her hand over the cover in the dark, needing to know the full story and the hidden history of Rhamiel's great grandfather's fight against the evil he had unleashed.

"Amille, mama, I'm scared." The small voice whispered in the dark room, breaking Naomi out of her thoughts. She felt a tear fall down her cheek as she snapped her fingers to light the torch she knew was across from them.

She smoothed back Taion's hair from his face and carefully placed a kiss on his forehead as she rocked him in her arms, the soft torch light flickering over them.

They were doomed.

Chapter One

Riverstone

Riverstone Keep was Tir Siorghlas' southern stronghold. Now cared for by Lord Callum and his wife, Morena, it had become a bustling port city, humming with activity. Callum and Morena had grown under the watchful eyes of Queen Alyndria's parents, Taeral and Tawny who hailed from Tir un Uisce. Their knowledge of the networks of commerce had breathed new life into the southern lands, attracting merchants from far and wide.

The once quiet harbor was now a vibrant hub, filled with the sounds of bustling activity and the salty tang of the sea. Callum and Morena had proven their worth to the land, and in return, the land and its inhabitants flourished.

The cliffs around Riverstone were a marvel of natural creation. They weren't just a picturesque backdrop; they were the city's first line of defense. Over centuries, the relentless pounding of the ocean had sculpted the coastline, creating a natural harbor where the cliffs dramatically split, forming a narrow, guarded entrance.

This natural formation provided a safe haven for ships while simultaneously acting as a formidable barrier against any potential seaborne attack. Riverstone itself was a tapestry of landscapes; lush forests, teeming with life, climbed the hillsides, their emerald green a contrast to the golden hues of the open plains that stretched as far as the border of Riverstone went.

Where the land met the sea, the scene was a symphony of textures and colors: sandy beaches, shimmering with sunlight, gave way to rocky coves, where the waves crashed against the cliffs with thunderous force.

The summer solstice was fast approaching, and the merchants were bustling with trade from all corners of the realm that they lived in; trade agreements with Locrya and Tir un Uisce to the east had been cemented years past, resulting in the hustle and bustle. Ships were docked and unpacked, pallets of items that they had never seen before on Tir Siorghlas were traded amongst those with enough coin in their pockets.

As a large merchant ship docked, a muscular elven man stepped onto the dock. His long black hair moved in the breeze as his blue and purple iridescent eyes scanned the port, watching the commotion as his ship had its turn to unload the wares that they had brought from Locrya: woven tapestries, spun gold, unique crystals and more.

His face was stern as he watched over his crew unloading the precious cargo to barter with at Riverstone. He had come a long way to make his fortune and was determined to ensure that everything was handled with care.

He walked back on the plank, hoisted a square wooden crate onto his shoulder wrapped with rope and disembarked with it. He looked around, his eyes settling on his first mate, Frig, and instructed, "There are five of these boxes; ensure that they are transported to the names on them promptly and you'll find more coin in your purse."

Frig nodded and with a short bow, swung around to yell for messengers to deliver the boxes. He watched as his captain left the docks, signalling to the rest of the crew to continue unloading the goods.

Callum and Morena were in the gardens of the Keep, the day-to-day work of running the port left to those in their employ. The gardens were nestled in the back with access to a gently flowing stream. Morena hummed quietly, her blue eyes large as she picked weeds from the dirt as the sun beat down overhead.

The large brim straw hat Callum had bought for her from one of the merchant ships protected her fair skin. Her auburn hair was tied back with a pink ribbon, another small purchase Callum had surprised her with. Her pink dress was of the latest style in Tir Siorghlas, a cinched corset top with a flowing skirt, which allowed for her to move almost unrestrained as she worked.

Callum sat under a tree a small distance off, his legs crossed at his ankles, whittling a stick for their walk later. His hazel eyes wandered as he looked over their domain. His brown and gold hair, shaggy and a bit on the longer side now, flopped over his forehead, causing him to push it out of the way as he pushed the knife down the stick. A low whistle came from his lips of a tune that he remembered from his childhood in the Tempestus Clan.

He smiled as he watched Morena engrossed in her task; the dirt on her hands and a small smudge on her cheek from when she brushed the stray strands of her auburn hair off her face. They had just celebrated their 13th season of their hand tying, yet they still acted like it was the beginning of their courting.

He mused as he watched her, the tune no longer present as his mind went back to when he was rescued by King Damien, his sister and the other Clan leaders from Blackwood's black grasp. Before the rescue, he had lost his family in the blink of an eye, all because he and Annika fell victim to the siren's song, luring them to the battlefield.

He *stood in the middle of the battlefield, unsure how he had gotten there, Annika pulled him into her arms, shielding his eyes from the carnage surrounding them. His small body trembled in her arms as he screamed for his mother and father. He heard a soldier yelling at them, "Why are you two here? You should be in the castle behind the wards!"*

He opened his eyes to see Annika being pulled away by his parents. An otherworldly light circling Annika...then Annika disappearing as he screamed for them. The soldier holding him grunted in pain then fell with him in her arms, her lifeless eyes connecting with his as they tumbled to the ground. His mother cried out and ran towards them, but she was too far away.

He scrambled, trying to crawl to her as he looked behind him. Corvus, Blackwood's brother grinned as he bent down, grabbing Callum's ankle. As his hand tightened around Callum, he closed his eyes and let out a scream as his magick shuddered around his small body. Corvus flinched, knocking him out before the earth bending magick could do anything.

Callum woke up in a bed in Blackwood's manor, the fog letting in slivers of light through the window. He looked down to find iron shackles on his wrists, his magick muted.

"Welcome, little Prince." He looked up and Blackwood stepped out of the shadows, his inky grin etched across his face, "You'll be perfect. We will mold you to lead my army, to prepare to take the nightingale magick when your sister returns. She won't stay hidden forever."

Blackwood cackled as Callum looked around in horror, feeling the tendrils of black magick creep up his legs, like long spidery fingers. It caressed him, moving until it reached his head and then dug in.

His first memory of coming back was feeling Annika's hands on him, her gentle voice singing a melody that caused the dark magick inside his head to writhe and scream as her magick worked to push it out, to heal the years of evil corruption.

As the powerful healing magick pushed through the darkness, Callum remembered the fog lifting and seeing his sister again, finally, for the first time in centuries. He was home.

He shuddered involuntarily as the darkness tickled the far corners of his mind. He knew the black magick was gone but the memories seemed to stick around like a stubborn burr.

He sensed Morena looking at him and subconsciously shook his head, a beaming smile on his face as he locked eyes with his love. He did not want her to start worrying about him again.

She had seen him through the worst moments of his life, and he would work until the end of his immortal life to make it up to her. The last thing he wanted was for her to have to feel like she was to play nurse-maid again.

Morena's face was concerned for a moment and she softly smiled back, resuming her gardening. She checked the herbs growing and carefully snipped some of them to put in her basket.

She would make Callum a tea tonight to soothe the memories that he was struggling with again; some chamomile, a snippet of memory ease flower and some of her own magick added would make the perfect combination.

"Are we about ready to go for a walk, my little witchling?" Callum asked as he stood up from the ground and stretched, his slender yet muscular frame casting a shadow over the ground.

Morena smiled and dusted her hands together to try and get the dirt off of them. She laughed and looked up at Callum, "I am ready, darling. I just need some water to clean myself as I fear I've made quite a mess!"

Callum grinned, an idea forming in his mind. A smidge too late, Morena realized what he was thinking and let out a squeal of protest as he scooped her up, throwing her over his shoulder.

"Callum! Dinna dare think of throwing me in the river. I swear to the goddess I'll turn you into a toad!" Morena squealed again as Callum smacked her bottom.

"You said you were dirty. The only thing to do would be to clean you up...unless you like being a dirty girl?" Callum laughed as Morena gasped in surprise when he swung her off his shoulder.

"Callum, I'm not playing around. Do not..." Callum grinned at her and promptly jumped into the stream with her in his arms. Morena squealed in shock as the cold of the water enveloped her warm skin and she clung to Callum as he chuckled.

"Two can play at that game." Morena sputtered as her teeth chattered. She pushed away from Callum, floating in the shallow water and waved her one hand upwards towards him.

"Now, now, little witchling, I was only trying to have a spot of fun. Put the hands down..." Callum put his hands up in surrender, trying to swim towards her. Morena smiled as she whispered, much to Callum's protests.

"Morena, if you turn me into a toad, how am I going to keep you warm at night? Think it through, a leannan!" He yelped as a tidal wave smacked him, pulling him under the water.

He broke the surface, sputtering and turned to look for Morena. She was sitting on the riverbank, her dress dry and her hair neatly tied in a braid with a bright smile on her face as the last traces of magick swirled around her.

She pulled out a small bundle of herbs and a rose quartz crystal, whispering a thank you as she laid the bundle on the earth, then looked up at Callum.

"Are you done wasting time, my love? I'd like to go on that walk now."

Callum grinned and climbed out of the water, his sopping wet clothing dragging him down as he stalked towards Morena. She let out a squeal of delight as he pounced on her, claiming her mouth with his.

He ran his hand up her thigh and watched as Morena tipped her head back and relaxed against him.

The walk would have to wait.

Chapter Two

Clan Bayle

Not far from Riverstone Keep, the lands of Clan Bayle were a realm of breathtaking beauty; rolling emerald forests, sapphire lakes, and mountains that pierced the clouds like jagged teeth. Here, nestled amidst the towering peaks, lay the Clans' stronghold- a majestic castle carved into the very heart of the mountain.

Castle Leyebourne, a masterpiece of architecture, was proof of the Clan's ingenuity and reverence for nature. Its walls, seamlessly integrated with the rock face, made the castle an impenetrable fortress.

Saphielle was warm in Hagen's strong arms as they stood on a balcony overlooking the southeastern city of Oblor. The sun peeked over the mountains; the fiery red and pink hues splashing across the horizon signaled interesting weather for Clan Bayle to come that day.

Her brilliant blue eyes drank in the sky as she drank in the beauty around her. The sky would never cease to amaze her, all of those years of being an indentured servant in Efrana at the tavern had given her very little time to just relax and look at the sky. Now, she took every moment she could to memorize each constellation, each sunrise and sunset.

"It feels like rain today, little fox." Hagen murmured as he nuzzled

Saphielle's neck gently, pushing back her long auburn hair to get better access. She softly smiled and leaned back, closing her eyes as she mused.

"The farmers could use it, the heat this summer has been too much. Even though our power comes from harnessing fire, we do not need the countryside going up in smoke."

She opened her eyes and looked out towards the lands that she now looked after with him; the harvest wasn't as vibrant as it could have been at this time of year. Hagen turned her around to face him, and he levelled himself to look at her, his golden eyes to her sea blues.

She looked at him and memorized again: his strong angular jaw, the small scar on the right side of his cheek, from a battle gone past that made him look just a smidge more dangerous. The sensuous shape of his lips, and his long auburn hair that he wore loose. She felt her heart flutter again as he smiled under her scrutiny.

"It'll rain, little fox, we will not stress." He nodded and lifted his chin to get Saphielle to follow his gaze as a raindrop smacked her on the cheek. She let out a gasp of surprise as Hagen chuckled, sweeping the rain off of her cheek with his thumb carefully-reverently-as if she was the most precious thing to him.

He pulled her to him and slowly danced as the rain gently came down around them, humming the tune from their first dance. She sighed, resting her head against his chest as she closed her eyes, her hand resting over his heart.

She thought that even after all these years she would get used to the love that Hagen gave her, but she still was surprised to this day. Everything that had brought her any bit of joy had been taken away in the past. To know that he loved her and would never leave her, it was a strange feeling. Almost overwhelming at times.

Her soul bond mark, a jagged bolt beneath her collarbone, fluttered at his contact. He grinned as he felt it through his own. They were the only couple that had been gifted with such a mark in any of their histories because their soul binding was so powerful.

She giggled as the rain started to come down, at first a soft patter of drops before it suddenly turned into a downpour. Saphielle gasped with shock as the rain soaked them both head to toe before they could do anything. Hagen swept her up into his arms and spun around, quickly striding inside to dry her off.

"You can't be catching a cold, little fox. Not now. Off with the wet garments." He put her down gently, pulling the ties on the wet gown, releasing the stays and helping her step out of the hoop as it dropped.

"Hagen, my love. As much as I love how attentive you are, I do know how to take care of myself. I did it all those years on my own just fine." Saphielle protested as he shushed her.

He quickly used his fire magick to warm up the large cotton towel and drew it around her as she sighed in delight. He smiled at how small she looked, wrapped up in his large towel. He nodded for her to crawl into the bed as he followed behind.

The day could start in a bit; the time for listening to the court didn't start for another hour. He pulled her close and he felt her relax against him, her head resting on Hagen's heart.

"I love you, Hagen. Always," Saphielle murmured as she closed her eyes.

"I will forever love you, my little fox," he responded.

He sighed heavily. The last few years had been hard on her; relearning how to be elven royalty, reeling from the loss of her mother and the betrayal of her father. She was an orphan of unfortunate circumstances; however, her uncle Silvan had been amazing, stepping in to fill the void.

He thought back to when Saphielle was on the hunt and ready to burn Tir Siorghlas down during her one of her rages. Hagen had to pull her back from going to Bloodrose lands to kill the tavern owner, Feno, who had made her life hell. The years of her living as an indentured servant, her true identity hidden from her, had hurt her more than she had originally let on. When he could no longer deny her revenge, he had gone ahead to tend to unfinished business.

She didn't know still, but when they had found Feno's body battered and broken in a back alley in Efrana, his fingers snapped off and shoved down his throat, it had been because Hagen had found him first and ensured that the threat he had said years back was brought to reality.

He smiled at the memory of Feno seeing him walk into the tavern;

he knew that his time had come as his eyes connected with Hagen's. Hagen had asked him if he remembered his promise, watching as Feno blanched, falling to his knees as he implored Hagen to reconsider. His cries of pain and terror had fueled Hagen; each snap of his finger bones reminding him of what Feno had done to Saphielle.

As he shoved them down Feno's throat and watched him asphyxiate on them, he grinned darkly. When Feno's last gurgling breath was taken, he walked away, leaving the body for the animals to feast on. Hagen had no regrets.

When he had brought her to the back of the Tavern and she saw Feno, Saphielle had spit on his body and walked away, her eyes filled with unshed tears as she held her head high. Hagen had followed behind, cautious of the sparks of electricity snapping from her fingertips.

She had calmed down considerably once they had reached their horses and she had muttered, "Good riddance to that waste of skin. I'm glad he suffered, he did so much bad while he took breath." Feno had been part of the seedy underbelly that had taken hold in Bloodrose's lands; selling children and women to anyone with enough coin in their purse for whatever they chose.

She had looked at Hagen with such fierceness in her eyes that he fell in love with her all over again. No one would put hands on his woman and live to tell the tale. Ever.

He looked back down at Saphielle as she breathed gently, her slender hand on his chest. He carefully brushed away a stray strand of hair off her face and smiled to himself as he watched her sleep. The gentle swell of her belly was barely noticeable, but Hagen had sensed before she had told him.

They were finally going to be parents.

At the castle doors, a square wooden crate tied in rope was delivered. The guard accepted it, a frown on his face as he checked it over. He called another guard over.

"Was the Eldatár expecting anything of the sorts?" he asked the other.

The second guard shrugged, carefully running his hands down the joints of the box, trying to see if they could open it. The first guard grabbed his dagger and just as he went to cut the rope, it loosened and fell off the box.

Confused, they looked at each other, the second guard carefully lifting the lid of the box open to see a folded yard of exotic fabric and a container of spices. The first guard huffed, "It's just fabric and spices. It can go."

He closed the lid and put the rope back around the box while the second guard called a servant over.

"This can be delivered to the library for the Eldatár to open. A gift from a merchant, new to Riverstone it seems." The second guard handed the box to the servant who nodded and walked towards the library with the box.

Chapter Three

Clan Tempestus

Even though war was far from everyone's minds, King Damien had never stopped training. His Clan was in the middle of the realm; threats could come from any direction, and they would not be caught unprepared.

Asthemar, the heart of Tir Siorghlas, was a small city woven into the landscape. Nestled amidst rolling hills and the forest, it exuded an aura of tranquility that disguised its strategic importance.

The city's architecture was a mix of stone and timber, its buildings blending seamlessly with the surrounding landscape. A river, clear and sparkling, snaked its way through the city, reflecting the blue hues of the sky and the lush greenery that bordered its banks.

Just on the outskirts of the city stood Castle Dewmire, a majestic fortress of white stone that always seemed to shimmer in the sunlight. Its towering walls, adorned with intricate carvings, offered a formidable defense against any potential threat.

Damien remembered the last time they had known peace for this long. The quiet had lulled them into a false sense of security, a dangerous complacency that had almost cost them everything. He vividly recalled the frantic scramble, the fear that had choked him as he watched the darkness attack.

He had almost lost Annika, his love, as quickly as he had found her. The memory still sent a shiver down his spine, a chilling reminder of the fragility of peace and the ever-present threat that lurked beneath the surface.

For centuries they were separated. Annika was spellbound and sent to the earth realm to keep her safe while Damien had stayed back, stepping up to the throne for Clan Tempestus, waiting for the day he could call her home.

They had spent precious time reconnecting and working through the spellbinding that her parents had put on her, making sure her magick could not be found by those who wanted to use it for evil. They had still found each other and their love had never faltered. Even with the spellbinding, their souls had connected again.

He looked at his wife, his Queen. Her face was fierce as she swung her practice sword towards him in an arc, the muscles under her training clothes straining as she attacked him. Her long brown and gold hair, braided in a warrior braid, swung around as she launched, her hazel eyes flashing with fire.

She was every inch the warrior Queen the prophecy had said. Her nightingale flew above her, a cry of delight as it felt its master fight. Annika's magick was one of the most unique that had ever been blessed on a Royal by the goddesses.

The Clan's base magick was the control of the water element; however, Annika could control all of the elements and then some, drawing in power that was beyond anything they had encountered.

Damien, being an heir from Clan Aether, had the ability to control both fire and water elements. This was very different from what his wife had control over, but he was proud to have such a strong woman by his side.

He grinned and blocked, grunting as he realized he would have to dodge her quickly as she swung again. She feinted and swung around, kicking Damien square in the chest. As she knocked him onto the ground, his breath left him with a woosh.

Annika quickly jumped onto him and held her hand on his neck. She bent down and whispered in his ear, "Dead."

He grinned as he grabbed her waist, and she sat up on him with a serious look on her face. "Just what were you thinking, my love? Distraction is what will get you killed. You know that; you taught me that." She smoothed back his shorter thick black hair, grazing the tips of his elven ears.

Damien quickly flipped Annika under him as she squealed in surprise, landing with an oomph on her back as he straddled her. "I was thinking about how lucky I was to find you again, a mhuirnin. How many times I almost lost you when you came back through that portal because we were not prepared enough." His chocolate brown eyes, flecked with caramel, swirled with the memory of what they had gone through.

Annika softened and reached up to Damien's face, cupping his cheek as he closed his eyes. Those memories, however faded, still woke him up from time to time in the middle of the night. Immortal or not, they could still die.

A shout startled them, and they both looked over to the edge of the training mat to see Gabriel and Ilyana, now in their elven youth, fighting each other with training swords, sweat glistening on both of them as they relentlessly went through the paces the way their amil had taught them.

They looked almost identical: their hair, shades of brown and black, with Gabriel's shorter in the style of youth in Asthemar and Ilyana's long and braided. Their eyes, chocolate and emerald, sparked with gold as they fought. Each had a smattering of freckles across the bridges of their noses and their bodies were lithe, muscular and agile. They were already beautiful beings, and they hadn't reached their mature age yet.

Ilyana screamed as she swung around; with a swift kick she sent Gabriel across the mat, tumbling as his body hit the ground. He pushed back, using his air magick to stop his feet from sliding as he himself swung up, his eyes shining like molten gold. The wind howled around him, tossing items around the training ground.

"That wasn't fair, and you godsdarned well know it, Ilyana!"

He growled as he ran towards her, his sword raised as he swung at his sister. The wind propelled him as he pulled his water magick forward, icicles flying.

Ilyana laughed, "All's fair in battle, Gabby. You know that!"

She ducked just in time and flung her free arm up, creating a wall of earth between them. Gabriel grunted as he connected with it and the icicles shattered. He groaned and sat, leaning up against it as he panted, trying to regain his breath as the wind receded.

Ilyana smirked and walked around it to sit next to her brother. She laid her head on his shoulder as he grinned and rested his head on hers. Their chests heaving, they moved together, pulling out small bundles of sage and sweetgrass, tied with cordage from their pockets. Gently placing them on the ground as an offering for their magick, they thanked the goddess quietly.

Annika and Damien chuckled as they watched them. The twins had been a handful since they could start walking; this was no different.

"They both will be formidable when they are of age if they keep practicing like that." Damien mused.

Damien carefully got off of Annika and pulled her up against him as they stood. He paused, his eyes drinking her in. He whispered as he looked at her, ""Do you even know, after all this time, how you take my breath away, a mhuirnin? It's like the world stops turning. Everything fades and all that's left is you."

He put her chin in his hand and tilted her head upwards to look at her, memorizing the freckles that splashed across the bridge of her nose, how she flushed when he looked at her.

He continued, his voice low, "This...consuming need to be near you, to hear your voice, to just *be* with you. It's never faded, even after all the bairns; you are my everything."

Her eyes: they were like wandering through the forest in the evening with little bursts of moonlight filtering through the leaves. They swirled when she was excited and darkened when she was mad. Her lips slightly parted, and she swallowed hard.

He leaned his head forward and carefully brushed his lips over hers. "I could love you for ten thousand years, and that would still not be long enough."

Her eyes closed as her body melted against him. "Our lives are intertwined like the roots of our ancient trees here my love, inseparable and strong, for I am yours until the goddess takes me, and even then, I will always be yours," she whispered as she felt his hands sweep over her ribs.

He claimed her lips and just as he almost lost himself in the moment, they both heard simultaneous groans of disgust from their youthful children. Annika and Damien rested their foreheads together as Annika laughed.

They broke apart and walked towards Ilyana and Gabriel. Annika pointed at the earthen wall.

"Ilyana sweetheart, remove the wall please. It'll impede any other forms of practice in the training area. Gabriel, you'll clean up anything that got tossed around from that display of wind as well. Good job remembering to lay your offerings after you were done. It's important to not forget that after a battle."

Damien added in, "That was a great show of power from the two of you today. I think it's time for us to consider sending you to receive more magickal training to better hone what the goddess has gifted you."

Ilyana's eyes lit up and Gabriel's shoulders sank. That meant they were going to be sent to the Silver Lands, far from home.

"Does that mean we can see Piper again too, amil? She's my age and I think it would be nice for us to get to know each other better, since she's related to your best friend?" Ilyana's eyes lit up as she danced on her toes, her hands behind her back with her fingers crossed, hoping her father would say yes.

Gabriel looked at Ilyana out of the corner of his eye, his lips pursed. He didn't want to go; he'd much rather be home with his family and see his friends in the city.

Just as Gabriel was going to speak up, a commotion could be heard from the castle, most specifically the kitchen. Annika and Damien looked at each other and then grinned, running together to ensure that the castle didn't cave into itself from the mischievous twins inside currently causing trouble.

They opened the door from the gardens that connected to the kitchen to find the entire space covered in powdered sugar.

Innocently sitting in the middle of the room were two covered twin girls and a small critter, the family pet, who shook itself off, powdered sugar floating in the air. It licked its paws and coughed, the powder dusting its nose. The girls giggled and one of them pulled the winged beast into her arms as the other tickled under its chin. The little beast purred at the attention. "Lucky! You got it all over us!"

Annika cleared her throat, her arms crossed as she tried to keep her face stern. Damien didn't even bother, he chuckled as the girls looked up, Lucky following suit.

The girls blinked their large green eyes at their parents and smiled as they licked the powdered sugar off of their lips. Aywin and Rina, the younger royal terrors. They were mini versions of Annika; freckles dusting their cheeks, pouty lips and bright brilliant eyes. The only trait they were gifted from their father was their raven black hair that reached down to their hips-now white from the explosion.

Mrs. Perch sat in a chair, equally covered with powdered sugar and looked at Annika and Damien with pursed lips, her arms crossed as she huffed.

"If the two of you ever think of having more bairns, I strongly recommend against it. You're making me hairs grey!"

Annika burst out laughing as Damien's jaw dropped from Mrs. Perth's comment.

"Mrs. Perth, I'll have you know..." Damien started before being interrupted by a shout from the palace guard warned Damien and Annika that someone was entering the castle gates; a horse and a rider approached. On the back of the horse sat a square crate tied in rope.

The messenger stopped short at the steps and nodded to a guard who grabbed the box. The guard walked towards the steps of the castle and brought it to Maelyrra, Clan Tempestus' General.

She frowned as she took it, feeling the weight of the box. She nodded at the guard, "Cut the rope, this seems a bit suspicious." The guard pulled his dagger out and as he went to cut the rope, it slipped off the box. The guard looked up at Maelyrra, confusion reaching his eyes, "General, I didn't barely touch it."

Maelyrra's frown deepened as she put the box down carefully, pulling out her long sword, "I don't feel any magick on it but let's be cautious." She carefully lifted the lid with the tip of her sword as the guard and her peered into the open box.

Nestled inside was a folded yard of fabric in a vibrant green, a container of spices nestled on top.

Maelyrra visibly relaxed as the guard chuckled, "All that for nothing but a cloth and spice, general."

She looked at him and shook her head as she sheathed her sword. She carefully put the lid back on the box and pulled the rope back onto it.

"Come take this to the Eldatár and Elentári, leave it in the sitting room." She instructed to the servant waiting at the doors of the castle.

The servant bowed and grabbed the box, running it inside. A slight glow emanated from it, subtle enough that no one noticed.

As the servant reached the sitting room, Damien entered the hallway and walked down towards the sitting room. The servant put the box down and turned around, quickly bowing as they saw Damien in the doorway.

Damien looked at the servant then at the box on the table. "Where did that come from?" he inquired as he walked over to it.

"General Maelyrra cleared it, it came from a messenger. She had said something about spices and fabric, Sire." The servant responded.

Damien smiled and picked the box up, "Thank you, I'm sure the Elentári will love the gift." The servant bowed and exited the room.

Damien paid no mind as he left the sitting room, leaving the wooden box unattended. As the room emptied, a blue glow emanated from it.

Chapter Four

Clan Empereal

The western part of Tir Siorghlas was a land of harshness. The sun beat down relentlessly, turning the rolling hills into a sea of shimmering gold. Yet, a cool breeze, laden with the salty tang of the ocean, swept in from the west, tempering the heat and creating a refreshing respite.

Castle Greywood, the Clans' stronghold, stood perched precariously on the edge of a towering cliff. The wind, a constant companion, had worn down the castle's walls over centuries, leaving the stonework weathered and scarred. Yet, the castle remained strong, much like their people.

To the north of the castle lay the city of Estia, a vibrant tapestry of cultures. Witches, with their goddess-given powers, coexisted alongside the graceful elves, their magick interwoven with the rhythms of nature. The city, a bustling hub of trade and commerce, reflected the mix of its inhabitants. Falcons soared above the city, their presence expected as Clan Empereal held the honour of breeding and raising the realms' messengers.

The land surrounding Estia mirrored the eastern reaches of Tir

Siorghlas, a vast expanse of rolling hills minus the heather. As the hills gave way to the distant horizon, the Silver Lands could be seen, the mountains creating a breathtaking background.

King Silvan sat in the throne room, his long auburn hair tied into a braid today, his usually brilliant sea blue eyes were tired; the line of petitioners was long today and he had something on his mind. Thankfully the line was moving quickly as most of the requests and updates were items that were easy to act upon.

He let his mind wander back to what was plaguing his sleep lately. His dreams centered around one thing every time he closed his eyes-Death. He had, many years back made an irreversible agreement with the goddess Death to save his wife from being taken from him.

She had been caught in the clutches of the shapeshifters in Stonecastle lands. Riverstone Keep had been surrounded by a creeping evil that had almost consumed half of Tir Siorghlas before Alyndria had given her soul up to the grandfather tree, the epicentre of where the shapeshifters had started. His plea to bring her back had been answered by Death, who in turn, vanquished the evil shapeshifters and removed the blight from Tir Siorghlas. Alyndria had lived, his soul bond survived, but his cost was high.

At some point, his agreement was going to be called in. He wasn't ready yet. Not when he had only been able to spend so little time loving Alyndria.

He shook his head and focused on the merchant in front of him, asking for an allowance for the new merchant wares that were coming up from the Riverstone port. He nodded and a new parchment with the agreement was signed.

Later in the hour, a younger mother approached, a small child holding her hand and another babe in her arms. She explained that her mate had left them one evening and hadn't returned.

"Eldatár, I come to you for help. I wouldn't if it wasn't for the wee ones. If you can't help me, at least help them. I beg you."

She was unable to meet his eyes; however, the small child watched Silvan with wide bright blue eyes, barely blinking as she watched him. Silvan couldn't help himself; he stepped off of the dais and bent down on his knee in front of the young girl. Her long auburn hair was in desperate need of a brush and braid, her clothes, some mending.

"Gods", he thought to himself, "she mustn't be more than 5 turns." He smiled as he twirled his hands in the air and a water bubble came forth from his magick. Silvan had been practicing little surprises with his water and wind magick, preparing for the children he and Alyndria had hoped for.

The young girl gasped in delight and stepped away from her mother's skirt. Enraptured, she touched the ball, and it burst, creating little snowflakes around her. She squealed in delight as Silvan grinned, watching the pure childlike wonder.

Silvan looked up at the mother and without standing up, he softly replied to her request as he pulled out a small bundle of sweetgrass with a falcon feather.

"You and the bairns can live at the castle. We will find you gentle work while the babe is young. The children will want for nothing while they are under our care. Is that satisfactory for you?"

The woman looked shocked. She wordlessly nodded in agreement and Silvan tapped the little girl on the nose with a grin before standing to his full height, his strength evident in his build.

He looked down at the woman who was now under his care. As he walked towards the windows, he laid the bundle down and patted it, thanking the goddess. He turned and looked at the woman again.

"Do you have a name? And the bairns?"

"Sire," she stuttered, "I am named Cyra, the young one is Erawyn. The babe has no name yet." She curtsied as she spoke. The babe in her arms fussed for a moment then resumed sleeping.

Just then, Alyndria swept into the room. Her long jet-black hair shone radiantly in the sunlight that streamed through the throne room and the dark purple of her gown set off her bright green eyes. They sparkled as she looked at Silvan and she walked purposefully towards him, her hips swaying in the gown, her curves on display.

Silvan's breath hitched as he watched his bride walk towards him. It was as if she was glowing from within when he laid eyes on her. The years had done nothing but make her even more beautiful in his eyes. She flushed as she saw him staring intently at her.

Cyra turned and instantly curtsied when she saw the Queen. The young girl, Erawyn, looked up in awe as Alyndria came and stood beside Silvan. Alyndria looked down at Erawyn and smiled as she bent down to look at her,

"Hello, little one." Her green eyes connected with Erawyn's bright blues and Alyndria felt her heart hitch. She smoothed Erawyn's auburn hair and gently patted her shoulder then stood up and turned to Silvan, smoothing her skirts out.

"My love, the petition time is now closed. We have more to do today, and I was hoping to have a moment with you?" Alyndria threaded her arm through Silvan's as he smiled down at her. He patted her hand and kissed the top of her forehead before turning to Cyra.

"Report to the kitchens. The head staff will be there and can instruct you on what they need help with. They will also show you the lodgings. Welcome to Castle Greywood."

He turned and winked at young Erawyn, who was absolutely enraptured with the King and Queen now. Her bright blue eyes were large with wonder as Silvan swept Alyndria from the room, little snowflakes lingered in the air, dusting her cheeks.

Alyndria and Silvan slowly walked the long hallway towards their private rooms. She looked up at Silvan and sighed. Silvan heard her and turned his head ever so slightly to glance at her.

"Don't start now, Alyndria, it was the right thing to do, nymph. Her mate left her and the bairns. We can always use more hands for the castle."

Alyndria kept pace with Silvan's steps as she replied, "My love, I just sometimes wonder if you are just too kind, and the people take advantage of it. Her mate has an obligation and should be brought to account for not taking care of his family. Are we sending a scout out to bring him back so he can face a trial?"

Silvan frowned and nodded, "I will call for Ashryn to come and send out a scout. It is worth seeing if we can do that. The bairns deserve better."

"I do not bemoan the fact that we now have more mouths to feed; in fact, the more the merrier." Alyndria replied, "I just want to make sure that you are not going to hurt your heart when one day the littles are no longer here. They don't belong to us," she continued as she carefully watched her husband's face.

Silvan faltered a bit in his steps. She had seen right through him, yet again. He recovered and continued to walk to their private quarters before choosing to speak again, lest someone hear them.

As he closed the door behind them, Alyndria stepped into the middle of the room and clasped her hands in front of her. Silvan kept his back turned to her for a brief moment to collect his thoughts and then turned towards her, his face kind as he spoke.

"Nymph, I keep forgetting how much you can see through me and read my mind. I would be remiss if I didn't admit that the sounds of littles in the castle have soothed my heart lately. They are..."

He paused as he watched Alyndria. Her face betrayed no emotion but the tears that fell down her cheeks said it all. They had tried for years and to their disappointment, had not produced an heir for the Clan. Alyndria and Silvan together had prayed, sought out herbalists, mystics, spell makers, and still nothing.

They knew that at times, elves struggled to produce heirs, but Alyndria watched as Damien and Annika had two sets of twins, Sarya and Carwyn were now on their fourth child and Saphielle and Hagen were expecting.

She couldn't help but wonder if they were just not meant to be goddess-blessed. She also wondered if the promise that Silvan had made to Death had anything to do with her not being able to produce heirs. Those bargains were sometimes tricky in nature, and she didn't put it past the goddess.

He strode to her and pulled her into his arms, tightly holding her as she sobbed.

"I didn't mean to upset you, my nymph. I am sorry. I will have them removed from the castle if it hurts too much. It was extremely rude of me to not think of your own pain seeing the wee ones in the castle."

He kissed her cheeks and continued, "I was selfish and only thought of myself at that moment. Alyndria, little nymph, I'm sorry."

Alyndria spoke, her voice muffled from her face being pressed against Silvan's chest. "My love, I would never cast out the wee bairns from the castle because I myself will never experience that joy. I only cry because I will never be able to see that same joy on your face that I saw today, holding your own heir in your arms."

Silvan pulled her away to look at his love and she looked up at him as he gently squeezed her arms.

"Alyndria. You are all that I need. If that is what the goddess has chosen for us, I am happy with that blessing." He pulled her back to him again and captured her lips to his. She melted into him and reached up into his hair to tug on his scalp as he scooped her up.

She wrapped her legs around his hips, and he walked towards the chaise to sit. They explored each other with soft movements and Silvan traced his mouth against her olive skin, licking and nipping where he knew she liked.

She moaned and let him pull her dress out of the way. Silvan flicked his hands and the click of the lock on the door broke the silence. He looked at Alyndria, his eyes dark with hunger as she bit her bottom lip.

She traced his face and then leaned down to kiss him again and Silvan felt her consume him- her smell, her body on his as she ground herself against him. He groaned as he kissed her neck and quickly got up, still holding onto her and strode into their bedchambers.

A messenger on a horse trotted into the castle courtyard, a box tied in rope on the horse's back. He slowed the horse down and dismounted, patting the horse's sweaty neck as he turned to grab the box.

He turned back around and made two steps to the castle stairs before he was stopped by a female with long braided auburn hair wearing the outfit of a highly decorated general.

Ashryn walked up to the messenger, blocking him from going further, and crossed her arms. "Where did this come from?" her eyes scanned the wooden box, the rope tied around with the folded paper, the scribbled words with 'To be delivered to the king of Clan Empereal'.

The messenger shrugged, "Just take the package, miss, I don't get coin unless you take it." He held it out expectantly, nodding his head towards her. She sized him up; he wasn't in official messenger attire, he looked more like he worked the docks in Riverstone.

"Where did you say you came from?" she asked.

"Riverstone, ma'am. I came straight from there with the instruction that this was for the Eldatár."

Ashryn carefully took the box and watched as the messenger swung himself back onto the horse, taking off with a shout, the trail of dust flying up as he left the courtyard.

Ashryn looked down at the box in her hands, puzzlement on her face as she tried to figure out what was in it. The rope slid off unexpectantly as she touched it, and she frowned as she carefully lifted the lid to see a yard of blue fabric and a container of spices nestled on top.

"This is quite odd." She said to herself, "why would we get a delivery of fabric and spices to the king?"

A guard approached Ashryn and looked into the box, "I heard there was a new merchant that docked at Riverstone, perhaps they're trying to see if their wares would be received here?"

Ashryn closed the box, "Perhaps." She turned and called out to a servant who was in the entrance of the castle, "Come take this to the Eldatár and Elentári's sitting rooms."

The servant nodded and took the box under her arm as she walked through the castle. As she stepped into the shadows of the hallway, the box started to glow. Unaware, she stepped into the sitting room and placed it on the sideboard as instructed.

Chapter Five

Clan Aether

The land of Clan Aether was perched on the easternmost point of the realm. The castle afforded a breathtaking view of the horizon, where the sky met the sea in a dance of colors. Castle Elden was built strong, stone walls carved from the very cliff upon which it stood. The eastern walls were so seamlessly integrated with the rock face that it was as if the castle had grown organically from the earth itself.

To the west of the castle the landscape consisted of rolling hills, carpeted in a vibrant tapestry of heather. The purple hues of the flowers created a beautiful image, especially when bathed in the golden light of the setting sun. As the eye followed the gentle rolls of the hills, it was met with a dense, ancient forest that stretched southward, its dark canopy a contrast to the purple expanse of heather.

This forest was a space of mystery and intrigue, a place where the whispers of ancient magick lingered in the air. Deep within its heart, a small portion of the forest had been granted to the Baobhan Sith, a Clan of shadowy creatures who answered to the Queen of Clan Aether, Amodra.

Clan Aether royals harnessed all of the elements with their magick and Osian was King, the eldest of the Aveum line. Orin, the adult son of Amodra and Osian, held his own unique powers of portal making and of bringing beings back to life before their last breaths left their bodies. He was under guard at all times because these powers were sought after by folk both good and evil.

Today, the land basked in the summer sun, the waves lazily stroking the shoreline as Orin walked through the water with Atmos, their Nephilim spy. As Atmos walked beside him, his black wings were tucked against his back, avoiding touching the ground.

He carried himself regally, his years of being both a soldier and now a spy evident. His black hair was cropped on the sides and longer on the top, his dark eyes shimmering as he looked over at Orin. He kept his one muscular arm on top of the hilt of his sword, the other freely swinging at his side. He wore looser clothing today, being a day off from his duties. His dark pants were tucked into high boots and his shirt hung open at the top, letting his tanned muscular and lithe frame enjoy the breeze.

His mind went to his mate, Ephyra, who was waiting back at their quarters for him, having the day off as well. He knew she'd be in the gardens in the back by now, her purple hair in a bun, wearing her favourite loose gown as she prepared a meal. But he knew that something was bothering the prince, so he had told her he'd be a few hours.

"Did you ever think when you were growing up that you'd end up doing what you do?" Orin asked, a handsome young man; his dark hair flopped over his face, his chocolate eyes swirled with hints of red and gold. His frame had filled out and he was no longer a lanky half elf; Orin had worked to ensure that he could hold his own.

As the Crown Prince, he was well versed in battle; he had completed his mandatory three years of military service to the Clans and now was looking for where he fit in. He was done feeling lost and he was tired of waiting to see where his father would place him within the Clan. Would he take the title of lord like his father did or would he simply sit beside him, waiting to take the crown?

Atmos paused with a smile and looked at Orin as they continued walking.

"To be honest, if it wasn't for your amil, I would be dead. It was because of his kindness and willingness to give me a chance that I have been able to spy for the Clans. I had sworn fealty to the Night Prince of Tenebris before this and when he was defeated, so was most of our army."

Atmos continued, his voice laced with a hint of bitterness, "I wish I could have refused the Night Prince; he caused so much destruction. Your amil, bless his soul, he saw something in me, something I didn't even know I possessed. He gave me purpose, gave me a reason to fight for something more than just survival."

Orin nodded, understanding what Atmos was saying. "You found your place with him, didn't you?"

Atmos smiled, the bitterness fading slightly. "Yes, I did. And I wouldn't trade it for the world. But you, you're a Prince. You have a destiny to fulfill."

Orin sighed, the weight of his royal lineage settling heavily upon his shoulders. "But what is it? My amil, he keeps me close, but I feel like he doesn't let me truly participate. I feel like I'm waiting, all while not having the freedom to explore."

Atmos placed a hand on Orin's shoulder, his grip firm yet gentle. "You're still young, Orin. You have time. But, true, you can't wait forever. You have to find your own path, your own purpose. Don't let the expectations of your parents define you."

Orin looked at his friend, a smile tugging at the corner of his mouth. "You're right."

He thought back to the villagers he had met during the last court session he had sat in on, their faces etched with worry, their hopes pinned on the promises of their leaders. Maybe he could find a purpose there. Orin looked to his friend and confidante, the spy who had been with him since it was discovered he was the heir to Clan Aether.

Years before when his mother and amil had found each other again, she had told Osian about their son: how he had been hidden from Osian's life because of his parents' arrangement to send Amodra away, having not been of royal blood. They couldn't imagine their son marrying someone who was not able to trace their lineage- soul bond or not. His grandparents later realized their error when they saw the heartbreak they had caused their eldest child. They embraced Orin when he had come home and treasured their eldest grandchild.

As they continued walking down the beach, Orin's gaze was drawn to where the vibrant green of the castle gardens stretched towards the distant horizon. "It's like I'm a bird with clipped wings," he muttered, his voice laced with exasperation. "Trapped in this gilded cage."

Atmos raised an eyebrow. "Where did that come from, Orin? You seem more restless than usual."

Orin stopped pacing and kicked the sand, running a hand through his hair. "I... I can't do anything. I can't even leave the castle grounds without a dozen guards trailing behind me like a pack of hounds, unless I use my magick and they don't realize I use a portal to get out."

He gestured towards the horizon. "I long to explore, to see the world beyond the castle, to truly experience the lives of my people and not be sneaking around using my magick to taste freedom. I want to go sit in a pub and shut the place down like my amil used to with his friends. I want to know what it feels like to kiss a female..." he trailed off.

Atmos nodded, concerned that Osian and Amodra would be keeping their grown son under such strict conditions. Carefully he responded. "I understand, I'm sorry, I didn't realize. It must be frustrating to be so restricted."

Orin sighed and lowered his eyes as he shoved his hands into his pockets. "It's more than frustrating. It's suffocating. I feel like a puppet, dancing on strings, my every move dictated by my mother."

Atmos bumped him with his shoulder. "Hey, look at me, it'll be ok."

Orin looked over at Atmos, a flicker of gratitude in his eyes. "Thank you, for coming to visit... For being a friend, for sharing your stories as you soar above Tir Siorghlas, for reminding me that there's more to life than these stone walls."

Atmos smiled, his posture reserved. "Always a pleasure, Prince Orin. Besides, someone has to keep you sane, clearly. I wish I could do more."

Orin chuckled, a small, rueful sound. "You do a better job than you think."

He knew Atmos understood. He had seen firsthand the constraints of royal life, the suffocating weight of expectation that came with being a Prince. But Atmos, with his easygoing nature and his adventurous spirit, offered Orin a glimpse of a world beyond the castle walls, a world of freedom and possibility.

Atmos looked at Orin again; something was clearly wrong. There was an odd shift in the atmosphere and this was just another complex issue to add to the feeling he had. Atmos sighed and decided he was going to have to talk to general Solana to find out just how to approach the King without setting him off.

Orin and Atmos continued walking the shoreline in silence, back towards the castle, the royal guards trailing behind them.

Amodra lifted her head and licked her lips, little rivulets of blood trailing down her chin. She closed her eyes and inhaled deeply as she savoured the taste.

Her fangs retracted and she laid back in the bed with a satisfied grin as she brushed her pale hair away from her face, letting it fan across the pillow. Royal blood gave her such a buzz that she could barely contain herself when she fed on Osian, her lawful husband and the King of Clan Aether.

All the better that she ensured he was drugged and unaware; she had been feeding increasingly knowing it was more than they had agreed to keep her hunger at bay. When they had first married, Osian and Amodra had mad an agreement; that she could feed when the hunger was too much for her and they hadn't been able to hunt.

As a Baobhan Sith, her Clan had been hunted for centuries. With the marriage agreement, it had meant peace for her Clan at long last. She didn't want to ruin it yet; not when she had claimed the most powerful throne in Tir Siorghlas; she had other plans.

Amodra watched in the dark as his chest rose and fell, a rhythm that blended with his heartbeat. She looked over at the balcony as the sun slowly rose in the east and carefully rose out of bed to look over the land that she ruled along with Osian.

This was the only time he looked innocent and young anymore. She smiled as she watched his chest rising and falling, the muscles still there even though he had lost a fair bit of weight over the years.

She gently traced a fingernail down his chest and Osian opened his eyes, locking with hers as she smiled at him. Osian grunted and pulled away, rolling out of bed. He sat on the edge of the mattress and clenched his jaw as he rubbed his face.

His spine was evident as he leaned over to pull on his pants. As he stood up, he walked over to a plush chair, grabbed his shirt and pulled it over his head. He looked over at Amodra, her naked body bared to him. He watched as she got onto all fours and crawled towards him on the bed until she was touching him.

Amodra carefully ran her hand up his chest, towards his neck and he quickly pulled away. She sat back and pulled the sheets to cover herself as Osian looked at her again, his eyes dark and shuttered.

"My love," she said, letting confusion and hurt swirl in her red eyes, feigning innocence. "Whatever I did, please tell me so I can make it right."

Osian frowned and shook his head. He wasn't ready to speak yet and was afraid that any noise he made would betray him.

He turned away and walked towards the washing room and closed the door. Amodra sat back against the headboard and pondered what she had possibly done to receive such a cold reception.

As she wracked her brain, wondering if he knew, if somehow her façade was up, he stepped out of the washing room. His shorter dark brown hair was wet from his bath and his face was scrubbed clean. He had new clothing on, the white and gold colours of his Clan, looking every bit the elven Aether King as he walked towards the doors of the bedroom. His dark chocolate eyes flashed with flecks of gold, the only thing showing his barely restrained anger.

"Find me General Solana, immediately," Osian growled at one of the guards at the door. The guard bowed as he walked towards the barracks to find the general. Osian didn't look back as he closed the bedroom door, leaving Amodra alone. A red tear slowly ran down her cheek.

Osian walked down the stairs to the front of the castle where a servant was holding a wooden crate wrapped in rope. The servant bowed and handed it to Osian.

"Where did this come from?" Osian asked, a touch of uncertainty in his voice.

"A man approached the castle gates this morning, Eldatár, instructing that this had to be in your hands. It was cleared by a guard, nothing but white fabric and a spice container." The servant bowed and walked away with Osian holding the box, confusion swirling around him. Why would he want spices and white fabric?

Atmos and Orin walked in the doors just as Osian went to unwrap the box. Atmos lunged, "No, Eldatár! Don't open that box!"

Osian stopped, the rope partially unwrapped and locked eyes with Atmos.

"Sire, I beg of you. Put the crate down." Atmos' eyes were wide as he held his hands out, his palms upwards. "I'll take it and put it somewhere for safekeeping."

"What exactly is this that has you so afraid, Atmos? The box holds nothing but fabric and spices." Osian frowned again as he looked between him and Orin who was standing, transfixed on the box.

"Sire, I'll explain when it's just you and I, I swear. Just do not proceed in unwrapping that box, there's more than meets the eye."

Osian nodded and carefully re-tied the rope, putting the crate down carefully. Atmos walked up and gently picked the crate up. He nodded and walked towards the front door of the castle and took flight.

Orin looked at his dad, "Amil, what was that about?"

Osian shook his head, confused more than ever. "Seldo, I am not sure we will ever know. I'll leave that to Atmos to take care of for now. That's why he's our spy; he keeps us safe."

He nodded towards the throne room, "Would you like to listen to petitioners today, seldo? I could use some guidance."

Orin grinned and nodded, "Thank you, amil. I will assist today. Is general Solana there too?"

Osian nodded, "Speaking of, I may need to pull her aside today for a moment. Can I trust you to take care of listening to the villagers and making the correct decisions based on their requests while I do so?"

Orin was surprised. His father was trusting him with more than he ever had imagined. He swallowed hard and nodded with a smile, determined to make Osian proud. His father was finally giving him a purpose.

Osian smiled at his grown son and mused. He had grown up to be a smart and handsome man; if only he had the spirit of adventure like he had when he was that age. Orin was always walking around the castle grounds or sitting in the library reading. He never saw him entertaining friends or females. He needed to talk to his wife, Amodra, about this. It wasn't right for the prince to be so isolated.

With her in his head, his thoughts went dark again. He quickly shook it off before Orin noticed. They walked towards the throne room to prepare for the petitions.

Solana stood at attention and bowed at the King and Prince as they entered the room. She nodded as Osian tilted his head towards the back room. She wasn't sure he was ready to hear what she had found out, but it had to be said, as unbelievable as it was.

Solana turned around in the room and took a deep breath. Osian stood firmly, his feet apart and his arms crossed against his chest. She quickly noticed that he had lost weight; a tad bit more than she had thought.

"Osian, are you eating at all?" Solana asked gently. Osian rolled his eyes and, for a moment, looked away. When they locked eyes again, all Solana could see was pain.

"Food has lost all flavour for me for now, General. Until I know the truth and the answer, which I am hoping you have for me today, the world is no longer full of anything bright." His eyes shimmered in the candlelight, and he cleared his throat.

Solana shifted her feet and decided that pacing would be the best way to deliver the news that she had for him. Osian watched as she paced. He counted to ten then impatience got the best of him.

"Solana, I love you like a nésa but if you don't say something I'm going to lose my patience." He growled.

Solana stopped pacing and looked at him. He had never seen her look so serious before. She tucked her white hair behind her ears and cleared her throat as she clasped her hands in front of her.

"Sire. There is no delicate way to put this so I'm just going to spit it out. Please forgive my straightforwardness."

Osian nodded and felt a wave of coldness flow through his body as Solana spoke.

"Amodra misled you, sire, just as you had suspected. Orin is indeed your true son, but not hers. The twist is that the woman that you were in love with centuries ago is still very much alive, as you suspected, but it is not the woman that you married." Solana paused.

"The woman currently in your bed has been sucking the lifeforce from you for years-without your consent- even though you and she agreed to feedings if you both couldn't hunt for fresh blood. She will one day kill you, that is her destiny as a Baobhan Sith. She had somehow taken on the form of Amodra to trick you. Ever since you found her in the forest years back, Osian, that was by design. She's not the woman that you had fallen in love with as a young Prince. This creature sharing your bed was never Amodra."

"You need to proceed with caution if you want to find Orin's real mother and not die in the process. We know the tales- a Baobhan Sith, once they know that their glamour is no longer working, has nothing to hide. She *will* kill you and take the crown. I think her intention this entire time has been to claim the strongest throne in Tir Siorghlas and create and army of Baobhan Sith to destroy everything"

Osian felt the blood rush from his head and quickly found a chair to sit in. He stared ahead, absorbing the information that Solana had told him.

"I... I.." he hunched over, placing his hands in his head. "What in the gods have I done, Solana? How did this happen? Have I been dreaming the last many years? How do I get out of this?" He looked up at Solana as she bent down, putting her hand on Osian's knee.

"You are well aware, there is only one way to remove the hold she has on you and the glamour, Sire. You need to stake her, cut her head off. But be prepared, for Orin does not know the truth and I am not sure how he would react to seeing you kill his amille; his powers are so strong he may react before he realizes what is happening. We would do best to find his true amille first before we proceed, to confirm, and then kill the false Amodra and her mates."

Osian felt the bile rush to his throat at the thought of the female currently in his bed; how he went to bed every night and would wake up with healed over puncture wounds on his body.

How he had reached out to a local healer to find a way to remove the spell and having done so, had lain next to the monster for the last few weeks, realizing what she had done to him for years, unsure how to proceed. The hardest moment was realizing that the woman he had actually loved, the mother of Orin, was trapped somewhere all this time, taken from her child, from him. It was all too much for him to process.

Solana watched as Osian struggled with the news, knowing full well how he was feeling. She was shocked at the news herself, but the Baobhan Sith Clan that Osian had given land to had spilled all of it as she had taken one of them to force the truth out of.

When she was done, there was one less Baobhan Sith to spew lies. She was truly impressed with the length that the leader of the Baobhan Sith had gone to procure her hold on the throne. She had done it so well that none of them had been the wiser. Until now.

Osian's true love was buried in a dungeon in the Silver Lands; Solana's new mission was to get her out.

Chapter Six

Clan Basalt

Puck groaned as he opened his eyes, the bright sun piercing them through the sliver in his curtains. He pushed his tousled jet-black hair out of his eyes and gagged at the smell that wafted from the movement.

The echoes of laughter still lingered in the air as Puck stretched and smiled, the lingering thrill of their escapade still buzzing through his veins. It had been a night of adventure, a whirlwind of daring acts, all orchestrated by the mischievous minds of Puck and Kilyn. Orin had been a begrudging participant, the more responsible one of the group.

These three, bound by a childhood of shared secrets and a thirst for excitement, rarely saw each other due to their vastly different responsibilities. Yet, when they did, it was inevitable – chaos would ensue. He sniffed and the smell assaulted his nostrils again. He instantly regretted not washing before crawling into his clean bed in the wee hours of the morning.

A suspicious creak from outside the door sent a jolt of adrenaline through him. He wasn't about to be caught off guard. As Puck bent down, his brilliant cerulean blue eyes flashed as he formed a ball of fire in his hands and waited, leaning against the bedframe for the door to open.

"I know you're here" the voice said.

Puck grinned and held his breath. He could see their feet walking towards the bed. With a shout he jumped out and tossed the fireball towards the figure who in turn squealed in indignation, blocking the magick with his hands, turning it to dust.

"Puck! Stop or I'll tell Ma!" Ward whined as he dusted off his jacket from the embers floating around the room. "You're supposed to come down for breakfast so that we can start eating. Amil and Ma are waiting."

He looked Puck up and down and scrunched his nose. "Maybe you need to have a bath first because you smell like a swamp creature. What did you all do last night?"

Puck carefully sniffed his arm and grimaced as the smell wafted up his nostrils. "We were messing around with Kilyn's water magick," Puck explained, "and we accidentally angered something in the pond. Luckily, Kilyn was able to handle most of the attack."

"When will I get to come and hang out with you all? I'm old enough now and I know how to use my powers." Ward crossed his arms as he looked up at his older brother who was quickly undressing and walking towards the bathing room.

Puck grinned back as he flicked his wrist, and the sunken tub slowly filled with steaming hot water. "Ward, you ARE only a wee half elf, you're not past the youngling stage. I'm of age and Orin and Kilyn are both older than I am. We don't want any selda clinging on. You should find someone your age to hang out with."

Ward frowned and watched as Puck lowered himself into the tub. "Maybe I won't be as good at keeping your secrets anymore then. You know that amil and ma would want to know about your magick." He turned and walked out the door, slamming it behind him as hard as his slender body would allow.

Puck groaned and rolled his eyes. His parents were still oblivious to his teleportation abilities, and he wasn't eager to break the news. Whenever he tried to broach the subject of his lineage, his mother would shut down the conversation, suggesting they discuss it at a later time.

Why should he trust them with his secrets when they couldn't even be open about his own heritage? He was getting tired of the arguments or refusal to talk about what the other half of his genetic makeup was; he had a right to know. Maybe he needed to just get the answers himself-without his ma.

He nodded to himself as he decided the next time they would talk, he would bring up his magick and give them an ultimatum; tell him or he'd leave. They should open up then, he was the crown prince: if he left, they would have to prepare Ward for the crown.

As he lathered up the soap to clean himself, he mused about how to keep Ward safe while still being able to enjoy his time with his friends. Puck leaned his head back and dunked his whole body into the water, holding his breath. He rotated his hands under the water, creating bubbles under the surface and watched as they floated to the top. He held his breath and closed his eyes. He was feeling stifled lately and wondered if it was time for him to leave, to expand his horizons. Maybe Kilyn could use another man on his ship.

He blinked open his eyes to find a face, iridescent eyes flashing as they connected with his, hovering over him. Water filled his lungs and he coughed, sputtering, as he scrambled to sit up. Panic surged through him as he looked around, but the room was empty.

He scrambled out of the tub, wrapping a towel around him and pushing back his hair. A cold dread settled over him as he felt a presence, unseen yet undeniably there.

"Seriously, take your haunted spirit and shove it somewhere else, please and thank you." He muttered as he rummaged through his pile of clothes to find a semi-clean tunic and pants.

As he pulled his clothes on, he looked in the mirror and frowned. With a flick of his wrist, the wrinkles in the clothing smoothed out and his jet-black hair was dry, tousled just right to give him an air of mischievousness.

He smiled as he admired his reflection, his brilliant blue eyes looking back at him. "The ladies will enjoy the view tonight," he declared, though a self-conscience glint in his eye hinted at his true feelings.

He chuckled as he pulled on his boots and made his way downstairs. Who was he kidding? He turned redder than a beetroot at the slightest female attention. He'd be lucky if he could even form a proper sentence if a woman approached him. No, he was much more comfortable in the dirt and the mud with the guys.

He strode out of his room and took the stairs to the main level two at a time, his long legs effortlessly carrying him. As he quickly walked down the hallway, he could hear voices from the breakfast room. Sarya and Carwyn looked up as Puck entered, slightly out of breath.

"Good morning, Ma and amil. Sorry for the delay."

He bent down to pet his dog, Comet. Now old and slow, he preferred to stay close to the warmth of the fires on the main level of the castle.

Sarya beamed with pride as she watched her eldest son. Her eyes were the same as Puck's, wide and brilliant blue, framed with dark lashes. Her long curly brown hair hung down her back, almost touching the back of her legs, the curls framing her heart shaped face and her signature red lips.

Carwyn, his golden eyes taking in his eldest child's attire- looked him up and down with a knowing grin. "Off on a grand adventure tonight, are we, Puck?" he leaned forward on the table, his cream-coloured shirt loose and pushed up at the elbows, a ring on one of his fingers. His brown wavy hair was loose around his face, making him seem younger than his age. He had just come in from the morning check of the barracks and found his soldiers in fine form.

He raised his one eyebrow as Puck leaned down and kissed the top of his little sister's head and reached over to muss the hair of Ward who protested out loud.

"Ma! Make him stop!" Ward smoothed down his wavy brown locks and scrunched his face as he glared at his brother.

Sarya sighed and put her elbow on the table, resting her chin in her hand. "Boys, I do not want to have to put you both in a timeout again. Behave, for the goddess' sake."

She looked at Ward, "Did you give an offering to the goddess for using your magick with your brother upstairs? The both of you?"

The boys groaned and searched their pockets for the bundles that their ma always ensured they had. They pulled them out and walked over to the sideboard, placing them in the large shell as they whispered their thanks. Sarya smiled and nodded as they returned to the table and sat.

Carwyn leaned over and carefully stroked Sarya's belly, which was swollen with their fourth child, due within the next month. Sarya smiled and leaned into Carwyn as he kissed her forehead then looked towards Puck.

"Once you're done eating, we have a name day gift for you, Puck."

Puck stopped shovelling his cooked oats into his mouth and swallowed hard. "But, amil, that's in a week, not now."

Sarya laughed, "Son, it's not normal for you to not want a gift. What exactly is going on in that head of yours? Are you suddenly too grown up?"

Puck flushed and quickly recovered. He shoveled the rest of his food into his mouth, walking quickly to the sideboard to put his dirty bowl there to be cleaned up later and stood tall. Would they be giving him a sword so he could stand with Clan Bayle's armies this season?

Carwyn chuckled and got up. He walked towards Puck and thought about all the years that had passed: how little Puck had been when he came into their lives, the struggles and trials that they had all gone through to get to today. Losing his grandma and the entire Silverbark coven had been hard on all of them, but it seemed to have affected Puck the most.

He knew Puck was hiding something and thought maybe with the early gift, Puck would tell him before it got him into trouble, and before Sarya figured it out. Carwyn slung his arm around Puck's shoulder and smiled at Sarya.

"We will be back shortly, mo chroí. Call if you need help wrangling the bairns."

Sarya rolled her eyes and shooed Carwyn and Puck out the door of the dining room with a laugh. She turned around and waited for her other two children to look at her.

"Ward, Emery, I will only ask this once. Clean up your plates, put them on the sideboard. If you do that, I'll conjure up a vision from a book of your choosing. I feel like I have some magick I can spare today."

Ward and Emery both gasped with delight. Their ma's storytelling was magickal and when she had the energy to do so, she transported them across realms, through all of the neat things that they didn't have at Clan Basalt.

Emery's bright blue and gold eyes lit up as she thought about finding the book with unicorns and dragons in it. Ma would surely read that one this time. She giggled as Ward helped her off her chair.

They quickly cleaned up and ran out the room together, running down to the library, hand in hand. Sarya followed slowly, her pregnant frame still radiant as she ran a hand over her belly, feeling the babe move.

"You're the last heir, little one. Your amil needs to give your ma a break." As she pressed her hand on the small of her back to relieve an ache, she sighed. Soon, her age would start showing.

Unlike the elves with their immortal lives, witches only lived for about 400 years; her mortality weighed on her mind as she watched her children grow. Each passing year was a precious reminder of the fleeting nature of time. But she wouldn't change anything in the realm for what she had been blessed with.

She chuckled as she felt a foot press against her hand, pushing her out of her thoughts. She looked up and watched as Ward and Emery disappeared around the corner of the castle hallway.

If she didn't pick up her pace, they'd be tearing the library apart trying to find the books with dragons in them. After the last encounter with Elara and her dragon, Sarya wanted no part of another one for a long while.

She felt her heart clutch as she remembered her dear departed friend; a friend who succumbed to the evil darkness in Tenebris, north in the Silver Lands. She had struggled to forgive her for killing her coven and almost ripping the realm apart; the darkness had been clever, consuming such an innocent and kind soul. Elara hadn't stood a chance.

She still wrestled with the memories of watching the carnage, Prince Rhamiel standing in the clearing, his face alight with glee as he watched Queen Elara kill Sarya's coven. She closed her eyes for a moment, thanking the goddess for saving her, Morena and Puck from the death that so many others had succumbed to.

She shook her head and reminded herself that going back to the past served no purpose. She pulled her skirts up and walked a bit faster as she heard Ward yell, "Aw not that dumb book again!"

Chapter Seven

Clan Basalt

Carwyn and Puck walked down the hallway through the back doors, heading away from the castle gardens towards the training ground. Puck looked at his father, confusion etched on his face. "Amil, are we practicing today? If so, I'd better change. Ma will have a fit if I ruin this tunic."

Carwyn chuckled and shook his head. "Just keep walking, seldo. I have a question for you."

Puck's stomach lurched. He had a feeling Carwyn was onto him, after all, he hadn't been careful at times with the magick.

"How you answer it will determine your future, seldo," Carwyn continued, his voice serious. "Think carefully before you speak."

Carwyn kept walking casually towards the training grounds, but Puck froze. Should he confess everything? What if he disappointed his father? Carwyn wasn't the type to fly off the handle, but Puck knew he'd may be deeply disappointed.

Puck took a deep breath, trying to calm his racing heart. 'Amil, stop,' he said firmly.

Carwyn halted, turning to face him. Puck met his father's gaze, a goofy grin spreading across his face. Then, with a snap of his fingers, he vanished.

Carwyn stood, shocked. He spun around and frantically looked for his first son. That was not what he thought the secret was. Gods and goddesses did he have some explaining to do with Sarya. And with her delicate state... he cursed under his breath.

The sound of Puck's laughter echoed through the training grounds and it sent a jolt of adrenaline through Carwyn. He quickened his pace, his heart pounding in his chest. Sarya would have his head if anything happened to Puck.

As he approached the training ring, the sight that met his eyes left him speechless. Puck stood in the center of the ring, a mischievous grin playing on his lips, his arms crossed over his chest. But it wasn't Puck's expression that stole Carwyn's breath away. It was the magick around him.

The air crackled with an unseen energy, and the very ground seemed to tremble beneath Puck's feet. Carwyn stared in disbelief, his mind reeling. He had never seen such raw, untamed magick, not for centuries...and the last time it was seen was not a pleasant time for the realm.

Puck, sensing his father's gaze, turned to look at him as he placed a bundle of herbs at his feet. Their eyes met; the young man innocently unaware of what he had unveiled. Carwyn's initial shock gave way to a wave of protectiveness. This changed everything; he had to protect Puck. They had to guide him and ensure that his power was used for good, or he could fall into the clutches of evil so easily.

He took a deep breath, forcing himself to remain calm. He couldn't let Puck see how scared he was, how overwhelmed he felt by the sheer magnitude of his son's power.

"Well, seldo," Carwyn said, his voice firm despite the trembling in his hands, "I see you've been quite active."

"Amil, wasn't this what you were going to ask me about? I know you weren't going to ask me to be in the army and I didn't intend to hide it from you and ma, I wasn't prepared to utilize it for anyone, or..." He faltered as Carwyn stood there, captivated, utterly silent.

Carwyn quickly blinked and recovered, "Seldo, I thought you had a woman! I never thought in a million turns that you were hiding that! Gods! Are you trying to give me more grey hairs?"

Puck relaxed and started to laugh as Carwyn chuckled, which then turned into a full-blown belly laugh as he came up to Puck and hugged him.

"Puck, what a surprise. Well, that beats anything that I was going to get you for your name day then." He waved his hand and whistled as a beautiful horse came out of the bushes, his dark grey coat speckled with white glistened in the sunlight. Puck stood in awe as the horse approached him and nickered, nudging Puck for attention.

"Seldo, meet your new friend. He doesn't have a name yet, but he will become an extension of your being. Take care of him and he will defend you with his life. As a man, it is important that we have a steed to call our own as we go forth in the realm and, gods forbid, into battle."

The horse, knowing that Carwyn was talking about him, stepped back, reared up and suddenly massive white wings burst out of his back. Puck gasped and stepped back in shock as the animal stomped his feet, whinnying and shaking his head.

Puck turned back to Carwyn, "Amil! Where did you find a Pegasus? I thought they were extinct?"

Carwyn grinned. The circle of Mystics in the Silver Lands still had a small herd and his brother, Gaeleath, making amends, had parted with one of their best mounts.

Carwyn's relationship with his older twin brother was still slightly strained because of what had happened with him and their parents. Years of not knowing that he was a twin, his brother trapped in a room in the wing of their castle, under his nose. All because of a blood oath their father had made against his firstborn grandchild to protect his Clan during times of darkness. A mistake their father acknowledged before death had claimed him.

Gaeleath had made a secondary blood oath to destroy the first which resulted in their parents' lifeblood being sold to cover the debt, releasing his own child that no one had known about.

Carwyn, Sarya and the children had travelled to Gaeleath's home in the Silver Lands a few times in the years since to get to know his wife, Magnolia and their daughter, Piper. After learning why Gaeleath had done what he did, Carwyn had to respect it; he would have done the same to protect his family. But at the time, he had been prepared to murder his own brother for how he had gone about it.

He came back to the present and smiled at his son, "Don't worry about that, seldo. Just give him a name to make him proud and spend time with him."

Puck nodded and reached to pet the Pegasus. The animal bowed his head and nudged Puck again. Puck laughed and pressed his head against him and whispered, "Atlas."

Atlas nickered in agreement at the name chosen for him. Puck turned to Carwyn.

"Am I able to ride him?"

Carwyn smiled and crossed his arms. "Don't ask me, talk to Atlas. He'll tell you what he wants."

Atlas whinnied and bent his front knee, allowing Puck space to get onto his back, between his massive wings. Puck carefully mounted and patted Atlas' neck. Atlas nickered and then with no warning bounded forward, the air under his wings catching as they soared upwards.

Carwyn watched carefully, ensuring to have time if he had to create a safety net out of vines so that Puck wouldn't die on his first flight. Puck had his hands threaded in Atlas' mane and was leaning low; almost if he had instinctively known what to do.

He beamed with pride. Though Puck wasn't his biological son, he was just as cherished as his other children, and his love for him was boundless. He considered it a profound honor to be Puck's amil and took the responsibility with the utmost seriousness.

Carwyn shook his head, a mixture of awe and apprehension washing over him again. A young warlock with the power of teleportation? Tir Siorghlas was stirring ancient magick, and the implications were both terrifying and exhilarating. He'd been so off-base about Puck hiding a woman.

He chuckled to himself as he watched Atlas land and Puck dismount. He walked away from the training ring to let Puck have some time alone with Atlas.

Now was the time to break the news to Sarya about what Puck had been hiding, fully realizing there was no way to tell her gently. He braced himself for a reaction very different from what he would have expected if it had been a woman.

He mused if he would be able to break Sarya's silence about Puck's lineage so they could better prepare for the future. Clearly, Puck was more than half a warlock: the magick never lied.

That was a topic that she tended to clam up about and Carwyn hated the look she got in her eyes when it was brought up. As he walked across the gardens, suddenly the side of the castle where the library stood burst forth with light and images of unicorns danced across the lawn.

"It looks like Emery won in the book choosing again," Carwyn chuckled to himself.

Carwyn navigated the hallway when something in the front foyer arrested his attention. A wooden crate, bound with rough rope, sat precariously atop the table, a single card affixed to its surface. He approached, extracting the card. It bore a simple inscription: *"To be opened by Eldatár Carwyn."*

Carwyn frowned, returning the card to its place. He scrutinized the crate, his fingers tracing its contours, attempting to work out its contents. Despite the prevailing peace of the land, a lingering unease-a shared sentiment amongst the Kings- permeated the air. The crate felt profoundly out of place, and it sent alarm bells ringing within him.

He summoned a servant, who materialized promptly, bowing respectfully. Carwyn gestured towards the crate. "Do you know how this arrived?" he inquired.

The servant, eyes darting between the crate and the King, stammered, clearly flustered.

"Eldatár, I was instructed to leave it there for you. I did not recognize the messenger, but they were insistent it was for you and it was cleared by the guards, they said it was a brown cloth and spices? I apologize, should it go somewhere else?" the servant went to grab the crate, but Carwyn stopped him.

"No, that is fine, thank you. I will figure out what to do with it for now. You can go."

The servant bowed and walked away, wringing his hands as he worried that he had done something wrong.

Carwyn settled into the chair opposite the crate, subjecting it to another critical appraisal. His gaze roved over the rough-hewn wood and the coarse rope binding, a puzzle piece refusing to fit.

The rope, he realized, was unfamiliar, not the style typically used within Tir Siorghlas. And the wood; it bore no resemblance to any species he could recall from the surrounding forests. And why would he want anything to do with fabric and spices? Was it possible that it was under an illusion?

He rose, pouring himself a generous measure of spirits. He savored the potent liquor, his gaze lingering on the crate. An unsettling feeling urged him to proceed with caution, to resist the temptation to open it.

Instead, he resolved to secure the crate in a safe, undisclosed location. He would talk with the other Clan leaders, check whether they too had received such unexpected deliveries, and then, and only then, would he consider opening it.

Carwyn flung open the window, the cool breeze whipping through the room. With practiced speed, he penned five missives, then whistled sharply. A flurry of motion answered his call as a squadron of falcons, perched atop the army barracks, took to the air. Stepping out onto the balcony, Carwyn swiftly affixed the letters to their legs.

With a flick of his wrist, each falcon launched itself into the sky, their powerful wings carrying them towards their respective Clans. The birds seemed to relish the mission, eager to serve.

Carwyn sighed, draining the last swallow of the liquor from his glass. His gaze followed the retreating falcons, each a feathered messenger bearing his concerns. Then, his eyes returned to the crate, its presence on the table now unwelcome. A tremor, a low thrum of unease, snaked through him, unsure of the mystery that lay within.

Chapter Eight

Riverstone

The captain's eyes wandered, assessing the port. Years of work, countless sacrifices, had led to this point. He would not be deterred, not now, not when the culmination of his efforts was so close.

He strode across the cobblestones towards the stable, a sturdy structure nestled against the tavern. As he entered, he noticed the air was thick with the scent of hay and horse sweat. He frowned as he looked around, finding the stable manager leaning against a pitchfork, taking a break.

The stable manager, a grizzled man, regarded the visitor with a gruff, "What brings you here?"

The captain grinned, a glint of amusement in his eyes. "I require a mount." He tossed a small pouch of coins onto the hay-strewn floor. "The finest you have."

The manager, eyes widening at the sight of the Locryan gold, gestured towards a magnificent creature occupying a stall at the far end. At nineteen hands high, the stallion dwarfed its companions, its coat a deep, lustrous black that shimmered in the dim light. The captain chuckled as the horse nipped at the manager's sleeve. Feisty, indeed. Just as he preferred.

He pulled the reins taut, bringing the horse's head level with his own. Their gazes locked, an unspoken understanding passing between them. The stallion, a low nicker rumbling in its chest, patiently waited for the captain to mount his back. With a practiced ease, the captain swung himself into the saddle, his legs finding their place naturally.

As the horse settled back on its hooves, the captain patted his neck affectionately. "What is your name, magnificent beast?" he inquired.

The stable manager, eyes fixed on the imposing creature, uttered a single word, his voice tinged with a hint of fear, "Diablo."

The captain threw his head back and roared with laughter as Diablo, in a sudden burst of energy, reared back, his hooves flashing in the air. The startled manager scrambled out of the way as the magnificent pair thundered out of the stable, leaving a trail of dust in their wake.

"Good riddance," the manager grumbled, brushing himself off. He hefted the heavy bag of coins, a satisfied smile playing on his lips. With a mischievous glint in his eye, he disappeared into the depths of the stable.

The captain, astride Diablo, guided the magnificent beast back towards the bustling port. One final task remained before he could embark from Riverstone. His first mate, a seasoned sailor that had spent many years with him, approached, bowing respectfully. "Captain," he saluted, "all preparations are complete as you instructed. What further orders do you have for us?"

The captain, a mischievous glint in his eye, nodded. "You are free to indulge in whatever pursuits your hearts desire until my return."

"However," he added with a stern glance, "I expect to find this port intact upon my return. Don't forget to check in with your wife!"

With a grin, the first mate caught the heavy sack of coins the captain tossed towards him. A wave of excited murmurs rippled through the crew, their imaginations already ablaze with the possibilities that lay before them.

The captain reined Diablo around, preparing to depart. "Captain," the first mate queried, his voice low, "What of our plans? Are they aware of your arrival?"

A feral grin spread across the captain's face. "Oh, they will be keenly aware of my presence," he declared, his voice a low growl. "I am coming to reclaim what is rightfully mine. And when those crates are opened by the kings, all of Tir Siorghlas will tremble at the knowledge of my return."

Diablo, sensing the surge of his master's power, whinnied and reared dramatically, his hooves striking the cobblestones with a thunderous sound. In an instant, the magnificent beast and his fearsome rider vanished from the port, leaving behind only a trail of swirling dust and the echoes of the captain's chilling laughter.

The first mate looked at his crew with a grin. "Time to find ourselves some luscious Riverstone minxes to bury ourselves into, mates! The coin will let us feast for weeks!"

The crew yelled and jeered as they stormed off the ship towards the village.

A shipmate approached the first mate hesitantly, "Frig, where is Captain Taion going?" he watched as Diablo thundered away down the main road.

Frig shrugged, his gaze following Diablo's receding form. "None of my concern, Jep. The Captain will return when he's good and ready. Until then, I intend to indulge in the pleasures of elven pussy – deeply and without interruption!" He roared with laughter, his dark eyes crinkling as his voice echoed through the port. The crew, emboldened by their newfound wealth and the promise of revelry, surged towards the Fiddler's Inn.

Women, clutching their children close, hastily retreated into the safety of nearby buildings, their eyes wide with apprehension as the motley crew descended upon the street. However, one woman, her face etched with defiance, stood firm, blocking their path as they attempted to force their way into the tavern.

Her dark hair was draped over her shoulder, her pointed ears decorated with hooped golden earrings. Her corset was tight around her ribs, giving her a classic hourglass figure, a perfect body for the men to appreciate. Frig's eyes roamed over her, his eyes hungry as he grinned.

"Sirs, kind sirs," She nodded with a gentle but firm smile as she draped her arms across the doorframe. "Now, I wouldn't want to have to kick you out before you've even stepped foot into my inn, would I?

So, before you choose to cross this threshold, there are some rules for the lot of you."

She looked across the group and laid eyes on Frig. Her smile widened as she continued, "First of all, the pussy which you so loudly speak of Mr. Frig? Well, that lovely Riverstone pussy is some of the best that we have here, and I wouldn't want to have to call upon our guards to toss any of you out for damaging the goods, yes?"

She crossed her arms, a formidable figure despite her diminutive stature. Stepping down in front of Frig, she raised her head, her gaze unwavering, and he felt a shiver down his spine. This woman was no pushover, and he loved it.

Frig swallowed hard, his bravado momentarily shaken. He quickly handed her the heavy coin purse, which she deftly caught. A fleeting smile touched her lips as she assessed the rowdy crew, her gaze lingering on each man.

"Well, lucky for you lads," she declared, her voice surprisingly melodic, "it seems Mr. Frig has generously provided the means for you to drown yourselves in elven hospitality, if you so choose-but be careful with the witches."

The men exchanged hesitant glances, unsure of how to react to this unexpected turn of events. Amara rolled her eyes, a gesture of both amusement and exasperation.

"That means the ladies will be expecting your company after you've freshened up, boys!" she announced, her voice echoing through the street. The men erupted in cheers, anticipation filling the air as they surged into the inn.

Stepping aside, Amara waited for Frig to join her, their gazes meeting once more. "Mr. Frig," she began, her voice firm, "the agreement is clear: food, lodging, and the unwavering consent of our ladies. No coercion, no exceptions. Understand?"

Frig nodded eagerly. "Yes, ma'am, I understand. I agree to your terms, and I assure you, my men will abide by them."

Amara scoffed, a hint of amusement in her eyes. "Amara," she corrected, her gaze unwavering. "Just Amara. And that's an agreement you won't soon forget, *husband*."

A slow grin spread across his face. He crossed his fingers over his heart, a silent promise. "Amara, my sweet, wonderful, understanding wife," he responded, her name rolling off his tongue with the ease of years being together. "I swear."

Amara tossed her long brown hair over her shoulder, a mischievous glint in her eyes. With a final, lingering look at him, she turned and disappeared into the inn, Frig hot on her heels.

Chapter Nine

Riverstone &
Clan Basalt

Taion inhaled deeply, the crisp mountain air filling his lungs. The scent of cedar and pine needles, sharp and invigorating, scented the air as they rode further north, leaving Riverstone behind. Even at this altitude, the peaks remained crowned with snow, promising a steady supply of fresh water for the villages nestled in the valleys below.

Determined to remain undetected, Taion guided Diablo along the less-traveled paths, though a brief encounter wouldn't derail his plans, merely introduce a minor delay. He allowed Diablo to set the pace, mindful of the thinning air as they climbed deeper into the mountain pass. Overexerting the magnificent beast would prove detrimental to their journey, and he was partial to the animal.

Relaxing slightly in the saddle, Taion scanned the rugged terrain with his iridescent purple and blue eyes, searching for any sign of sentries or scouts. The mountain pass remained eerily quiet, a welcome relief. A grin touched his lips as he patted Diablo's neck, acknowledging their good fortune.

He nudged Diablo forward, urging the horse to increase his pace.

Lingering in the open pass was a risky proposition. His imposing figure and the sheer size of Diablo were bound to attract unwanted attention; they stuck out like a third eyeball on a human.

Years had passed since he last stepped on Tir Siorghlas' soil, and while returning felt like a homecoming, the memories that clung to the land were anything but welcoming.

A weary sigh escaped him as he forcefully banished the haunting images from his mind. Now was not the time for such unwelcome intrusions, he would deal with those later.

As they rode, a small forest materialized ahead, an unexpected obstacle in the familiar landscape. He frowned, puzzled. This grove of trees had not been present during his last journey through this region. Had the land changed so drastically in his absence?

The earth trembled beneath them, and the surrounding woods groaned in protest as they pressed further into its depths. The forest, it seemed, resented his intrusion. Taion braced himself, the sudden swaying of the trees confirming his suspicion: a sentry lay in wait.

"Hold!" A voice, sharp and commanding, echoed through the trees. Taion swore under his breath, but pressed on, guiding Diablo deeper into the treacherous terrain. He would not be deterred.

"Sir, in the name of Clan Basalt and our Eldatár, Halt!"

Taion paused, Clan Basalt? He had veered too far east, too soon. He carefully tilted his head back a bit to assess how many sentries were on his tail. Two guards wearing the Clan Basalt crest sat on steeds, waiting with their swords drawn. Taion sighed and reached down to stroke Diablo's neck while responding, "I bow to no King."

With a roar, Taion urged Diablo forward. The stallion, muscles rippling, exploded from the forest, hooves pounding the earth as they fled the pursuing Basalt sentries. Their shouts echoed behind them, growing fainter with each thunderous stride. Finally, bursting into the open, they emerged from the canopy of the forest and into the blinding sunlight of the plains.

Reining in Diablo, Taion slowed their pace. He surveyed the vast expanse of grassland, a frown creasing his brow. How, in the gods, had he strayed so far off course? His ruse was over. The sentries would undoubtedly report his presence to the King of Clan Basalt. He hoped that by then, the boxes would be opened by them.

"Again, not exactly according to plan," Taion muttered to himself, a wry smile playing on his lips. Time for a little bit of theatrics. With a snap of his fingers, he vanished into thin air, leaving the sentries staring in disbelief.

The sentries stood frozen at the edge of the forest, their eyes wide as saucers. The large black horse and its rider vanished without a trace.

"Did... did that just happen?" one sentry stammered, his voice trembling.

The other, his face pale, rubbed his eyes vigorously. "Sermo, I think we need to report this to the King immediately. Magick of that caliber... it can only bring trouble to Tir Siorghlas."

"Didn't the last man who wielded such power..." The first sentry's voice trailed off as the second raised a warning hand.

"Don't speak that name, sermo, not here. Not now." The second sentry's voice was hushed, laced with apprehension. "We don't need to stir up unnecessary fear among the Clans. And for the love of all that is holy, let's not jump to conclusions."

The first sentry, still bewildered by the events that had transpired, followed his companion as they cantered back towards Ochor and Castle Stowerling. He hadn't realized that the name still held the power to stir such deep-seated fear within the Clans.

Years had passed since the darkness had been vanquished, along with its monstrous minions and the soldiers who had succumbed to its influence. He glanced back, searching for any sign of the rider, but the road remained eerily empty.

As they approached the castle, they reined in their horses, nodding to the guards stationed at the entrance. They dismounted, moving with the ease of seasoned soldiers. The first sentry removed his helmet, tucking it under his arm and mirroring the gesture of his companion.

"Let me handle this," the second sentry muttered under his breath, anticipating the questions that would undoubtedly follow. The massive oak doors creaked open, revealing the castle's butler, his expression a mask of impassivity.

The second sentry cleared his throat, attempting to compose

himself. He was about to begin to ask for the king when the first sentry, growing impatient with his hesitation, blurted out, "We encountered a rider on a large black horse deep within the forest. When we ordered him to halt, he vanished into thin air, right before our very eyes!"

The butler's carefully maintained composure shattered. His eyes widened in shock, and he took a startled step back, his hands instinctively clutching at the lapels of his jacket. A silent nod of acknowledgment passed between him and the guards, then he turned and hurried down the hall, summoning a servant with a frantic wave of his hand.

Whispered conversations erupted among the guards as the servant, his face pale, hurried towards the library where Carwyn and Sarya were visiting with their children.

The second sentry frowned at his companion, a sigh escaping his lips. "Peace in Tir Siorghlas," he muttered, "it seems to be hanging by a thread."

"Sorry," the first sentry mumbled, "but you were taking a bleedin' eternity to get to the point."

Carwyn and Sarya emerged from the hallway, the servant struggling to keep pace with their hurried strides. Sarya, her hand gently resting on her swollen belly, attempted to maintain a calm façade as her one hand held her royal blue skirt up so she didn't trip, but her eyes betrayed her anxiety. Carwyn, on the other hand, barely suppressed his fury.

"What in the name of the gods is this charade?" Carwyn demanded, his voice booming. "You claim someone vanished into thin air? Such magick has been absent from Tir Siorghlas for generations. Explain yourselves!"

The sentries exchanged nervous glances. The second sentry stepped forward, his voice trembling slightly. "Sire, we swear on our oaths to the Clan. The horse... it was enormous, at least nineteen, perhaps even twenty hands tall, dark like the devil. And the rider... we couldn't see much other than his eyes, but he snapped his fingers, and just like that..." He snapped his fingers, a chilling echo of the impossible event. "...he was gone. Vanished without a trace."

Sarya's face paled, her hand instinctively clutching at her belly. Fear, cold and sharp, pierced through her. She stumbled back, her knees buckling as her mind spun back to that fateful time. Carwyn, his heart pounding, quickly caught her in his arms, his gaze locked with hers, confusion swirling around them.

"Carwyn, what are we going to do?" Sarya whispered, her voice trembling, her face buried in his chest. He held her close, his chin resting on her head, his gaze fixed on the sentries.

"Maintain absolute silence," he instructed them. "If you encounter anything unusual, report directly to me immediately. And triple the border guard patrols, now." The sentries bowed, their faces grim. They strode out of the castle, mounting their horses, spurring them into a gallop. They disappeared towards the barracks to gather reinforcements.

"Sarya," Carwyn said gently, pulling her back to face him. He held her arms firmly, forcing her to meet his golden gaze. He paused as he watched her wide blue eyes fill with tears. "Do not speculate. Do not allow yourself to panic. We do not know the true nature of what those men witnessed."

He sighed, a deep furrow creasing his brow. "There's something I need to tell you about Puck, mo chroí. I believe he should be here."

Sarya frowned, tilting her head in confusion as she wiped her tears. "I am completely lost, Carwyn. What is happening? What does Puck have to do with this display of ancient magick?"

Anxiety surged through her, and she spun around, rushing to the window. She scanned the courtyard, searching for Puck. Relief washed over her when she spotted him, his hand gently stroking the neck of his new Pegasus, Atlas. The tension that had gripped her began to ease.

Puck looked up and smiled, waving to his mother. Sarya returned the wave, a soft smile gracing her lips. He softly stroked Atlas's cheek. "Well, Atlas," he murmured, "it seems it's time I had a little chat with ma and amil about what I've been up to and make my demands. You'll wait for me here, won't you?"

Atlas whinnied softly, nudging Puck's shoulder playfully. "Willing to let me walk to my figurative death already, Atlas?" Puck chuckled, shaking his head. "True friend, you are." Atlas whinnied indignantly, stomping his foot on the ground, causing Puck to burst into laughter.

"I only tease, Atlas," Puck said, a playful grin on his face. He shoved his hands into his pockets and began walking towards the castle, his gaze drawn to the window where his mother stood, worry etched deeply on her features. His amil stood behind her, mirroring her concern.

Puck frowned, puzzled. There was no reason for such grave concern. Unless...unless they had received some disturbing news. He pulled his hands from his pockets and broke into a jog, reaching the door to the breakfast nook in a few strides.

"Ma! Amil!" he exclaimed, bursting through the door, "What is it? What happened?"

Carwyn nodded towards the chairs nestled in the corner, gesturing for them to sit. Puck, ever the independent spirit, crossed his arms stubbornly. "I'll stand, thank you, what's going on?"

Carwyn nodded, his gaze unwavering as he waited for Sarya to join him. He gently took her hand, ensuring she was comfortable before speaking. Sarya looked at him, her face a mask of worry, her blue eyes reflecting her unease.

Carwyn cleared his throat, his voice firm. "Puck, seldo, I believe it's time you demonstrated your newfound abilities to your mother. Please."

Puck's face fell. Anger surged through him at his father for cornering him like this. He swallowed thickly as he realized he had been caught off guard.

He sheepishly grinned at Sarya, his hand rising slowly towards his chest. Sarya watched intently, her eyes wide with anticipation, waiting for her firstborn to reveal the secret he had been keeping.

With a sudden snap of his fingers, Puck vanished, leaving Sarya staring in stunned silence at the empty space where he had stood.

She fainted.

Carwyn swore as he dove to catch her before she fell out of the chair. With Sarya cradled in his arms, he looked around to see where Puck had decided to show up and looked outside to see him standing by Atlas.

Carwyn stood up, Sarya in his arms as Puck looked back at his ma and amil, a frown creasing his face. He whispered something to Atlas who bent at his knee, allowing Puck to climb up.

Sarya's eyes fluttered and she opened them, quickly looking around as Carwyn groaned out loud, "For the gods. Puck, don't be a stupid lad."

Sarya caught Carwyn's line of sight and watched as Puck and Atlas took to the skies together, until they could see them no longer.

Sarya's sob caught in her throat as Carwyn pulled her closer to him, tenderly stroking her hair as she cried. She sniffled suddenly and Carwyn felt her body tense with anger.

She shoved Carwyn, "Put me down, immediately."

Carwyn quickly put Sarya on her feet and went to speak and she raised her hand up, "Unless you want me freezing you to the spot for the next however unforeseeable future, keep those lips shut, Carwyn."

"OHHH! I am so angry! At you! At Puck! You should have told me!"

She spun on her heels and paced, flinging her arms around her as she ranted. "We have a teleporting half warlock in our midst! Of all the godsdamned powers Puck could have inherited, it had to be the ancient one that quite literally can tear the threads of our existence apart if not used properly."

Carwyn lifted his finger up to interject and she whirled around on him, her finger pointed at him. He stood straight and gulped as she stormed over to him.

She stood toe to toe and jabbed him in the chest, her small frame radiating anger as her magick swirled around her, lifting her hair off her shoulders, creating a shimmering outline around her.

He looked at his wife; she may be small but right now he would bet the universe that she would be able to destroy everything in her path right now.

"Do," poke "not," poke "try me," she snarled as Carwyn watched her. He put his hands up in surrender and stepped back.

Sarya took a deep breath and closed her eyes, caressing her belly as she breathed long and deeply, in, then out. She opened her eyes and her magick subsided.

"I know you were there the day that I was found in Blackwood's cells, my love. I know you know what happened." Her eyes glistened with unshed tears as she walked over to a chair to sit down. Carwyn had guessed as much but until now had not determined who could have sired Puck.

Carwyn carefully pulled a chair towards her and sat in front of her, pulling her one hand to rest in his. Sarya sighed and looked at Carwyn.

"I had hoped that Puck would have been spared receiving something from his parentage from the man who sired him. I don't even know where to start to understand the magick that he now wields, and so carelessly! Carwyn! What do we do?" she looked up at him, her face sorrowful as a tear rolled down her cheek.

Carwyn used his thumb to gently remove the tear off her cheek and she let him cup her face in his hand. As Sarya closed her eyes she whispered, "Magick takes. If he does not replace what he has taken from using it, we will lose him, just like my ma. The grey death will slowly work its way to his heart, and we won't be able to pull it back."

He looked at his wife; his strong, fierce wife and pursed his lips, formulating an answer.

"I'll find him, mo chroí, I promise. We'll make an offering to restore the balance for the magick that he's used. We will not lose him. But you need to sit down with him and have an honest discussion about his sire."

Soaring above the land, Puck surveyed below, searching for the invisible boundary that marked the edge of their lands.

The lands of Clan Basalt stretched out on the southwestern peninsula of Tir Siorghlas, woven between the rugged coastline and forests. Rolling hills, carpeted in lush green grass, gave way to fields of golden hay, shimmering under the summer sun. The ocean, a vibrant turquoise, lapped at the rocky shores.

The forests, a patchwork of emerald and jade, were scattered throughout the landscape, offering a haven for countless creatures. As his eyes roamed the land, they rested on the small mountains to the east of the border, their rounded tops dusted with fresh snow.

A pang of apprehension, a flutter of rebellion, stirred within him.

The thought of leaving his home and striking out on his own no longer seemed so daunting, even though it wasn't the way he had planned.

He didn't need his ma or amil to dictate how he used his magick. He had been honing his abilities for months when he had first discovered it, and nothing untoward had occurred. He felt invincible, untouchable, and resented the thought of them wanting to control him.

A wave of anger surged through him leaving a bitter taste in his mouth. How dare his amil corner him like that, forcing him to reveal his secret like that? It wasn't fair.

And now, he feared, his mother would recoil from him, horrified by the knowledge that the magick coursing through his veins might be a tainted inheritance, a legacy of the unknown man that had sired him. Why wouldn't his ma tell him anything about it? What could be so awful that he didn't deserve the truth?

As Atlas glided closer to the invisible border, Puck faced a choice.

Chapter Ten

Clan Aether

Solana strode into the barracks, her presence commanding attention. Her gaze fell upon a seasoned soldier who was cleaning the swords after their last training session Solana waved and stomped the ground, getting the attention of the soldier. She looked up and paused from cleaning the sword as Solana signed, "I need you to pick a small team of ten. This is a covert assignment, and I need complete discretion."

The soldier, Nala, put down the sword and returned sign, her brow furrowed. "Understood, General. I know the soldiers for this mission. But the objective...?"

Solana stepped closer, her gaze piercing Nala's green eyes. "What I am about to reveal must remain strictly within the confines of this team, Nala. The Eldatár's throne hangs in the balance."

Nala blinked rapidly, the gravity of Solana's words sinking in. She nodded decisively, signing, "We need to discuss this elsewhere."

Solana nodded, her eyes scanning the room. "Follow me out there," she signed, gesturing towards the door.

Nala, understanding the need for secrecy, followed Solana until they reached the outer wall of the castle. "Meet me here with your chosen team," Solana signed. "We will convene outside the walls. I will provide you with all the necessary information. Prepare yourselves accordingly. Travel light. Bring the earplugs the Eldatár crafted just in case and as much iron as you can bear without hindering your movement."

Nala's eyes widened in apprehension. "Understood," she signed, bowing her head before swiftly departing towards the training grounds to assemble her team.

Solana sighed, the weight of the mission settling upon her. As she surveyed the castle, her gaze was drawn to a particular window. Their eyes met – hers and those of Amodra, the Baobhan Sith. Solana schooled her features, a serene smile gracing her lips as she returned the gaze and waved.

Amodra looked back at her and didn't bother to return the wave. She turned around and walked the room, a thin robe thrown over her body while she had been pacing. She had heard Osian instruct the guards to not let her out and no matter how much sweet talk or cajoling she had tried, they were not budging.

She wasn't used to men being impervious to her charm. Had they been made aware of what was going on in their king's chambers? She wondered if she could turn the charm on a bit more and manage to escape them before she was betrayed by the man she had married.

King Osian was almost outliving his usefulness; Amodra had estimated that he should have died years ago, yet he kept on living, almost as if he had protections placed to keep his soul from leaving his body.

Each night as she pressed her fangs to his chest and drank her fill, she could feel a barrier keeping her from fully taking what she needed; no, what she wanted, what she was due.

She needed him dead before the Clan started to break free from the glimmer and illusion she had placed on the court. Once Osian was dead, she would be the sole crown of Clan Aether; she could release her

Baobhan Sith mates and together they would feast until they couldn't anymore. The task of taking over the Clan would make up for the years she had denied herself true pleasure.

She missed the erotic sex and blood high that she could only get when she was with her mates. It had been a necessary evil to pull the true Amodra out of Osian's grasp to get this far. The child was a bit of a pesky issue, however his brain had been malleable and any memories he had of his true mother had been spellbound.

Orin only knew the pretend Amodra as his mother; he thought he was half Baobhan Sith. The truth was that no Baobhan Sith had ever given birth; they were already dead, made only by the trading of blood. It was almost laughable that she had easily convinced Osian that it had happened. Men. She rolled her eyes.

Amodra stopped pacing, an insidious grin spreading across her lips. If they wouldn't let her leave as a Queen, she'd show them the true beast within.

With a low growl, her eyes ignited, a malevolent yellow fire burning within them. She dropped to her knees, her body contorting with unnatural speed. Bones snapped and shifted, fur erupting from her skin. In a matter of seconds, she was transformed, a magnificent, predatory wolf, her eyes gleaming with savage hunger.

A commotion erupted behind the heavy oak doors, warning shouts and the sound of weapons being drawn. She padded towards them, growls rumbling deep in her chest. The scent of fear, thick and pungent, rolled off the guards in waves.

With a deafening howl, she launched herself at the doors, her massive frame shattering the wood like kindling. The heavy oak doors splintered, one crashing down on the startled guard, while the other, sword drawn, scrambled back in terror.

Amodra chuckled darkly in her wolf form. "I always loved to fight for my breakfast, elf." she hissed, saliva dripping from her fangs. The guard, eyes wide with terror, swung his sword, but the blow was clumsy, easily evaded. With a savage lunge, Amodra sank her teeth into his neck.

Her wolf form faded away as she continued to feed on the guard's body, feeling his heartbeat slowing down until just before it took its last beat, she released herself. She wiped her mouth with her arm and watched with glee as the other guard who had been pushed under the door was dragging himself towards the stairs.

"Sound the alarm! For the love of the gods, sound the godsdamned alarm! The Elentári..." his last words garbled as Amodra ripped his head off of his body.

His body slumped and tumbled down the stairs, a grotesque show of limbs and blood. It bounced and slid, finally coming to rest in a heap at the bottom of the staircase. Amodra watched with a grin, enjoying the macabre spectacle as she heard gasps from the elves who had just left the throne room.

Amodra licked her lips, a predatory gleam in her eyes. "Blasphemy against the Elentári," she purred, her voice a silken whisper, "appears to carry a rather... severe penalty."

A peal of laughter, chilling and cruel, escaped her lips. With a casual flick of her wrist, she tossed the severed head aside as if it were nothing more than a discarded toy.

"It seems many of you are guilty of this most heinous crime," she observed, as she walked down the stairs, her gaze sweeping over the small group of elves. "Simply by bearing witness to the... unfortunate demise of that guard."

One of the elves, his face pale, stammered, "Your Highness! We beg for mercy!" He threw himself to his knees, followed by the others, a pathetic display.

Amodra narrowed her eyes, assessing the potential victims. How many could she subdue, how many could she drag back to her kin, those unfortunate souls imprisoned on the other side of the magickal barrier?

The ruse was clearly over now. Osian, soon to be nothing more than an empty shell, would no longer be a hindrance. And why not indulge in a little recreational feeding? After all, what were a few more casualties when victory was so close? She would savor the moment, each delicious bite, until finally, she could claim her rightful prize – Osian's lifeblood... and perhaps the Prince's as well.

"Get up, you pathetic creatures," Amodra sneered, wrinkling her nose in disgust. "Lucky for you, I've already indulged in my breakfast. Otherwise, you'd all be nourishing my hunger by midday."

Fear radiated from the cowering elves, their eyes wide with terror as they scrambled to their feet, avoiding any direct eye contact with their now monstrous Queen.

Amodra, satisfied with their display of abject fear, strolled amongst them, pausing to poke one unfortunate elf in the ribs with a long, crimson-stained finger. "As a matter of fact," she purred, her voice a silken caress, "I suggest you leave the castle immediately. Head directly towards the border with the Baobhan Sith Clan."

Her gaze, cold and predatory, lingered on each of them, their minds already reeling under her hypnotic influence. They nodded mutely, their movements robotic, as if under a spell. One by one, they shuffled out of the castle, their footsteps echoing down the cobblestone steps, forming a silent, terrified procession.

Amodra leaned against the imposing oak doors, watching them go with a satisfied smirk. All that killing and feeding, while exhilarating, had left her with a different kind of hunger.

Amodra paused, a mischievous glint in her eyes. An idea began to form. Who, she wondered, would be the most... willing... accomplice in her plans?

As she ascended the stairs, another guard emerged from the back hall. Her eyes lit up. Standing at the top of the staircase, she beckoned with a single finger, her other hand casually tracing a suggestive path up her stomach to fondle her breast.

The guard, his gaze locked with Amodra's, saw only a vision of his forbidden desire –his betrothed, transformed into a creature of ethereal beauty. He grinned, his weapon clattering to the floor as he moved towards her with an urgency that bordered on desperation.

Amodra, her touch a whirlwind of sensation, ran her hands up his chest, swiftly undoing the clasps of his armor. The metal pieces clattered to the floor, a symphony of release. With a seductive purr, she pulled him towards the King's chambers, her touch a burning brand against his skin.

The guard whispered, "My love, I didn't think you would give yourself to me until after the wedding."

Amodra rolled her eyes and pretended to care, "I just cannot hold back any longer, my love, please take me, ravage me."

The guard groaned and pulled Amodra onto him as she quickly

released him from his pants. He swiftly buried himself into her and Amodra sighed in pleasure, feeling herself being filled by the guard. As he thrust, holding onto her hips, she pushed him to lay down on the bed so she could ride him.

She slowly ran her hand up his chest until her hand was on his neck. Her nails elongated as she tightened her grip on him, making the guard grunt with the cut off airflow.

She grinned down at him as he bucked against her. She leaned her head down and with a growl whispered, "Would your beloved really ride you like a seasoned whore, guard?"

The guard pulled back, his eyes widening in horror as he saw Amodra's true form, her red eyes sunken in her head; her body thin and bony. He let out a strangled gasp, his body stiffening in fear. Amodra, sensing his distress, quickly dispelled the illusion, her form shifting back to that of his betrothed.

The guard relaxed, his fear subsiding, and he resumed his embrace, his mind clouded by the lingering effects of the illusion. He ran his hands over her hips, his movements clumsy as he bucked under her; believing he was making love to his beloved.

With a feral grin, she tightened her hand around his neck until he could only wheeze, her nails digging in. She was enjoying the feeling of his cock sliding in and out of her and she wasn't ready to lose her climax.

She groaned as she felt herself tighten. She quickened her pace and felt the guard stiffening under her. She grinned again and bent her head towards his neck, purring, "You won't last long once you come." She quickly increased her rhythm until she felt her climax approaching; pressing her fangs against his neck.

As she broke the skin, she heard him sigh with ecstasy. She grinned as she slowly lapped the blood up, creating an image of pure unadulterated bliss for the man as she took his life force.

With a final thrust, she moaned against his neck as her climax overtook her. She bit down hard and sucked as he gurgled in panic. The guard in his weakened state tried to claw her hand off of him but she held his neck tight as she took her fill.

She slid off of him, her hand still tight around his throat, keeping him immobile as she continued to drink until she felt the last breath leave him. She smiled and sat back, looking at the lifeless body on the King's bed and laid back on her elbows, playing with her nipples.

She flipped around to her belly and propped her head on her hands. She brought her calves up and slowly swung them as she mused what her next step would be. It was time to find Osian. She was done waiting and the throne was calling.

Chapter Eleven

The Whisperwoods

Taion materialized in the heart of what he knew to be the Whisperwoods, his senses instantly assaulted by the sight of dilapidated huts and overgrown gardens. Confusion washed over him. Where was the vibrant energy he remembered? Where were the witches? Where was Matron Constance? He had expected a much different welcome.

He dismounted from Diablo, his gaze sweeping across the desolate landscape. He approached the apothecary, the once-vibrant shop now shrouded in dust and decay. The dried herbs hanging from the ceiling swayed listlessly in the breeze, releasing a stale, lifeless scent. Taion inhaled sharply, the air devoid of the vibrant magick that should have permeated this place.

With a frustrated growl, he slammed the door shut and stepped back, his gaze sweeping across the space again. He closed his eyes, whispering an ancient incantation, allowing the earth to unveil the secrets of the past as he raised his hands.

A vision unfolded before him: Constance, her face alight with wisdom, guiding Queen Annika through her first tentative steps back into the world of magick. Sarya and little Puck, their laughter echoing through the woods, chased each other along the banks of the stream, Comet chasing Puck's heels. Morena, her hands deftly weaving spells, gathered herbs in the sun-dappled garden. The other witches, their voices a melodic hum, celebrated the solstices, their magick weaving a tapestry of light and life around the coven.

Then, the vision shifted, the idyllic scene shattered by a wave of violence. Elara, the Nightsinger's chosen vessel for the darkness stood defiant in the face of a terrifying onslaught, her laughter echoing through the woods. The witches, their faces contorted in terror, were scattered and fleeing, their homes reduced to smoldering ruins. Sarya and Puck, their faces streaked with tears, dragged the injured Morena through the chaos.

And then, he saw Rhamiel, his arms wrapped around Elara in a passionate embrace. A low growl rumbled in Taion's chest, a fierce anger ignited within him.

And finally, he watched as Sarya cradled Constance in her arms, the greyness of misused magick making its way to Constance's heart and stopping it.

A tear fell down Taion's face as he watched Constance's last breath. Just when he thought the vision was done, an image formed that stopped Taion cold. He watched as the image took the shape of a man and he gasped as he saw Carwyn, smiling. He gathered Sarya in his arms, and they kissed.

This unexpected turn of events shattered his carefully laid plans. Sarya had found her heart bond. Frustration boiled over as he cursed and kicked at the ground. The information he'd been given was hopelessly outdated, causing him to arrive too late. He could never speak to Constance again, nor share his tale with the coven.

Looking up at the sky, he scoffed bitterly. "A twisted sense of humor you have, goddess," he muttered, his voice laced with despair. "Bringing me back after all this time, only to find everyone I cared about already gone. They're dead!"

He turned around as he felt a pair of eyes watching him. Quickly he unsheathed his sword and carefully walked around the opening of the forest, "I can sense you, Stikini, come out before I decide to level this forest."

The Stikini cried out and flapped its wings, taking flight before landing in front of Taion, bent at the knee as she assumed half her human form. She looked up at Taion and tilted her head, her large eyes taking the man in.

"Did you find what you were looking for, 'Captain' Taion?" she grinned. "It's such a shame that you came too late. The realm doesn't need the likes of you back here in Tir Siorghlas." She spat on the ground and flexed her wings, her eyes darkening as she assessed him.

"Did you forget your place since your master has been gone, Stikini?" he replied, his voice low, laced with warning.

Taion growled, a savage arc of his sword suddenly flashing upwards. Agile as a shadow, she transformed into her full Stikini form, a mix of bird and woman, fleeing, her piercing shriek echoing across the wind as a warning of his arrival, praying the forest would relay the message before it was too late.

He cursed, a snap of his fingers teleporting him above her. She screeched, craning her neck to meet his gaze. Desperate, she twisted, talons extended, but it was too late.

His dagger found its mark, plunging into her chest. He twisted the blade with cruel satisfaction as she shrieked, her Stikini form reverting to back to her witch form, losing her wings. Her eyes widened in terror as she cried out, clawing at the dagger embedded in her chest, the dark tendrils spreading across her chest. Taion held firm, a grim smile playing on his lips as he pulled her close.

"You failed, Stikini." He whispered in her ear, his grip on her bruising.

With a final snap of his fingers, he vanished as her body plummeted towards the ground. He reappeared beside her body as it crashed to the earth, smoothing his tunic as if nothing had happened, a chillingly casual indifference in his demeanor.

He sneered as he looked down at her broken body, the life force draining away. "I didn't need you raising the alarm bells so soon, Stikini, darling. You saw too much."

He turned, "Diablo, come!" the horse nickered and came trotting through the forest to his master. Taion swung himself into the saddle and nudged Diablo forward.

"We might need another teleportation if these interruptions continue, dear Diablo," Taion murmured, a wry smile playing on his lips as Diablo snorted in disgust.

Back on the road, Taion couldn't help but admire the thriving landscape of Tir Siorghlas, a testament to the hard-won peace among the Clans. He wondered what lengths they would go to maintain this fragile tranquility.

A mischievous glint entered his eyes. "Time for a little chaos," he muttered, nudging Diablo forward. The journey continued northward, but Taion's mind was already plotting.

With Constance out of the picture, Tenebris in the Silver Lands remained his only potential source of information. It was time to stir things up a bit. With a grin he nudged Diablo forward and Diablo started an easy trot down the road again; this time headed due north.

Puck, perched atop Atlas, rode along the border of Clan Basalt's lands, a knot of uncertainty twisting in his gut. Should he have at least said his piece to his parents? The castle and city faded behind them, replaced by the vast expanse of the horizon. The wind whipped through his short black hair, mirroring the turmoil within.

It wasn't that his parents didn't love him, he realized that. But he was a young man, yearning for answers, which he rightfully deserved. His magick was his own, and he would decide how to wield it. If his mother saw him as a monster now, so be it. It would only make him more determined to get his answers.

With a decisive tug on the reins, Puck crossed the border, the castle now a distant memory. He would figure this out. Maybe proving his independence, his ability to make his own decisions, to fend for himself, would finally earn him the respect he wanted. He wanted to be a man like his amil, Carwyn: a strong leader. And to be a good wizard, not a mere product of his unknown sire's genetics.

Atlas nickered, sensing Puck's inner turmoil. They soared above the landscape, a patchwork of forests and fields, until Puck decided it was time for a break. They landed gently near a stream, where Puck allowed Atlas to drink his fill.

As he quenched his own thirst, Puck scanned the woods, a sudden wave of apprehension washing over him. He was woefully unprepared, armed with nothing more than a small dagger. He reached into his pocket, a few coins in his hands. That was something he should have thought of before he took off: his years in the Clan's army had taught him better. He sighed, cupping water to cool his neck and hair. Atlas nudged him gently, and Puck smiled, patting the horse's flank.

He wandered to a better spot by the stream and started pulling logs and dead underbrush into a pile to light; hopefully the fire would both keep them warm and also keep away any creatures lurking around. Puck whispered into his closed fist and slowly opened it, displaying a flame which he then softly blew into the pile. The pile of logs and dead underbrush caught on fire instantly and Puck smiled.

See. He could take care of himself; his magick would help him along the way. He flexed his fingers remembering his ma's warning about balance when using magick. He scoffed and rolled his eyes but carefully pulled some hair out of the nape of his neck, wincing at the pain and laid it down with a short prayer to the goddess, it wasn't a bundle, but it was still an offering. Just in case. He rolled his shoulders and looked around again.

Atlas laid down by the fire and Puck walked over to sit down and lean against him. Atlas nuzzled Puck's hair and Puck leaned up to pat his new friend.

"Well, Atlas, it seems like we're on an adventure now, aren't we."

Puck stretched out, interlacing his fingers behind his head as he leaned back against Atlas. So much had changed since the last battle years ago.

They had settled into a comfortable rhythm at Castle Stowerling. His mother was happier than he could ever remember, and he adored his younger siblings. Yet, a nagging sense of unease lingered. It had become louder and louder recently, almost hard to ignore.

It was like a siren's call, urging him to explore, to see what lay beyond the familiar, to stretch and discover. He knew, with certainty, that staying put would lead to profound regret.

He closed his eyes, a smile gracing his lips as he reminisced about the latest escapade with Kilyn and Orin; the chaotic encounter with a swamp creature. Their combined powers were truly formidable, an unstoppable force.

He sighed as he thought about all of the things he would be doing if he was at home. He shouldn't complain about the freedom he had, though. Orin's parents were far stricter than his own; having to secretly portal to get out of the castle.

Kilyn, on the other hand, had the life of his dreams. Captain of his own ship, he roamed the oceans, encountering exotic lands and captivating women. Puck couldn't deny a pang of envy, his imagination captivated by Kilyn's thrilling tales.

Kilyn's reputation as a heartthrob was well-deserved. His toned physique, olive skin, vibrant green eyes, and unruly long black hair made him a magnet for female attention. He regaled Puck with graphic details about his conquests, describing their bodies, their moans, and their passionate embraces.

Puck, however, still blushed easily at the mere glance of a female elf. The thought of being naked around one, of performing the acts Kilyn described, was utterly mystifying.

He could talk a good game, but the reality of intimacy filled him with apprehension. He admired the strong, independent women in his life, and Kilyn's tales often portrayed a disregard for female respect that made him question the act. Puck shook his head, a sigh escaping his lips. At this point, he would settle for a simple kiss. It was yet another reason to leave home, to experience life beyond the familiar.

As the sun dipped below the horizon, the clearing grew colder. Puck huddled against Atlas, the Pegasus wrapping a protective wing around him. Exhaustion finally claimed him, and he drifted off to sleep.

The fire crackled through the night, casting dancing shadows until the first rays of dawn touched the horizon. In the forest, multiple eyes blinked in the dark, observing the stranger and his magickal fire.

Chapter Twelve

*Somewhere in
Tir Siorghlas*

Puck groaned as Atlas nickered and shifted his wing, stretching after a night of immobility. As Puck attempted to rise, he stumbled and landed with a thud, groaning again. His body ached from the unnatural position he'd slept in, and he missed his bed back home already.

He scrambled to his feet, stretching his back and arms, then rolling his neck. As he turned his head, a pair of brilliant green eyes met his through the dense foliage.

He gasped, stumbling backward, shock flooding his veins. His fight-or-flight response kicked in, and he instinctively drew his dagger. But as he hit the ground for cover, he heard a peal of laughter – a melodious sound that didn't sound remotely predatory.

Shaking the sleep from his eyes, he saw her. A breathtakingly beautiful elf emerged from the forest, her body lithe and graceful. Her long, brown hair was loose, framing a face that men probably started wars over. Her olive skin accentuated the pearly whiteness of her smile as she looked down at him, offering a hand.

He sheepishly grinned and accepted it as she pulled him up to stand close to her, their bodies almost touching. He looked down at her and all thoughts suddenly vacated his brain. She smelled like a fresh cut meadow mingled with rain. How was that even possible?

The strange woman looked up at him and giggled again, "You sure move fast. Where are you from, elf with the fancy clothes?"

Puck blinked rapidly, his mind still aflutter. He stuttered and crossed his arms, stepping back slightly while he shrugged, "I... I, you know, just came from the south of Tir Siorghlas. My steed, Atlas, and I are just on a journey."

She extended her hand again, and Puck eagerly grasped it. "Lera," she declared, "wood elf, loyal to Tir Siorghlas."

Puck swallowed hard, his voice a mere whisper as he echoed, "Lera." His heart hammered against his ribs. The world seemed to slow down as he gazed into her eyes. They were a mesmerizing swirl of green, flecked with gold, a captivating depth that threatened to pull him under.

He blinked, startled as she cleared her throat. "Puck," he stammered, "of... er..." Did he really want her to know he was a Prince of Clan Basalt? He hastily withdrew his hand, rubbing it against his pants, unease creeping in.

Freedom or not, he was still royalty. Despite the peace in Tir Siorghlas, the threat of rogue Clans or even resurging evil always lurked beneath the surface, his ma had drilled that into his head. He stepped back, assessing their surroundings with renewed caution.

"Where did you say you come from, Lera?" he inquired, keeping a wary eye on her. "I didn't see any settlements nearby."

Lera crossed her arms over her chest, a playful tilt to her head as she raised an eyebrow. "What part of 'wood elf' did you not understand, Puck of Nowhere?" she teased, her hand resting on her hip as she gestured towards the dense forest.

Color surged up Puck's neck as he noticed a small group of wood elves observing them from the edge of the clearing. He gulped. "You said you're loyal to Tir Siorghlas, right? Which Clan do you pledge your allegiance to?"

Lera lowered her arms, recrossing them. "When I said loyal to Tir Siorghlas, I meant it. We're independent, but if Clan Basalt or

Tempestus called for aid, we'd answer. Does that satisfy your inquiries, Puck of Nowhere?"

She studied him intently. "Say, I can't quite place it, but you're more than just an elf, aren't you?" She circled him, her gaze sharp. Puck swallowed hard as she stopped before him. "I sense... something. An aura that doesn't belong to the Clans."

Puck scoffed, crossing his arms. "You're wrong. I'm just a lowly half elf, lost and wandering." He quickly moved towards Atlas. "In fact," he added, "I'll be on my way."

Lera raised her hands. "Hold on. How did you come by such a magnificent creature? A Pegasus? They're practically extinct in these parts. To acquire one, you'd need a bleedin' fortune, or..." Her eyes widened.

Puck swore under his breath and swung onto Atlas's back. "A Prince! Are you a bloody Prince, Puck of Nowhere?" Lera's voice echoed behind him. The wood elves emerged from the trees, their eyes wide with astonishment.

Puck gripped Atlas's neck, ready to bolt. He sighed, running a hand through his hair, making it stand on end. "Yes," he admitted, "I'm a Prince- of Clan Basalt. I'm trying to find myself, to discover who I am beyond the title." He gestured towards the dying embers of his fire. "Can you keep my identity a secret? At least until I know where I'm going?"

He carefully released Atlas' mane and slid off of him. Lera regarded him thoughtfully as she paused, her eyes taking in his tall, toned body, his gently tipped ears, the black hair that was dishevelled, giving him an air of mischief, his brilliant blue eyes wide with worry while he waited for her to respond. She grinned, approaching him as she surveyed Atlas.

"If you let me ride your Pegasus, I won't tell a soul where you went. Wood-elf's honour." She crossed herself over her heart and spit in her hand, offering it out to Puck. He grinned, relief flooding his features as he spit and clasped her hand.

Atlas rolled his eyes and whinnied as he pawed the ground. No one had asked him if he wanted other creatures on his back. Puck turned back and smiled, "Come on, Atlas, just one ride. Please." He offered his hand to Lera.

Atlas' eyes roamed over Lera, and he heaved a sigh as he bent his knee for Lera to grasp his mane and hike herself up.

The small group of wood elves gasped in delight as he shook himself, trying to unseat Lera. Much to his dismay, she laughed with delight and threaded her hands into his mane, massaging his sweet spot. Atlas begrudgingly decided she could stay. With a cry he shot to the sky as Lera yelled out in pure delight.

Lera was at a loss for words as she watched her world disappear below her. She closed her eyes and lifted her face to the wind, feeling her hair whipping around her, the highest she had ever been being the tops of the trees. Atlas swung up towards the clouds and Lera lifted her arms up, little whisps threading through her fingertips.

He whinnied a warning and suddenly plunged down towards the earth. Lera let out a squeal of surprise as she grabbed Atlas' mane and bent her body almost flush on his.

"You are a creature of pure beauty, Atlas." She whispered. Atlas caught it and nickered, slowing down enough for a gentle landing. Lera sat up and stroked his neck before he bent his knee to let her slide off.

Lera turned towards Atlas and produced an apple from her dress pocket. The Pegasus whinnied with delight, eagerly accepting the treat from her outstretched palm. He crunched into the apple with gusto, while Puck watched, mesmerized. Lera continued to pet Atlas, whispering soothing words that made his ears twitch as he responded with soft nickers back.

"What a good Pegasus you are, Atlas." She crooned as Atlas happily accepted another apple from her outstretched hand.

Puck's heart pounded in his chest as he continued to observe her. She was unlike any woman he had ever encountered. Her brilliant green eyes sparkled with laughter, her long hair cascading down her back like a river of molten chocolate. Delicate braids adorned her hair, interwoven with wired crystals and wildflowers, giving her an ethereal, almost other-worldly appearance. Puck's gaze involuntarily drifted downwards, taking in the graceful curves of her body. He was utterly smitten.

Sensing his intense scrutiny, Lera turned to find him staring at her, his mouth slightly agape. He flushed crimson as she caught him gazing at her, a slow smile gracing her lips as she continued to stroke Atlas's neck. Then, to his astonishment, she stepped closer, her body brushing against his. Her eyes met his, and she parted her lips.

All around him the sounds could be heard. The forest erupted in a cacophony of screams, the trees themselves wailing in agony, shuddering and drawing within themselves. Lera whirled, dagger drawn, and vanished into the depths of the woods with the other elves.

Puck was left alone with Atlas. The stallion whinnied nervously as Puck pulled his own dagger out, Atlas' ears flicking back and forth as they both scanned their surroundings.

The cries intensified, a deafening chorus of pain that pierced Puck's ears. He sank to his knees, clutching his head in an attempt to block out the horrific sound. Atlas whinnied in distress, pawing at the ground.

Then, as abruptly as it began, the cacophony ceased. An eerie silence descended upon the clearing. A long moments later, Lera emerged from the woods. Her face was pale, a single tear tracing a path down her cheek. Her arms hung limply at her sides, the dagger still clutched in her hand.

Puck rushed to her side, grasping her hand. "Lera, are you alright? What was that? What happened?" he demanded, his eyes searching hers for answers.

"We lost her," she whispered, her voice hoarse. "The last guardian of the forest. She's gone. The peace of Tir Siorghlas... it may not last. Who would kill the Stikini, Puck? She was guarding the Whisperwoods..."

She stepped closer, burying her face in his chest. Puck instinctively wrapped his arms around her, offering what comfort he could, still in shock of what just happened.

The Stikinis, the guardians of the Whisperwoods, the place of his childhood. Why would one still be there? Who would dare to kill such a harmless creature? A plan began to form in Puck's mind. He would find whoever had committed this heinous act and make them pay.

Before he could set off, Puck knew he needed to leave a trail. He let out a sharp whistle, a signal for his messenger. A cry echoed from the depths of the forest, and a magnificent falcon soared into view.

Puck grinned at Lera as he snapped his fingers; a quill and parchment appeared in his hands. Lera looked at him, speechless. "I thought you said you were just a half elf Prince, Puck from nowhere, not a mage."

Lera watched him quickly scribble a message, attaching it to the falcon's leg. He whispered a few words to the bird, and with a powerful screech, it launched itself into the air, disappearing towards the distant ocean. "I didn't feel safe telling you everything."

"What did you send off?" she inquired as she gauged Puck, interest building as she looked him over again.

He turned back to Lera with a sheepish shrug. "Bloke things," he answered.

Chapter Thirteen

Clan Empereal

The flickering torchlight cast long, dancing shadows across the stone floor of Silvan's study. Rain lashed against the windows, mirroring the turmoil within him.

He had been struggling to sleep, the weight of the agreement he made to Death many years ago resting heavy on his conscience. Alyndria was sleeping in the next room, and he needed to get it over with before she woke. Before she would try and change his mind.

He turned to the window and whispered an incantation, his head bowed as he sighed, clutching the small bundle of tobacco flowers in his hand. He gently laid the bundle inside the shell on the windowsill and waited.

A chill, deeper than the storm outside, swept through the room. Silvan whirled, hand instinctively reaching for the dagger at his hip. But there was no intruder, only a figure coalescing from the very air, shimmering and indistinct.

"You called, Silvan," a feminine voice softly spoke, ancient and chilling.

Death.

Silvan's breath hitched. He knew it was time, but the reality was far more terrifying than anticipation. "You... you came."

Death inclined her head, a seductive gesture. "Your debt is due. I even decided to let it wait out a few more years. You always were my favourite, King of the air and water."

Panic clawed at Silvan's throat. He had promised his life to spare Alyndria's, years back when the war against the shapeshifters had ravaged Riverstone. Death had asked for something more; and he had agreed. How could he not; Alyndria was his light, his reason for living, his heart bond.

"I... I," he stammered, "I don't know if I'm ready."

Death's eyes seemed to burn with an ancient, predatory hunger as she tilted her lips into a soft grin. "Silvan, dear. You must fulfill your bargain. What kind of terrifying being would I be if I let everyone get away with not fulfilling their promises they made to me?"

Silvan's heart hammered against his ribs. "I know you want my magick."

Death smiled softly. "Your magick was what made me agree to not take your life."

"Yes," Silvan said, his voice trembling. "I will be powerless, a mere mortal. But I will live, and I will still protect Alyndria." He tilted his chin upwards, his jaw set as he looked at Death.

Death studied him, an unsettling scrutiny. Finally, she spoke, her voice a whisper that seemed to seep into Silvan's very bones. "Very well. Your magick, it is yours to give, and you are giving it freely."

She walked around the room, assessing Silvan and continued, "But know this, Silvan. You won't always be able to protect Alyndria. One day, your mortal body will take its last breath, and you will see me again."

Silvan sank to his knees. He knew he had made a terrible bargain that day, a pact that would forever alter his destiny. But he had saved Alyndria. And for that, he would endure anything.

Death walked over to Silvan and bent one knee to level with him, her dark dress cascading around them. As their eyes met, she caressed his cheek and he closed his eyes, a single tear escaping. She smiled softly and pressed her lips to his. Silvan shuddered, his body shaking as he felt a part of his soul rip itself from him.

And then, as suddenly as she appeared, Death vanished, leaving behind an oppressive silence and the lingering scent of decay.

She stood and watched from the door of the study, invisible to Silvan's now human eyes. Her eyes held a depth of sadness that she hadn't felt in a very long time.

Silvan had always been one of her favourites of the troublesome elven boys; he was kind, morally upstanding, willing to put himself last to ensure those he loved were taken care of.

She had seen the great things he was destined to do but she had also seen this path; and she knew that at the end, he would always choose this: his love for Alyndria so great that he would sacrifice everything he had.

The things they would do for love, she mused, as she watched Alyndria rush into the room, her nightrobe swirling around her as she bent in front of Silvan, pulling his head against her shoulder. Silvan buried his face in her neck and wrapped his arms around Alyndria as she wailed.

Death felt a tear slip down her cheek. Surprised, she wiped it and looked at her now moist fingertips. She looked at them one last time, straightened her shoulders and vanished.

Alyndria looked up as she felt the study warm with the disappearance of Death and frowned through her tears.

The first rays of dawn, muted by the heavy drapes, filtered into the room, casting long shadows across the bed. Silvan stirred, blinking against the sudden intrusion of light. His eyes, once accustomed to the piercing clarity of immortal sight, struggled to adjust.

The room, familiar yet somehow seemed hazy, the edges of objects blurred. He squinted, trying to make out the details, a frustration he hadn't ever had to experience. He mused as he wondered how to go about asking for assistance with his aging mortal eyes.

A soft sigh beside him broke the spell. Alyndria, her face still drowsy with sleep, was watching him with an amused glint in her eyes. "Having trouble seeing, my love?" she teased, her voice a soft whisper.

He chuckled, the sound rough and unfamiliar to his own ears. "Seems my mortal eyes haven't quite caught up yet."

He swung his legs over the side of the bed, wincing slightly as his feet touched the cool stone floor. The feel of the smooth floor beneath his fingers as he pulled on his clothes was strangely grounding.

Alyndria, now fully awake, sat up and leaned against the headboard, watching him with a mixture of concern and curiosity. "Are you alright, Silvan?"

He turned to face her, a warm smile gracing his lips. "I am just fine, my nymph." He paused, "Just feeling my age a bit today, that's all."

"You do seem more... mortal," she agreed, her eyes tracing the lines of his face, the faint lines that had appeared overnight, a sign to his newfound mortality.

"I must get ready for court," he said, "and perhaps find a few more ladies in waiting for you. Your current entourage seems... overwhelmed."

Alyndria laughed, "I have enough ladies in waiting, thank you. Besides, I enjoy your company, and if I have any more ladies, I won't have as much time with you."

He grinned, crawling back into bed and pulling her close. "And I enjoy your company also." He leaned down and kissed her, a long, slow kiss that spoke volumes of the love that bound them. The kiss was different now, raw and passionate, a reflection of the knowledge that he didn't have infinite time anymore to love her.

As he held her close, a sense of peace, unfamiliar yet profound, settled over him. He would work to provide a lasting legacy so that when he took his last breath and met Death again, it was a life well lived.

He captured her lips in a soft kiss and trailed his hands down her hips to her thighs. Alyndria sighed and pulled him onto her as she spread her legs for him to lay between. She traced his face with her hands, memorizing the fine lines that appeared around his eyes, and the silver threading through his auburn hair at his temples.

Silvan captured her hand and pressed his lips to her skin as he reached down again and kissed her neck, his hand trailing down her body. She softly moaned as he gently slid his fingers into her, slowly stroking as he continued kissing her neck.

He pulled her hands above her head as he leaned down and captured her nipple between his teeth. Alyndria gasped and arched her back against the sweet pain.

He carefully replaced his fingers with the tip of his cock, slowly filling her up as she watched him. When he had filled her to his hilt, he paused.

"Don't close your eyes. Keep them on me, little nymph." He softly whispered as he slowly started to thrust into her. As he slid in and out, Alyndria let out a soft whimper, her eyes never leaving his.

He kept her arms captured above her as he used his other hand to hold onto her hip, his thrusts gentle and steady. Alyndria arched her back and wrapped her legs around his hips, angling herself for him to go deeper.

He groaned as he felt her tightening around him. She was delicious, her body glistened with sweat as he pumped into her. He watched her face as her mouth parted and her eyes widened. She tried to pull her arms out of his grasp, but he kept her pinned.

"You're mine, little nymph. Until the last breath leaves my body. You're." he grunted as he thrust harder, "Mine."

She moaned and bucked under him. He pinned her hip down and his eyes darkened as he looked at her.

"Say you're mine, Alyndria." He slowed his thrusts down and bent to crush his lips to hers. She moaned into his mouth, and he grinned against her lips as he rocked his hips into her.

He released her arms, and she quickly grabbed his hips as she arched under him, his slow movements creating waves of pleasure rolling through her. She reached down and grabbed his buttocks, urging him to go faster as she gasped, her mouth softly opening as she watched him sliding in and out of her.

"Say you're mine, little nymph." Silvan growled as he felt her clenching around him. He wasn't sure how much longer he could last but he needed to hear her say it.

Alyndria looked at Silvan and grabbed the back of his neck, pulling his head towards her and she cried out, "I'm yours, Silvan!"

He crushed his lips to hers and thrust himself into her again, hard, as he muffled her cries with his mouth. Her hands threaded into his hair, grabbing on like he was her anchor in the storm.

He could feel himself slipping over the end with each thrust and as he felt Alyndria clench around him, her orgasm sent him tumbling along with her.

Chapter Fourteen

Clan Aether

The air in the grand hall of Castle Elden was almost stifling, a mixture of the villagers' anxieties and Orin's own growing unease. He sat on the throne, the polished oak cool beneath his palms, his gaze sweeping over the assembled crowd.

The usual murmur of conversation had been replaced by an unsettling silence, broken only by the nervous shuffling of feet.

Orin missed Osian. His amil, with his quick wit and easy laughter, usually livened these proceedings, offering a reprieve to the often-tedious petitions and grievances. Today, however, Osian was nowhere to be found. He had vanished with Solana earlier, her whisper in his ear prompting them to step away. He hadn't seen his mother the entire day as well, which was very much out of the norm.

Orin glanced towards the door, his gaze lingering on the empty doorway that led to the private chambers. He had dismissed the looks that his amil and general Solana had traded, assuming it was a matter of minor court intrigue. But as the morning wore on, a growing sense of unease had settled over him.

The villagers, sensing his distraction, hesitated to approach. Finally, an elderly woman, her face etched with worry, stepped forward. "Your Grace," she began, her voice trembling, "my seldo, he has fallen ill. The fever... it won't break."

Orin, roused from his reverie, focused on the woman's plea and leaned forward. "Tell me, ma'am, what has the healer said?"

The woman shook her head. "He has done all he can, Your Grace. But the fever... it is strong. We heard of your powers and thought perhaps..." she trailed off.

Orin paused as he gazed into the woman's eyes. His unique powers sometimes caused him to be placed in uncomfortable situations; playing a god was not something he relished in. "Bring him to the castle. We will do everything in our power to help him."

The woman's face brightened. "Thank you, Your Grace. Thank you. We knew you held such kindness in you for your people, just like your amil."

One by one, the villagers presented their concerns: a dispute over land, a petition for repairs to the village bridge. Orin, surprisingly, found himself able to address each concern with a clarity and decisiveness he hadn't always possessed.

Perhaps, he thought, the absence of Osian's easy charm had forced him to rely on his own judgment; maybe one day he could actually rule over Clan Aether.

But as the last villager stepped down, a wave of relief washed over him, quickly replaced by a renewed worry. Where was his amil? The court session had been shorter than usual, but it felt like it had dragged on endlessly for Orin.

He rose from the throne, his movements unsure. He would find him, he decided. A nagging fear, cold and sharp, rolled over him as he heard noises in the front foyer of the castle. Were they being attacked? Was that why the general had pulled his amil aside?

He looked around for Solana amidst the scuffling noises and carefully cracked the door open, his hand ready to use his magick if needed.

What greeted his eyes made him stop cold. His mother, naked, covered in blood, instructing the small group of villagers to go to the Baobhan Sith lands as a sacrifice.

With a soft gasp, Orin closed the door quietly, leaning against it as his chest heaved like he had run a marathon. What in the gods did he just witness?

His mother... He quickly looked around and his head whipped back to the private chamber. He quickly jogged over and pulled the door open to see his amil, his head in his hands sitting down in the corner.

"Amil! What happened? What is going on! I just saw..." he gasped, still unsure of what he had truly seen.

"Orin, my seldo, I am so sorry." Osian whispered through his tears. It had begun.

Orin gently walked over to Osian and dropped to his knees, his one hand on his father's arm. Osian looked up and locked eyes with his son, his light, his heir, and could only manage a weak smile as he spoke.

"Seldo. I am not sure how to explain this. Your mother, the woman you know to be your amille... she isn't. We all knew that she is a Baobhan Sith. What we didn't know was that she had glamoured herself with the likeness of your true amille and had spellbound you to not see who she truly is, ensuring your memories were locked."

"She held me captivated for so many years until," he continued, "for some reason, her glamour stopped working on me. Perhaps it was my heart, knowing it wasn't truly her. I will never know. But Orin, you need to run. You need to get as far away from here as you can until I can fix this. I cannot lose you, my seldo."

Orin's ears were hearing the words but the roar in his head was making it hard to absorb what his father had just told him. The pain intensified as Osian launched into a spell, holding the side of Orin's head.

Orin squeezed his eyes shut hard, the pain intensifying until suddenly, a blinding flash of light appeared behind his eyes and his memories came flooding back. The Baobhan Sith Clan had found his mother and him in a cabin- capturing them and selling her off while one of them took on her form to infiltrate the throne, using Orin to make Osian easy to trick. The true Amodra was still alive.

Osian grabbed Orin's shoulders and firmly shook his son. "I am ordering you, get out of here and quickly. Take my steed, the unicorn, and get out of here before she realizes that we know. Because when she does..."

He trailed off, his eyes wide as he looked up. He quickly looked back at Orin and yelled, "Run Orin! For the love of the gods, RUN!"

Orin stumbled as Osian pulled him up and pushed him across the room, an incantation flowing from his lips as his fingertips flashed blue, his other hand dropping the bundle of herbs he had clenched tightly in his fist. As Orin stumbled, scraping his knee, he finally righted himself and ran. He moved across the room towards the door to the grand hall and he turned, catching a glimpse of Amodra.

The woman he thought was his mother all this time, gleefully smiled as she walked towards Osian. Blood drenched her naked body as she dragged a broadsword behind her, slowly walking, stalking her prey.

Orin sobbed as he continued to run. He yelled for Solana, for Atmos, for Ephyra, for anyone to save his father. He ran to the stables, grabbing his father's beloved unicorn as he released the others. He swung himself up on the unicorn, and turned around, trying to make himself go help his amil. The magickal wall pushed against him, preventing him from going back.

He yelled in frustration and swung the unicorn around again, his father had forced a command spell on him. He had no choice. He cried, his pounding heart matching the rhythm of the hooves of the unicorns as they fled Castle Elden.

As he turned to look back one more time, he saw Solana, dressed in full battle gear running to the castle, twelve of her elite deaf soldiers on her heels. Swords raised, iron bared, and stakes at the ready.

He prayed they would not mistake him for a coward, but he did what his amil compelled him to.

He ran.

The salt spray kissed Kilyn's face as he navigated his ship, the "Midas," (because everything he touched turned to gold) through the choppy waves. Laughter bubbled up from his chest; gods did he love the water. His dark hair whipped in the wind, framing his face, and he wiped the salt spray from his eyes with a bandana, tucking it securely into the waistband of his trousers.

"Starboard, first mate!" he roared, his voice booming over the crashing waves. "Set a course for Tir Siorghlas!"

The Midas, a sleek vessel with yellow sails that shimmered like gold in the sunlight, responded to his command. Tir Siorghlas. It had only been a week, but he was already itching to step foot on her soil again.

Tonight, he had plans. Plans that involved catching up with old friends, sharing stories, and perhaps, just perhaps, a bit of mischief if he could manage it. The closest port at this time of year was the old Blackwood Lands, a treacherous journey for most, but a mere inconvenience for a water elf like him. A few well-placed spells and he could be across the unkempt lands in a matter of minutes to Puck's doorstep.

His train of thought was abruptly interrupted by a screech. A messenger falcon landed gracefully on the railing in front of him. Kilyn frowned, intrigued. Who would send a message by falcon?

He carefully retrieved the parchment tied to the bird's leg. Unfurling it, he scanned the message, a slow smile spreading across his face. Puck.

Puck, his friend, the one who had always yearned for adventure, had finally left the confines of Clan Basalt. He was heading towards the Whisperwoods. Perfect timing, a coincidence. The port in the Blackwood Lands was a direct road to the ancient forest.

Kilyn grinned, a mischievous glint in his eyes. He whispered instructions to the falcon, his voice barely audible above the roar of the waves. "Find Prince Orin of Clan Aether," he commanded. "Tell him to meet us at the Whisperwoods tonight. Under the old oak at the edge of the clearing."

He released the falcon, watching as it soared into the sky, a dark arrow against the blue canvas. Tonight, old friends would reunite, just in a different area.

Kilyn hesitated. It wasn't normal for Puck to buck authority. He wondered what exactly had caused him to leave the Clan so suddenly.

He shook his head as a slender hand touched his shoulder, slowly trailing down his arm. He grabbed the hand and swung around, pulling the woman to him. Her long seafoam green hair was curled and bounced as he moved her, his eyes roving over her pale skin, her full lips, the light freckles amongst the paleness and green eyes that shimmered with mischievousness. She was a sea nymph through and through.

With a low growl as he nuzzled her neck he whispered, "Now now, little minx, ready for round two so soon?" She giggled and threw her head back as Kilyn trailed kisses down her neck and between her breasts, which were barely concealed with a poorly tied dressing gown.

"I have time for one more, then I'm afraid you'll have to go home." Kilyn swung her over his shoulder and patted her bottom as she giggled.

"I don't mind staying on the ship, Captain Kilyn, truly." She squeaked as he slid his hand up her leg and cupped her bottom.

He tutted, "If I leave you here, I have no doubt you'll have sampled half the crew before I get back. No, that simply won't do. They can find their own taste of Locryan delicacy. I will pay dearly for your time and your time is mine."

He shoved the doors to his chambers aside and walked to the mussed bed, tossing her onto it. She landed with a squeal, and he turned, with a flick of his fingers, closing and locking the door.

With a grin he turned back, "Now where were we?" he asked her.

She smiled seductively and leaned back on her elbows, pulling her knees up and letting them fall gently, her dressing gown moving out of the way to display what Kilyn was after.

With a groan he moved to the bed and crawled onto it, pulling her legs towards him as he buried himself between them. She sighed and arched her back as he ran his hand up to her belly, pushing just slightly as he dragged his tongue up her folds.

The woman's eyes fluttered closed and her mouth opened with a small gasp. Kilyn's brilliant green eyes darkened as he watched her arch, his tongue flicking and twirling over her clit. He carefully slid one finger into her as he pressed on her belly, increasing the pressure with the flat of his tongue on her. She moaned again, reaching up and grabbing the posts of the headboard.

"You'll need more than that to hold on to, little minx, once I have my way with you." Kilyn growled. He slid a second finger into her and she arched again, gasping as he flicked his tongue around her clit. He pressed his lips to her, sucking as he stroked her.

She rocked her hips into his face, and he groaned at the taste and feel of her around him. He could tell she was getting close as her rocking became more erratic; he kept the pace going, sucking and stroking while she moaned and writhed against his face.

With a cry she shattered around him, and he carefully licked her clean, then slowly pulled his fingers out, sucking one then he sat up and leaned forward, his other finger tracing her lip.

"Clean that finger up for me, little minx, I want you to taste yourself."

She moaned as she drew his finger into her mouth, sucking and licking. Kilyn's mouth opened slightly as he watched her. With a smile he pulled his finger out of her mouth and trailed it down her neck between her breasts.

"Naked, now. I want to bury myself into your sweet pussy," he instructed. She giggled again and dragged the robe off of her, flinging it to the side of the cabin as she rolled onto her stomach. Kilyn groaned again as he looked at her pert bottom, her knees on the mattress.

He quickly pulled his pants off and his cock sprang free. He ran his hand between her legs, feeling her wetness and he brought his hand to his cock, stroking a bit as he bent down to land a bite on her bottom. She giggled and arched her back again and turned to lock eyes with Kilyn.

"You know my name Kilyn. I want to hear you say it when you enter my sweet pussy." She pouted and Kilyn groaned again. That mouth was going to get her into trouble.

"Nyana, the only words I'll hear in this room will be you screaming my name as I enter you." Kilyn grinned as he slid his cock into her, slowly, inch by inch as she gasped and arched her back again. He ran his hand down her back and reached the nape of her neck, grabbing it gently, pulling her into a kneeling position as he filled her.

He pulled his hand around and rested it just below her chin, holding her there as he slowly pumped himself into her. She mewled as she arched against him again, her hands reaching for his head and his hair. He grinned darkly and whispered in her ear, "I want you to come for me Nyana, can you do that for me like a good girl?"

Nyana's eyes fluttered closed and he felt her clench around him; She was delicious. He ran his other hand over the small of her belly and found her breast, reaching to pinch her nipple as he tightened his grip on her neck. She gasped and bucked as he thrust harder into her.

Each thrust had Nyana gasping his name and Kilyn grinned as he felt her climax coming. He kept his hand around her neck and moved his other hand down to pull her close to him. He bent her back over and plunged himself into her, roughly as she gasped.

"Kilyn, oh my gods, please... oh please!"

She cried out as her climax slammed into her, Kilyn groaned as she clamped around him and he pressed his face into her back as he climaxed as well. He quickly released his hold on her and pulled her to him as he slid out of her, cradling her in his arm as he laid back, gasping for air.

Too bad she had to go back to Locrya before her father found out she was gone. He chuckled as he pulled her close to him, kissing the top of her head as she nestled into his chest. Such was the game of playing the rogue, he supposed.

Chapter Fifteen

Orin's brown eyes were blurred from the tears and fatigue as the unicorn trotted along the dirt road. He had no idea where he was anymore, and he bit back another sob as he flashed back to watching that evil creature stalk his amil.

Would he come back to an empty throne? Or to the arms of his father? He wiped his eyes with the back of his hand and sniffled. Suddenly a piercing cry overhead had Orin stopping the unicorn as he craned his neck, wondering what was going on. The sun was slowly setting on this hellish day, and he had a long ride to find Puck and Kilyn.

A falcon swooped into Orin's view, and he gasped. He flung himself off the unicorn and stumbled to where the falcon had landed; on a low branch of a tree. He sobbed as he stumbled again, unsure if he was receiving a message of good tidings or bad.

He wiped another tear as he reached up and unrolled the parchment to see both Puck and Kilyn's writing.

"I left the Clan behind me. Plans have changed. Meet me at the Whisperwoods. Something has happened." ~Puck

"Meet us at the Whisperwoods, the edge of the clearing there is a tall oak." ~Kilyn

Orin read it again and then dropped his arms, the parchment in his one hand as he looked around him. The Whisperwoods? He groaned and scrubbed his eyes again and bunched the parchment up and threw it, screaming as he balled his fists.

"The godsdamned WHISPERWOODS?! What about my amil?! Where in the hells is my mother?!" he swung his arms around as he yelled- to no one in particular- and stopped, his chest heaving from the effort.

He groaned and flung his head back as he forced himself to walk back to the unicorn who was patiently waiting for him, grazing on some clover on the side of the road.

The unicorn nickered as he came near and waited for Orin to mount him again. He stood, waiting for Orin to say something. Orin looked at him and sighed.

"I know you already heard me. We need to go to the Whisperwoods. I know the spell my amil laid hasn't been released yet or you'd be taking me back home." He swung himself back onto the unicorn's back and threaded his fingers through his mane.

The unicorn nickered and turned slightly south, picking up a canter and Orin groaned as he tried to hold on until he found his rhythm.

As they carried along the path, Orin heavily sighed and watched as the road continued on ahead for what looked like easily a day or two ride. The men said to meet tonight? The sun was already starting to set, that means they were using their magick. Orin stopped the unicorn and got off of him, patting his neck gently, placing his head on the unicorn's.

"I need to continue on my own, Grey. Go back to the castle if you can and save your herd from the bloodsucking beasts." The unicorn whinnied and turned around, trotting off back east towards Clan Aether lands.

Orin turned around west, back towards the road to the old Whisperwoods. He whispered, his hands outstretched as he closed his eyes, drawing in the power that he didn't play with enough. As he balled the magick in his hands, he pulled out a crystal from his pocket and laid it on the earth before whispering, "Echuia" and a portal opened.

On the other side stood the Whisperwoods; Puck stood with his new steed, Atlas, a grin on his face. Orin smiled back and walked through.

As the portal closed, Puck went to high five Orin but stopped as he watched Orin's face fall. He stepped towards Puck as Puck instinctively embraced Orin in a hug. Orin sighed, and with a muffled voice said something that he couldn't hear properly.

Just then Kilyn arrived on a wave of water, that with a flick of his finger disappeared as he glided into the clearing where the young men were standing, laying a crystal on the ground as he stretched. Confused, he looked at Puck, then at Orin, then back to Puck, shrugging with his hands up, "Anyone want to tell me what I waved in on?"

Puck looked at Kilyn with the same shrug and pulled Orin back and looked into his dark eyes, "What happened Orin?"

"Castle Elden has been courting a lying, glamoured Baobhan Sith this whole time. Amodra, well, whatever she actually goes by... she may have killed my amil. I don't know what happened, but he spelled me to leave the castle to save me. I can't go back until he releases it. I think that means he's still alive." Orin looked at both Puck and Kilyn, their faces identical looks of shock.

"Wait," Kilyn crossed his arms, "You mean to tell me your mum is trying to kill your amil? I mean their marriage seemed pretty good..."

"No," Orin shook his head and sighed, running his hands through his brown hair. "She's not my mother. She's been glamouring herself all this time to trick us. I think she's trying to steal the throne."

"By the god's bones!" Kilyn whistled while Puck still stood, shocked.

"So, what are we going to do then, Orin, what do you need?" Puck asked.

Orin shrugged and wrapped his arms around himself while he paced. "There is nothing we can do. In order to protect me, he placed wards to keep me away and hidden from her. I can't do a godsdamned thing until hopefully general Solana and her soldiers murder the bitch."

Puck watched as Orin paced, "Did he say anything about your real mum before he sent you away, Orin?"

Orin looked up at both Puck and Kilyn. "She's alive. That's all I know."

Kilyn whistled again. "Gods, I'm sorry, Orin." He clapped him on the back and then looked at Puck, gauging the gravity of the situation they were all in.

"Are you going to tell us why you decided to escape Clan Basalt, Puck?" Kilyn raised an eyebrow at Puck who flushed at the question.

He rubbed the back of his neck and sighed, trying to figure out the best way to explain, "Ma found out about the teleportation powers I have. She fainted. I think it has something to do with my sire. I don't know, I'm just tired of not knowing, you know? Of feeling like I'm missing something. Why does she think it's ok to hide that from me? I am done waiting for her to open up."

Kilyn patted Puck's back, "Puck, I don't think she's hiding anything. She really loves you. If anything, she's probably trying to protect you. You've at least let them know you are safe, right?"

Puck flushed again.

"Gods! Puck! You sent me a falcon, you couldn't think to send them one? They must be going out of their minds with worry! Do you want all of Tir Siorghlas called to find a missing prince because he couldn't be bothered to let his ma and amil know he was fine?" Kilyn flung his arms up in the air as he glared at him.

"I'll do it! I just... I just needed a minute." Puck muttered.

"I've already ruined our night out anyways," Orin replied.

Kilyn rolled his eyes, "Stop the whining. If there is nothing we can do to fix what is going on, can we at least take our minds off of it?" he wiggled his eyebrows as he grinned.

Orin looked at Kilyn like he had sprouted two extra heads, "Wait...You're thinking about sex NOW?"

Kilyn kept grinning, "When am I not, is the question, fair elven gentlemen." He laughed as Orin groaned. "And to be fair, that's what you assumed. We do, however, need to figure out what to do tonight."

"I am not in the mood for festivities while wondering if my amil is dead..." Orin paused and put his hand up as Kilyn went to protest. His eyes had caught a form lying on the ground a bit away from where they were standing.

"Um, Puck...Kilyn... do either of you have the ability to cast light? I think we need some right now." He pointed to the form and prayed it was not what he was thinking it was.

Puck nodded and whispered into his hand and opened it to a brilliant light floating above it. As he swung his arm around the light caught the form and all of the young men gasped as their eyes landed on a naked and mangled form of a half Stikini woman.

"The last guardian of the Whisperwoods." Puck whispered, remembering Lera's words.

Kilyn carefully walked up to the body and saw the gaping wound in her chest.

"Um, not to alarm anyone, but she's been murdered."

The three looked at each other uneasily, as the light in Puck's hand flickered. He quickly dissolved the light, and they were plunged into darkness.

"This, I think, tops the dumbest plan you have ever had by, I don't know, infinity at this point.' Kilyn muttered as he glared at Puck.

They were walking down the road, following the large hoofprints that were fresh on the trail. Atlas trailed behind Puck, nickering as he plodded forward, his white wings tucked on his back, trying to get the attention of the young men.

"We can't let a murderer go, Kilyn, that's not the way of Tir Siorghlas. That was the last guardian of the Whisperwoods, where I was raised, where my ma was raised, where my granny died..." he paused as his mind wandered to his granny Constance's soft smile. Atlas nudged Puck insistently and Puck absentmindedly patted Atlas on his neck, continuing to walk down the road. Atlas spluttered in indignation at Puck ignoring him. He pawed the ground and Puck turned around to look at his Pegasus.

"Come on, Atlas, now's not the time." Puck sighed and turned to continue walking.

Orin came and walked alongside them, "Why don't we track for a bit then I can create a portal if we can guess where the murderer is headed? Maybe head him off before he escapes?"

Kilyn grimaced standing on the other side of Atlas and Puck, "I am not ready for a battle. Actually, that is the last thing I'd like to ever do if I can be honest with you. I spent time in the naval army, however, it was merely to placate my ma."

Orin laughed at Kilyn, "Kilyn, we all have been trained, and with the powers we hold between us, there is very little that could stop us if we are smart about it."

Kilyn muttered under his breath, "NOT the way I envisioned spending my evening."

Orin reached over and smacked Kilyn on the back of his head. Kilyn growled and rubbed his head, readying to pounce when Puck suddenly stopped with Atlas in the middle of the road.

"Uh, guys... We need to run."

Standing in the middle of the road stood Diablo, pawing the ground as his rider sat, his cloak hiding his appearance. The young men could see only his iridescent eyes piercing through the darkness. Diablo snorted, the cool air creating steam as it left his nostrils. He pawed the ground again as the rider let the massive dark horse prance, his eyes tracking the three young men on the trail. Atlas whinnied as he pawed the ground back, determined to keep his owner safe. Puck pressed his hand to Atlas to shush him as he looked at the horse and rider.

The rider smiled under the cover of his cloak, assessing the young men. He lifted his hand, and a ball of fire formed. Puck's eyes widened at the magick that the rider displayed, and his mind raced back to the morning when he was playing around with his brother, Ward. How did someone have that kind of magick as well?

Orin swallowed hard and looked over at Puck and Kilyn. Kilyn's normally relaxed and aloof behaviour was nowhere to be found. His eyes were wide as he kept his gaze on the stranger.

Puck's eyes quickly darted around, trying to figure out a plan; a bead of sweat trailed down his back as he realized they were in danger, the rider being a variable he couldn't predict. Orin slowly pulled out his dagger and stood rooted to the spot. Puck quickly grabbed his two friends, wrapping his arms around theirs, shut his eyes and snapped his fingers.

Taion gasped in soft surprise as he watched the three young men who had been tailing him disappear right before him. He let the ball of fire distinguish as he looked at the Pegasus, left alone.

Atlas whinnied and pawed the air as he looked around frantically for Puck and his friends. He snorted and took flight, leaving the rider and the dark horse behind.

Chapter Sixteen

"Woah! What in the gods was THAT?" Kilyn yelled as they all fell in a heap as Puck released them.

Orin groaned and shoved Kilyn, "Gods, Kilyn, get off!"

"I'm sorry, it's the only thing I could think of to get us out of there quickly." Puck replied. He pulled himself up and groaned as a sharp high note ran through his ears. He bent and covered his ears, waiting for it to subside. He quickly looked at his fingers and sighed in relief when there was no indication of the grey death: the misuse of magick in their realm.

He paused and turned his hands over again... no misuse of magick. He hadn't laid down an offering so he should be seeing signs of it. He looked up at his friends who were looking at him with questions in their eyes.

"Are you ok, Puck?" Orin asked as he dusted himself off and sheathed his dagger.

Kilyn ran his fingers through his hair and lifted his chin at Puck, "I think he's realizing he doesn't have to lay down offerings for his use of magick." He bent down and grabbed his handkerchief that had fallen out of his waistband. "The Prince of Basalt has figured out his magick is beyond the rules of balance, somehow."

Orin's eyes widened as he watched Puck turning his hands over again and checking his chest. Just one more mystery to unravel.

"Sermo... do any of us know where we are?" Kilyn looked around at the unfamiliar landscape and raised his hands in frustration.

Puck gasped as he turned around. "I left Atlas!" he realized as he swung around again. He snapped his fingers and disappeared. Kilyn looked at Orin and sighed. Before he could say anything, Puck reappeared in front of him.

"Atlas is gone. That means my parents are likely going to think I'm dead."

Kilyn pointed a finger at him, anger written all over his face, "That wouldn't have happened if you had sent the bloody falcon to tell them! I don't know how hard it is to tell your parents, 'Hi ma and amile, I'm upset that you both cannot tell me about my sire and the magick I now wield, I'm leaving to figure this out.' You're not a child anymore, Puck. You may as well start planning your funeral, ya numpty."

Taion reeled from the shock of seeing the dark-haired young man grabbing his two friends and disappearing. What forces were at play that he would encounter someone that had the same power as he did?

He looked around, realizing that the cover of dark would prevent him from seeing how far the young man had been able to move them. He would track and see if he could pick up their trail in the morning.

He turned Diablo around and they continued on their path. He had more pressing things to take care of before letting that distract him.

Sarya sat and watched the spot where Puck had last vanished on Atlas' back, a knot of worry tightening in her stomach. She rested her hands on her swollen belly, chewing on her lip.

This was exactly what she had feared. After all, Puck had always been exceptionally powerful, a prodigy even as a child. That power couldn't have come solely from her lineage. To even think that he may be so powerful he wouldn't have to lay offerings made her head swim.

A sigh escaped her lips as she let the troubling thoughts swirl in her mind. What if she had been more open with him? What if she had explained who she believed his sire to be, reassured him that she would help him navigate his unique magick? She knew her reluctance to discuss the matter had driven him away, but the memory of what had happened to her still made her wake up screaming at times. How would she be able to sit and explain to her child that he was the result of that horror? To separate how much she loved him from the evil that had caused him?

Carwyn startled her, his hands gently massaging her shoulders before he pressed a kiss to the crown of her head. "Your worries echo across the castle, mo chroí," he whispered. "Not good for the babe."

Sarya turned to him, her eyes filled with concern. "Not knowing where our son is, Carwyn, that's not good for any of us."

He nodded understandingly. "Let him cool off, mo chroí. He'll return. Let him spread his wings, find his own path. There's no need to worry yourself to death, he's just looking for answers."

They both turned their eyes towards the gardens, where Atlas had just landed. But Puck was nowhere to be seen.

"Ok.... Now may be the time to start worrying." Carwyn said as he quickly rushed out to the Pegasus to see if he could find anything out.

Sarya was done waiting, she quickly walked through the castle, up the stairs and down the hall to their chambers.

"Can you help me pack a small bag, just essentials in case I go into labour with the babe." She instructed one of the maids.

The maid curtsied and quickly started pulling some clean cloths for the birth, a sharp knife and herbs, bundling them into a bag for Sarya as she pulled on a long cape, tying her walking boots and pulling a sword and dagger from the chest at the foot of their bed.

She nodded at the maid, "Thank you, I'm sure the King will figure this out quick enough but say nothing to anyone." The maid's eyes widened, and she bowed as she watched Sarya lay a bundle of herbs down on the floor and start an incantation. She raised her hands and whispered, "Echuia."

A portal appeared and on the other side stood Asthemar. She needed her dear friend Annika's help. Sarya looked back just as Carwyn came running into their chambers.

"Sarya, mo chroí! Just wait!" he shouted as he watched her turn to lock eyes with him.

She stepped through and shut the portal. Carwyn swore and kicked at the air as he stood watching the spot where the portal dissipated.

"That stubborn godsdamned woman, she'll be the bleedin' death of me one day, I swear!"

He ran down the stairs and marched down the hallway, grabbing a cape, his pack and his swords as he walked towards the doors.

Ward, hearing all the commotion, stuck his head out of the play-room and watched as his father stormed out of the castle. He looked back into the room and looked at Emery before quietly sneaking out.

He carefully jogged down the hallway on the balls of his feet to keep the stones from vibrating any noise. As he reached the castle doors he peered out and watched his father mount Puck's Pegasus and take to the skies.

He turned around and looked at the servants standing behind him, watching the same thing.

"I guess I'm in charge now?" he asked as they all looked at him and bowed, waiting for the young Prince to tell them what he wanted.

"Carry on, I'll figure out what I need in a bit," Ward waved his hand and walked back into the castle towards the throne room. He walked carefully to the throne, wary that someone was going to jump out and scare him- telling him he wasn't supposed to touch the throne.

He stepped up the dais and reached his father's seat. Carefully, hesitantly, he turned around and sat in the large chair. As he leaned back, he smiled.

It felt powerful being a king. He sighed and swung his heels on the throne. As he swung the second time, his heel connected with something solid. He frowned and got off the throne, bending down to see what he had hit.

On the ground under the throne sat the wooden crate wrapped in rope. Intrigued, Ward pulled the crate towards him and read the paper, *"To be opened by the King of Clan Basalt"*

"Well, I'm the Eldatár for now until amil shows up." He gleefully unwound the rope and tossed it aside. As he assessed how to get into the crate, he noticed a faint glow emanating from it.

He ran over to the private chambers attached to the throne room and found a small dagger. He ran back, excited to open the crate. "Maybe it's a fairy! Or some kind of light orb. Amil never told us he got presents all the time for being Eldatár."

His train of thought quieted down as he stuck the small dagger between the top and the rest of the crate and pried it open. He peered in and a blinding white light surrounded him as he screamed. The lid fell back on the crate and the dagger clattered to the ground. The white light receded.

Ward was nowhere to be found.

Chapter Seventeen

Clan Tempestus

Sarya stepped through the swirling portal, her feet landing with a solid thud on the stone steps of Castle Dewmire. With a decisive snap, she closed the shimmering passage behind her, whispering, "Avalyta," as she ignored her husband's startled shout.

She knocked firmly on the massive oak doors, tapping her foot impatiently on the stone. The doors swung open, revealing the castle butler, his face pale. "Your Majesty," he stammered, bowing low. "We were not expecting you. I... I apologize. Please, come this way." He straightened, leading her towards the sitting room.

"No need for apologies," Sarya said with a gentle smile. "Simply inform Elentári Annika of my arrival and request an audience."

"Of course, Your Majesty." He bowed again, swiftly disappearing to summon assistance.

Sarya surveyed the room, her gaze drawn to a new portrait hanging on the wall. It depicted Annika, Damien, and their four children – two sets of twins – a heartwarming scene. A wave of nostalgia washed over her as she remembered delivering all four of them.

Time flew, she mused. Gabriel and Ilyana were on the cusp of adulthood, their elven youth drawing to a close. Aywin and Rina, however, still retained the mischievous glint in their eyes that their father had always possessed.

"Everything alright, Sarya? Not that I'm complaining about a visit, but you're so close to your due date," Annika remarked, entering the room and enveloping her friend in a warm embrace.

"I wish this was a social call," Sarya said, pulling back from Annika's embrace. "But Puck is missing. He left the castle a couple of days ago on Atlas, the Pegasus that Carwyn gifted him, and... the Pegasus returned alone."

Annika's eyes widened. She guided Sarya towards a nearby settee, then moved to the sideboard where a pot of steaming tea sat ready. "Let me pour you some," she offered, stirring honey into two cups.

Sarya accepted the cup, inhaling the fragrant steam of clover and peppermint. "You always remember my favorite," she smiled warmly.

Annika sat beside her, taking a sip of her own tea. "What do you know so far?"

Sarya shrugged, setting the cup down on the saucer resting on her belly. "I left Carwyn at home, of course. I portaled here directly."

Annika let out a stifled giggle. "Sarya! You're going to give that poor man a heart attack!"

Sarya smiled again, then her expression sobered. "I know Puck has been sneaking out to meet his friends, the other young men, Kilyn and Orin. I understand that. But this is different. I know he's upset with me over not talking to him about how he came to be but...he wouldn't simply leave and not come back without a word, without sending a message, not even a falcon. And Atlas returning riderless... Annika," she paused, searching for the right words, "I fear for him. I fear he's been hurt, or worse, taken captive. It's been such a long time since we have had to worry about the peace being disrupted. I can feel it shifting. Something is wrong."

Annika gently placed her teacup on the table and took Sarya's hands in hers. "Sarya, as mothers, we always fear the worst. But Puck is strong, resourceful, and incredibly clever. He'll be alright. I know he will."

She paused, her gaze darting towards the door. "Perhaps we should try scrying for him? We have Damien's bowl. Maybe we can find him that way."

As Annika rose to her feet, the sound of a muffled scuffle and a childish giggle erupted from the hallway. Gabriel tumbled into the room, followed closely by his sister, Ilyana.

"Gabriel, Ilyana, you know better than to eavesdrop," Annika scolded playfully, pulling Gabriel to his feet. She reached up and tousled his hair, gently pushed him towards the door.

"Off you two go. Your amil has some memories of his own childhood misbehavior he can share with you and the punishment that happened for being caught." She warned with a grin.

The twins laughed and jogged away down the hallway. Annika turned back to Sarya, who was struggling to rise from the settee. With a groan, Sarya pushed herself to her feet, a small smile playing on her lips.

"I told the babe that it is the last. I do not have it in me to do any more." She laughed.

Annika smiled, "Did you inform Carwyn about that decision? The goddess only knows the man cannot keep his hands off of you!" They both laughed as they walked down the hallway towards the private study.

Sarya prayed that the scrying bowl would sense something; at least so she could feel like she could take a full breath again. Whoever said having children was easy clearly lied.

Gabriel and Ilyana walked slowly down the hallway, their footsteps echoing softly behind their parents.

"Puck is missing," Gabriel repeated, his voice barely a whisper. Ilyana, her eyes wide with concern, placed a hand on his shoulder, halting him. "We could look for him, Gabby. We're old enough now. We'd have to be quiet about it, of course, but I think he might have gone to the Whisperwoods. He talked about it a lot, you know, the place where he grew up. If I had chosen to run away, I'd go somewhere I'd feel safe."

Gabriel chewed on the inside of his cheek, a heavy weight settling in his chest. As the eldest twin, the future of Clan Tempestus rested on his shoulders. If something happened to him or Ilyana, their younger siblings would be thrust into the complexities of court life, perhaps even married off to strengthen alliances with other Clans. The weight of responsibility pressed down on him.

Ilyana watched him thoughtfully, her gaze filled with a quiet understanding. While she enjoyed a degree of freedom as the second-born, she knew the burden of leadership weighed heavily on Gabriel. They balanced each other, these two halves of a whole. And if anyone knew the depths of Gabriel's heart, it was Ilyana.

"Let's do it, but we need to be so careful, 'Yana. And you know when we come back that there will be more than hell to pay from our parents."

Ilyana let out a quiet squeal of delight and danced on her tippy toes; they were going on an adventure!

"Wait, Gabby, what do we pack for an adventure?" She loudly whispered to him as they took the back stairs to their rooms. Gabriel groaned and rolled his eyes as he walked up the steps, Ilyana hot on his heels.

He turned around as they made it to the second floor and held his hand up, pointing at each finger as he spoke, "Sword, something warm to wear for the evenings, a bedroll, a dagger, something to eat. Pack it all in a bag and meet me down by the back door of the castle in ten minutes."

She nodded and turned into her bedroom, then turned around before Gabriel opened his door, "Do I wear pants or a dress?"

Gabriel audibly groaned, "Ilyana, seriously?"

She scoffed, "Well, what if I meet someone on the way? I don't want them thinking I'm a boy! You know I'm going to be ready soon for my coming out."

Gabriel looked at her up and down. Ilyana was a younger version of their very beautiful mother. Her darker hair cascaded down her back in waves of curls and her eyes swirled with greens and golds. Her full mouth and high cheekbones showed her regal bearing.

"I doubt anyone would ever mistake you for a boy, 'Yana." Gabriel softly closed his door.

"Right, pants and tunic it is, well, I may as well just throw on my training leathers, add a cape and longer sweater…" her voice trailed off as she closed the door to her room.

Aywin and Rina poked their heads around the corner from Gabriel and Ilyana's rooms.

"Why do they get to leave and try to rescue Puck, but we have to just stay here?" Rina whined.

Aywin jabbed her sister and pushed her long black hair out of her eyes. "Let's go see what amil and amille are up to and maybe we can follow!"

Rina gasped with delight and nodded hard, her black braids bobbing on her head. She grabbed Aywin's hand, and they ran down the back stairs quietly and peeked their heads into the back study where Annika and Sarya were.

"Euchia" they heard as they quietly watched.

"Annika, this is the Whisperwoods! Why would he be... oh, Puck. That place held so many beautiful memories for us." Sarya paused.

"They're not there anymore though, Sarya, it looks like they disappeared. Let's try and push further out to see if the scrying can sense them."

They scanned the watery bowl, waiting, watching. The image filled slowly, and Sarya stepped back with a gasp. A large black horse and its hooded rider shimmered in the image.

"Oh no." Sarya gasped as her eyes locked with his. He smiled as his iridescent eyes swirled with anger, looking directly at her. Before the rider could say anything, Sarya flung her hand up.

"Avalyta!" she yelled as she pushed Annika back. The bowl tipped and they watched it in horror as it rocked itself over the edge of the table, shattering as it hit the stone floor.

Annika looked over at Sarya who was shaking, she looked down and saw the small puddle of water between Sarya's feet and gasped.

"Annika, I can't deliver now. Not when Puck is missing, and that man is on Tir Siorghlas soil... oh." She gasped and bent over, her hands on her knees as she felt a wave of contraction course through her.

"Missing or not, my friend, the babe is not going to wait for anything. Let's get you up to the room and I'll call a midwife." Annika carefully pulled her friend beside her, and they slowly walked down the hallway to the back where the healers rooms were.

"You're going to have to tell me why that rider scared you so, Sarya."

Annika softly said to her friend who was squeezing her hand hard through another contraction. Sarya looked at her friend and nodded frantically as she prayed Puck would stay safe.

They rounded the corner and disappeared out of sight. Rina and Aywin could no longer hear their mother, so they quietly walked into the room, stepping over the wreckage of the scrying bowl.

"Look at all the cool stuff in here, Rina!" Aywin loudly whispered, pointing to stuffed creatures and things in jars that she had never seen. Rina ran her hands over dusty tomes and suddenly tripped over something. As she sprawled to the ground, her shoe got stuck in the rope.

"Help me Aywin!" she cried. Aywin dropped the basket she was holding and rushed over to her sister. She tried pulling the rope off of her ankle, but it had twisted too much. She looked around and spied a small dagger and came back to her.

The crate and rope were pulsating with a blue light and Rina was captivated, staring at the light, speechless. Aywin read the note on the box, *"To be opened by the King of Clan Tempestus"*

"I need to cut the rope so we can get you out and get out of here before amil or amille find us!" Aywin loudly whispered "I don't think we're supposed to be in here." She dragged the dagger through the rope and with a few passes, finally freed her sister. They both stopped and watched as the rope flopped off of the box. The light started to glow brighter and Aywin looked at Rina.

"It wouldn't hurt to make sure that there isn't an injured fairy or sprite or Will-o'-the-wisp in there, right?" Rina slowly nodded at her sister.

Aywin carefully slid the dagger in between the lid and the box, opening it. They both looked inside, and their bodies disappeared as the lid snapped shut.

The dagger and Rina's shoe clattered to the floor. Just as the light subsided, Damien walked into the room, a frown creasing his forehead as he looked at the broken scrying bowl spread on the floor. He unsheathed his dagger and quietly stalked the room, his eyes scanning. They fell on the crate on the floor, the rope in a pile and cut and Rina's shoe discarded.

Damien picked her shoe up and looked back at the box. He cursed as he realized what he had put in his castle; a portal to somewhere and his precious children had just been taken. Realizing the portal must only activate once the box was opened by someone of the royal family of the Clan, he blanched.

He swore and ran out of the room, yelling for the guards as he stormed down the hallway towards the war room. As they assembled, Annika, unknown to the chaos happening down the hall, was busy prepping the room with the midwife for Sarya to bring her last babe into the world.

Gabriel and Ilyana snuck out the back door, packs on their backs. Gabriel carried a broadsword along with a dagger and Ilyana a bow and a quiver full of arrows.

Chapter Eighteen

Clan Bayle

Aria entered castle Leyebourne, her old home, and smiled. Her entourage trailed behind the princess, their heels sounding out across the tiled floor. She thanked the butler who opened the door for them and turned to walk into the sitting room. As she looked around, realizing it was deserted, she frowned slightly. Turning around. she shrugged off her cape, handing it to a lady-in-waiting. She walked across the hallway to the library, noticing it was empty too.

Confused by the lack of servants, she emerged into the hallway. Suddenly, sounds drew her attention. Whispering erupted among her ladies as they approached the sitting area and throne room, a scene of vibrant activity.

Her parents, King Cohnal and Queen Salihn, were engaged in animated conversation with their son Hagen and wife Saphielle by the fireplace. They turned as she entered, smiles on their faces. The court bowed respectfully as they noticed Aria's arrival.

"Aria, my sweet selye! You are finally here!" Salihn embraced her as Cohnal placed a kiss on top of her head. Salihn pulled away and looked behind her daughter, Aria, confused. "Where is your lovely husband, Theo?"

Aria cleared her throat and put on a bright smile. "He is staying at home this time. He said he had too much to take care of."

Salihn frowned as she sensed more to the story and Cohnal muttered as he went to sit back down, shaking his head.

"Nothing is more important than family, selye. Don't forget that."

Aria nodded and self-consciously rubbed her arms before she smiled brightly again, rushing up to Saphielle, grabbing her hands.

"Is it time to announce the news, nésa? Oh! I'm so excited!" She danced with Saphielle as they both laughed, their dresses swirling around them. As they stopped, Saphielle looked up at Hagen who looked down at her with a grin.

She looked back at Aria and nodded as they placed their foreheads to each other. "You are going to make the best aunt, Aria. I have something else to ask you later as well." Aria giggled again and they pulled away as Hagen guided Saphielle to the front of the room, the thrones behind them. Cohnal and Salihn followed, smiles wide on their faces.

Hagen cleared his throat, and the room quieted. All faces turned to them, waiting.

"Clan Bayle! We asked you all here today to make an announcement of great celebration." King Cohnal's voice boomed through the room.

"Prince Hagen and Princess Saphielle are carrying our kingdom's next heir." He trailed off as the crowd started to stomp their feet, a message of acceptance from the Clan leaders and their partners. The stomping started softly then became louder and louder as shouts and claps joined. Cohnal felt a tear fall down his face as the sea of men and women joined together to welcome the news.

Salihn smiled, clapping her hands to the rhythm while they placed Hagen and Saphielle in the centre of the room. A circle formed as the younger women danced around Saphielle, a way to ensure good luck to the pregnant Princess.

As the women circled her, they placed their hands on her shoulder as they danced by, whispering wishes to her, Aria joining in. Saphielle smiled and closed her eyes as she felt the warmth surrounding her.

Hagen stepped back and watched as Saphielle's magick started to swirl around her; the power emanating from his beautiful wife was breathtaking: swirls of electric blue softly dancing around her, sparks flying.

Cohnal and Salihn observed as Hagen and Saphielle were embraced by the Clan. Cohnal pulled Salihn's hand, and they walked out of the room and down the hallway.

"I do think it may be time for us to step down, my love." Salihn sighed with happiness. "They have all of the support that we have, why not give them the throne before the bairn arrives?"

Cohnal looked down at his love, a smile on his face as well. "I think that is a grand idea. I'm getting a bit tired of having to get up in the morning to govern. We could use a bit of downtime before we become grandparents."

"Then it's decided. We should do this while Aria is present as well; tomorrow?" Salihn turned and stopped Cohnal, her hands running up and down Cohnal's chest. He gathered her hands in his and nodded, pulling her towards him for a kiss.

As the celebration continued, Aria stepped out of the room to gather her thoughts, walking up the stairs to her old chambers. She opened the doors and walked to the bathing room, carefully pulling a few cotton towels over to the washing basin.

She ran her hand over the water and whispered; the water warmed to her touch, and she carefully pulled her top down, pulling the stays loose so she could remove the panel and corset.

Bruises bloomed across her ribcage and a cut between her breasts had dried. She winced as she took a corner of the towel, soaking it into the water and dabbing the wound. She looked on the counter for a balm and carefully dabbed it onto the cut, covering it with a strip of cloth that she tore from the towel. She pulled her top back on and started to retighten her stays and corset.

Sighing, she looked at herself in the mirror. Looking back was a woman she didn't recognize; the loveless marriage with Theo, its undercurrent of violence, had taken its toll. When he had first courted her, he was a different male- he brought her flowers, lavished her with gifts and now... well, now she was lucky if he looked her way without the back of his hand following.

She couldn't bear to let her family or parents know- there was nothing they could do anyways. The marriage contract was unbreakable in their realm. Death was the only way out.

A wave of despair washed over her as she pushed her hair back and straightened her small crown on her head, plastering her happy smile on her face again.

She walked back into the bedroom, readying herself to go out to the joyous celebration again. Saphielle was standing in the middle of the room, her hands gathered at her small belly with a slight frown on her face. Startled, Aria stopped then smiled again, patting her hair and smoothing out her gown.

"Saphielle! You gave me quite a fright!"

Saphielle looked at Aria, quiet as she walked up to her. She watched, noticing the corset was not tied as tight as it normally should be, a bruise barely peeking above the top. Her eyes connected with Aria as she softly spoke, pulling the top up a bit to cover the bruise for her.

"Aria, nésa, I am going to ask this just out of concern, and I will never ask again."

She pulled Aria's hands to her, "How long has this been going on." She asked. Aria's eyes widened as she tried to keep her composure, her smile faltering as her eyes started to water.

"He doesn't mean it, Saphielle, he only does it when he's angry at me." She feebly said and winced as she heard the excuse leave her lips. What kind of elven Princess said that about their partner?

"I mean, sometimes I say things that I shouldn't, I should know my place..." she trailed off as Saphielle gently placed her hand on Aria's face, cupping her cheek.

"Melethel, no man should ever lay a hand on his wife. No matter how angry he is." Saphielle paused, trying to assess how to navigate this and make sure Aria felt she was still in charge. "What do you need, Aria? Whatever you need, I am here to help you."

Aria smiled and slowly pulled her hands out of Saphielle's. "Thank you, Saphielle, but I promise, he doesn't mean to." She forced another smile on her face and lifted her hand towards the door, "They will miss us shortly if we are gone any longer, and knowing my hano, he'll be stalking the halls looking for his love."

Saphielle returned the smile and nodded, realizing that if she pushed any further, it would do no good. She turned and pulled her gown up to walk along with Aria as they returned to the party.

Hagen was talking to one of the Clan leaders and paused as he watched Saphielle and Aria walk back into the room. He locked eyes with Saphielle, and she gently tilted her head and walked around the outskirts of the party.

"Thank you for the update on the border patrols, please excuse me," Hagen said as he turned away from the leader and walked over to where Saphielle was standing. She had her hands at her front and quietly waved, stopping Hagen from asking what was going on. Instead, he followed her line of sight and looked at Aria.

"I would like Aria to stay with us until the bairn is born, my love."

Hagen frowned and looked at Saphielle's face. Her elven features were serene, and she had a gentle smile etched on her face, however underneath, he could sense a tremor of something.

He leaned down, his lips close to her ear, "Am I going to get to know the reason why, little fox?"

She turned her head and looked at him with her bright blue eyes as she whispered, "No reason, just needing some sisterly love since I'm an orphan, you know."

Hagen nodded and stood to his full height, scrutinizing his sister now, trying to assess what the women had up their sleeves.

Aria was talking with a small group of younger women and men, her laughter could be heard through the din. He smiled as he watched her; she would always be his baby sister, no matter how many centuries passed. To know that she was married and happy was a relief to Hagen.

The music turned to a romantic ballad; the lyre, harps and fiddle played beautifully together, and Hagen smiled down at Saphielle as she realized it was the song they had first danced to. He placed his hand out to her, his palm up and half bowed.

"May I have this dance, little fox?" Saphielle smiled and placed her hand into his waiting one and he spun them onto the floor. The party goers made space and chord by chord, more couples joined, but the Prince and Princess stole the show. Their magick intertwined again like the first night they had danced together: fire and electric storm.

As they spun around the room, all eyes on them, Aria felt her heart hitch and she turned away, walking out of the grand room and down the hall. She stood against the wall, clasping her hand over her mouth, strangling a sob.

She turned, running down the hallway, tears streaming down her cheeks, her gown swirling around her. Her crown fell from her head, and she continued running until she made it to the library. She slammed the doors behind her, leaning up against them as her chest heaved. She sobbed again, her tears blurring her vision as she held her hands to her heart.

She sunk down on the floor, her knees up as she cradled herself, letting the tears flow. A small noise interrupted her, and she quickly lifted her head, looking around as she wiped her tears with the back of her hand. She pulled herself up and pushed down her skirts to walk around the library.

"Hello?" she called; nothing. "I heard you, you can come out." Still nothing. She kept walking along the walls and furniture, looking around. She pointed at the light fixtures and whispered, lighting them, one by one as she placed a crystal on the floor.

The library lit up, she surveyed the space, realizing no one was there. As she looked around, her eyes dropped to a wooden crate on the table wrapped in rope that she didn't remember seeing there the first time she came in.

Intrigued she walked over and sat down on the settee, pulling the crate towards her. Maybe it was a gift for Hagen and Saphielle? She looked at the paper tied to the rope, "To be opened by the King of Clan Basalt"

Her father? She held the paper in her hand and the rope fell off of the box. Confused she looked down, she hadn't removed the rope, how did it move?

A light pulsated from the cracks of the lid and Aria couldn't help herself. Almost as if in a trance, she gently opened the lid and peered inside. Suddenly the light was so bright that Aria cried out and covered her eyes, blinded.

Chapter Nineteen

Tenebris

As she blinked her eyes open, she was sitting in a dark dungeon, slivers of pale moonlight through the small window above her. Across the cell were three sets of eyes in the shadows.

Aria gasped and scrambled backwards, hitting the rough wall. "Princess Aria?" she heard a young boy's voice in the dark.

"Ward?" she gasped and crawled forward as Ward, Aywin and Rina stepped into the moonlight, their faces dirty and their clothes ripped.

"Where are we?" she gasped as she pulled them into her arms. Aywin cried as Rina shushed her, "Don't do that, remember they don't like that!"

"What do you mean, 'They' don't like that, Rina?" Aria asked as she looked at them all.

Ward looked up at Aria and whispered, his eyes wide. "We're in a jail somewhere in the mountain. That's all I could figure out. I lifted Rina to look out the window above us when they first came."

Aria smoothed back his wild hair from his face and cupped his cheek. Ward was trying to be brave, but he was terrified. From what, Aria wondered.

"How long have you three been in here?" she asked. They pointed to the wall and Aria counted five lines scratched into the wall."

"Five days?" she raised her eyebrows as she looked around again. The dungeon was nothing that she had ever seen. They weren't in any of the castles that she was familiar with. Where were they?

As they all stayed huddled together, a flash of light blinded them again and Ward nudged Aria, "that's one more, Princess." She looked up as the light receded and in the middle of the cell stood a young girl that she didn't recognize. As the little girl looked at the four strangers, tears welled up in her eyes and her lips pouted as she started to blubber.

"I want my amille!" she wailed as Aria got up and pulled the young blue-eyed girl to her. Rina's eyes went wide, and she shushed Aria and the little girl. "They don't like that! Be quiet!"

Aria smoothed the little girl's auburn hair away from her face and chucked her chin with a smile. "And what is your name, little one?" she asked. The little girl hiccupped and whispered, "Erawyn."

Aria nodded, "I am Aria, over there is Aywin, Rina and Ward. Where do you come from little Erawyn?"

Erawyn drew in a ragged breath and her shoulders slumped, "I don't know. My amille and nésa live with me in a really, really big castle. We live with King Silvan and Queen Alyndria. She's really pretty."

Aria brought her head up and looked around the room again as realization dawned on her. She counted; Clan Bayle, Clan Basalt, Clan Tempestus, Clan Empereal. They were missing only Clan Aether.

All of the Kings were supposed to open the boxes to be sent here, wherever 'here' was. What strange plan was being put into motion that innocent children were being used for now?

She cuddled Erawyn closer and smiled at the other children. "Come closer, melethel, it's a bit chilly in here and none of us are wearing enough garments to ward off that cool air coming in."

Aria sat up against the wall again as the children huddled next to her, the cold of the walls seeping into her back. She looked out through the bars of the dungeon, at a loss for what to do next.

Suddenly a flurry of activity could be heard down the dark hallway and the twins and Ward tensed up. Footsteps continued to grow louder while a light grew brighter and brighter until the torch was directly in front of their prison. Aria squinted as she tried to make out the holder of the torch but all she could hear was a voice.

"Heir of Clan Bayle, welcome to Tenebris."

She swallowed hard and gathered the smaller children closer to her. Tenebris? The last time she had heard anything about Tenebris was when the Night Prince, Rhamiel, and his Queen Elara rampaged through the Whisperwoods. They were both dead, the darkness was gone and had been for a long time.

What did Tenebris want with the Clans?

Clan Empereal

Silvan and Alyndria ran out of their quarters to screams from the servants. As they rushed down the stairs and into the sitting rooms, Cyra was standing over a box, sobbing.

Silvan paled as he pushed Alyndria back. He turned his head and looked at her, "Do not come closer, I no longer have the powers to keep you safe as I used to."

Alyndria glared at him, "Then I should be the one protecting you, Silvan!"

She moved him out of the way and approached the box carefully. Cyra kept sobbing beside it, Alyndria looked over at her and then grabbed Cyra by her arms, shaking her. "Enough of the crying, what happened? Where is little Erawyn?"

Cyra sobbed and pointed to the box. Alyndria looked at Silvan and he sat down heavily, completely unsure of what could be happening.

She released Cyra who collapsed by the box and walked over to Silvan. She sat beside him and grabbed his hand. "My love, even though I have been on Tir Siorghlas for but a wee time, I need you to tell me what that box could have done."

Silvan looked at her then over at the box again. "I didn't think anything of it, little nymph, it was just a box tied in rope with instructions for me to open it. The guards had cleared it as fabric and spices. There wasn't anything leading me to think it was a gateway designed to pull someone through, or I would have ensured it..." he cut himself off with a strangled gasp, "I would have made sure it wouldn't have put a wee bairn in danger. I couldn't feel the magick around it anymore."

"But where would it have sent them, my love?" Alyndria asked him. He looked at her with his mortal eyes and sighed, "At one point in time, I would have known as they would have left behind a magickal residue, a hint directed to the Eldatárs, but without my powers, I cannot help."

Alyndria looked across the room to the servants standing around and stood up. She traced her hands around the box, feeling for the magickal residue that Silvan had mentioned and softly gasped as she realized where Erawyn could have possibly gone. She looked at Silvan, her face pale.

"Tell no one of this. If this gets out it will create chaos within the Clan." She turned to her lady in waiting. "Find the falcons, send missives to each of the Clan Queens. We need to find out what others know." The lady in waiting bowed and rushed off.

She turned to Cyra. "Enough crying, Cyra. Save your strength for the return of your hina. We will find out who is behind this, do not worry."

Silvan watched as his love took command of the room, directing each person to a job, tasking her ladies with comforting Cyra and removing her from the room. He watched as she checked the box, asking a guard to lock it in their dungeon and was proud. She would be able to handle the kingdom when he was gone. Heir or not, their Clan was in safe, strong hands.

She walked over to Silvan, and he stood up, taking her hand as they walked out of the room towards the throne room. There was nothing more to do but wait for information. He had an idea to introduce Alyndria to the work he did.

"I would like for you to sit with me today during the summons and petitions, my little nymph." He said as he kissed Alyndria on the head. She looked at him, surprised.

"I never have, why would I start now, Silvan?"

"I want you beside me, that's all." He said as he guided her into the room. The entourage, already waiting, bowed as Silvan directed his Queen with him to the dais and he sat her on her throne. He turned and sat down in his and they started the official petitions and summons hour.

The falcons soared out of Castle Greywood, the wind beneath their wings with missives to the Queens of the Clans.

As Alyndria listened with half an ear to the petitions, she pondered the reliability of what she felt. Tenebris. Why Tenebris? What could they want with their children or was it the kings they were truly after?

She looked over at her love, her mortal king, and fear coursed through her. He wouldn't survive a battle the way that they fought- not without his magick. She had a few things she needed to do now.

Across in Asthemar in Castle Dewmire, Sarya held a brand-new baby boy in her arms. She had been moved into her old suites in the castle when she stayed with Annika years past and watched the sun rise again. Another day that she had no idea where Puck was.

She looked down at her beautiful little boy, his soft pointed ears, his shock of dark brown hair and his gorgeous long lashes. Another cute little Solterra child to terrorize the castle and to woo the girls when he came of age. She smiled and looked up as Carwyn stepped into the room.

He had cleaned himself off after days of travelling on the back of Atlas; even though flying had its perks, he had sworn he would never do it again. He walked over quietly and bent over the bed, kissing Sarya on the forehead.

"Mo Chroí. You have blessed me yet again."

He looked down at the little baby boy and smiled. He looked like his ma and Carwyn was certain that little boy would be the one to keep them on their toes.

"My love, drink it all in, that's all you get for heirs." Sarya chuckled as Carwyn joined in, his laughter lighting up his face.

He walked over to the fireplace and pulled the soft plush chair over to the bed and sat down with a sigh.

"I have some news that you are not going to like." He put his hand up to stop Sarya as she sat up straighter ready to talk. "Let me talk, mo chroí. I need you to understand that we are all working to figure out what is happening. The Clans are preparing our soldiers as I speak which is why I am heading out right away. I just couldn't leave without saying this."

He looked at her and held her hand, reaching out with his other to stroke the hair on his new son. "Ward was taken." Sarya gasped and Carwyn shushed her. "No tears yet, mo chroí. Something is happening and I know without a doubt the bairns are all alive."

Sarya paused, "Wait, you said bairns. What do you mean?"

"Aria, Aywin, Rina, Ward and another child from Silvan's castle were all taken through this portal that was contained in each of the boxes that the families received. It seems that the portals only activated when someone with royal blood opened the box. With some help with the witches in each of our Clans we were able to pull the small threads of magick that were left behind for the Eldatárs to sense, and Alyndria sent letters to all the Elentáris. They're all in Tenebris."

Sarya's eyes went wide, and she pulled her hand away from Carwyn. "What in the seven hells is going on Carwyn! Are you telling me everything? Where is Puck? Why Tenebris? That throne has stood empty for a long time, and for good reason!"

Carwyn sighed, "That's what we are still working out. We know for certain that the boxes were meant to trap the Eldatárs, however, for some unknown reason it seemed to have taken whoever was compelled to open the box. Again, I am almost certain it's targeting those with royal blood."

"We are still trying to find Puck. There has been no answer from King Osian or Clan Aether. Damien is heading that way first to find his hano as he's been met with nothing but silence, a small troop with his general has gone ahead of them. To top things off, Gabriel and Ilyana were found a day's ride away trying to look for Puck."

Sarya looked towards the window, watching the sun as it rose into the sky. "It's a full-scale war again, isn't it, my love? But our children are in the middle of it now. And we don't know who we are fighting."

Carwyn gruffly responded, "They will be fine. We will make sure of it. There is no one on Tir Siorghlas left that would harm a child."

Sarya lifted her eyebrows, pressing her lips together firmly. She needed a moment to sit, to use her magick to see if she could look into the future. She needed to know if she would be mourning the loss of her children or not.

Carwyn looked at her, "Don't be thinking of doing any of your magick to figure out what you can see ahead, mo chroí. That is dangerous all on its own."

Annika appeared at the doorway, her face puffy from crying. Carwyn bent down and kissed Sarya again before walking across to Annika. He gave her hand a squeeze and a brotherly kiss on the cheek.

"We will find them, Annika, we swear. They will come home safe."

Annika nodded and looked over to Sarya who was silently crying, tears rolling down her cheeks. She rushed over and pulled Sarya to her, much to the protest of the babe in her arms.

Carwyn walked out of the room, rubbing his sleeve across his eyes to hide the tears that he had also shed. There was no time for emotion. They had an unseen enemy to fight, and children to bring home.

Chapter Twenty

Clan Aether

"Why did we have to come along for this, amil?" Gabriel asked his father as they crested the hill, Castle Elden finally in sight. Damien growled as he looked back at his twins; he was still angry at the fact that they had tried to sneak off.

"Because we clearly cannot trust you to be alone, so you're going to help me find your uncle and cousin. We haven't heard from them, and it's been too long since we've visited."

Ilyana groaned and rolled her eyeballs. She stretched in the saddle and checked that her quiver and bow was still on her bedroll.

Boys stank, she wanted to be back in the castle in her bed, cutting flowers with her amille and enjoying fresh baked food. This travelling was for the peasants. She curled her upper lip as she sniffed her armpit inconspicuously and groaned. She'd murder for a bath.

"I don't understand why the punishment was us having to travel anyways." She whined.

Damien looked back at them with a death stare and Ilyana snapped her mouth shut. "We're almost there. When we get into the castle courtyard, I want you both to watch for anything that is out of sorts. General Solana and Atmos should be greeting us along with your Uncle Osian, Aunt Amodra and your cousin, Orin. Anyone else approaches you, you get back on that horse and get out of that courtyard as fast as you can. Do you both hear me?"

Ilyana and Gabriel both looked at each other and together responded, "Yes, amil."

Damien glanced back at both of them and smiled. He nudged the horse, and it broke into a canter as they neared the castle. His general, Maelyrra, was waiting outside the castle walls. Her nod confirmed that Osian was inside.

"Sire, we're still clearing for safety but so far, all is quiet." she announced, "Nothing out of the ordinary. It should be fine to proceed."

"Thank you, General. Call back the troops to guard the entrance." Damien replied, confusion at the lack of response from his brother evident.

Maelyrra nodded and turned her horse to call her troops back to stand sentry at the entrance. Was bringing Gabriel and Ilyana with him a smart choice? He was starting to second guess himself, but he thought if all was right, then they could spend some time with their cousin. He trusted that if something was truly amiss, Atmos, Ephyra, or Solana would have reached out.

As he entered the courtyard ahead of the twins he looked around, and nothing seemed out of sorts, just as Maelyrra had said. He brought his horse to a stop and dismounted, nodding to Gabriel and Ilyana who were hesitantly stopped outside the castle gates.

Damien paused and looked around again. It was quiet. Too quiet. He pulled his sword out and readied himself. Gabriel went to move forward, and Ilyana put her hand out, stopping him.

"Amil said to keep an eye out, Gabby. We can't if we're right next to him. Watch the doors and the windows." She pulled her bow from behind her and notched an arrow. She whispered and the tip of the arrow started to glow.

Damien walked towards the steps of the castle towards the doors and stopped as the door swung inwards. He gasped as he watched his brother, drenched in blood, stumble through the doors.

Osian was grasping his sword, coated in blood in one hand. In the other was a grotesque head of a dead Baobhan Sith. Her long pale hair was plastered with blood, her eyes white and vacant. Her sharp fangs could no longer harm anyone.

Osian looked at his brother and sadly smiled. "It seems like my happy ending had other plans, hano." He tossed her head across the courtyard and sat heavily on the steps.

Damien carefully walked over and sat down beside him, shock on his face as he looked at the severed head. "Dare I ask what happened?"

Osian looked down in shame, "She glamoured herself to all of us, stole Orin from his real amille and pretended she was my heart's desire. I guess I had wished so hard, the Baobhan Sith fed off of it and I succumbed to her glamour."

He looked over to where the false Amodra's head had rolled, "And I finally got out from under the spell to find that she had planned to kill me and take over the Clan, releasing the Baobhan Sith to feast their way through Tir Siorghlas." He shuddered as he looked over at the head again. "I can't believe I fell for it! I even had the iron bracelet that I kept on me warning me, and I still..."

He paused, looking around as he took a breath to center himself. "Everyone is safe. General Solana and my elite soldiers were able to kill the Baobhan Sith that were a part of the plan, and the others scattered to the four winds. We will hunt down every last one of them, if it's the last thing I do."

Damien looked at his brother, a frown etching his face. "Wait, hano, where is the real Amodra?"

Osian glanced over at him, "That's the next thing I have to find out. I need to clean this blood off and figure out what to do with the inside of the castle." He looked up and saw Gabriel and Ilyana on their horses, now in the courtyard.

He pointed to them and looked at Damien, "Do not let them inside the castle until I have had it cleaned up. They do not need to see the carnage; they are still too young."

He got up and walked back into the castle, calling the servants for assistance in cleaning up. Damien stood up off the steps and looked at Ilyana and Gabriel who were staring at the Baobhan Sith's head in horror.

"Ilyana. Gabriel. Eyes on me please." Damien said softly. The twins simultaneously swiveled their heads toward their father, their eyes wide. Gabriel swallowed hard while Ilyana looked like she was going to throw up.

"That is not your aunt. That is a bloodsucking Baobhan Sith that took over Amodra's image. Your uncle is fine, Orin is safe. You can dismount and we will wait to go inside."

They nodded at Damien and slid off of their horses. Ilyana rushed to her father and buried her head into his chest, her hands clenching his shirt. He held her tightly and waved Gabriel over who also came in for a hug.

Damien looked out around the castle as the twins clung to him. What in the hells was going on with Tir Siorghlas?

They knew that Amodra was Baobhan Sith, but the story she had woven for them was different. It was one of redemption, love and so far from the natural order of what they were; that was why she had agreed to segregating her Clan from the rest of Tir Siorghlas. She had stated she wasn't like them; she was different, and Osian truly was in love with her.

How did no one see through that and realize that she had glamoured herself to them? Oh, what fools they all had been.

What was worse was what Osian had just been through: realizing that the woman he loved was not who he had married or shared his bed with these last years. That his overwhelming desire for love had left him open and vulnerable to the wretched creatures. Would he come back from that so that he could find the real Amodra?

Damien walked over with the twins, sitting them down on the front steps of the castle while they waited for entry. They could hear Osian cursing softly from behind him. Ilyana stood up and put her hand on Damien's shoulder as he opened his mouth to tell her to sit back down.

She looked down at her father, his handsome features shadowed with stress and confusion. She looked up to see her uncle on his hands and knees, scrubbing away at the blood on the tiles in the front entrance. Tears streamed down his face as he scrubbed like a man lost in the storms, untethered and no anchor to bring him home.

A soft hand touched his shoulder, and he stopped wiping the floor. He carefully looked up to see Ilyana on her knees beside him, her hazel eyes swimming with unshed tears as she placed her hand on his and took the bloody rag from him. She placed a gentle kiss on her uncle's cheek and started to clean the tiles. He choked back a sob and grabbed a new cloth, soaking it and continued scrubbing.

He heard more footsteps behind him and glanced to see Damien and Gabriel bend down to clean the blood up as well. The servants paused as they watched them together, working to remove the result of betrayal from their home.

As they wiped and wiped, it got to the point where Osian leaned back on his heels and proclaimed, "I think it's time to use our magick to finish cleaning or we'll be here until our eternal lives end." Ilyana and Gabriel frowned as they thought; Osian cracked a smile, "Which means forever, young ones." Damien chuckled and patted his brother on the back.

"That's a great idea, sermo. Who has the offering for this one? What are we doing? I'd imagine a water spell coupled with some wind?"

Osian nodded and looked over to a servant who walked over to a sideboard in the entrance. They opened up a drawer and pulled out a bundle that was complete with herbs, a feather and a small vial of sand. The servant walked over and placed it in Osian's hand as he thanked them.

"Alright, hang on while we remove all traces of what happened here today!" his voice rose as he flung his hand out, coercing the air around him to swirl as his other hand reached down, pulling the water from the ground.

Together the elements swirled around the castle as Damien muttered, placing his hands out as well, adding to the magick. Ilyana and Gabriel stood, transfixed as they watched their uncle and father show off their powers.

Within minutes the castle was swept clean of the carnage and righted to the way it normally was. Osian and Damien both wiped the sweat from their brows and helped each other off the floor.

Damien kept his hand clasped over his brother's forearm as they pressed their foreheads together. "Now, you're going to find out where Amodra really is right, hano?"

Osian sighed and pulled back. "I don't know if I'm ready for that, Damien. I...," he trailed off as he ran his hands through his hair, "I don't know if I can go through that shit again."

"Orin deserves this though, Osian." Damien insisted. "Where is he?" He looked around realizing that Orin hadn't made himself known.

Osian grunted as he walked towards the kitchens, Damien and the twins on his heels. "I spelled him away while I dealt with the Baobhan Sith filth. He's the heir of this Clan and heir to my throne. I would imagine he would have met up with the boys..."

Damien cursed under his breath. Now two heirs were missing; all while chaos was underfoot in Tir Siorghlas, no direction on who was causing it yet.

Chapter Twenty One

North of the Whisperwoods

Kilyn, Puck and Orin were filthy, hungry and grumpy. It had been days since they'd landed gods knows where in Tir Siorghlas and Puck refused to transport them further for fear of them all winding up somewhere else. He was unsure if his teleporting abilities worked for places that he had never gone, and he was starting to worry about maintaining the balance.

Orin didn't have the energy to open a portal as the only places he could go to were places he had been, and none of them wanted to wind up at any of the Clan houses yet to face the wrath of the parental units for taking off without proper protocol. No guards and no plans meant trouble, that had been taught to them from a young age, and they had broken every protocol so far.

They had to figure this out alone, together and quickly. As they walked along the dirt road, Orin side-eyed Kilyn and finally broke the silence.

"You have water magick, can you at least clean us up?"

Kilyn turned and glared at Osian while simultaneously raising his hand, a wave of water coursed from him and slammed into Orin, dragging him off the path into the grass and to the edge of the woods. Kilyn calmly pulled a crystal out of his pocket and placed it on the ground.

"There's your damned bath, you baby." Kilyn growled, pushing his hair out of his face while he cleaned himself up. His anger was partially out of embarrassment that he hadn't done it sooner and the other part was because he was tired of them being lost.

Orin spluttered as the water disappeared around him, leaves and grass plastered to his clothing. He stumbled to get up and flapped his hands, pulling at his wet clothes and groaning.

"You know, if I felt like it, I could make your life very uncomfortable you arse!" he groaned and pulled a stick out of his hair and tossed it beside him, grumbling as he felt his feet squishing in his boots.

"You wanted to be clean, well there you go." Kilyn retorted, crossing his arms over his chest as he stood on the road, daring Orin to try something.

"Alright, alright, I think we can all agree we need to sit and figure this out. Clearly the walking isn't doing us any good and we can't move forward if we're just going to fight." Puck sighed and sat down on the side of the road, crossing his arms over his raised knees.

"You boys wouldn't be able to fight your way out of a wet bag at this point." A female's voice echoed through the clearing, the laughter following behind made them all stand at attention, scanning the area, trying to figure out where it came from.

Kilyn, Orin and Puck all pulled their daggers out of their sheaths, prepared to attack. Puck swung around while Kilyn scanned, leaving Orin ready to use his powers.

A small wood elf with olive skin and bright green eyes jumped out of the tree above where Orin had just been laying, a smile on her lips as she stood, assessing the trio looking back at her with shock.

"Lera?" Puck said with awe. Kilyn and Orin exchanged glances while Kilyn mouthed, "Who the hell is Lera?!" Orin shrugged and sheathed his dagger looking at the woman as she approached with a confident stride, her hips swaying rhythmically, causing her jewelry to clink and clack. Her loose pants couldn't conceal her curves, high-lighting her strength and femininity.

Her shirt was tied high, revealing a hint of toned stomach and leading the eye to her breasts, draped in a vibrant green linen. Her long hair, adorned with intricate braids, wired crystals, and feathers, cascaded down her back. But it was her eyes, a mesmerizing shade of green, that truly captivated the young men, holding them spellbound for a fleeting moment.

Reaching Puck, she placed her hands on his chest, arching her back and rising onto her toes. A soft kiss landed on his cheek. Kilyn and Orin, speechless, watched in astonishment as a blush, the color of a ripe tomato, spread across Puck's face.

Puck had found himself a woman? This time Orin turned to Kilyn to mouth, "What is going on?" and Kilyn shrugged, a goofy smile on his face as he assessed.

"Are you going to introduce us, Puck, or do we just make assumptions here?" Kilyn finally found his voice. He sauntered over towards Lera and offered his hand out. She smiled and placed her hand in his as he bowed and kissed the top of it. He looked up at her with his devilish grin and whispered, "At your service, wood sprite."

She pulled her hand back and looked at Kilyn, assessing him. He stood up and put his hands behind his back, grinning at her, waiting to see if his charms would work on her.

She suddenly threw her head back and laughed. As she covered her mouth, she looked at Kilyn with mirth. "Oh, you're good, water boy, really good." She waggled her index finger at him. "I've danced a few dances with the likes of men like you."

Kilyn laughed, he liked her. She had a light in her that he'd love to know how to tame, if she'd let him. He watched as she looked him over again, a small spark of interest lit in her eyes.

Kilyn smirked, anticipating the amusement to come. Orin, elbowing him sharply in the ribs, muttered, "For the love of the gods, show some restraint!" Kilyn rubbed his chin, a mischievous grin playing on his lips, which he attempted to conceal.

Orin turned, a slight bow accompanying his introduction, "Orin of Clan Aether. A pleasure to meet you, Lera."

Lera, captivated by Orin's striking appearance – dark eyes, raven hair, and tanned skin – found herself mesmerized. This man held some interesting power in his body, she could feel it.

Her gaze swept across the three men, a playful glint in her eyes. A hand on her hip, she jutted it out slightly, then pointed at each of them in turn, a mischievous smile playing on her lips.

"So, let me get this straight. We have Puck from nowhere which I actually found out after some persuasion was Clan Bayle, Orin from Clan Aether... and from the looks of you you're also royal blood... and Kilyn, the water boy from...?" she trailed off as she looked directly at Kilyn.

Puck looked from Lera to Kilyn and his shoulders dropped a bit. She liked Kilyn; he didn't stand a chance next to the daring, more experienced young man. She stood expectantly, her arms crossed under her chest with a seductive smile on her face.

Kilyn grinned again as he looked her up and down again. He leaned his arm on Orin's shoulder as he replied, "Tir un Uisce, ever heard of it? It's across the ocean, to the east." He lifted his hand towards the east with a flair and continued, "I could take you for a boat ride you'd never forget, wood sprite. I have some nice wood that you could ride." He winked. He couldn't help himself.

Lera assessed him again, her green eyes vibrant as she looked Kilyn up and down. She shrugged and walked closer to Puck, looking at Kilyn as she grabbed Puck's hand. Shocked, Puck looked down at where they were joined and looked up at Kilyn who was equally surprised.

"I think I prefer to play with the unknown, water boy." She looked up at Puck who was still staring at her in awe. Orin barked out a laugh as Kilyn dropped his arm, unsure of what was happening in front of him.

"Not quite the paramour you think you are, hey, 'water boy'?" Orin continued laughing until Kilyn smacked him over the head. Orin flinched and rubbed the back of his head still laughing.

The world ceased to exist for Puck at that moment. All he could see was Lera, her hair cascading down her back, little wisps caressing her face, her thick eyelashes framing the most beautiful eyes he had ever laid his own on. Her flushed cheeks, which he gently caressed with his free hand.

He watched those brilliant eyes close as she leaned into his hand, her lips forming a slight smile. His heart stopped in his chest. He forgot how to breathe. He forgot how to exist. He leaned down and pulled her head towards him, his lips gently brushing across hers.

"You may want to tether yourself to something, Puck, old boy, before you and Lera decide to breach the atmosphere..." Kilyn said from a distance.

Puck blinked and inhaled deeply as Lera's eyes fluttered open. She gasped and grabbed Puck, her legs swinging around him as she wrapped her arms around his neck. Surprised, he looked down, they were floating multiple feet off the ground.

Lera's eyes were wide as her mouth fell open. Puck craned his neck to see what she was looking at. His eyes set on a massive pair of black angel wings that were attached to his shoulder blades. Shocked, slowly, Puck felt himself lowering his body back and they gently touched back down on the ground.

"When were you going to tell us you had wings?!" Orin exclaimed, gesturing wildly as he circled Puck, examining the two massive black wings that had erupted from his back. "Gods, they're even bigger than Atmos'! What does this mean? Are you part Nephilim? This makes no sense!"

Orin reached out to touch the tip of a wing, but Puck instinctively folded them in protectively. "Don't touch." He growled. He looked at them again over his shoulder as he continued.

"I don't even know how this happened," Puck admitted, bewildered. 'These powers... they just keep appearing. And the further we travel from home, the more I discover about myself, and it's all happening so suddenly." He released Lera, who stood mesmerized, her gaze fixed on the newly revealed appendages.

Kilyn spoke softly, his voice grave, "We need to understand this. We can't let more of these unexpected abilities surface without knowing the full story."

Chapter Twenty Two

The Silver Realm

Taion pulled his cloak around him, the wind howling and whipping around him as Diablo plodded closer and closer. The imposing face of the mountains that housed the Night Realm, and more specifically Tenebris, loomed before him.

He had finally made it; all of the answers to the questions he had would finally be answered. The centuries of not knowing, of feeling incomplete were ending. He urged Diablo on as they made their way through the pass to find the entrance.

The boxes had done their jobs as he felt the trickle of magick make its way back to him. The only box not opened was Clan Aether; which he assessed must mean that someone who knew what the box would do stopped the king from opening it.

He mused; that simply wouldn't do. They all had to answer to what had happened. All of them were complicit in what had occurred, and he would make them pay for what they had done to his family.

As they entered the entrance to Tenebris, he dismounted from Diablo and held the reins as they walked together, the light from the earth slowly disappearing as they walked further and further into the mountain.

Slowly the sunlight turned into what almost looked like moon-light. Taion looked up at the high ceilings and gasped in awe; it was lit up and sparkled in the fading light. He looked forward and noticed torches on the walls, lit with never-ending firelight. He smiled as he walked towards the stone railing and looked down at Tenebris, his home.

The city was a hive of activity today; on the ground level, merchants were selling their wares, the gardens along the hills were being tended to and children were running through the streets.

He could see birds and winged creatures flying around in the mid level of the cavern. As his eyes wandered, he noticed the castle carved into the mountain itself. He would have a small walk to get to the castle gates and steps as he observed, choosing how to make his entrance into this world.

A sentry was guarding the entrance to the city, his skin a dark green with scales. His black eyes looked Taion up and down and he frowned slightly.

"Are you here on trade or pleasure?" he inquired, his voice carrying a slight accent.

Taion answered in his native tongue, a whisper carried on the breeze, "lá caritas, navin, alasaila ná. I would choose very carefully how you choose to respond, sentry." Diablo snorted and stomped his foot in agreement.

The sentry's jaw dropped, and he scrambled to bend his knee.

"Sire, I... I, please, forgive me. We did not know to expect you..." He stood up and bowed again.

Taion nodded, "Lead me to the castle, sentry. I have business to attend to."

The sentry placed his two fingers in his mouth, letting out a shrill whistle. Two Nephilim came from the air, landing beside him and looking expectantly at Taion.

The sentry pointed towards the castle, "Take the Sire to the castle, directly."

They turned and bowed to Taion who nodded, as they turned, the one stood still and put his hand up. "The horse has to stay behind, he cannot live in Tenebris. The land is not meant for an animal like him."

Taion frowned, "He comes with me." His iridescent eyes started to glow as his anger rose. The winged creature looked at Taion and repeated, "He cannot live in Tenebris, Sire."

Diablo snorted, nostrils flaring, sensing danger. Taion, eyes fixed on the Nephilim, mirrored his steed's unease. A feral grin spread across his face, his eyes glowing with an eerie intensity. "No one tells me no," he hissed.

With a snap of his fingers, the winged creature that had defied him gasped, clutching at his throat, struggling for air. Taion watched impassively as the guard writhed in agony, his partner recoiling in fear, uncertain of what to do. The Nephilim clawed at his throat, his eyes bulging in terror as he stared at Taion, his silent screams echoing in the air.

Taion raised his chin, his gaze cold and unwavering. He refused to relent, his magick tightening its grip. Finally, with a strangled gasp, the creature collapsed, life draining from his eyes as his soul departed.

The remaining Nephilim bowed and looked at Taion, "I believe you wanted to go to the castle, Sire?"

Taion smiled and patted Diablo's neck. The Nephilim guard turned around and started to walk, stealing glances here and there, observing the tall stranger with the strange iridescent eyes walking next to the horse.

As they made their way around the side of the mountain through the tunnels, Taion took in the city again. His eyes roamed as he looked over at the Nephilim area of the city, still two tiers: one for the fighting, one for their homes. A mother called her children who came half flying and running towards her, cries of joy as they reached her. He frowned as another memory assaulted him.

Taion running towards his mother, Naomi, her smile lighting her face up as he flung his arms around his mother's neck, placing a kiss on her cheek. She laughed and kissed Taion back as she pushed back his long black hair.

"You need to go and practice your flight, little 'Tai, go on, see your amil. He's waiting for you. I think he said that he may have a small surprise for you." She winked at him as he gasped in delight.

Maybe they'd visit the market, and he could play with the other young Nephilim that he had met. He didn't have a lot of friends, being the only young boy in the castle.

Naomi smiled as she watched Taion run towards his amil who was waiting at the entrance of the castle. He bent down and opened up his arms, his eyes lighting up as Taion squealed in delight as he swung his son up. Their wings flapped as he twirled Taion around, grabbing his hand as they jumped off the ledge.

Naomi watched as they soared over Tenebris. Her Night Prince and his heir.

He looked over at the bustling marketplace. Merchants hawked their wares – vibrant fabrics, gleaming metals, and exotic spices – while citizens of this subterranean city browsed, their baskets overflowing with the most colorful fruits and vegetables imaginable.

He looked up, noticing an ingenious feat of engineering: the mountain face was punctured with an opening, allowing the filtered light of the surface world to penetrate. Hammered steel plates, curved and polished, redirected the precious light, cultivating a thriving ecosystem within the mountain itself. Small, meticulously tended gardens, bursting with life, provided sustenance for the inhabitants.

As he walked closer to the wall, a breathtaking sight unfolded before him. Butterflies, their wings iridescent and shimmering with colors unknown to the surface world, flitted around him like living jewels. One, bold and curious, alighted on his hand.

He smiled, a rare moment of softness washing over him. He quickly dismissed the butterfly, however, reminding himself of his mission. There was no time for such distractions. Diablo snorted in derision as a butterfly landed on his face, snuffing as he tried to shake the butterfly off.

Finally, the imposing figure of the castle loomed before him. Built into the very heart of the mountain, it was a fortress of dark stone, a monument to the city's past. Decades of neglect had taken their toll, leaving the castle with an air of brooding menace.

Rhamiel, the so-called 'Prince of the Night,' barely held onto the throne before the Clan kings deposed him. The fool! He had the audacity to capture one of their queens which had been a grave miscalculation. He should have known better than to provoke such a powerful enemy.

He walked up the steps, Diablo plodding behind him. As he came up to the doors he sighed as he placed his hand on it. So many memories, unwelcome memories.

The heavy doors creaked open, revealing Atmos standing patiently, a singular box cradled in his arms. With a deep bow, he carefully deposited the box at Taion's feet.

Chapter Twenty Three

"What is the meaning of this, Taion?" Atmos demanded, his wings tight to his body as he kept his hands by his side, fists that he was clenching so tight the veins stood out.

Taion's eyes roamed over Atmos, and he finally made eye contact with his half brother. "What do you think, little Atmos? All these years, all this time I was sent away, I deserve answers."

"Not at the expense of what you have caused, hano!" Atmos yelled, his rage barely contained. "Do you know what you did with those boxes? There are godsdamned CHILDREN in the dungeon right now, terrified out of their minds! And I couldn't do anything to get them out because the first thing the Princess that you trapped there would think would be that I am in alliance with you!"

He angrily pointed his index finger at Taion, his anger making him seethe. "They are innocent! And what you did just made you the villain in the story. I hope you know how to make this right."

Taion laughed, his eyes flashing as he looked at his half brother, "Make it right? When do the righteous Kings get to answer to what they did?" he yelled back, stepping up to him. They were now nose to nose and Atmos refused to back down.

"I am not a child Taion. I have every right to inherit this throne as well, and I will be damned if you are going to be the one to take it if you are going to be as much of a bastard as our sire was."

Taion grabbed the back of Atmos' head and held him, their foreheads pressing together now. "Brother, I am not beyond beheading you and putting your head on a stake for all to see. Do. NOT. Test. Me."

He released him and Atmos stepped back. His eyes filled with sorrow as he assessed his older half brother. "I expected better of you, Taion. Especially after all you went through, after what I went through... and after what our younger brother went through. I'm glad our mothers are not alive to see this."

Red flared into Taion's vision as he clenched his fists.

"Do not bring my mother into this."

He growled as he flung his hands forward. Atmos was prepared and he crossed his forearms, holding them up to combat the wave of fire magick that coursed over him, intent on taking him down. He flung his arms down, dissipating the power around him.

"I will play no part of this, Taion. Release those children. I will take them home." He turned around and walked into the castle, his footsteps echoing down the hallway. "Do something with that black beast you brought here and lay down an offering too for what you're spending in magick, lest the goddesses choose to take that from you as well." He yelled.

Taion flung his middle finger up at Atmos' retreating back. He'd deal with him later. He walked into the castle and looked around. A guard walked up to him and Taion pointed to Diablo, "Please find him a place to relax, some water and find him some feed, I realize there are no real stables, but I want him comfortable."

The guard nodded and hesitantly looked at Diablo who snorted as he looked down at the guard. He begrudgingly let him lead him away, back down the steps towards the ground level of the inside of the mountain where there was water.

Taion turned back and looked at his home. The castle, even though it was buried in the mountain, was full of light, the rays of what little sun they were given from the hole in the mountain made the dust motes dance in the air as he walked down the hallway. He stopped and turned to the statue of Life and Death, intertwined and carved from white granite, tucked in an alcove of the hallway. He pulled a grey feather from his pocket and gently laid it at the base of the statue.

He turned and walked, the memory of when he was last here assaulting him; *a small child, terrified, holding onto his mother's hand for dear life as they walked towards the throne room. He looked up at her, his eyes wide. He had to come to be presented to his father; the Night Prince.*

His mother looked down at him, her gentle smile on her face as she bent down and looked into Taion's eyes. He remembered they shared the same eyes; iridescent shades of purple and blue; unique to her lineage of Nephilim.

She was one of the last of their kind; all the others had been hunted to the brink of extinction from the outside world for their magickal abilities and the fable of the power of their wings.

Her white wings were folded behind her as she stroked her son's face. "My son do not be afraid. For you are destined for great things. Your amil sees that. It's time for you to learn how to rule."

He nodded and turned towards the throne room.

Taion blinked the tears back quickly as he realized he was standing at the throne room doors. He shoved them open, the power behind his action making the doors slam against the brick walls, almost taking them off of their hinges.

He snarled as the dust settled and he looked at the throne up on the dais. He stalked towards it, checking for any signs of the darkness having reared its head in recent years; nothing.

He looked around and noticed more layers of dust on everything; it seemed no one wanted to be in this room. He glanced down and observed stains on the floor. Upon further inspection he realized it was blood that had leeched into the stone. He grinned, realizing he was standing where his father had met his fate.

"I had to come to make sure that what Atmos said was true."

A quiet voice reached across the room. Taion slowly lifted his head up. His face softened as he took her in. Ephyra, one of the Nephilim that he had played with as a child and Atmos' mate. "Yes, little Pyre. I'm here."

She smiled as she walked across the room, and they embraced in a hug. She pulled back, her eyes searching his.

"Atmos also said you refuse to release the children, Tai. You need to let them go or you're no better than the rest of them."

Taion sighed and brushed Ephyra's purple hair back from her head and stepped away from her.

"They won't be harmed. I'm not prepared to let them go quite yet, even though they were not my intended target. Their fathers need to be held to account for their ignorance."

Ephyra sighed and turned, slowly walking back through the throne room doors. She placed her hand on the door and turned, softly responding, "How you choose to start your reign will solidify your worth as a leader, Tai. Choose wisely."

She walked out, her dark wings closed behind her. Atmos was standing in the shadows of the hallway, watching their interaction. Ephyra walked up to Atmos, and he wrapped his arms around her. She sighed as she sank into his embrace.

"Unless he lets go of the anger, we are just going to repeat the same pattern all over again, Atmos. The darkness will claim him." He rested his chin on the top of her head, watching Taion in the throne room, standing alone, looking up at the throne and legacy that they were all tied to. Taion felt the memories swirl around him again. This room was filled with them.

Constance and Naomi, Taion's mother, met at the edge of the Whisperwoods, young Taion was asleep in his mother's arms. She had his small bag hanging on her arm as she passed Taion over to Constance. A younger witch stood beside Constance, checking their surroundings with keen ears.

Taion, half asleep, vaguely heard his mother. "Please promise me, Matron. Get him as far away from here as you can. It's the only way we can save him. Rhamiel is changing, the darkness is starting to thread its way into his heart, and I cannot let my child near that. He cannot be corrupted."

Constance nodded and gathered Taion close to her. She looked down at him with a soft smile. "We will make sure that he is safe, that he is sent away from Tir Siorghlas, away from the prince's darkness. I promise you, Princess Naomi."

She paused, "What about little Atmos? Does Prince Rhamiel know that Atmos is his heir as well?"

Naomi shook her head no, "Atmos' mother has been very smart keeping him hidden in the city, where the Nephilim live. Because it was only one night, I'm not even sure if Rhamiel remembers bedding her... should we be worried? I can go retrieve him as well."

Constance shook her head, "I will trust that Marion will keep her son safe and out of Rhamiel's sight. If something changes then we will move to extract him."

She paused. "I know how hard this is, Naomi, love. But the darkness is an evil entity that we are still trying to understand, and we cannot risk another innocent soul being dragged down by it until we know how to vanquish it."

Taion's eyes fluttered as sleep took over again. His mother had spelled him to keep him from crying for her. Naomi handed Constance the small pack for Taion; his blanket, his small stuffy, a white feather from her wings and a small necklace of her tears for when he would need to tap into his magick.

She pulled a small box out of her bag that was slung across her chest and placed it on the ground, "Please keep an eye on the egg, it is the last of its kind, and it's meant for Taion. It's the last piece of my home."

She watched as Constance nodded and instructed the young witch to come and pick up the box with the dragon egg in it. The young witch bowed towards Naomi, and they turned away from the Princess of Tenebris, Taion bundled in Constance's arms, fast asleep as they faded into the Whisperwoods.

Naomi watched until she could watch no longer, a tear tracing its way down her cheek. She brushed it away and straightened her shoulders. She turned back and took flight, heading back towards Tenebris.

As she touched down at the entrance, the royal guards were waiting for her. She lifted her head and strode into the tunnel, pulling her arm away as one of them tried to grab it.

"I will go to my husband on my own two feet. You would do well to remember I am still a Princess of the blood. Do not touch me." She snarled

at the guard, her claws bared. The guard removed his hands and quickly bowed but stayed close to her.

As they walked through the tunnels, they made their way into the castle by the back way to avoid the city, and Naomi stormed into the throne room where Rhamiel was sitting, waiting.

"Where is my heir, sweet wife?" Rhamiel inquired, his eyes swirling pools of dark ink.

"Far from the reaches of the darkness that swirls inside you, sweet husband." Naomi retorted as she stood defiantly in the middle of the room.

Rhamiel's eyes slowly faded back to his regular chocolate brown, he looked around and blinked, confused.

"Naomi? What is going on? Where is Taion?" he stood up from the throne and walked towards his wife, his hands outreached to embrace her.

She stiffened as his arms reached around her, bringing her close to him. She squeezed her eyes shut, willing herself to not let her guard down.

But he felt and smelled like the Rhamiel she had fallen in love with, musky amber with the faintest hint of the smell of frost. His embrace was gentle and strong at the same time, just like how she remembered.

She carefully looked up and their eyes met; hers a swirling combination of iridescent blues and purples, his, a chocolatey brown.

She bit back a sob as she realized the darkness had stepped back; its venomous tendrils pushing back from their hold on her love.

Naomi reached her hand up carefully to Rhamiel's face and watched as he closed his eyes as she touched him. A small smile crossed his face as he looked at her again.

"We should go for a walk through the city tonight, Mo ghaol, it's the solstice and the moon will light Tenebris up. I know they'll be holding a dance in the city centre..." he trailed off as he brushed a strand of her light hair off her face.

"It's been a while since we've danced, mo ghaol." He mused as his eyes roved her face, as if he was memorizing her. She kept a close eye on him, waiting for the smallest hint that the darkness was returning before she responded.

"I would love that very much, Rhamiel, mo ghràidh. You are right, it has been a while since we've danced. Shall I ask my ladies to pick out *matching outfits for us? Which do you prefer?" She smiled, pulling away from him as she walked towards the doors.*

She turned around to wait for his answer so she could instruct her ladies who were waiting outside the throne room for her.

"Choose what you like, Naomi, I'll wear whatever you want." He paused, a frown taking over his face. He looked up and his face contorted, a look of desperation as he stepped forward.

"You know I love you with all of my heart, Naomi, I need you to know that. You and Taion, you both are the reason I exist, the very breath that fills my lungs. Taion is the reason I want to see Tenebris enter a new dawn."

He looked at her as his neck muscles started to tense, as if he was fighting something. He grunted and stopped walking. She started to step back, her eyes wide with horror. Her ladies gasped and one of them pulled Naomi to them.

"The lengths I would go to, to keep you both safe... I hope you know, Naomi.... No matter what." He groaned as he grabbed his head with both hands, falling on his knees to the stone floor.

Naomi gasped as she watched him, "No, no, Rhamiel, mo ghràidh, no!"

She pulled herself out of the hands of her ladies and she ran to him. She fell to the floor and pulled his head up to look at him. As they locked eyes, she realized her fatal mistake.

For looking back at her, Rhamiel's eyes were inky black pools. The darkness had come back, and its voice slithered out of Rhamiel's mouth.

"Sweet wife. How very naughty of you to keep secrets." He reached up and grabbed her neck, forcing her close to his face. She grunted and grabbed his arm, trying desperately to pull away as he stood up. He roughly dragged her body across the floor, her wings desperately trying to find leverage to pull her out of danger. They flopped uselessly as she tried to pull away, her nails clawing his arm as her eyes widened, gasping for air.

As he made his way to the throne, Rhamiel pulled her up against his body and looked at her one more time, his predatory grin slashing his face.

She looked at him, her eyes wide with horror as she tried one more time, gasping, "Mo ghràidh, fight it. Fight for me, fight for your son!"

She sobbed, "I love you, Rhamiel. I will always love you."

A high-pitched giggle left his lips, and he suddenly bent his head, his teeth connecting with her neck as he bit, hard. She cried out, her claws scraping against his chest as he chuckled darkly, her blood pouring around his mouth, staining her white dress. He lifted his head to take a breath, blood spraying as he barked orders at the ladies standing in horror at the doors. "Leave or you'll be next! You whores, you liars!"

His spittle sprayed her white wings as he screamed. She dimly could hear her ladies running away as she felt herself drifting away.

Her last magickal act before she took her last breath was to spell the darkness to always being hungry, to never finding the right host to fulfill its desire to take over the realm, to plunge Tir Siorghlas into chaos. Rhamiel, or rather the darkness known as the Nightsinger, howled with anger as it felt the magick bind it.

It flowed out of Rhamiel, growing larger and larger, screaming in rage. It desperately tried to stop the blood from flowing out of Naomi, to make her reverse the spell.

Rhamiel gained awareness for a brief moment, only to lay his eyes on his love. His face filled with sorrow as a tear slowly rolled down his cheek.

Naomi looked at him and softly smiled as her eyes fluttered closed for the last time.

Chapter Twenty Four

North of the Whisperwoods

Puck's new wings were a pain in the arse. He flexed his back muscles as he rotated his arms, trying to figure out how to get them to do anything but flop uselessly on his back. They dragged behind him as he grumbled, twin trails in the dirt behind his footprints.

Lera walked beside him, touching his wing here and there in pure wonder. Each time she touched his wing, Puck groaned as if he was in pain. He couldn't figure it out, but the touch was causing him to feel like he was going to orgasm every time she stroked them.

He finally couldn't take it anymore and stopped Lera, his hand on her arm as she went to reach up again. Kilyn and Orin, unaware, continued walking.

Puck leaned down and with a voice that was foreign to his ears, growled lowly at Lera, "Keep touching my wings and I'm going to take you and claim you as mine, little wood-elf." Lera stiffened in shock and then softened, a smile growing on her face as she looked up at him from under her lashes.

"Such fun threats, Puck of nowhere." She murmured as she leaned forward. Their lips were a breath apart now and Puck's chest went still as he waited, his grip on her arm relaxing as she brushed her lips over his.

His entire world tilted on its axis as his heart painfully clenched in his chest. He quickly pulled Lera to him, his hand threading into her hair as he ravaged her mouth. Lera gasped and wrapped her legs around Puck's hips, softly bucking as he explored her mouth with his tongue.

He gently tugged her hair back, exposing her neck to him as he trailed his tongue down to the centre of her breasts. She moaned and gripped Puck's shoulders as she closed her eyes, ready for him to take her.

Through the haze they heard someone clear their throat. They both turned and looked over to see Kilyn and Orin standing in the middle of the road, looks of bemusement on both of their faces.

"Maybe, Puck, the right thing to do would be to...oh, I don't know, have a proper bath, take her for a meal before you treat her like she's a common whore?" Kilyn chuckled as he watched both of their faces colour varying shades of red.

Puck carefully put Lera down, her body dragging down his as her feet touched the ground. She patted his chest and cleared her throat.

"Who says I need to be wine and dined, water boy?" she flicked her hair back behind her shoulder and strode through the two men, walking down the dirt road.

"If it's a room you want us to find, pick those feet up, because I need one."

Kilyn, Puck and Orin watched as she walked away, her body swaying seductively as she disappeared down the road. Kilyn and Orin both swung their heads to look at Puck who was watching Lera with a drunk love look on his face.

Orin rolled his eyes and smacked his lips, his arms crossed as he grumbled, "Great. Love struck, unaware of his powers, parents thinking he's dead. Anything else we want to add to the pile?"

Kilyn laughed and decided to catch up to Lera. Maybe she'd soften up to him if he had a chance to talk to her one on one. Lera looked over at him as Kilyn jogged up to her, matching her pace with his as his eyes took her in. He needed to understand why she was there, what her motive was; especially after seeing the look on Puck's face.

Casually he asked, "So, is this something that you do a lot? Hang out with strangers?"

Lera gave him a side eye, "For a moment I thought you were going to ask if I had sex with a lot of strangers. Smooth move, water boy." She smirked as he stammered.

"I just want to look out for Puck. He's young, inexperienced..." he trailed off as Lera looked at him with a frown that he was certain scared off lesser beings.

"What does young and inexperienced have to do with what I feel about Puck? I like him. He's at an age most of our parents found their lifetime partners. He's sweet, shy and I don't give a godsdamned if he is inexperienced. It's not like I have a long line of lovers trailing me, water boy. If you think that talking like this was going to encourage me to add you to the list, you've got the wrong wood elf." Her eyes started to shine as her magick started to unfurl around her, the green whisps floating off of her body.

He stepped back and put his hands up. "I'm sorry, Lera, that wasn't what I meant."

She tossed her hair over her shoulder, a storm brewing around her. Furious, she marched away, offended that he would dare to judge her character based solely on her appearance. She could dress however she darned well pleased, no male was going to change that.

Kilyn groaned, running a hand through his hair in frustration. He quickly caught up with her. "Lera, please. Let's try this again. I apologize. I usually don't have trouble conversing with women, but you... well, there's something about you."

Lera slowed her walk and looked up at Kilyn, "What is it about me, water boy?"

"You're intriguing," Kilyn admitted, his gaze intense. "No-nonsense. I just... I don't understand your plan, or why you're here." He halted their walk, gently restraining her arm with his hand. "I'm just saying, and I can't believe I'm actually saying this, but don't hurt Puck. If you do... well, I may have to resort to more... drastic measures."

He pulled her hands into his, his green eyes searching hers for any sign of deception. Lera hesitated, a flicker of amusement in her eyes, before a soft smile touched her lips. She nodded, a silent agreement.

Puck, observing their interaction from a distance, felt a surge of murderous rage. Orin, sensing the shift in his friend's demeanor, quickly stepped in front of him.

"Puck," Orin cautioned, "Kilyn is simply talking to her. Don't start anything while we're on the road over a woman. Please."

Puck looked down at Orin's arm, taking a deep breath to quell the surge of rage that threatened to consume him. Where had that sudden, inexplicable fury come from?

As they approached Lera and Kilyn, she moved with a graceful fluidity, her arm threading through Puck's, her hand resting possessively on his. A challenging smile played on her lips as she addressed Kilyn. "Kilyn and I have decided to be friends, haven't we, water boy?"

Kilyn returned the smile, a hint of amusement in his eyes. "Indeed, wood sprite."

Lera looked up at Puck again and smiled at him, patting his arm with a reassuring tap and she pulled him forward. "The walking is not going to do itself, Puck from nowhere. Let's go."

They turned and continued their walk down the path, suddenly feeling a cold wind hit them. As they kept walking, the mountains to the north came into view.

Puck gasped with awe; the mountains were massive, unlike anything he had seen in his years, making the mountains back home seem puny. They looked almost as if they were spearing the sky with their jagged tops.

As they halted, a piercing screech echoed through the air. Puck shielded his eyes, scanning the sky. There it was – a magnificent falcon, diving towards them with deadly precision.

"Oh shit," Kilyn muttered. "You're in trouble now, Puck."

The falcon landed with a confident thud, shaking out its feathers before fixing its gaze on Puck. It seemed to regard his newly sprouted wings with a mixture of curiosity and disdain, raising a single leg at him. A small note was tied to its leg, a message that he knew was from his ma.

Puck gently stroked the bird, which responded with a soft chirp. He unfurled the note, a grimace twisting his features as he recognized his mother's elegant script. After a quick read, he flipped the note over.

With a flick of his finger, a quill materialized. He hastily penned a reply, then fastened it securely to the falcon's leg. "To Asthemar," he commanded. The falcon let out a sharp cry and soared south, disappearing into the distance.

Turning to his companions, Puck announced, "Apparently, we've been heading north this entire time. Mother knows our whereabouts. She's... not pleased, to put it mildly. But we'll address her concerns later. For now, we press on, she said that there should be a border town coming up shortly and we can rest there."

He paused and thought for a moment, "She's apologized as well. She mentioned that it's likely that Tenebris will hold the answers I seek."

He started walking and Orin cleared his throat. Puck stopped and looked at his friend.

"I need to go home, Puck, the barrier has released, the Baobhan Sith is dead. Or at the least, I need to figure out where my own mother is. I think this is where I need to leave you."

Puck walked over to Orin and embraced his older friend. They pressed their foreheads together and Puck whispered something which caused Orin to step back, a look of sheer want crossing his face. Orin nodded and Puck held his hand out, waiting.

Orin placed his hand upwards in Puck's and cut his finger. Shocked, Kilyn stepped forward, "If that's blood magick, this is where I'm going to be leaving you as well, friend or not. That's dangerous to do, no matter what level of mage you are, Puck. You don't know what forces you are playing with. You know the raw power derived from blood magick can be addictive. You could start craving the feeling of control and strength, which will lead you down a dangerous path of escalating sacrifices and self-destruction."

Puck look at the blood welling on Orin's fingertip and without hesitating continued his spell while responding to Kilyn. "If it means finding his mother, then I'd go to the ends of the earth for him, I'd do all of the magick I could to help him, Kilyn, just like I would you if you ever needed it, because you two are my hanos, blood or not."

Kilyn whispered, "That's the very reason why I said that, Puck." He stepped forward anyways and helped close the trifecta, his hands on his friends' shoulders.

Puck whispered an incantation as he waved his fingers over Orin's blood, watching it dance and float in the air. As he finished the spell, the blood drifted, as if waiting for a call. It floated above Orin then danced and took off northwards.

Orin and Puck looked at each other and then at Kilyn; confusion on their faces. What were the chances that Puck's journey would converge with Orin's?

Lera shivered, her gaze drawn to the stark, snow-capped peaks of the mountains. "That is no place for a wood elf," she whispered under her breath, her voice laced with apprehension.

Puck stepped closer, his arms encircling her in a warm embrace. Lera leaned into him, seeking solace in his warmth. "You'll be fine," he murmured, his voice a low rumble in her ear. "Besides," he added with a mischievous spark in his eyes, "where's the fun in an adventure without a little sense of danger?"

Lera rolled her eyes, a small smile playing on her lips. "You have a point," she conceded, "I suppose you'll play my knight in shining armour?"

Puck chuckled, his chin resting on the top of her head. "That's the spirit," he whispered, his gaze fixed on the distant mountains, a sense of anticipation stirring within him.

The lanterns of the border town shone as the sun slowly set. Lera excitedly bounced on the balls of her feet, "Oh gosh, please tell me that's the border town and that they have hot water. I'd KILL for a hot bath."

The men laughed as Puck grabbed Lera and they took off in a jog towards the town.

As they found the tavern in town, Puck searched his pockets and realized that not only had he left with no provisions, but he had also barely enough coin in his purse. Kilyn watched and scoffed.

"Good thing I'm the grown one in this group." He pulled a full purse out of his pocket, the coin jingling as he tossed it to Puck.

Puck smiled, "Thank you, Kilyn, I owe you."

Kilyn nodded, "Yes you do. I'll add it to the tally." He chuckled as he shouldered Puck as they entered into the doorway.

"Are you going to be a gentleman tonight?" his eyes roamed over to Lera who was standing at the bar, animatedly talking with the maid behind it.

"I'll behave," Kilyn chuckled as he looked around the room. He had a secret that he wasn't quite ready to tell his friends about, now was not the time.

As the men walked up, they caught the tail end of the conversation, "...so I opened my eyes, and he had wings!" Lera's arms flew up. The maid gasped and a shadow fell over her face as she looked at Puck.

The tavern slowly hushed around them and Puck, Kilyn and Orin looked at the small group inside as they looked back.

Orin spoke up his eyes assessing the group, "Are we going to have a problem tonight?"

The group at the table shook their heads quickly and turned back to their meals, avoiding eye contact with the four of them. Lera looked at the men and grimaced, "Sorry, I completely forgot about the general attitude about Nephilim."

Puck smiled and walked up to her, putting his arm over her shoulder as he politely asked the barmaid, "I am in need of four rooms please."

The barmaid walked back to the kitchen and came back with a tall Elvin man who looked the small group over with critical eyes.

"We don't have four rooms." He paused. Puck sighed and went to turn around. "We have two rooms, one with one bed and one with two beds. You'll have to make do, Nephilim."

Lera stepped forward, her hands fisted as she questioned, "Do you know who you're talking like that to?" she stuttered as Puck put his hand on her arm, praying for her to be quiet.

She looked up at him and closed her mouth. She nodded and looked down at the floor.

Puck turned back to the owner and smiled as kindly as he could, "I thank you, sir. We'll figure out the arrangements between the four of us."

The man nodded and held his hand out while Puck counted the

coin, pressing a few extra in his hand. The man looked back at him and pocketed it with a nod, wordlessly handing the keys to Puck.

They walked up the stairs of the tavern towards the back of the hallway. Orin and Kilyn looked at each other as Kilyn whispered with a devilish grin, "One bed, eh? Wonder what's going to happen there?" Orin chuckled and nudged Kilyn in the ribs.

"Don't you dare think of sneaking out to find a woman to bring back Kilyn. I don't want to hear you moaning all night."

Kilyn threw his head back and laughed as they grabbed the key to the room with the two beds, disappearing inside and closing the door.

Puck looked at Lera, "I can go sleep in the room with the boys. If something happens, you scream as loud as you can, and I'll be there." He handed her the key and went to reach to open the door that the men had gone into.

He felt Lera's hand on his arm, and he looked down to where she touched him. Her face was serene as she leaned towards him, tilting her face up to him.

"You, Puck from nowhere, need to finish what you started."

With a yelp, Puck was pulled into the room, Lera's hands on him as her lips crashed to his. He slammed the door behind him and fumbled as he tried to pull his shirt off around his wings.

"That shirt is definitely ruined," he muttered as his lips broke contact for a moment as Lera stepped back slowly. Her eyes on Puck's as she slowly untied her top, a small smile on her face.

Puck gulped as he watched her hands trail down and grab the hem of her shirt, pulling it over her head, leaving her top naked.

Her breasts were full; the nipples tight as the air caressed them. Puck's eyes took in her half naked form and felt himself hardening painfully. He groaned and stepped forward, his hands aching to cup her breasts and savour her.

Lera put her hand up and whispered, "Not yet."

Puck, unsure, stopped. "Sorry, I... I didn't mean to make assumptions..."

Lera laughed, "You aren't making assumptions, Puck from nowhere. I want to take this slow. I want you to watch me as I undress in front of you."

Puck's eyes widened as he watched her slowly slide her pants down, her legs stepping out of the pants one at a time and she tossed them to the side. A seductive smile worked its way across her face as she looked up at him through her eyelashes, her pupils large with arousal.

Her body was stunning; supple, curvaceous, her little stomach led down to a soft swell of her hips and Puck felt himself almost drooling.

"Your turn," she whispered as she slowly walked to the bed. She crawled up onto it on all fours and Puck internally groaned at the sight of the swell of her backside as she turned around and laid on the bed.

Puck pulled his pants off as fast as he could, tossing them to the side as he sat on the bed. He carefully touched her ankle and watched her face as he pulled her closer to him, his hand trailing up her calf to her thigh.

Lera sighed and tilted her head back, her hands slowly reaching up to her breasts as Puck drank her in, his other hand carefully caressing her other leg until he had both hands on her hips.

He prayed that all the things that Kilyn had told him were true. He bent down and carefully kissed the apex of her thighs and Lera stilled.

He breathed her scent in, and his mouth watered. He carefully pressed his tongue against her and with one movement slid his tongue up her folds and found her clit. Lera jolted and let out a soft moan as she grasped Puck's hair in her hand.

Puck paused, waiting for Lera to say something. When she tilted her hips up, he grinned and continued, his tongue gently pressing against her clit as he figured out what pressure she liked.

"Yes, just like that, Puck." She moaned breathlessly as she reached her hand up to play with her breast, her other hand finding purchase on Puck's short hair. He pulled her down and wrapped his arms around her thighs, spreading her legs more as he settled in between her, stroking her clit with his tongue.

As he placed his mouth over her again and gently sucked, she gasped, her eyes flying open as she clapped her hand over her mouth, a muffled moan escaped.

Puck quietly thanked Kilyn in that moment. He hadn't lied. He carefully ran his hand on the inside of her thigh, slowly inserting one finger into her wetness. She groaned again and bit her fist as she arched her back.

Puck continued to suck on her clit as he pulled his finger back to insert two, carefully and slowly stroking them inside of her, pressing his fingers upwards. Lera gasped at the pressure and writhed under Puck's mouth.

Suddenly, Lera pulled on him as she breathed out in ragged gasps, "I want the first time I come to be with you inside me, Puck, please." She begged as Puck pulled himself up, his elbow holding himself up as he cradled her in his arms.

His wings flexed out behind him as she reached down and wrapped her hand around Puck's cock. She grinned as she felt the size of him. She leaned up and their lips met as Puck groaned against her slow strokes up and down his length.

She murmured against his lips, "Take me, Puck. Make me yours." And Puck's vision clouded as she guided him into her wet centre. He slowly pushed as she arched her back, gasping as he paused. Gods, she felt so good. He pushed again and slowly felt her open up to him as his cock filled her. She wrapped her legs around his hips as he carefully pulled out and slid back into her, their hips meeting as he filled her.

As they started a slow rhythm together, Lera carefully slid her hand over Puck's shoulder and stroked his wing. Puck groaned and felt his cock twitch as he plunged into her. She grinned as she realized what she had been doing to him on the walk. She held onto his wing as he thrust into her, his face buried in her neck as his lips found the spot that made her melt.

She moaned as she felt herself tightening around him, his strokes slowly creating a heat that unfurled in her lower belly. She gasped as he dipped his head, capturing one of her nipples in his mouth. As he grazed his teeth over her nipple, she arched her back and cried out.

She felt herself clenching around Puck as he continued to thrust into her, both of them lost to the pleasure as they both let go together, wrapped in each other's arms.

A falcon approached Asthemar, landing in the window of the room Sarya was staying in. She rushed over to retrieve it, her heart pounding. As she unfurled it and read it, she clutched the paper to her heart like it was a lost love. Tears of relief streamed down her face.

As she read it again, she knew that she needed to tell him everything; no matter how much it hurt.

"I will always love you, ma. I need to know who I am. Trust me. I will come home. Let me figure this out- please don't send anyone."

Chapter Twenty Five

Tenebris

Aria flexed her hands, the rough stone of the dungeon floor digging into her palms. No magick. Nothing. Just the cold, damp air and the echoing silence. Disappointment washed over her. She had hoped, foolishly perhaps, that her magick would still function and she could get the children out of here.

Then, a soft voice, like the whisper of leaves on a summer breeze, startled her. "You there," the voice murmured, "the one with the children."

Aria squinted, trying to pinpoint the source of the sound. Across the hallway, a faint glow emanated from another cage, revealing the silhouette of a woman within.

Relief washed over her, quickly followed by a surge of cautious apprehension. At least she wasn't alone.

"The iron wards," the woman continued, her voice barely a whisper, "they'll keep us trapped."

Aria nodded, her voice a mere breath in the oppressive silence. "I've tried. No magick."

"Are you... do you belong to one of the Clans?" the woman asked, her voice hesitant.

Aria paused, weighing her words carefully. What information was safe to reveal? What could she gain from this stranger? "I... I am," she finally admitted, her voice barely audible.

"Which Clan?" the woman pressed, her voice a touch more insistent.

"That... is not important," Aria deflected, "What is your name?"

"Amodra," the woman replied. "I'm Amodra, I come from Blood-rose lands."

The blood ran cold in Aria's veins as the name sent a shiver down her spine. Amodra wasn't from Bloodrose lands, she had come from across the ocean with Orin in tow. She had married King Osian...What was Amodra doing in the dungeon of Tenebris?

The woman, almost as if hearing Aria's thoughts, responded, "The Baobhan Sith captured me a long time ago, they stole my son and when they couldn't figure out how to use my power for themselves, I was sold to the Night Price of Tenebris."

Aria collapsed onto the cold, damp stone floor, her hands gripping the iron bars of her cage. "What do you mean... wait... you're Orin's amille?" she gasped, her mind reeling. What tricks were being played in the dark? She was so confused. Was it the iron wards? The dark space playing with her mind?

Amodra smiled faintly in the darkness, a single tear tracing a line through the grime on her cheek. "Thank the goddess, he's still alive," she whispered, her voice thick with emotion.

She pressed her face against the bars, her eyes desperately searching Aria's face. "Bayle," she breathed, her voice barely a whisper, "You're Cohnal and Salihn's selye, Aria."

Aria gasped, pulling back. "How... how do you know that? Just by looking at me?"

Amodra shook her head, a sad smile gracing her lips. "The resemblance is undeniable. Your amille's eyes, your amil's mouth... it's uncanny."

Aria stared at her, speechless. This Amodra didn't seem anything like the Queen that King Osian had married. From what she had heard from Hagen and Saphielle, she was aloof and mysterious. They had never officially met, so how could the woman know that Aria was the daughter of the King and Queen of Clan Bayle? Questions swirled in Aria's mind, a whirlwind of confusion and disbelief. It had to be trickery down here, an illusion.

Aria's eyes narrowed as she took in the woman across the hallway, trying to figure out what to do. Amodra, sensing Aria's turmoil, softly smiled again, opening her mouth to speak. Then, a sudden commotion erupted down the hallway, a cacophony of shouts and the clatter of metal on stone. Amodra's eyes widened.

"Go back to the children," she whispered urgently, "Protect them. I'll try to distract the guards. Hurry!" She waved Aria towards the children, her voice filled with a newfound urgency.

Aria, having no one else to turn to, decided to trust this stranger, illusion or not. She nodded frantically and scrambled back towards the children. She huddled them close, her heart pounding against her ribs. Rina and Aywin whimpered as they watched for the shadow to appear. Erawyn buried her face into Aria's dress and Ward kneeled beside her, his hand on her shoulder, defiance in his eyes as he watched.

Aria looked at all of them then towards the sounds coming down the dungeon hall. What was happening?

A figure emerged from the shadows at the end of the hallway, a cloaked guard dragging a spiked club behind him. Aria felt a cold dread grip her heart. They didn't mean to harm them, did they?

She clutched the children close, watching in horror as the guard advanced, stepping closer and closer. The air crackled with a sinister energy, and she could feel her own fear rising, threatening to choke her. The guard stopped in front of their cell, his chest rising and falling, not a sound coming from him.

Rina and Aywin sat silently, terror holding their little bodies captive. The guard had visited before, and his threats were still swirling in their heads.

Aria looked up at the guard through the cell bars, her magick spluttering as she felt the fire growing around her, trying to push outwards, to protect them, but it couldn't push past the wards that were placed on the cell.

As her magick fizzled down again, her heart continued to thud dangerously fast, her pulse quickening as she watched for the guard to do something, anything other than stand in front of the cell breathing and staring at all of them.

She glanced at Amodra, who was now pressed against the bars of her cage, her eyes narrowed in concentration. A low hum emanated from her, a strange vibration that seemed to ripple through the air.

The guard turned and glanced at Amodra, his footsteps heavy and deliberate as he stepped closer to the cell Aria and the children were in. As he drew closer, Amodra's hum intensified, the air growing thick. He grinned, a cruel, predatory smile that sent a shiver down Aria's spine; she could do nothing but helplessly pull the children closer as she watched the guard.

Suddenly he stopped and turned, storming over to Amodra's cell, surprising them all. Reaching through the bars, he quickly grabbed a fistful of Amodra's pale hair, yanking her head towards the iron.

She cried out in pain, her head snapping back against the cold metal. Just as his face neared hers, his knees buckled beneath him. A guttural cry escaped his lips as he crumpled to the ground, the spiked club clattering to the stone floor.

Aria gasped, her eyes widening in disbelief as she tried to keep the children's faces turned away. Amodra, her face pale but resolute, pulled a small knife away from the bars. Blood trickled down her wrist, a crimson stain against the grime. Her face displayed no emotion as she watched him.

The guard laid on the ground, his body convulsing. Then, as abruptly as it began, the tremors ceased. He lay motionless, dead.

Amodra looked at Aria. "Now," she hissed, her voice low and urgent, "You need to move." She reached through the bars, stretching her hands as far as she could, searching the guard.

He wore a simple uniform, a leather jerkin and rough-spun trousers. A small pouch hung from his belt, and Amodra carefully retrieved it. Inside, she found a few coins, a small knife, and a set of keys.

Aria, still reeling from the unexpected display of violence, hesitated. "But... but what about you?" she whispered, gesturing towards Amodra's cell.

Amodra shook her head. "You can't risk being caught. You need to find a way out of here." She tossed the keys across the hallway and watched as they fell to the ground in the cell that Aria was in. "Whatever reason the Night Prince has you all trapped here, you need to get out of here before the darkness takes you as well."

The Night Prince? Aria's mind spun again. The kings had killed Rhamiel years ago- was it possible he had been resurrected? The thought sent chills through her as she remembered Saphielle being captured by him, his plan to take a royal to create a vessel for the darkness that swirled around him. She couldn't let that happen to the children.

With a renewed sense of urgency, Aria stood up quickly and gathered the children close. She grabbed the keys from the ground and unlocked the cell door, cautiously approaching the fallen guard, her eyes darting around the hallway. The air was thick with tension, and an eerie silence had descended upon the dungeon.

Her heart pounded with a mixture of hope and fear. She could get the children to safety, to kill the Night Prince if she needed to; they couldn't let him destroy Tir Siorghlas again. She turned and moved to Amodra's cell, moving to insert the key into the lock as Amodra cried out, her arms reaching, "No, Aria, don't!"

Suddenly the dungeon lit up with a blinding light, the force slamming Aria against the wall. She hit her head and slumped down onto the ground, unconscious.

Ward yelled out, Aywin and Rina ran to Aria, checking her breathing, shaking her as Erawyn stood crying, her little fists clenched together.

Amodra looked around at them, unable to do anything. She reached through the bars desperately, "shush, little ones, please. It'll be ok! Just breathe..." her eyes darted over to Aria, laying on the floor then she sized the children up.

"You, Clan Basalt," she pointed at Ward, her voice strong. He gulped and looked at Amodra and pointed at himself. She nodded, "Good boy. Now, you grab the smaller one, Empereal, I feel? You get the Tempestus twins to follow. Make sure you all stick together. There is not a lot of time left. Listen very carefully to me."

Ward, Aywin and Rina nodded together, their eyes huge. Erawyn clung to Ward as he scooped her up.

"Now, there is a set of stairs down the hallway on the right. You will take those and go down, not up. Keep going until the stairs stop, then you will take a left. It will lead you to a hallway. Do not look back. Keep following the hallway, always staying to the right. You'll start to see the sun. That's when you'll know you're almost at the surface."

"Whatever you do," Amodra urged, her voice barely a whisper, "do not lose sight of each other."

The children, their faces pale but determined, nodded solemnly. "Go!" she commanded, her voice firm. The children, without hesitation, turned and fled down the hallway, their small figures disappearing into the shadows.

A loud clatter echoed from the opposite end of the hallway, sending a jolt of fear through Amodra. "Please, be safe," she whispered, her gaze fixed on the direction the children had vanished. She tried desperately to reach Aria, to pull her closer, but the iron bars remained an insurmountable barrier.

A figure emerged from the shadows, a man with obsidian wings that seemed to absorb the meager light. He bent down, his face obscured from Amodra's view. She watched in horror as he scooped Aria up in his arms, whispering something to the guard standing beside him.

"You need to make right what your father did, Nephilim." Amodra whispered, tears welling up in her eyes, "before all of this gets out of hand and neither you nor the heir can fix it."

He paused and turned his head slightly, looking at her. "I cannot let you out, I'm not the one destined to do so." He whispered, his voice pained as he looked down at Aria's still form.

Atmos turned and walked away, Aria's limp form dangling in his arms. Amodra watched until they vanished from sight, her heart sinking into the depths of despair.

The guard remaining scoffed, his voice dripping with contempt. "When will you learn, bitch? You can't escape from this cell, no matter what tricks you try, ain't no one with the right magick able to release you." He extinguished the torch, plunging Amodra back into the suffocating darkness.

Amodra sank to the floor, pulling her knees to her chest and wrapping her arms around herself. Tears streamed down her face, a silent, anguished cry in the oppressive darkness.

Chapter Twenty Six

Tenebris

Taion surveyed the throne room, his gaze finally settling on the imposing throne that dominated the chamber. A wave of revulsion washed over him.

"Remove that abomination," he commanded, his voice low and dangerous. Two startled guards hurried forward, struggling to dislodge the heavy throne from its dais.

As they began to drag it across the room, the throne groaning as it slowly moved, Taion halted them. "No," he said, his voice sharper. "Leave it. I'll deal with it."

The guards, visibly relieved, quickly obeyed, depositing the throne unceremoniously on the floor. With another curt nod, they scurried from the room.

Taion circled the throne, his eyes narrowed. He raised his hands, whispering an incantation. A low hum filled the air, suddenly, the throne erupted in flames, the wood crackling and spitting. Taion watched impassively as the flames consumed the tainted object, the intense heat pushing him back slightly. His eyes reflected the fire within: hot, angry, betrayed.

When only charred remains were left, Taion turned and strode from the room, his footsteps echoing in the sudden silence. In the aftermath of the flames, a low, guttural screech echoed through the chamber.

The darkness had awakened, having been imprisoned in the throne all this time. She licked her lips, tasting the air. The heir had arrived; the time for a new age of darkness had come. Her inky form slithered along the walls, waiting.

Atmos walked along the hallway, an unconscious Aria in his arms. He had been horrified when he came across her seemingly lifeless body in the dungeon and had cursed a stream under his breath until he felt her pulse under his thumb.

He had arrived too late to get the children to safety and explain what was going on. He only hoped that he could stop everything before Tenebris was nothing but an empty mountain.

He stormed down the hallway until he came to the royal chambers of the castle. He pushed open the double doors to one of the rooms and tilted his head to the servants that had followed him.

"Air the room out, I want the windows opened and a bath drawn, please." He gently placed Aria on the bed, the mattress soft under her.

He looked her over one more time in the light that came from the windows; aside from being covered in dirt, he couldn't see any other wounds. He carefully walked around and noticed her dress was ripped. The portal shouldn't have caused them any harm, he mused.

Underneath he could see older bruises on the side of her exposed ribcage. They were splayed across her ribs, and he growled as he looked closer.

"Gods, to lay your hands on such an innocent being..." he trailed off as he realized who it was. Someone had some explaining to do. He wondered if Hagen had found out that his little sister was being abused under the hand of her husband, Theo.

He looked up as he felt a presence at the door. Taion had quietly come upon him, and he leaned against the door, his arms crossed. Atmos turned around, Aria's unconscious form hidden from him as he frowned at his brother.

"What are you doing in the chambers meant for the royal family, Atmos? Did you decide that you were going to follow me?" Taion teased with a grin as he pushed himself off the door frame, his muscles moving under his shirt as he moved to walk into the room.

Atmos crossed his arms, his wings splayed out a bit further as he contemplated if he should reveal to his brother who was on the bed. At this point, someone needed to shock some sense into him.

With a sigh he drew his wings in, "Your plan is unravelling, brother, the children..." He said as he turned to look back at Aria. Hearing a strangled sound from Taion, he quickly turned back and looked at his brother again, his brows knitted in confusion.

"What's wrong?" he asked as he looked at Taion.

Taion stood frozen in the doorway, his breath catching in his throat. His eyes were frozen on the woman in the bed. He had never seen such beauty. Aira lay sprawled across the bed, her chest rising and falling in a gentle rhythm.

Her long, red hair cascaded over the pillow, framing a face that was both delicate and strong under the dirt from her time spent in the dungeon. Her skin was pale, too pale, and her lips were slightly parted.

Taion felt a strange warmth spreading through him, a feeling he had never experienced before. It was as if something within him had been awakened, something that had been dormant for far too long, his chest hurt from the feeling. He felt an overwhelming urge to reach out and touch her, to feel the softness of her skin beneath his fingertips.

But he resisted the urge, afraid that he might disturb her. He didn't want to wake her, to take away from this moment of pure innocence. He wanted to savor this moment, to commit every detail of her face to memory.

He studied her for what seemed like an eternity, his heart pounding in his chest. He had never felt this way about anyone before. He was captivated, enthralled, and utterly bewildered by the intensity of his emotions.

Finally, he tore his gaze away from her, his heart heavy with longing. He knew he could never touch her, never possess her. She was a creature of light, a goddess, while he was a blight, a shadow lurking in the darkness, only meant to destroy, that was his destiny. He was meant to be alone, ruling Tenebris while ensuring the safety of his people.

He turned and left the room without a word, his footsteps echoing in the silence. He didn't know where he was going, or what he was going to do. He only knew that his life would never be the same again. He had seen her, and he would never forget her.

Whatever plans he had were slowly going up in smoke now that he knew who he had captured: it was different when he hadn't seen their faces. What Aria didn't know was that she had unwittingly captured his heart as she laid there, unconscious.

Atmos had watched the interaction with surprise and amusement; unsure what to make of what just happened. He turned to the servant and whispered strict instructions to keep an eye on the Princess, ensuring that when she came to that he would be alerted.

He quickly walked down the hallway, opposite of where Taion had rushed down. He had to find the children before they fell into any danger. As he retraced any steps of where they could have gone, he realized the prisoner would have sent them to the eastern entrance; the only way to exit the dungeons from that path.

He had to get to them before they froze to death. The children were not dressed for the weather that the mountain controlled. He ran over to the servants who were cleaning the entrance of the castle. They bowed and he looked at the both of them.

"I need either blankets or cloaks if we have them, hurry." The servants bowed and hastily ran over to the side of the entrance, revealing a small room full of garments. They pulled out a few cloaks, thick and lined with fur and a large black blanket.

He thanked them and with his arms full, ran out the front doors of the castle, taking flight as he jumped. He flew over the city and soared over to the southern entrance. As he touched down, the guards at the entrance bowed. "Sire Atmos, will you be gone long this time?"

Atmos looked at both of the guards and without a word, his eyes flashing, whispered an incantation and knocked them both out. He didn't need them knowing what he was going to do, lest Taion had already instructed them to let no one enter or exit.

The children needed to go home, and he needed to sort this mess before it became a full-scale war. He ran down the large tunnel and as he saw the opening, he jumped and took flight, swinging around the mountain towards the eastern entrance.

As his eyes roamed over the entrance, he coasted and calculated his landing. His feet touched the cold stone, and he drew his wings in as he looked around the entrance, the bundle of cloaks and blanket in his arms.

"Ward? Aywin and Rina? It's Atmos. I've come to take you home." He looked around and patiently waited.

"You're safe now, please come out. Your parents will be missing you by now."

Out of the shadows, Rina and Aywin stepped forward, their hands held tightly as Rina looked back and nodded. Ward came into the light, holding Erawyn.

Atmos looked at the little girl with confusion, unable to place her as a royal and Ward offered, "She's from Clan Empereal. Her ma works at the castle for Eldatár Silvan and Elentári Alyndria."

Atmos nodded in understanding, unsure though of how a child without royal blood had been pulled into the portal: the magick was very specific, it had to be of the Clan's royal blood to activate.

He got down on one knee, his arms out as he looked at Ward. He softly said, "Prince Ward, I'll take little Erawyn, I have a blanket for her. Take the cloaks and get yourself and the girls warmed up."

Ward assessed Atmos and carefully walked towards him, Erawyn whimpering as Ward pulled her arms off of his neck, giving her to Atmos. Atmos quickly wrapped her in the blanket and breathed some heat with his magick to warm the little girl up. Her big blue eyes looked at Atmos, assessing him warily.

He smiled gently at her and tapped her nose, "It's time you go home, hey, little one?" She giggled and buried her face into the soft warm blanket. Atmos grinned at her adorable movements.

He looked at the other three children, trying to assess how he was going to get them all to safety. His eyes fell to their feet which thankfully still had shoes on them. It was going to be a bit of a journey if they had to walk. He just needed to get them to the border town where the guards were stationed.

Ward watched as he realized Atmos was assessing how to get them all out and he stepped forward, "I can walk down the mountain, Atmos. I'm old enough to do that. Take Erawyn back to her ma, she's too little to walk. Rina and Aywin can do the walk down as well, we aren't babies."

A rustle at the entrance of the cave had Atmos carefully putting Erawyn down as he turned to block the view of the children from whoever had entered.

"Atmos? Are you here?" a female voice echoed through the tunnel. Atmos' shoulders dropped as he sighed with relief, answering back, "Ephyra, my love, we're over here." She came around the corner and gasped as she saw the children standing, looking back at her.

"They need to go home, Ephyra." Atmos looked at her as he gathered Erawyn in his arms again.

She looked at Atmos and scrubbed her face with her hands before dropping them at her side, "You're really putting yourself in a precarious situation, Atmos. How are we going to get all of them down the mountain before Taion sounds the alarm?"

Atmos shrugged, "I'll die trying at this point, Ephyra. We cannot start another war over something like this, I swore a promise to protect the Clans. Now, come help me get the twins down." He turned and looked at Ward, "I'll come back for you as soon as the twins and the bairn are down at the border town, ok? Do not move."

Ward swallowed hard, trying to hide how scared he actually was. He nodded, his eyes wide as he moved back into the shadows of the tunnel and sat down to wait, pulling the cloak around him.

Ephyra bent and pulled the twins to her as they scrambled to grab each other, holding tight to her. She muttered as she felt the additional weight on her. Her wings were going to be unimpressed at her for a while after this.

She swung around and dove over the mouth of the cave. The twins closed their eyes in terror as the plummeted downwards. With a gentle woosh, Ephyra spread her wings out and they coasted over the land, the clouds flying by.

Rina cracked an eye open and poked Aywin who opened her eyes and gasped with delight. They both looked down in wonder as Ephyra soared over the land, aiming to put the kids at the edge of the border town so the guards would find them.

They gently flew down and Ephyra landed carefully, Atmos right behind her. Atmos handed Erawyn to Rina who bundled her up. He pointed to a large tree close to the town, "Go wait over there until I bring Ward back. Ephyra, stay with them please."

Before Ephyra could say anything, Atmos shot up, flying back towards the eastern cave entrance. His mind was trying to reconcile how he could persuade his brother to actually listen, to see that the anger was misplaced, that he could still claim the throne, make things right and not cause a war.

He flapped his wings and landed in the entrance, "Ward, I'm here to take you now, let's go. The others are waiting for you."

Out of the shadows, Puck emerged, rage dancing in his blue eyes as he held his brother's hand. Ward looked up at him and back at Atmos, unsure where he should go.

Atmos stepped back, shock etched across his face. His gaze fell upon Puck's black wings, identical to his own, and his jaw dropped. "Puck?" he stammered, "Why... why are you here, in Tenebris?"

Anger surged through Puck. "Why is *my* hano here, Atmos?" he demanded, his voice low and dangerous. Atmos, realizing the futility of any explanation, raised his hands in a placating gesture.

"Ward can confirm," he said, his voice strained. "I'm merely escorting them to the border town. The guards will take them home from there. There was a misunderstanding."

Ward, still reeling from the sight of Puck's wings, nodded mutely in agreement. Atmos, seizing upon Ward's silence as a sign of agreement, gestured towards the opening of the entrance. "Let's get you to the girls," he said, "and I'll alert the guards."

Ward stepped forward, but Puck intercepted him. Orin emerged from the shadows, Kilyn and Lera trailing behind.

"There really is a whole city down there, Puck! Did you see the other Nephilim..." He halted abruptly, his eyes widening in surprise. "Atmos?" he exclaimed, "What are you doing here?"

Atmos, equally startled, bowed his head, his mind swimming as he tried to piece together what the hells was going on.

"Prince Orin," he acknowledged, then straightened, his gaze hardening. "Why are *you* in Tenebris, Prince?" he countered, realizing that Ward was clearly not going anywhere with him anytime soon.

The group all looked at each other, confusion surrounding the circumstances. Atmos sighed as he crossed his arms, "We all need to say something but I really need to get Ward down to the twins so they can get home before there is a war over the missing heirs. Ward, come, your brother will let you go."

He frowned at Puck, hoping he would realize he was being serious as he put his arms out.

Puck weighed the situation and nodded, releasing his hold on his brother. "Tell ma and amil that I'm fine, Ward. I'll come home soon. I promise."

Ward turned and looked at his brother with a wry smile on his face, "I guess I can tell them you have wings now." Atmos quickly grabbed Ward and stepped off the cliff ledge to get him to the twins before Puck changed his mind.

As they soared over the Silver Lands towards the border town, Atmos's mind swirled. Why were the young men in Tenebris? What else did Taion have brewing that he didn't know? He needed to get back up to the eastern entrance before they started wandering the city, causing even more chaos.

Chapter Twenty Seven

Tenebris

Taion paced the length of his private balcony, his gaze fixed on the city below the castle. The light slowly dimmed, allowing the bioluminescent flora to come out, casting a shimmering glow over the city and castle.

The city seemed to come alive, the light dancing and flickering like a thousand tiny stars. He watched the lights for a moment, struggling to piece together what was happening as his mind went back to when he would stay in his mother's lap, watching the lights with awe from the window before bed.

His mind was consumed by the image of Aria, her face etched in his memory with precise clarity. He had seen her only once, yet the impact was profound on him.

A strange warmth had spread through him, an unfamiliar emotion that both terrified and exhilarated him. It was a feeling he had never experienced before, a yearning that threatened to consume him, weaving its way around his heart as it took hold.

His life had been dedicated to the pursuit of power; The throne of Tenebris was his birthright, a destiny he had embraced his entire life, guided by Constance, Frig and his wife. But now, this unexpected emotion threatened to derail those carefully laid plans.

How could he conquer all that he wanted when his heart was already captured by a woman he barely knew, a woman who he had unwittingly captured through the portal meant for her father?

He struggled as he pushed against the magick surrounding him. His small frame slowly being captured by the bubble that was tightening. With a grunt he whispered an incantation, and the bubble shattered around him.

"Well done, Prince Taion." Constance smiled as she walked towards him.

Taion flexed his wings and looked at Constance, a scowl on his face. "I want to go home, Matron. Release your hold on my teleportation powers. I demand it!"

Constance's face fell and she kneeled down to level with Taion. "Prince, we cannot do that. To do that would mean certain death to you. The darkness, the Nightsinger, has taken your amil."

She stood up and pointed to a carriage. "This was the last of the lessons I had time to provide to you. The plan has to move forward, and you need to go. We are sending you to another coven on the island of Locrya, to keep you safe and hidden from your amil."

Taion looked at Constance and protested, "Wait! I don't want to go! I want my amille! I want my friends, Atmos and Ephyra! Why can't you all just protect me here?"

Constance sadly looked at Taion as she whispered an incantation. Taion's eyes widened and he dropped to the ground. Constance nodded to the three men who were waiting, and they gathered the little Prince, placing him in the carriage.

Constance handed them the bag with Taion's belongings and sternly looked at Frig, "You take extreme care of your ward, Mr. Frig. Under no circumstances can you let him back on Tir Siorghlas soil until the darkness is vanquished. We cannot have another vessel for the darkness to corrupt, not until we can figure out how to contain it."

Frig bowed, "Ma'am, Matron. You have my solemn vow that my wife and I will take care of the bairn. We'll raise him to know the sea, to be a strong leader for when the time comes and to know his magick. I promise."

He bowed and turned back towards the carriage, directing them towards the east, towards the coast. Constance hugged herself as she watched them drive away, praying that Locrya was far enough to keep Rhamiel and the darkness from finding Taion.

Taion woke days later, the rocking of the ship causing him to fall off the bed and promptly vomit all over the floor. As he wiped his mouth and looked up, his eyes connected with the kind face of Frig.

"Welcome aboard the mighty Lancaster, bairn. We're heading to Locrya, and you'll meet my wife."

Taion groaned and laid prone on the floor as his stomach rolled again. What had he done to deserve this?

As he wrestled with the memories, a movement caught his eye. Out of the corner of his vision, a swirling darkness began to coalesce in the air, a malevolent presence reaching out from the shadows.

A cold dread gripped him. He knew the tales of the darkness- the Nightsinger- all too well, the insidious power that had corrupted his father and plunged the kingdom into seasons of chaos. With a surge of adrenaline, Taion raised his hands, channeling his own power to counter the encroaching darkness.

He felt a familiar tingle, a surge of energy coursing through his veins. With a focused will, he reached out, shaping the energy into a protective barrier. The swirling darkness recoiled, her tendrils lashing out against the invisible force field.

He could hear the soft screeching as the Nightsinger realized what was happening. His lessons with Constance, learning about the darkness and the spells required to contain it were important now, he prayed it would be enough.

Taion, his breath catching in his throat, willed the darkness back, compressing it into a smaller and smaller form. Finally, as he strained, sweat dripping down his back, he imprisoned the malevolent energy within a crystal vial, the swirling mass now a still, ominous object in his hand.

He stared at the vial, his heart pounding. He would not succumb to the darkness, not like his father, he was stronger. He sat down heavily on the floor and carefully put the vial next to him as he breathed a sigh of relief.

He leaned against the column holding the roof of the balcony up and closed his eyes as he caught his breath. He went over his plan in his head one more time, pushing aside Aria's image in his mind.

As long as the vial contained the darkness, he could proceed with cleansing Tenebris and bringing the Kings to account for their lack of support for his family. He stood up and rolled his shoulders and neck, willing his wings out of hiding. He groaned as he felt them flex out of his back, the grey feathers unfurling as his wingspan spread out.

He rolled his shoulders again; it had been too long since he'd taken flight. As his wings settled in place he turned and leaned against the balcony railing, looking at the city below him again. His fingers bit into the stone railing. His city. His people. His land. His throne.

The silence that had descended since the children vanished was odd. Enough time had passed, a gnawing length of days that stretched into weeks, for the initial shock and disbelief to give way to a plan being made. The Clan Kings should soon be banding together and making their way to Taion.

He envisioned it clearly – a gathering of warriors from all of Tir Siorghlas and the five Clans- The Kings at the front of their forces. They would march upon the mountain, their swords gleaming, arrows notched, moving with a single, unwavering purpose: to reclaim their children. And Taion would be at the front of his winged army, ready to destroy them: to make them feel the pain he had felt his entire life.

The weight of this impending conflict, oddly enough, settled heavily upon him. He knew that the battle would be a bloody one, lives would be lost. But he could see only that path forward.

He strode out of the bedroom and walked down the hallway, his wings tucked behind him. He nodded as two guards quietly followed him as he marched towards the doors to the dungeon. He quickly stepped down the stairs that lead to the main level of the dungeon beneath the castle. He continued walking down the hallway, frowning when the smell of the damp earth hit his nostrils.

Taion peered into the inky darkness and snapped his fingers; the torches down the length of the dungeon sparked, flames dancing to light up his path. The guards stood behind him, their eyes adjusting to the sudden light.

He quietly walked to where the children were imprisoned, thinking about what he was going to say to them, so they understood why they were there. As he reached the bars, he looked over and noticed the cell door was open. He frowned and growled lowly as his eyes assessed the space, noticing the scuff marks in the dirt floor.

He walked over and he stopped as his eyes traced the slight outline where Aria had landed after being knocked unconscious. A slight roll of guilt panged through him. He shook it off as he looked back at the empty cell, his brows knitting together as he frowned: he hadn't realized that with Aria out, the children had also been released. Without them, his plans were dashed: they were the bargaining chip that he had to get the Kings to heel. His vision clouded as he tried to figure out a way to salvage everything.

A soft voice behind him made him turn quickly, his iridescent eyes assessing as he listened to it, unable to see who it belonged to, he walked over to the cell, a couple of feet down from where he had stood. "The children are never the answer to punishing someone for the mistakes of the father, Taion. You should know better."

Taion's frown deepened as he stepped closer to the bars. "Show yourself, you shadow."

The woman stepped out, her dress white, her wings tucked behind her back and her blonde hair braided to lay over her shoulder.

"My little stargazer, I thought I raised you better." She softly said, her eyes filling with unshed tears.

Taion grabbed the bars tightly, his grip on them slowly bending them. "Mother?" he looked through the bars in horror as she walked towards him. She looked down where his hands were tightly clenching the bars and gently touched his hands, "Let go, Taion. You can rule without making them pay that way. Let me out and we can figure this out together."

Taion, deaf to what she was saying looked around for the keys to the cages. His eyes fell to the ground, and he saw them, covered in dirt from the floor. He bent down and grabbed them, flipping through to find the right one. His heart beat frantically as he held onto the door, his eyes searching for the key.

"I... I didn't know you were here the whole time, mother. I...

Matron Constance had told me you died in a letter she sent to me in Locrya." His eyes blurred with tears as he struggled to find the right key, desperation taking over.

"I'm sorry, I'll get you out. I'm so sorry, mother." He choked out hoarsely as he dropped the keys into the dirt. He reached down and grabbed the heavy iron keys again, his fingers trembling. But before he could insert it into the lock, a hand clamped down on his shoulder. Atmos was looking at him, his face etched with sadness.

"Taion, brother, stop." Atmos' voice, usually calm and reassuring, was laced with urgency. "It's not your mother. It's the siren."

Taion whirled around, his eyes blazing with anger. "What do you mean? Can't you see my mother standing there? How could you leave her in there all this time, Atmos?"

Atmos sighed, the weight of years and seeing the destruction the darkness had caused, settling on his shoulders. "She was imprisoned here long ago by your grandfather, a creature of illusion and deceit. She feeds on the hope and despair of those who fall under her spell."

Taion scoffed. "You're wrong. I know my mother. I can feel her presence."

Atmos gently but firmly shook his brother. "Look again, Taion. Really look."

Reluctantly, Taion turned back to the figure in the cell. The torchlight flickered, casting the woman in an eerie, shifting light. As his eyes adjusted, the illusion began to unravel. The sorrowful expression morphed into a grotesque parody, a chilling smile twisting her lips. Her eyes, once filled with maternal love, now glowed with an unnatural, predatory light.

A low, guttural chuckle escaped the creature's lips, a sound that sent shivers down Taion's spine. It was a sound of triumph, of a hunter savoring its prey. "Interesting that the son of Rhamiel wasn't protected by the spell around my cell." She hissed, "So close, but little Atmos had to ruin all the fun."

Horrified, Taion stumbled back, dropping the key with a clatter. The illusion shattered completely, revealing a grotesque, skeletal figure huddled in the shadows. It let out a shriek that echoed through the dungeon, a sound of pure, malevolent anger.

Shocked, Taion swung around and stormed out of the dungeon, racing up the stairs as his cheeks burned with shame, Atmos on his heels. "Taion, wait!"

Taion whirled around on Atmos, "What do you want, Atmos? Other than to constantly undermine me, is it the throne you really want? Just spit it out!" he roared, his hands clenched into fists as his eyes flashed with danger.

Atmos stopped short and put his hands up, "I want nothing to do with that throne, Taion, I've said that since the day I found out who my sire was. We have another problem."

Taion growled, "What is the problem?"

Puck stepped into the hallway from the front entrance of the castle, his wings tucked behind him neatly. Holding his hand was Lera, her eyes were wide in shock as she took in not one, but three men that all bore a slight resemblance to each other.

Kilyn and Orin came up behind them, having watched the altercation between Taion and Atmos. "This is a lot of family drama for me." Kilyn muttered to Orin. Orin frowned and jabbed Kilyn in the ribs. "Shut up, Kilyn."

Puck looked at Taion and Atmos, his face hiding any feeling as he assessed both of the winged men. His list of questions just got significantly longer.

Taion gave Puck a once over, recognizing the resemblance and groaned, pressed his fingers to the bridge of his nose, "You have got to be kidding me. What in the hells else could happen, really."

He pushed through the group and stormed to the throne room, the one place that was large enough that he could think and still have the others in the room. He stood at the door and waved his arm towards the room, indicating for them to follow.

Atmos lead the way, Puck and Lera following and bringing up the rear, Kilyn then Orin. Orin warily sized Atmos up again as Atmos walked towards him when they all entered the large room.

"Have you been playing the Clans, Atmos? This whole time? Are you going to revive the darkness and the Night Court? What are you doing? I thought I could trust you!"

Orin swung at Atmos who ducked just in time. He didn't want to have to fight Orin but could sense the pent-up aggression and anger in the prince and sighed, preparing himself for a fistfight.

Orin squared up and swung again, this time connecting with Atmos' face. His face swung and Atmos grunted at the pain, tasting blood in his mouth. He turned his head back and looked at Orin as he wiped the blood off his lip with his thumb, assessing it darkly.

"I'm not going to trade punch for punch but don't think for a second, Prince," Atmos spat, "that I'm going to just bow down to you and let you beat me. I am a prince in my own right."

Orin's face was a mask of furious rage, his eyes burning with a dangerous intensity. With a guttural roar, he launched himself at Atmos, a whirlwind of limbs and fury. Atmos, anticipating the attack, braced himself, his body a coiled spring.

The collision was violent, a thunderous impact as their bodies slammed together, sending them tumbling to the cold, hard stone floor. The air crackled with the violence of their struggle. Fists flew, a blur of motion in the dim light.

Orin, fueled by rage, struck with savage force, but Atmos, years older and wiser, was a whirlwind of controlled aggression. He dodged, weaved, and countered, his movements fluid and precise, his wings sweeping around him as he moved.

Finally, with a surge of strength, Atmos seized the opportunity, twisting and turning until he had Orin pinned beneath him, his arm locked around his throat.

Orin's face contorted, his eyes bulging with panic as he gasped for air, his struggles growing weaker with each passing second. He thrashed beneath Atmos, his fingers clawing at the air, desperate to break free. Atmos, his face grim but controlled, tightened his grip slightly, the pressure building. Orin's body went limp, his struggles ceasing as he tapped out.

Atmos released the pressure, and Orin fell to the ground, coughing as he drew air back into his lungs. He laid on the cold floor, his chest heaving as he swore, "Fuck you, Atmos. You dirty liar."

Atmos stood overtop Orin and put his arm out to pull Orin up, "We need to talk, Prince Orin. It's not what you think it is."

Orin slapped his hand away and rolled onto all fours and pulled himself up, standing on his own, his chest still heaving as he glared at Atmos.

"Nothing you say is going to change..."

Atmos interrupted Orin, his voice steady despite the rising tension in the room. "I'm your friend, Orin. You know that I have always been. The throne of Tenebris belongs to three Heirs. You're looking at three of them right here in this room. I'm not a traitor, I have never laid claim to the throne, even though I could have."

Orin's jaw dropped, the words hanging in the air between them. Shock, raw and unfiltered, washed across his face, his eyes widening as Atmos's confession sunk in. He stumbled back, his gaze darting to Puck, who mirrored his own astonishment. Puck's mouth hung open, his eyes wide with disbelief.

Kilyn, who had been observing the exchange with an amused detachment, let out a low whistle, shock written on his face. "Well, well," he muttered, "that's certainly one way to announce a family reunion."

Lera shot him a withering look, her eyes narrowed to slits. "Kilyn," she hissed, her voice a low growl, "if you don't zip your lip, I swear I'll-"

She trailed off, raising a finger to her lips in a gesture of warning. Kilyn, despite the threat, couldn't help but grin, the tension in the room broken by a flicker of amusement.

She turned to Atmos, "Aside from the wings, elven ears and the obvious resemblance you three have, what proof do you have that Puck is related to you two?" she put her hands on her hips and waited.

Atmos sighed, the weight of the past heavy in his chest. He looked at Puck, his gaze filled with a mixture of sympathy and regret. "Your mother... she would be the better person to explain this. But when the first war with Blackwood erupted, Rhamiel, our sire, was still consolidating his power. He joined Blackwood's forces. He was one of the soldiers that..." Atmos trailed off, the memory of the atrocities committed by his sire too horrific to articulate.

Puck swallowed hard, the pieces of the puzzle finally falling into place. It all made sense now – the hushed whispers, the way his mother's eyes would cloud over whenever he brought up the war. The realization hit him like a physical blow. He had lived with this shadow hanging over him, unaware of the true source of his mother's pain, and expecting her to just open up about an event that had shattered her.

A wave of sadness washed over him for the burden she had carried for so long. He wondered if every time he entered a room, if every time he laughed or smiled, she was reminded of that night, of the creature who had sired him, a monster who had taken everything from her. Did she feel the same about Puck?

He rubbed his arms and walked towards Atmos and Taion. He looked at Taion then at Atmos, his brilliant blue eyes shining in the soft light.

"I don't want to claim the throne, I came here because I just needed to know who I was. Who sired me." He gestured with his hands as he talked, nerves taking over as he was painfully aware that Taion was watching him carefully. "I thought it would give me answers to questions that I had been asking my whole life, to make me whole. But now...gods, I owe my ma a lifetime of apologies."

He paused as he turned his head and looked at his friends, "Orin's blood travelled here when I did the blood bond spell. His amille is somewhere in the castle. Do either of you know if an elven woman named Amodra is here?" He needed to put Orin first for this, his answers could come later, he had time.

"She's in the dungeon next to where that arsehole put us." An angry female's voice interrupted the group. Taion's heart stopped as his eyes connected with a pair of very rage filled but beautiful golden eyes looking right back at him.

Atmos muttered under his breath and then brightly replied as he walked towards her his arms open in invitation, "You're awake, Princess Aria, I apologize, I asked the servants to let me know..."

She didn't take her eyes off of Taion as she interrupted, putting her hand up, "Atmos, kindly shut up. I am beyond enraged right now. Don't try and downplay this. Where are the children?"

Kilyn raised his hand and quickly put it down when Aria whipped her head in his direction, her eyes glowing like embers. He swallowed and shook his head quickly, crossing his arms and stepping back. He'd let the more grown adults handle this one.

Atmos cleared his throat to answer and Puck, seeing that she was going to take her anger out on him, stepped beside Atmos to offer some support. Aria quickly blinked in surprise.

"Puck? You have your amil and amille worried sick! Wait...what are you doing here?" She ran to him to hug him and stopped short, "Are those wings?!" she looked at him and back at the black wings on his back.

Puck smiled sheepishly, "Yeah, they appeared when we reached the border to the Silver Lands. The children are all with the border guards right now, likely almost all home. Atmos and Ephyra ensured they were safe. He had nothing to do with you all being captured."

Lera watched the interaction between Aria and Puck, a strange, unsettling sensation coiling in her gut. It felt like a tiny, green demon of jealousy, its claws digging into her insides as she witnessed the easy camaraderie between them.

Puck's cheeks were flushed, a warm pink tinge coloring his skin, and his eyes, when they met Aria's, sparkled with an almost... joyful light. Lera felt a pang of something akin to despair.

Puck, sensing her discomfort, looked over, his eyes meeting hers with a reassuring smile. He beckoned her closer, his gaze lingering on her for a moment longer than strictly necessary. Lera hesitated, her heart pounding a frantic rhythm against her ribs, before cautiously approaching.

Aria, meanwhile, stood a little apart, observing them with a detached air. She straightened, her spine ramrod straight, and clasped her hands gently over her hips, an almost regal bearing that made Lera feel oddly intimidated. She looked like a Princess, indeed, a porcelain doll come to life, albeit a little dirty.

Puck, oblivious to the undercurrents of tension, introduced Lera. "This is Lera," he said, his voice warm. "She came from the woods when I left home, and she has been with me the entire journey."

Aria, with a slight tilt of her head, acknowledged the introduction. "A pleasure to meet you, Lera. I am Princess Aria of Clan Bayle."

Puck, his smile faltering slightly, turned to Aria. "Wait, Princess," he said, his voice laced with concern. "Does... does Lord Theo know that you are missing?"

"Theo," Aria replied, her voice trembling slightly as she carefully kept her arms at her sides to hide the rips in her dress and the bruises underneath, "he... he was busy. You know how it is. Lords of estates have their duties. Meetings, inspections, the endless demands of the land."

Taion's head snapped up, his eyes blazing with a fury he couldn't quite control. "Busy? Is that what he called it? While you were imprisoned here, enduring this... this nightmare, he was 'busy'?"

The words tumbled out, rough and bitter. He immediately regretted them, the harshness of his tone cutting through the already tense atmosphere, realizing that he was the reason. Aria's eyes widened, anger flashing across her face.

"He didn't know," she said, her voice low and defensive. "And those are some harsh words considering you're the reason why I am imprisoned here." She paused as she spat, "enduring this *nightmare*." Her fire magick danced over her fingertips as she flexed them, itching to throw the flames at him.

Taion flinched at her words, the anger within him boiling over. He stood tall, glaring at her as he crossed his arms and widened his stance, "Then let him know. Send a message. Let him know where you are. Let him come and rescue you. I'd like to see him try." He'd be damned if another male was going to go near this woman.

"Who the hells do you think you are," she continued, her voice rising as she stormed over to Taion, her golden eyes flashing as her fists started to glow brighter. "I am not a damsel in distress waiting for a knight in shining armor to save me. I am strong. I am capable."

She looked him up and down as she sneered, "And I will not sit idly by and wait for someone else to get me out of this. Whatever problems you have, whatever this cock fight is for the throne or for Tir Siorghlas, figure it out yourself and stop using innocent people as an excuse for your terrible behaviour. You should be ashamed." Their bodies were almost touching: Aria's chest heaving from her rage, Taion's from the emotions swirling around him with her so close.

Taion couldn't stop himself, he grabbed Aria by the back of her neck and crushed his lips to her. She stiffened, grabbing the front of his shirt and clenching her fist against him, smoke slowly escaping from her hands.

Then, it was subtle, but she softened against him as his lips gently explored hers. Suddenly, just as she had softened, she froze and shoved him back.

She looked at him, her eyes blazing with indignation as she swept out of the room, leaving Taion standing, his anger replaced by a profound sense of shame. He had hurt her, and he knew, with a certainty that chilled him to the bone, that he might have irrevocably damaged any chance of getting to know her, bonded or not.

Four sets of eyes were looking at him, speechless. He growled and stormed out, following Aria. He found her standing in the great room, her back turned to him; the air crackled with tension. Aria, her fiery hair a defiant halo around her face, turned and glared at Taion.

"You think this is some kind of game?" she spat, her voice low and dangerous. "That you can just lock me away like some... some bird in your dark castle?"

Taion, leaning against the door, regarded her with a chilling indifference, shoving down the overwhelming urge to grab her, to claim her, to make her his. He felt the contract to another on her skin when he had touched her. She wasn't his to claim that way.

"You are a weapon, Aria," he said, his voice a low growl. "A weapon against those who wronged my father."

"Your enemies are my family!" Aria retorted, her eyes flashing, flames licking behind the gold. "I did nothing wrong, those other children did nothing wrong!" she felt her fire magic heating up her fingers as her hands clenched.

"Innocence is a luxury you can no longer afford," Taion countered, his gaze hardening. "The kings of Tir Siorghlas betrayed my father, helped plunge our kingdom into chaos. And you, their blood, will be part of their downfall."

Aria scoffed, her anger boiling over. "You think I'll help you? After what you've done? After you've imprisoned me, stolen innocent children?"

Taion's hand tightened around the doorframe, the veins in his hand pronounced. "You have a choice," he said, his voice low and menacing. "Cooperate, and perhaps, just perhaps, I might release you after all this is done." He didn't want to release her, but he was scrambling for words.

"Release me?" Aria echoed, her voice dripping with sarcasm. "What, are you going to sell me to the highest bidder in the realm? Or perhaps use me as a bargaining chip to escape? You know if you go through with this, you will not have a safe harbour to go to. All of Tir Siorghlas will hunt you down as they did your father."

Taion's eyes narrowed. "Your defiance is admirable, but it will not serve you well." He took a step closer, his gaze intense. "I will break you, Aria. I will bend you to my will."

Aria felt a surge of rage, her fire magick flaring to life, the air around her shimmering with a dangerous heat. "You will never break me!" she yelled, her voice echoing through the chamber.

"Others have tried; I will fight you every step of the way!" The image in her head of Theo looming over her made her heart skip a beat. She would be damned if another would make her feel the way he had.

Taion watched her, a flicker of something akin to admiration in his eyes. He had expected defiance, but not this raw, untamed fury. It was intoxicating, addictive.

He took another step closer, the distance between them shrinking. "Then let us see how long you can resist," he murmured, his voice a low growl.

He reached out, his hand brushing against her cheek, sending a jolt of heat through her, striking her heart. Aria gasped, her eyes widening. He leaned closer, his breath fanning her face.

"You are fire, Aria," he whispered, his voice husky as his eyes darkened with desire. "Wild, untamed, dangerous. And I... I am being consumed by you, little firecracker."

He lowered his head, his lips brushing against hers. Aria, despite her anger, found herself trembling, her body reacting against her will. He carefully pressed his lips to hers and she moaned. His kiss awakened something inside her, heat coiling around her as his lips claimed hers.

They clung to each other, their bodies pressed together, their breaths mingling as he claimed her lips to his. The air crackled, the tension between them reaching a fever pitch.

Finally, they broke apart, their chests heaving, their eyes locked. The anger, the defiance, the simmering hatred – it all seemed to fade away, replaced by a raw, primal need.

Taion, to his own astonishment, felt a strange sense of peace. He had faced countless enemies, conquered countless foes, but none had ever affected him like this. Aria, with her fiery spirit and defiance, was unlike anything he had ever encountered.

He knew this was a dangerous game, a game they were both playing, she wasn't free to take a male; she was bound by a marriage contract, a contract that would rip her soul in half if she broke it. But as he looked into her eyes, a dangerous glint reflecting in his own, he realized he might not be able to resist the temptation for much longer, but he refused to stoop that low.

He quickly turned and walked out of the room, leaving her behind. He stormed down the hallway, dragging his hands through his hair as his grey wings flexed behind him. He was aroused, frustrated, and decided he had enough. He walked into the throne room to find them all standing around still.

He turned and looked at Puck and Orin. "I will walk you down to the dungeon, Orin, to ensure that you make it past the siren's cell to find your mother, I'm not sure if the cloaking spell is working to keep the siren's magick suppressed. Let's go, I have work to do and all of you with your problems are starting to really irritate me." He said, his voice gruff.

"Puck, you and I are going to have to talk." Puck nodded and subtly reached out, looking for Lena's hand. She grabbed it and looked up at Puck, realizing he was scared.

Orin swallowed hard. It had been a whirlwind since he had left home; finding out the woman he had grown up with was a glamoured monster who had sold his mother and taken her identity, to finding out that somehow, the path that Puck needed to take also converged with his.

Orin nodded and Taion strode out of the throne room towards the dungeon.

Chapter Twenty Eight

Tenebris

As they walked down the hallway, Orin cautiously looked at Taion as they walked together. He was taller than Puck, but the family resemblances were there.

The bright eyes; Puck's were blue, but Taion also had blue mixed in the purples that were swirling right now. Their noses were the same, regal was the only word Orin could put to it. Their high cheekbones and full lips, square jaws, how did no one piece together that Atmos and Puck shared the same father this whole time? Tir Siorghlas wasn't that large, they had all seen each other.

Maybe the same reason why no one had figured out the Baobhan Sith's plan; it was all right in front of them in plain sight, they just refused to see it.

"Why are your wings grey, while Puck and Atmos have black?" Orin blurted out and then cursed to himself when Taion slowly pursed his lips and glared at him sideways.

"Sorry, I was just curious. My knowledge of Nephilim is very limited." Orin shrugged and smiled at Taion, hoping to disarm him before he put him down in the dungeon.

Taion sighed, "Both of my parents were Nephilim, my mother was the light class while my father was the dark class. It's simple genetics."

Orin nodded as if he understood, "So she had white wings, right." Taion rolled his eyes and continued walking. How did the kings sleep at night knowing their heirs were this uneducated on the species of the realm?

The heavy stone doors of the dungeon loomed closer, their iron-work glinting ominously in the dim light. As they approached, Orin's gait slowed, his mind a whirlwind of conflicting emotions.

He nervously smoothed his dark brown hair back, attempting to restore some semblance of order to his appearance. Dust from their journey clung to his tunic, remnants from the long road they had traveled to get here.

Taion, keenly aware of the nervous energy radiating from Orin in waves, mirrored his pace. He paused, his gaze softening as he studied Orin's face. He understood the weight of this moment, the fear and trepidation that gnawed at Orin's core.

Like Taion, Orin had lost his mother. The thought brought a pang of sympathy. To have the chance to see her again, to perhaps even bring her back from the depths of this forsaken place, would be an immeasurable gift.

The air grew heavy and thick as they descended into the depths of the dungeon. The stone walls seemed to press in on them, the musty smell of damp earth and forgotten things filling their nostrils. Orin's heart pounded in his chest, a drumbeat echoing the rhythm of his footsteps.

The light from the torches flickered, casting long, dancing shadows that writhed and twisted like spectral creatures. The air grew colder, the chill seeping into his bones. He shivered, not from the cold, but from the fear that gnawed at him.

They passed a cell, its bars thick and rusted. Inside, a creature sat huddled in the shadows, its eyes glowing with an eerie green light. It let out a bloodcurdling scream, a sound that seemed to tear at their souls. Orin flinched, his body reacting instinctively to the raw, primal evil that emanated from the creature.

Taion, ever vigilant, flicked his wrist, and a shimmering barrier of energy materialized between them and the cell. The creature's screams were muffled, the sound no longer able to penetrate their defenses.

"Now we don't have to worry about the siren, that barrier will hold for a long while," Taion smiled at Orin.

Orin took a shaky breath, his heart still pounding. He glanced at Taion, who gave him a reassuring nod. Then, with a deep breath, Orin stepped forward, his eyes fixed on the cell ahead.

Inside, a figure sat slumped in the corner, her face obscured by the shadows. As they drew closer, Orin's heart began to race. He could barely breathe, his entire being focused on the woman within the cell.

Finally, they stood before the bars, and Orin's breath caught in his throat. The woman was more beautiful than he could have ever imagined, even though her skin was pale and translucent from who knows how long of deprivation from the sun. He looked her over, her long, pale hair hung limp around her shoulders, and she sat motionless, her eyes closed, as if she were asleep.

Orin sank to his knees, his hands trembling as they reached out towards the bars. "Amille?" he whispered, his voice hoarse with emotion.

The woman stirred, her eyes fluttering open. Tears streamed down her face, tracing paths through the dust that clung to her cheeks. She looked at Orin, her gaze filled with a mixture of disbelief and longing.

"Orin?" she whispered, her voice a mere breath, raw with emotion.

He could barely speak, his throat constricted with emotion. "Amille," he choked out, his voice thick with unshed tears.

Amodra reached out a trembling hand, her fingers brushing against the bars. "Orin," she whispered again, her voice gaining strength. "Oh, my sweet, sweet Orin."

Tears welled up in Orin's eyes, blurring his vision. He reached out, his fingers grasping through the bars, desperate to touch her, to hold her, to assure himself that this was real, that she was truly here, alive.

Amodra's lips trembled. "I thought..." she began, her voice breaking. "I thought I would never see you again."

Orin shook his head, tears finally spilling down his cheeks. "I didn't know, amille, I'm so sorry."

Amodra's eyes, filled with a mixture of joy and sorrow, searched his face. "You grew," she said, her voice filled with wonder. "You've grown into a fine young man."

Orin managed a weak smile. Amodra's gaze softened as she looked up at Taion. "Thank you," she whispered, her voice filled with a love so profound it seemed to shatter the silence of the dungeon. Taion felt his heart clench painfully as he watched their reunion, a lump in his throat causing him to swallow hard. He pulled the keys out of his pocket and held them by his side.

Orin leaned closer, his forehead resting against the cold bars. "I'm here now, amille," he whispered. "I'm here to take you home, to amil."

Amodra's hand reached out and gently touched his cheek. "My seldo," she whispered, her voice filled with an overwhelming sense of sadness. "My brave, beautiful son. I am so sorry, but I cannot leave this prison."

Orin's eyes widened in disbelief and Taion looked down at Orin then at Amodra, confusion written on his face. "What do you mean, you can't leave? It's just a key, we'll-"

Amodra shook her head, a single tear tracing a path down her dust-streaked cheek. "It's not that simple, Orin. This prison... it's not just stone and iron. It's a cage for my soul as well."

Orin's confusion deepened. "I don't understand."

Amodra sighed, her voice weary. "When the darkness, the Nightsinger, imprisoned me, she didn't just lock me away. She bound my magick, my very essence, to this place. I am tethered to this dungeon, my power intertwined with its very being."

Orin stared at her, his mind reeling. "But... how? Why?"

Amodra closed her eyes, the pain etched on her face. "They wanted my power, Orin. When I refused to use it for the Night Prince and his attempts to impregnate me failed, he spelled me here. He was angry and resentful as he wanted his hands on my magick; the power to bring lives back from the dead, to create an invincible race. The Baobhan Sith stole you away as they knew that you had that very same power. They just didn't know how to activate it with you being so young."

Orin felt a surge of rage course through him. "I'll get you out, amille, he's no longer here to do anything to you."

He reached out for the keys, his fingers trembling with a mixture of anger and determination. "We'll find a way to break the spell, amille. I promise." He snatched the keys from Taion's hand, his movements frantic.

"No Orin! Don't try and open the doors, the magick could kill you! Taion, stop him!" Amodra cried out to Taion as she reached out to Orin.

Before Taion could stop him, Orin had inserted the key into the lock and turned it with all his might. A blinding flash of light erupted from the cell, momentarily plunging their vision into darkness.

Orin stumbled back, a searing pain exploding in his chest. He crashed against the wall, the air whooshed out of his lungs. Taion rushed to his side, his heart pounding. Orin lay motionless on the ground, his face pale, his breathing shallow and rapid.

"Orin! Godsdamnit" Taion yelled, frantically checking for a pulse. Relief washed over him as he felt a faint thrum beneath Orin's skin.

Amodra, trapped within the cell, watched in horror as her son lay unconscious on the floor. Tears streamed down her face, a helpless sob escaping her lips. She could do nothing, trapped and powerless, while her son lay injured before her.

Taion gently lifted Orin into his arms, his heart heavy with worry. He rushed through the dungeon, the cold stone floor a blur beneath his feet, taking the stairs two at a time. He burst through the heavy doors, ignoring the startled gasps of the servants who were standing in the hallway.

"Help!" Taion yelled, his voice hoarse. "Get the healer! Quickly!"

The servants, their faces pale with worry, rushed towards him, their hands outstretched to help. Taion let them take Orin and watched as they rushed down the hallway towards their healers quarters.

He burst into the throne room, the sight of Atmos talking to Puck and Lera doing little to quell his anger. "Atmos!" Taion roared, his voice filled with fury. "We need to talk, now." his last word a roar.

Atmos, startled by Taion's sudden appearance and the anger radiating from him quickly walked to him. "Taion? What happened? Is Orin hurt?"

"He's unconscious!" Taion snarled, his voice trembling with rage.

"Because our sire along with the darkness placed a curse on his mothers cell!"

Atmos's eyes narrowed. "A curse? What are you talking about? The darkness wasn't that strong..." he trailed off as he realized who had done it.

Taion watched Atmos' face, and he growled, "Start talking."

Atmos, sensing danger in Taion's voice nodded. "We need to sit for this. It's a long story and think I have to go back to the beginning."

Taion strode over to the fireplace where there were chairs and settees. He waved his hands theatrically and pronounced, "Sit your asses down, Atmos has a story time for us."

He sat down heavily on the chair and waited. Atmos looked at him and sank into the settee, sighing.

"It wasn't always this way, Taion......"

Chapter Twenty Nine

*To know the past is
to know forgiveness*

She called herself Amodra

The Bloodrose lands were a world away from the glittering halls of Clan Aether. Here, the air was thick with the scent of pine needles and damp earth, the only sounds the rustling of leaves and sometimes the distant call of a hawk. Amodra had found solace in this secluded cottage, a haven away from the prying eyes and whispering tongues of the court.

She clutched her newborn son to her chest, his soft breaths matching the beating of her heart. Orin, her son, a tiny bundle of warmth and innocence, was the only reminder she had of the whirlwind romance that had swept her off her feet.

Prince Osian, with his eyes the color of molten chocolate and a smile that could melt glaciers, had stolen her heart. Their love had been a forbidden flame, a secret whispered in the dark of the forest where they met. She had taken the name Amodra to keep her identity a secret.

The consequences of their love had been swift and severe. Osian's parents, the King and Queen of Clan Aether, had been adamant.

Amodra, an elf of uncertain lineage, was deemed an unsuitable match for their son. The scandal would be too great, they had decided.

Heartbroken but resolute, Amodra had agreed to their terms. She would leave Clan Aether, raise Orin in secrecy, and never reveal his true parentage. The pain of leaving Osian, of denying her son his rightful heritage, was a constant ache in her heart.

This life was simple yet isolating. She had to suppress her magick, to blend in with the ordinary elven folk. She became a healer, her touch mending broken bones and soothing fevered brows. Over the few years she lived there, she earned the respect of the villagers, but she remained an outsider.

The news however spread through the Bloodrose lands like wildfire. Word got out one day of a healer who had miraculously brought a child back from the brink of death after a bout of fever. The villagers whispered, their eyes wide with awe. Amodra, their quiet healer, suddenly became a legend.

But the whispers soon turned to screams. As the sun dipped below the horizon, casting long, eerie shadows across the land, the door to her cottage was ripped open with a deafening crash. Amodra, startled, turned to see a group of shadowy figures silhouetted against the fading light. Before she could react, they were upon her, their hands rough as they seized her, tearing her son, Orin, from her arms.

Terror, cold and paralyzing, gripped her. She struggled against her captors, her cries lost in the chaos. They were Baobhan Sith, creatures of shadow and night, their eyes gleaming with an unnatural light. She heard their chilling laughter, their voices echoing through the darkening woods.

"We have found what we seek," one of them hissed, their voice a rasping whisper. "She will be a valuable bargaining chip."

Amodra, her heart pounding like a trapped bird, was dragged into the depths of the forest. She remembered the last thing she saw – the face of one of the Baobhan Sith, her features contorting, her skin shimmering and shifting, transforming into her own likeness. Then, darkness. A suffocating, all-consuming darkness.

When she awoke, she found herself in a cold, damp cell, the air thick with the stench of wet dirt. A single torch flickered precariously, casting long, eerie shadows that danced on the walls. A tall figure loomed over her, his wings, like those of a fallen angel, cast a shadow over her. The man's eyes, burning with an unholy light, fixed upon her with a wicked gleam. Terror, cold and paralyzing, gripped her once more.

The Night Prince, a creature of shadows and ambition, was obsessed with Amodra's magick. He spent countless hours poring over ancient tomes, his eyes burning with a feverish intensity as he sought the incantation, the spell that would unlock the secrets of her power. The darkness, his insidious companion, whispered promises in his ear, urging him on, fueling his insatiable hunger.

But Amodra resisted. Her will was as strong as her magick, an unwavering force that defied his attempts to drain her power. Frustrated, the Night Prince resorted to other means. He sought to possess her, to claim her body as his own, to use her as a vessel for his dark ambitions. But his attempts were met with the same defiance, his seed unable to take root within her.

Rage, a consuming fire, ignited within him. He tried to kill her, to silence the defiant spirit within her. But Amodra, blessed with a life force that defied death, always returned. She would lie on the cold stone floor, her body ravaged, her spirit broken, begging him to end her suffering. Yet, he couldn't.

Years passed, a torturous eternity for Amodra. Then, one evening, a figure descended into the depths of the dungeon. Elara, the new ruler of Tenebris, the darkness swirling inside her, stood before Amodra, her eyes gleaming with hatred.

Amodra, weary and broken, met her gaze, hoping that another female would take pity and release her. Elara, controlled by the darkness, instead, whispered an ancient blood spell, designed to bind Amodra to never leave the dungeon. With a chilling satisfaction, the darkness inside Elara watched as Amodra's form shimmered, her life force tethered to the cold stone cage, forever imprisoned.

Only a true death would release her... or if someone with a pure heart spoke her birth given name.

Atmos recounted the story that his mother had told him as a youth, a chilling tale whispered in the dead of night after he had been bound to service to Tenebris and the Night Prince. The story had haunted him for years, a recurring nightmare that came true as he watched the evils Rhamiel performed in the name of the crown.

He continued, his voice dropping to a hushed tone, the room blurring slightly as he delved into his memories. He needed to make sure Taion knew, that Puck knew. Their lineage did not mean following the same dark path as their sire.

"I was born on a full moon in the north of the village where the Nephilim live..."

Aria had quietly walked back towards the throne room, pressing her back against the cool stone in the hallway, listening as Atmos continued to speak. She chewed her bottom lip with worry as he continued.

Marion

The sun pushed its rays through the portal in the mountain, shining on Tenebris as Marion, a young Nephilim woman, spread her wings, letting her shadow magick swirl around her as she soared down the hillside towards the bustling village market. Her mother had sent her on a simple errand: to find a loaf of fresh bread, still warm and fragrant, and the six brightest, reddest apples she could find.

Her father, a renowned Tenebris warrior, was returning home after a month-long security detail to the east of the mountain pass, and her mother wanted to bake him a welcome-home pie.

Marion, eager to please, tucked her black wings neatly against her back as she entered the market. A familiar warmth spread through her as she greeted the vendors, her smile a beacon of light in the crowd. She selected a loaf of bread, still warm from the oven, its crust crackling invitingly. Then, with a discerning eye, she chose six magnificent apples, each one a vibrant shade of ruby red.

As she reached for the last apple, a large hand gently covered hers. Startled, Marion looked up into the most captivating eyes she had ever seen – deep, rich brown, filled with a mischievous glint. It was the Night

Prince, Rhamiel, his presence commanding attention even in the bustling marketplace.

Marion gasped, her heart pounding against her ribs. She quickly curtsied, her cheeks flushing crimson. Rhamiel chuckled, a low, melodious sound that sent shivers down her spine. He gently removed his hand from hers, his touch lingering like a phantom warmth on her skin.

"Such fine apples," he remarked, his voice a silken caress. "For a special occasion, I presume?"

Marion, still flustered, stammered, "F-for my father. He returned from his patrol today."

Rhamiel smiled, his eyes twinkling. "A hero's welcome, indeed. Let me help you with these." He insisted on carrying her basket, his long fingers gently brushing against hers as he handed her the apples.

They walked together in comfortable silence, the sounds of the market fading into the background. As they neared Marion's house, Rhamiel turned to her, his gaze intense. "I will return later," he said, his voice a low promise. "To see your father, of course."

Marion, speechless, could only nod, her heart hammering against her ribs like a trapped bird. As Rhamiel continued his walk, she watched him go, his figure fading into the distance.

Marion's mother stood at the door, her face etched with concern. "Marion," she began, her voice laced with apprehension, "you need to be careful. The Night Prince is married. To Princess Naomi and they have a child together, little Prince Taion. Nothing good will come of this visit. Your magick has caught the eye of someone we never wanted it to."

Marion, her heart pounding with a mixture of excitement and trepidation, shook her head. "Mother, he only wants to meet Father. To thank him for his service. He doesn't want anything to do with me or my shadows."

Her mother sighed, her gaze lingering on her daughter's flushed cheeks. "You're too trusting, child. The Night Prince is not a man to be trifled with."

Marion, however, was oblivious to her mother's warnings. Excitement bubbled within her. She couldn't deny that the Night Prince intrigued her, his presence a whirlwind of both fear and fascination.

Her mother, realizing the futility of further arguments, ushered her inside. "Very well," she conceded, a touch of resignation in her voice. "But be cautious, Marion."

They spent the rest of the afternoon preparing for her father's arrival. Marion, despite her mother's warnings, found herself constantly glancing at the window, her heart fluttering with anticipation. Finally, the sound of hooves on the dirt road broke the afternoon stillness.

Marion and her mother ran to the door, opening it to see her father standing on the path to the house, a radiant smile on his face as they ran to him. He embraced Marion's mother with a tight hug and a kiss while he gathered Marion to his side, a gentle kiss on the top of her head while she closed her eyes in contentment. They walked back into the house together, the smells of the apple pie wafting through the small home.

A firm knock on the door later that evening had Marion's heart stop. Hope, a fragile bud, bloomed within her. Her father, his face weathered but his eyes twinkling, rose to answer the door.

Standing on the doorstep was the Night Prince, his presence commanding attention even from a distance. He nodded respectfully to Marion's father, his voice a low rumble, "Thank you, sir, for your service to the kingdom. Your courage is an inspiration."

Marion's father, a man of few words, simply bowed, his eyes wary. "Welcome, Your Highness."

The Night Prince then turned to Marion, his eyes holding a mischievous glint. "May I have a word with your daughter, Marion?"

Her father, knowing he couldn't refuse the Night Prince, bowed his head in submission. As he looked up, he saw the darkness swirling in Rhamiel's eyes. "Of course, Your Highness." He whispered, fear clutching his heart.

Marion, her heart pounding a frantic rhythm against her ribs, stepped out of the doorway, her gaze fixed on the Night Prince. As she walked beside him, she felt a strange sense of foreboding, a whisper of danger in the air.

The Night Prince, however, maintained a charming facade, his smile captivating, his voice a silken caress. Marion, despite her misgivings, found herself drawn to him, her defenses crumbling under the weight of his charisma.

As they walked further down the path, away from the watchful eyes of her parents, Marion knew that this encounter was far from over. The Night Prince, with his enigmatic smile and captivating presence, had woven a spell around her, a spell she feared she might not be able to resist.

The path wound through the woods, the bioluminescent light shone through the leaves, casting dappled shadows on the ground. Marion, still somewhat dazed by Rhamiel's presence, walked beside him, her heart pounding a frantic rhythm against her ribs.

Suddenly, he stopped, his eyes darkening as he turned to face her. Before she could react, he pulled her close, his arms encircling her waist as his wings encircled around her. Marion gasped, her breath catching in her throat. She remembered her mother's words, a chilling warning echoing in her mind.

"No," she protested weakly, her voice barely a whisper.

But Rhamiel ignored her protests, his lips capturing hers. The kiss was unexpected, a whirlwind of sensation that swept her off her feet. At first, she stiffened, her body resisting his touch. But then, something within her shifted. The resistance melted away, replaced by a strange yearning, a longing she didn't understand.

Marion's hands, initially hesitant, reached up to touch his hair, her fingers tracing the dark, unruly strands. The kiss deepened, a passionate dance of lips and tongues. She lost herself in the sensation, the world fading away, leaving only the intoxicating scent of him and the thunder of her own heart.

As the kiss deepened, a shiver ran down her spine. It was a strange sensation, a mixture of fear and exhilaration, of danger and desire. She knew she shouldn't be doing this, that this was wrong, but she couldn't seem to pull away.

Rhamiel, sensing her surrender, pulled back, his eyes burning with a possessive intensity as they swirled black. He gazed at her, his lips curving into a satisfied smile. "You," he murmured, his voice a low growl, "are far more delicious and intriguing than I anticipated. Your shadows taste like dark cherries, delicious."

Marion, breathless and dazed, could only stare at him, her mind reeling. Realizing she was in trouble, she protested, trying to push away as Rhamiel's arms tightened around her.

After he was done, the Night Prince left her lying beside a large oak tree, her wing broken and her dress torn to shreds. Marion sobbed as she curled up in a ball, waiting for the pain to take her away, her magick cloaking her in darkness as she wished she could die. Her father found her hours later, his face contorted in a mask of rage as he looked over his broken daughter. He swore he would murder the man, Prince or not.

Marion had to beg her father to not do anything, her voice trembling as she pleaded, "Father, please... if you confront him, I will lose everything. You, and our family's peace."

Her father, his face a mask of fury, looked at his daughter, his beloved Marion, her eyes wide with a mixture of fear and pain. He saw the desperation in her gaze, the love that shone through despite the fear. With a heavy sigh, he nodded, the weight of his unspoken rage settling heavily on his shoulders.

The next day, her father was called for sentry duty, a routine assignment that should have had him home that evening. He never returned.

Marion's mother, her face pale and drawn, knew what had happened. The whispers in the village, the hushed tones, the knowing glances – they all spoke of the Night Prince's ruthless hand.

A wave of grief washed over her, a grief that quickly morphed into a bitter, consuming anger. How could she forgive the man who had taken her husband, the man who had shattered her daughter's innocence?

The discovery that Marion was pregnant with the Night Prince's child only served to deepen her despair. The thought of her daughter bearing the child of the man who had destroyed their lives filled her with a profound sense of sorrow and a simmering rage that threatened to consume her.

The arrival of Atmos under the watchful gaze of a full moon brought a sliver of light into Marion's life. His cries, full bodied and loud, filled the room as he was born. Marion held her son, his tiny face, framed by a shock of raven hair, and the delicate flutter of his infantile wings, a flicker of love ignited within her.

It was in that moment, cradling her son, that Marion's mother let go of the anger and found her love for her daughter rekindled. The joy that radiated from Marion's face, the tenderness in her eyes as she gazed upon her son. They would make a better world for him.

From that day forward, Marion's mother dedicated herself to protecting her daughter and grandson from the shadow of the Night

Prince, weaving protection spells around the hut. She vowed to shield them from the darkness that had threatened to consume their lives, ensuring that Atmos would never turn into the same monster that his sire had. She placed a ward around Atmos' soul to keep him safe, her final gift.

Sarya

The battle raged across Tir Siorghlas. Sarya, a mere slip of a young woman with eyes like brilliant sapphires and curly hair the color of molten chocolate, watched the battle unfold with a mixture of awe and terror. Her mother, Constance, a formidable witch Matron, fought alongside the other members of their coven. She watched as their magick weaved a shimmering shield around the Clan warriors, desperately fighting against Blackwood's dark magick and monsters.

Sarya, though young, was no stranger to battle. Her bloodline pulsed with the magick of the ancient wood, and she had been training since she could walk. But this was different. This was a war that would determine the fate of Tir Siorghlas; if Blackwood got his hands on Annika, all was lost.

Her eyes darted across the chaotic scene. She saw Annika and Callum, huddled together, a guard yelling at them to get back to the castle. Their parents, the king and queen of Clan Tenebris, pulled them apart, and then, in a blinding flash of light Annika vanished. Callum was clutched in his mother's arms as she fled across the battlefield, Blackwood's young brother, Corvus, hot on their heels, his cackle of morbid glee echoed across the field.

Then, her gaze fell upon Damien, the young Prince of Clan Aether, betrothed to Annika. As he swung around, his face contorted in a scream of terror as Lord Blackwood himself bore down on him. Adrenaline surged through Sarya. Fear was forgotten. She had to help.

With a cry, she launched herself into the fray, her magick crackling around her, a whirlwind of emerald and silver. But as she ran, a searing pain erupted in her chest, and the world exploded into darkness.

When she awoke, she found herself in a cold, damp cell. Iron shackles bound her wrists, and her magick, once so vibrant, now flickered weakly, restricted by the iron.

Across the hallway, she could hear Damien's screams, raw and agonizing. The sound tore at her heart. If they would torture a future King, what would they do to her? A wave of nausea washed over her. She pushed herself to the corner of the cell, pulling her legs up and laying her head on her knees.

She whimpered, the fear now a cold, suffocating presence within her. The sound of heavy boots echoed down the dungeon hallway, breaking her silence. Sarya whipped her head up, her heart pounding against her ribs like a trapped bird. The footsteps halted abruptly in front of her cell door.

She scrambled to stand, her hands braced against the cold stone wall as she watched a group of men enter the room. They parted, revealing the Night Prince standing amidst them. His black wings were tucked tightly against his back, and a feral smile played on his lips as he slowly advanced towards her.

Sarya felt a wave of nausea wash over her. The Night Prince, with his obsidian eyes and a power that chilled her to the bone, was a creature of nightmares. He was the embodiment of darkness, a force of nature that could crush her with a single touch because of the darkness that had claimed him.

He stopped a few feet away, his gaze sweeping over her with a predatory gleam. "Well, well, well," he purred, his voice a low growl that sent shivers down her spine. "The young Whisperwoods witch. I've heard whispers of your power, child. A shame it seems to have deserted you, your coven deserted you."

Sarya remained silent, her gaze fixed on the ground. She refused to give him the satisfaction of seeing her fear.

The Night Prince chuckled, a sound that frayed her nerves. "Don't worry, little butterfly," he said, his voice dropping to a conspiratorial whisper. "We'll find a way to use that magick of yours. After all, a witch as powerful as you could be quite...useful."

His words sent a jolt of terror through her. What did he mean by "useful"? The thought of falling into his clutches, of becoming a tool in his wicked schemes, succumbing to the darkness, filled her with dread.

He leaned closer, his breath hot on her face. "You see, little butterfly," he hissed, "we have plans for this kingdom and mine, and a witch of your caliber could be a valuable asset. But first," he leaned back, his smile widening, "we need to break you, make sure that you realize who owns you."

The Night Prince raised a hand, signaling to one of the men behind him. Sarya braced herself, knowing that whatever torture awaited her, it would be far worse than anything she could have imagined. The last thing she remembered was his face hovering over hers.

When she came to, her dress was ripped and stained. She curled up into a ball, sobs wracking her body. The betrayal, the violation, the memory of the Night Prince's cold, predatory touch – it all crashed over her in a suffocating wave.

She wasn't sure how long they were down there; she could hear Damien's screams often, and a blur of activity as the Night Prince would visit her again.

Finally, the day came where she heard the Clans outside the castle. They had come to rescue her and Damien. As the cell door softly opened, she opened her one eye to see Damien's father, King Aerion bend down at the door, assessing Sarya before he said anything. "Sarya, we're here to take you home to your mother, to the Whisperwoods. Is it ok that I send a soldier in to retrieve you?"

She opened both of her eyes, panicked at the thought of a man touching her. King Aerion put his hands up, seeing the terror in her eyes. "It's Prince Carwyn, you know him. I swear we will only do it if you so choose, Sarya."

She felt tears stream down her face as she nodded: Carwyn was safe, he was her friend. She closed her eyes again as she heard his footsteps and soft voices. When she opened them again, young Carwyn was bent down, his eyes filled with sorrow as he took in her battered body.

He carefully put his hands out, gathering her body to him. He stood up and cradled her against his chest as they walked out of the cells, out of the dungeons and into the sunlight.

A month later, back in the Whisperwoods, surrounded by her coven, she realized she was pregnant.

Chapter Thirty

Tenebris

Atmos looked at Taion, his voice thick with emotion as he finished speaking. Tears welled up in his eyes, reflecting the pain and grief he carried within him having to hold those stories. Puck and Taion watched him intently, their faces etched with concern as they absorbed the weight of his words.

Puck sat back, the weight of finding out what had been done to his mother feeling like a brick on his chest. How she had come back from that, how her and his amil had found each other again and created a life. How, even though she may not have fully known, she loved Puck—Carwyn loved Puck—with all of their hearts.

"I know the tale of your mother as well, Taion," Atmos said, his voice softer now. "Would you like me to speak to that?"

Taion frowned, the memory of his mother a poignant ache in his heart. Matron Constance, his wise and unwavering mentor, had been his lifeline to Tir Siorghlas, sending him letters each full moon filled with news and insights.

She had always known that he would one day return to claim his rightful place. When her letters abruptly ceased, a chilling certainty washed over him. It was time; time to return home.

"I think that's enough storytelling for now, brother," Taion said, his voice firm. He turned away from them, unable to stomach hearing about his mother, striding towards the tall windows that overlooked the sprawling landscape.

Aria carefully peeked around the door as the room went quiet, her eyes glistening with unshed tears after hearing Atmos speak about how they had come to be. She took in Taion standing in front of the tall windows, his silhouette dark and imposing. She hung her head and quietly walked away. There was way more to this mess than she had realized and it was all going to come to a head.

The fairy lights of Tir Siorghlas twinkled below, a mesmerizing display against the velvet backdrop of the dark mountain. He watched, his hands clasped behind his back, lost in thought.

Soon, the Kings of the neighboring Clans might be on his doorstep ready to start a war of his making. He had yet to officially claim the throne, to gather his forces, to prepare for the inevitable conflict. But as Atmos spoke, sharing his own burden of pain and loss, the anger that had fueled his journey began to recede, replaced by a growing sense of responsibility and a newfound understanding.

The fact that all of those years, the kings left Tenebris to its own devices, letting the darkness consume complete family lines while they stood idly by was still unforgivable for Taion. They could have stepped in and stopped the darkness from killing, from taking his mother from him. Instead, they turned a blind eye and let her die. He lost his mother because they chose to protect themselves instead of the people that needed help.

He left the throne room quietly, his wings tucked behind him as he mused over everything that had happened. The group sat in front of the fire, lost in their own thoughts, absorbing everything that had been said.

As he walked through the castle, he stopped in front of the sitting room. He remembered his mother's favourite spot, the bay windows and the soft cushions piled around to create a space for her to lay and watch the city below her.

She would pick Taion up and point out the birds and name them for him as they cuddled together. He blinked and the vision disappeared as he realized Aria was sitting in the same spot as his mother, her long red hair cascading down her back.

He walked in and watched her. She had her hand pressed against the window, her eyes scanning below at the city as the day went on. She softly smiled as a bird flew by, her eyes following as it flew upwards towards a ridge in the mountain.

"It was a castle filled with love at one point." Taion softly said. Aria stiffened, her hand slid down the window as she carefully turned her head.

"Tenebris is beautiful, I don't understand why we didn't learn anything about it growing up." She responded softly.

Taion put his hands behind his back and gruffly responded, "I can take you for a tour if you would like? Show you what the city is all about?"

Aria fully turned and smiled, her eyes excited as she stood up. She paused and composed herself, placing her hands together at her waist.

"I would love to, but I'm afraid I am not quite in the right shape for viewing a city as a visiting royal."

Taion cursed to himself, realizing she was in a ripped dress still, her skin streaked with dirt.

"If you'll follow me, I'll show you to the chambers where you can clean yourself up and find a change of clothes."

She nodded and they walked together down the hallway towards the chambers where Atmos had laid her. Taion stopped shortly at the threshold, faltering as he looked around fully for the first time.

His mother's room hadn't changed much from his memory. Her perfumes were gone, and the bedding had been changed; otherwise, it looked the same. He put his hand out and guided her into the room, walking towards the large bathing chambers that were modified for his kind to accommodate their wings.

"Please, help yourself to whatever you want here. There should be dresses in the armoire. You'll need a cloak as they likely all are sleeveless."

His throat constricted as he watched Aria look around the room, her hand gently tracing the ornate woodwork on the armoire. How was he going to let her go when the time came? She didn't belong here, to him, even though she unknowingly held his heart in her hand.

He walked out and left Aria in the centre of the large bathing room, her eyes following him as she wondered why he all of a sudden was being so kind.

A couple of hours later, she walked out of the room, having found a beautiful blue sleeveless gown, the skirt shimmered with sparkles, and she couldn't resist. She had let her hair down, so it rested over her one shoulder, a small circlet crown on her head that had been left on the bed when she had come out of the bath. As she pulled the dark blue cape over her shoulders, she saw Taion step out of the shadows of the hallway, a small crown on his head.

His eyes roved over her, and she saw a spark of approval in his eyes as he held his hand out for her to slip her arm into. They walked down the hallway towards the front doors, and he opened them for her.

Taion and Aria descended the many steps of the castle, the crisp mountain air filling Aria's lungs. She gazed around in awe, captivated by the beauty of their surroundings. The market was alive with activity, a bustling hub of commerce on market day.

Fresh fruit from Tir Siorghlas overflowed from stalls, and a nearby vendor displayed vibrant fabrics and threads, recently acquired from a ship that had arrived at the southern port weeks prior. Women excitedly examined the textiles, their voices lively as they haggled with the vendor.

As they navigated the busy market, citizens stopped and bowed their heads respectfully as Taion passed, their eyes watching him. They stood in awe as they viewed a younger version of Rhamiel walking through Tenebris. After all this time, the lost prince had come home.

He frowned, wondering if their reverence was a lingering echo of their fear of his deceased father, Rhamiel and the darkness, or if they were truly happy he had come home.

The reign of darkness had cast a long shadow over Tenebris,

plunging the city into an age of isolation and despair. The once vibrant city that had overflowed with life and laughter when Taion was a child, had lain desolate for so long.

The people of Tenebris had lived in constant fear as the darkness played cruel games with the families of Tenebris, snatching away loved ones in the dead of night, leaving behind only whispers of their fate.

The screams of the abducted in the dungeon of the castle echoed through the city, a haunting reminder of the Nightsinger's insatiable hunger to consume every soul it could grab.

Trade had long ceased, the bustling markets had been deserted, the vibrant streets eerily silent. The people were cut off from the outside world, their cries for help unheard, their plight ignored. They were left to fend for themselves, to face the darkness alone, their spirits slowly being eroded.

Yet, even in the darkest of times, a flicker of hope had remained, a faint glimmer of resilience within the hearts of the people of Tenebris. When Rhamiel and Elara fell, the suffocating grip of darkness lifted, allowing the city to begin its slow, arduous recovery.

Atmos, with Ephyra by his side, played a pivotal role in this revival. He quietly spearheaded the reopening of trade routes, his mother as a guide, ensuring the survival of his people while the throne remained vacant, awaiting the return of the rightful heir. He had regularly updated Taion as he made his way back to Tir Siorghlas and Taion wasn't sure how he would be able to thank Atmos for his part in keeping their home alive.

Noticing his somber expression, Aria linked her arm with his and offered a bright smile, greeting several women standing nearby. The women were startled, their eyes widening in surprise. They then looked towards Taion, and recognition dawned.

A slow self-conscious smile spread across his face as he returned their gaze. The realization that they stood before their long-lost Prince sent a ripple of murmurs through the market. The women smiled brightly and bowed towards Taion and Aria.

He approached a stall and picked a small necklace with a round cast, two vines trailing around it, the gemstone reminding him of her eyes and fire. Turning around he looked at Aria. "It looks like it belongs to you." He muttered. Aria smiled and turned around as he carefully clasped it around her neck, his fingers softly grazing her skin. Aria felt her skin burn where he touched her.

She gasped softly as her heart clenched. She had never felt like that before when she had been touched by another male or her husband. She turned, the small necklace nestled between her fingers. The fiery gemstone within the round silver setting shimmered in the fading light, looking like burning gold embers, a reflection of Aria's eyes.

He watched as she gazed at it with wonder, then lifted her eyes as the first fireflies emerged, twinkling like tiny stars against the darkening sky. As the sun dipped below the mountain peaks, the inside of the mountain cavern began to glow.

Thousands of tiny lights, like a celestial dance, illuminated the ceiling, leaving her breathless. He watched her face, mesmerised as she twirled around the open market, her skirt reflecting the fading light, shimmering as she spun.

As she stopped twirling, she looked at him and her face stilled, her eyes serious again as she placed her hands at her waist. "I apologize, I got a wee bit excited, I suppose."

She paused as she looked up again. "Does it always look like this at night, Taion?" she looked up at him again and he wordlessly nodded, terrified to speak lest he say something he couldn't take back.

They walked along the path towards the Nephilim village and Aria watched as the mothers gathered their children to them, standing along the road as they wordlessly watched the heir walk through the village. They bowed and touched his shoulder with reverence as he walked by, a welcome home for a long lost son.

As they walked towards an old hut in the Nephilim village, Taion stopped Aria and smiled, "I need to do something, I just need a moment."

Aria nodded, curious, as she watched Taion stroll over to the small garden where an older Nephilim woman was bent over, smelling the flowers. She turned and her face lit up as she recognized Taion.

He got down on his knees and hugged the woman. They pressed their foreheads together and she gently pressed her hand to his cheek. Taion closed his eyes and whispered something to her, and she smiled.

Aria watched as he got up and walked towards her. Curiosity got the best of her as they started walking towards the castle. She looked up at Taion who kept his gaze ahead of them.

"Who was that, Taion?" She softly inquired.

Taion continued walking as he responded, "My aunt. She's Atmos' mother. I had to thank her and offer my debt to her for what they did."

Aria gasped and turned back to look again, realizing the woman was standing and watching them walk away. She smiled at Aria and waved gently. Aria was so shocked that she wordlessly waved back and turned around to catch up to Taion.

"I cannot believe how much I never knew about all of this. I am sorry, Taion. Truly."

Taion grunted in response as they continued walking back to the castle. They walked together, their hands almost touching as Aria looked around at the evening flowers opening up in the gardens out front of the castle. She bent down to smell one, the fragrance strong and enticing. Taion felt his chest hurt again as he drank her in. He wished he could say something, but he knew that unless her marriage binding was destroyed, they could do nothing.

As they walked up the stairs, Aria tripped on the hem of the gown, her hands flying out to stop her fall. Taion quickly grabbed her, and she winced as his hands spanned over her bruised ribs, nausea rolling though her.

Taion felt her flinch and carefully stood her upright as he put his hands on her arms, "Did I hurt you? I didn't mean to..." Aria looked at him, her face pale and her eyes wide as she shook her head, trying to figure out how to respond.

"No, it's not you...I... well, I'm just a little bit clumsy and I had hurt myself a while back," she chuckled self consciously as she twisted her cape in her fingers. Taion frowned, his gaze darkening as he looked her over.

"Clumsy is one thing, and it's evident you are, but how did you hurt your ribs?"

Aria opened her mouth and Taion interrupted her, "I don't want to ask again, Aria. Tell me the truth."

He sat her down on the steps and Aria hung her head as she twisted the cape between her fingers, frantically trying to figure out what to say.

He carefully put his hand on hers and stopped her fidgeting. She looked up into his blue and purple eyes and his face softened as he repeated himself, his eyes intent on her as he carefully pushed the stray strands of hair away from Aria's face, his touch gentle.

"What happened?" He cupped her chin with his hand.

She closed her eyes and sighed as she responded, "My husband, Theo."

A flash of murderous rage crossed Taion's face as he scanned her; her closed eyes, her flushed cheeks. As she opened her eyes, he quickly masked his anger with a chillingly neutral expression.

He nodded curtly and assisted her up the remaining steps to the castle doors. He'd kill him. He'd fix her bruises, her internal turmoil. He'd do anything to erase what had been done to her.

As they entered the hallway, Taion stopped suddenly, angrily running his hands through his hair as he paced in front of Aria. He couldn't take it any longer. He stopped, dropping his hands to his side as he looked at her, anguish in his eyes.

"If you can love Theo, even though he's so evidently wrong for you," he paused and watched as Aria wrapped her arms around herself, suddenly self-conscious as he stared at her.

"Imagine if you let the right one love you, Aria. Listen to me, just for a moment. I know you've built walls, I can see them. They're high and thick, and I understand why they're there. You've been hurt, more than I can even imagine. You've learned to protect yourself, to keep yourself from dreaming. And part of that protection, I see now, is hiding what he has done to you."

He walked up to her and pulled her hands into his, gently rubbing his thumbs over the tops of her hands. Aria's head bent down to watch his hands on hers as she felt her emotions swirling around her.

"Imagine waking up in the morning with someone who genuinely cherishes you, who sees the real you." Taion continued, hoping he could get it all off of his chest, "Someone who finds you endearing, your vulnerabilities beautiful. Someone who makes you laugh until your sides ache, and holds you close when you cry. Imagine sharing your secrets, your fears, your dreams, without fear. Imagine being truly seen, truly heard, truly understood."

Aria looked up at him, her golden eyes wide and shimmering with unshed tears as she listened to him tell her all of the things that she had prayed for. He smiled as he watched her, his iridescent eyes staring into hers, also filled with tears as he carefully cupped her face in his hand.

He softly whispered, "Imagine a love that isn't a battleground, but a safe harbor. A love that isn't conditional, but unwavering. A love that lifts you up, encourages you to grow, and makes you feel stronger, not weaker. Imagine someone who celebrates your triumphs, who comforts you in your failures, who stands by you through thick and thin, not because they have some ulterior motive or are bound by a marriage contract, but because they *want* to."

"I know it's hard. I know it's scary. Trusting someone again after being hurt is like walking on broken glass. But what if, just what if, the reward on the other side is worth the risk? What if the love you've been longing for is waiting for you, just on the other side of those walls? I'm not asking you to tear them down all at once. I'm just asking you to imagine. Imagine what it could be like to be loved, truly loved, by the right man. And then... maybe, just maybe, you'll find the courage to fight, to realize your worth."

Taion gently kissed her forehead and stepped away from Aria. He abruptly turned and strode away, disappearing down a shadowed corridor. Aria stood alone, the heavy oak doors swinging shut behind her. The sudden darkness, both physical and emotional, enveloped her.

Chapter Thirty One

Taion stood in the middle of the great room of the castle, frustration radiating off of him in waves. How could a man put his hands on a woman like Aria? Were there not rules in place in Tir Siorghlas now that prevented that from happening?

Just one more piece of the neglect that the Kings turned a blind eye to, marriage contract or not. He scoffed as he crossed his arms and looked around the room.

He walked over to the balcony and rested his hands on the railing, surveying the city below again. He had made his peace with his aunt Marion. She knew that he would take the throne and work to bring Tenebris into a new era, he owed her and Atmos a debt of gratitude for the work they had done to revive Tenebris, with no help from the rest of Tir Siorghlas.

What he didn't know the answer to was fixing the burning, deep seated anger he had towards the Kings; their negligence and neglect towards Tenebris, the way they turned a blind eye to what had happened.

That anger had fueled him for years when he had received the letters from Constance detailing what had happened to his mother.

He stepped off the ship in Locrya, a newfound sense of ease replacing the initial sea-sickness of the past three weeks. Frig's orders had kept him busy: scrubbing the deck, learning the ship's inner workings – the difference between port and starboard, how the wind affected its course, and, most thrillingly, the art of boarding an enemy vessel.

They came back to Locrya with jewels and fabrics from other parts of the continent that he had never heard from. As their ship was unloaded, the harbour master handed Frig three purses full of coin and Frig shook his hand.

He walked up to Taion and nodded his head towards the tavern. "Time to meet the missus, little one." Taion swallowed and nodded, following behind Frig as he looked around. The port city was different than Tenebris. The cottages were built practically one on top of the other, not a tree or grass to be found. The dust swirled around them as the wind picked up, causing Taion to cough as he inhaled.

Frig chuckled and handed Taion a handkerchief, "Press it over your mouth, lad, it'll help. You'll get used to it."

They made their way to the doorstep of the Inn and Amara stepped out.

She sighed and crossed her arms as she looked Taion up and down then looked over to Frig. "When are you going to tell the Matron that we are done being an orphanage? I have another tavern to run in Riverstone that I need to be at as well, I can't be bothered raising another bairn, Frig!" She put her hands on her hips and Frig walked up to his wife as he put his hands on her shoulders.

"This isn't an orphan, technically, love. He's the Night Prince of Tenebris' heir…"

Amara gasped and smacked Frig. "What in the goddess are we doing with the lad here, Frig! I swear, sometimes, you have nothing but cotton between those ears. Do you want to die?"

Frig chuckled as he placed a kiss on her forehead, "The matron spelled the child so any scent of him is hidden from the Night Prince and the darkness. We just need to raise him, train him and then one day his time will come."

Amara sighed and turned to size Taion up. She shook her head then smiled, "Welcome to your new home, Taion. Now, listen here. I will not be playing favours because you're a Prince of the blood. You'll work hard, you'll train hard, and you'll earn your keep, just like any of the other lads who came through these doors, understood?"

Taion wordlessly nodded his head, watching as Amara swept her arm to the inside of the Inn.

"Upstairs, end of the hallway on the right. That is your bedroom. Go clean yourself up then we'll talk."

Taion walked into the inn and his life as he knew it changed.

The salt spray kissed Taion's face as he scanned the horizon, his gaze sharp and practiced. The years had flown by, skin had been kissed by the sun and by battle. He'd grown tall, his frame lean and muscular from years of hauling ropes and battling the unforgiving sea.

But it wasn't the physical strength that set him apart. It was the uncanny way he seemed to sense the invisible currents, predict the wind's whims, and anticipate the movements of other ships.

Frig, ever the shrewd opportunist, had quickly recognized his ward's talent. Taion, with his innate sense of direction and an almost preternatural ability to read the stars, along with his ancient magickal abilities, became an invaluable asset. Frig, a seasoned sailor, saw potential beyond mere muscle. He saw a hunter.

Under Frig's tutelage, Taion blossomed. He learned to navigate, to decipher the subtle shifts in the ocean's rhythm. He became a ghost on the waves, appearing and disappearing without warning with a snap of his fingers, a shadow with wings that haunted the dreams of merchant captains across the seas.

By the time Taion reached manhood, he was a legend. Whispers of the "Dark Angel of the Sea" spread through every port, striking fear into the hearts of sailors and merchants alike. He was a master of his craft, a predator who moved with the grace of a shark, his strikes swift and decisive.

But beneath the ruthless efficiency lay a flicker of something else – a yearning for something more than the life he was living. A longing for home, for his mother's arms and the twinkling lights under the mountain's canopy.

As the call became stronger and stronger to come home to Tenebris, he finally pulled Frig aside as they made their way to Locrya. He needed to go back home, to claim what was his.

Constance had kept him apprised over the years of what was going on in Tir Siorghlas, how the darkness had spread, the wars that were happening. What always sat with him was how the Kings chose to turn a blind eye to help Tenebris against the darkness. They saw only enemies.

He had written to Constance one more time, letting her know that he was intending to come home, and it was left unanswered. Months went by and Taion decided to move forward, warning or not.

The throne had stood empty, unbeknownst to him; for years. It was only through rumours that he had heard his father had been beheaded by the Kings which furthered his rage against the Clans. The darkness was still free, the creature still corrupting everything it touched, and they chose to let it go.

The weight of loss pressed down on Taion's chest again, a suffocating blanket of anger and despair. He paced his chambers, the polished stone floor echoing with each heavy step. The kings, those self-proclaimed protectors of Tir Siorghlas, had failed. They had failed his mother, failed his father, ripped away his childhood, and ultimately, failed his people.

The memory of his father, twisted and consumed by the Nightsinger, still haunted him. The once vibrant man, filled with laughter and warmth, had become a vessel for the darkness, his eyes black, his soul consumed by the creature. And it was the Nightsinger that had taken his mother- not his father.

The Whisperwoods, once a sanctuary to witches and others was destroyed, the Silverbark Coven no more. The darkness, like a malignant disease, had spread, corrupting more innocent lives. Elara, the Night Prince's second wife, had become the newest vessel. She lost her life because of it, shortly after Rhamiel's head rolled.

But perhaps the most unforgivable sin was the willful blindness. While the Kings battled for their own Clans, protecting their innocent people, the Nightsinger flourished, growing stronger with each soul she consumed. Tenebris, the source of the corruption, the heart of the darkness, was left untouched, a festering wound ignored.

Taion's fists clenched. They had abandoned him, his family, his people, to the mercy of an unseen enemy. How could he ever forgive that?

Aria needed some time to digest what Taion had said to her, especially after he let her alone in the hallway, watching him walk away before she could respond. Her chin had lifted, a plea almost escaping her lips, but she'd swallowed it down. What was the point? Any response, any action, would only amplify the ache in her chest. The brutal truth remained: she belonged to another.

She turned away, needing to escape the suffocating weight of that realization. Her heart throbbed with a dull, persistent pain as she wandered down the hallway, searching for a place to clear her head. Drawn by the soft glow of light spilling from an open doorway, she found herself descending a circular staircase that spiraled downwards.

As she stepped off the last stair, her eyes lit up in wonder at the volumes of books surrounding her. They filled multiple shelves from the bottom of the floor all the way to the top of the 20-foot ceilings, ladders placed on each section for those without wings to access them.

She carefully ran her hands down the spines of the books, whispering the titles on the spines as she browsed. She looked over and saw a soft chair by the fireplace, a pile of books resting on a small table beside it. Intrigued she walked over and looked at the cover on the first book. "The Littlest Dragon and the Lost Star." She smiled as she opened the first page to read a scrolled inscription: 'To my little stargazer. Love always, your mother and father'

She sat down as a wave of sadness rolled over her, the image of Taion with his parents as a small child, reading the book together. How could it have all gone so wrong? She lifted the next book, realizing that it was one that would detail the emergence of the Nightsinger and the history of Taion's family, the Valran royalty.

A rustling sound made Aria lift her head, looking around as she tried to ascertain where the noise was coming from. She carefully closed the book and put it back on the pile. She stood up and walked down the length of the room, until she found another chair, laying on its side.

She grunted as she lifted it and sat it back on its feet, her hip hitting the wall as she stumbled. The wall let go and Aria turned around, startled at the noise. She carefully bent down and flicked her fingers to create a small flame to look into the room.

Dust and cobwebs covered the room, she coughed as she inhaled the dust accidentally, putting her other hand over her mouth as her eyes adjusted to the room. She looked around to see a bed that had been laid in, many ages ago. She glanced to the floor and noticed the small wooden dragon on the floor, next to a large family album.

What she had found had broken her heart; half ripped pages, photographs of Naomi and little Taion wrapped in Rhamiel's arms, their smiles bright. Then a shift. Ripped letters from Constance to Naomi, spells for removing the shield over someone... and then nothing.

Aria had come up out of the library, her eyes opened with newfound knowledge and a profound sense of sadness for what had transpired. She understood Taion's anger and knew what needed to be done to change the path they were all moving headlong down.

A small hand touched his shoulder, startling him from his reverie. He looked down, his eyes meeting those of Aria's. He turned to face her fully, his heart pounding in his chest. His hand, almost unconsciously, reached out to gently brush the stray strand of fiery red hair from her cheek.

Aria looked up at him, her gaze steady and unwavering. "I think... I think I understand what happened, Taion," she said softly, her voice laced with a hint of understanding. "Walk with me?"

Taion, unsure of what she was going to say, nodded slowly. He felt a strange lightness in his chest, oddly- a flicker of hope- where despair had been seated. He fell into step beside her, the silence between them heavy yet strangely comforting.

She looked up at Taion again, taking in his tall muscular frame, the way he held himself as his wings flexed behind him, the soft curve to his lips and how his long black lashes frame those mesmerizing eyes. Maybe one day she would be able to tell him how she really felt.

As they walked down the hallway, Taion kept his hands behind his back, stealing glances at Aria as she kept her face forward, marvelling at the lights as they danced overhead, creating what looked like stars for the mountain dwellers.

He smiled as he watched her look in childlike wonder over the balcony at Tenebris below them, the bioluminescent glow of the plants and bugs creating a show.

As he stood at the balcony with her, she softly whispered, "They're not coming."

Taion frowned and turned his head, looking at Aria, "Pardon me?" he asked, his hand clamping on the railing.

She turned and looked at him, her hands clasped in front of her. "The Eldatárs," she began, her voice calm but firm, "they are not coming. I sent falcons while you were busy talking with Atmos. The children are safe, and our fathers cannot fix what was done here, Taion. None of this was their making or doing."

She paused, her eyes searching his face which remained chillingly neutral, "Our families never harmed anyone in Tenebris, and I know that if they had known how bad things had been, they would have stepped in to help. Just because they didn't know, didn't come to try and destroy the Nightsinger; this is not worth starting a war over, look at what you have now: two brothers, a throne, and a city of people welcoming you home."

She stopped, a flicker of apprehension in her eyes as she saw Taion's eyes darken, the rage simmering. He stepped towards her, his gaze intense, his face inches from hers. "You had no right to interfere with my plans, Princess," he spat, his voice low and dangerous.

Aria, her heart pounding against her ribs, met his gaze without flinching, her golden eyes unblinking. "I had to," she said, her voice unwavering. "Your anger, your thirst for revenge, it would have consumed you. You would have become the very thing you swore to destroy, that your mother died for."

Taion's eyes narrowed, his grip tightening on the balcony railing. "And you think you know better?" he growled, his grey wings flexing behind him.

Aria took a deep breath, her voice steady. "I know what it means to lose control, to be consumed by darkness. I know what it means to fight for what you believe in, even when it seems hopeless. But I also know that sometimes, the greatest strength lies in forgiveness, in choosing a different path. You don't want the anger to consume you or the darkness to exploit it. Find a different way, Taion."

Taion remained silent, his gaze locked with hers, a silent battle of wills unfolding between them. Aria held his gaze, her stubbornness stopping her from walking away even though her brain screamed to run. Finally, he looked away.

"You may be right," he conceded, his voice rough. "But I will not forget or forgive what you did. You interfered when you shouldn't have." He pushed away from the balcony and opened the door of the room. He looked back at her before he walked through and down the hallway, his movements quiet and defeated.

Aria nodded, her heart aching for him. After hearing the story of what the other women had gone through and how the young men were brought into the world, the way they were used as pawns, she started to suspect that Taion was more of a pawn than he realized or was letting on.

Constance shouldn't have kept feeding him the information she did. And while she felt that the Kings could have done something to help, if they didn't know, could they really take blame the way Taion saw it?

She turned and with a low whistle called a falcon who responded with a soft cry. It flew over and landed on the railing, a note tied to its leg.

Aria opened the note and frowned as she read it. A wave of dread washed over her as she realized the gravity of the situation.

"Shit. Shit, shit shit shit shit," she muttered as she grabbed her skirt with one hand and she ran. She had to tell Taion, to warn him, to prepare him for what was to come. With a sense of urgency, she turned and ran towards the direction where Taion had disappeared.

"I may have just put my foot in it instead of making it better," she muttered to herself as her feet carried her down the hallway, her hair flowing behind her.

Chapter Thirty Two

Tenebris

She reached his chambers, her heart pounding in her chest from the run. She knocked on the door, her knuckles rapping against the wood in a frantic rhythm. The door creaked open, revealing Taion standing in the doorway, his shirtless torso glistening with sweat. Her eyes followed the muscles of his arms rippling beneath his skin down to with the muscles on his stomach that lead down to a very defined V above his pants. His grey wings were spread out, turning him into a fallen angel.

Aria's breath caught in her throat, and she swallowed down a lump as desire coursed through her. She had never seen him like this before, his raw masculinity laid bare, his eyes dark and intense. Thoughts swirled in her mind, a dizzying mix of fear, arousal, and a strange sense of longing that she had never felt before.

Before she could compose herself, Taion reached out, sensing her arousal, his hand gently cupping her cheek. His gaze, a smouldering look as the iridescent colours of his eyes danced, held hers captive. "Aria," he breathed, his voice husky with desire.

In a moment of impulsive surrender, Aria pulled him down to her, crushing her lips to his in a searing kiss. The world around them faded away, replaced by the intoxicating sensation of his touch, the taste of him on her tongue.

As their lips met, a surge of forbidden desire coursed through her, something that she couldn't deny. She clung to him, her fingers tracing the contours of his chest, her body trembling with a mixture of fear and exhilaration.

Taion deepened the kiss, his hands exploring her back, his touch sending shivers down her spine. She lost herself in the moment, the urgency of her warning forgotten, replaced by the pull of his embrace.

He wrapped his wings around her and stepped back into his chambers, closing the door. The kiss deepened as he turned them around, Aria stepped backwards until the back of her legs touched the bed.

Aria reached up to touch his hair, her fingers tracing the dark, silky strands. The kiss deepened, a passionate dance of lips and tongues. She lost herself in the sensation, the world fading away, replaced by the scent of him and the thunder of her own heart. He lifted her onto the bed, and they paused. He looked at Aria and ran his hand up her thigh, watching her as she tilted her head back and moaned.

That was all he needed from her, contract be damned. He crushed his lips to hers, and a surge of desire coursed through him. She clung to Taion, her hands threading behind his neck, as if she was holding on for her life.

Taion deepened the kiss, his hands exploring her face, down to her neck then as he brushed the tops of her breasts a flicker of memory, the reason why she had come to him in the first place, pierced through the haze of passion. The note, the warning, the impending doom. She broke the kiss abruptly, both of them gasping for breath, their eyes locked.

Taion, his eyes now dark and intense, searched her face, his expression a mixture of confusion and desire. "Aria, why did you come here." he whispered, his voice rough with barely suppressed need.

Aria, her mind reeling, tried to speak, to warn him, but the words caught in her throat. She looked into his eyes, the depths of which held a dangerous allure, and knew that she had lost control when she shouldn't have. She would pay for disrespecting the marriage bond when Theo found her.

Suddenly, a tremor shook the ground, a low rumble that echoed through the castle. Taion's eyes narrowed, his gaze hardening. "What was that?" he demanded, his hand instinctively reaching for the dagger at his hip.

Aria, her heart pounding with a mixture of fear and anticipation, looked towards the window. "I think... I think the Elentáris of Tenebris have arrived." She grimaced and smoothed down her hair with one hand.

The tremors intensified, "The Elentáris?" Taion growled pulled Aria close, his arm instinctively shielding her from the unseen danger. "We need to get to the throne room," he said, his voice low and urgent. "Now."

As they raced down the corridor, the tremors continued, the castle on alert for the assault. The fate of Tenebris was unknown. Amidst the chaos, Aria knew that her life, forever intertwined with Taion's, would never be the same.

The air crackled with tension as the four queens stood before the castle gates, an imposing force of nature; the guards knocked unconscious at their feet. Annika, queen of the Sky, her voice a sweet melody, called upon the wind, her song stirring the leaves of the ancient trees that ringed the castle. Alyndria, queen of the Waters, raised her hands, and the earth trembled as water erupted from the ground, forming a surging torrent that threatened to engulf the castle walls.

Saphielle, queen of the Storm, her eyes crackling with electricity, unleashed a barrage of lightning bolts, each strike sending tremors through the very foundations of the castle. And Sarya, witch queen of the Sun, her skin radiating an ethereal glow, summoned the power of the sun, bathing the castle in a blinding light.

With a synchronized harmony, the queens unleashed their combined power. Saphielle, sensing an opportunity, focused her attack, a bolt of lightning arcing towards the heavy oak doors. The wood cracked, the doors exploding outwards in a shower of splinters. Their power, a whirlwind of wind, water, lightning, and light, crashed against the ancient stone walls. Guards, alerted by the commotion, poured from the castle, forming a hastily assembled line of defense while the Nephilim guards scrambled to find a way around the air pushing them back.

A tempest of swirling air, summoned by Annika, ripped banners from their moorings and sent them spiraling behind them as she kept her hand up, the wind turning into a cyclone, sweeping the Nephilim warriors away. Alyndria commanded a surging wave, a miniature tsunami that crashed through the castle, cracking the wood and sending guards scrambling as they lost their footing.

Lightning crackled from Saphielle's fingertips, illuminating the chaotic scene with flashes of blinding white, each bolt striking a guard's weapon or armor, momentarily incapacitating them with jolts of raw energy. And at the heart of the storm, Sarya moved like a dancer, her movements fluid and graceful, her curls flying around her, radiating a blinding light that forced the guards to shield their eyes, disorienting them.

Swords clashed against summoned shields of water, the spray glistening in the flickering torchlight. Arrows, loosed from the battlements, were intercepted mid-air by gusts of wind, redirected harmlessly into the courtyard. The ground trembled as Alyndria manipulated the very earth beneath the guards' feet, creating fissures and cracks that sent them stumbling.

Saphielle's lightning danced across the ranks, arcing between shields, creating a chaotic web of electricity that made it impossible to maintain formation. Annika, meanwhile, weaved through the melee, her movements a blur, creating miniature tornadoes that lifted guards off their feet and tossed them aside like rag dolls.

Sarya, her presence a beacon of hope amidst the chaos, focused her energy. A beam of pure light shot forth from her hands, not to wound, but to disarm, melting the steel of swords and the fastenings of armor, leaving the guards defenseless.

Aria ran out of the throne room, her breath catching in her throat. The sounds of battle echoed through the castle corridors – the clash of steel, the roar of wind, the crackle of lightning. She had to stop them. The formidable queens, fueled by their righteous fury, were tearing the castle apart.

While she understood their anger, she knew they wouldn't stop until they'd achieved their objective, and that meant potentially destroying everything, and everyone, in their path to get to Taion.

"Stop! Please, stop!" she cried, her voice barely audible above the din of the battle. She dodged a stray bolt of lightning that seared the wall beside her, the smell of ozone stinging her nostrils. She had to reach them, had to make them see reason. She realized that her hastily written note had only incited the women-and rightfully so- but this was out of control.

As they stormed down the hallway towards the throne room, she turned to Taion, her voice trembling, "I can stop them!" she pressed her hands together, pulling all the sadness, the rage and the pain from her past into her fire, creating a massive ball as she pulled her hands away, preparing to throw it at the queens, praying that it would make them stop and look.

Before she could act, Taion pulled her back, his hands extinguishing the ball of fire, his grip firm but not unkind. "Stay here," he commanded, his eyes narrowed as he assessed the situation.

Saphielle looked over and saw her sister-in-law, her gaze falling upon Taion as he pulled Aria behind him. Her brow furrowed, a flicker of annoyance crossing her face. "You." she hissed, her voice crackling with electricity. With a flick of her wrist, she unleashed a bolt of lightning, aiming directly at Taion.

Taion, agile as a panther, dodged the attack with a practiced ease, pushing Aria out of harm's way. He landed lightly on his feet, his wings his partner in the fight. His eyes blazed with a fierce determination. "You have no idea what you're doing," he growled, his voice a low rumble.

The battle erupted with a fury that shook the very foundations of the castle. Taion, a whirlwind of motion, fought with a ferocity born of years of training. He deflected blasts of water, dodged bolts of lightning, and sidestepped the powerful gusts of wind. He flung his own magick out, fire raging around him, snapping his fingers as he could, teleporting around the space. But the queens were formidable opponents, their combined power a force to be reckoned with.

Taion, realizing he was fighting against a never-ending onslaught of royal elemental magick, began to tire. He felt the first prickles of exhaustion, his movements slowing, his defenses weakening and his wings slowing. Just as he felt himself on the verge of defeat, a familiar voice echoed through the chaos.

"Enough! Ma! Stop!" Puck's voice rang across the hallway. Puck and Atmos, their faces grim, stepped forward, their presence radiating an aura of power that momentarily stunned the women.

The battle abruptly ceased, the air thick with the lingering scent of their magick. Sarya, her face pale, rushed towards Puck, her arms instinctively wrapping around him. "Puck, oh my son! Are you alright?" she cried, her voice trembling as she reached up to run her hands over his face.

Puck, his eyes still wide with the shock of the battle, nodded slowly as he tried to stop his mother from checking him over, carefully pull her hands to his. He glanced at Taion, who was struggling to regain his breath, the effects of the women's combined assault still lingering.

Saphielle, her expression a mixture of concern and annoyance, rushed towards Aria. "Aria! Are you hurt?" She turned to look accusatorily at Taion.

Aria, still shaken by the intensity of the battle, hugged her sister-in-law tightly. "I'm fine, Saphielle. How did you convince Hagen to let you out of his sight?"

Saphielle looked back at her sister-in-law and smiled, "He didn't have a choice, a woman was in trouble. What on earth are you doing here still?"

Alyndria, arms crossed over her chest, surveyed the scene with a critical eye. Her gaze lingered on Taion, assessing him with a mixture of curiosity and suspicion. She could sense a bit of turmoil between Aria and Taion and pondered to herself, her eyes narrowing as she watched them.

Annika stepped forward, her voice commanding attention. "What is the meaning of this? Who are you?" she demanded, her gaze settling on Taion.

Taion, regaining his composure, stood up and flexed his wings as he straightened his shirt, frowning as he expected them to know him. "My name is Taion," he announced, his voice firm. "I am one of the Heirs of the throne of Tenebris."

Atmos, however, corrected him. "He is Taion Valran, one of the Heirs, yes," Atmos said, his voice calm and measured. "He is the Night Eldatár of Tenebris. Queen Annika, we are working to make things right with Tir Siorghlas, to usher in a new chapter of peace and understanding."

The Queens exchanged stunned glances. The Night King? This man standing in front of them was the son of the very being that had plagued their nightmares, the source of countless terrors and deaths, the reason why they had lost Elara, the Whisperwoods, Sarya's coven. They all turned to look at Atmos and Puck as the men stood together.

The air crackled with a tension that was far more potent than any of the spells they had just unleashed. Lera stepped out of the throne room and cleared her throat, looking around at the group, her eyes wide as she recognized the Queens. She quickly bowed at each of them, unsure what to do.

Puck sighed and walked over to her, grabbing her hand as he pulled her back so he could stand with his brothers. He looked at his mother.

"I think we have a lot to discuss. I left to find out who I was, ma. I know you were doing everything you could to protect me, but it was like a piece of me was missing. I needed to know what was being kept from me. And I'm sorry that I left."

"However," he continued, "Along the way, I met Lera."

He paused as he looked down at Lera his eyes filled with love, she squeezed his hand as she looked back at him, the same look in her eyes.

Sarya stayed silent, assessing that her son was in love and waiting for Puck's discovery, willing it to not be true as she suspected where Puck was going with his announcement.

Puck voice was rough as he declared, "I'm an heir to the Tenebris throne as well, Rhamiel was my sire." Sarya bit back a sob and Annika rushed to her, pulling her to her side as Sarya watched her son continue talking, "I am not claiming the throne ma, I want to come home, if you'll have me."

Sarya nodded frantically and opened her arms, walking towards him as he pulled away from Lera, rushing to her. She pulled him into her embrace, and they sank to the floor. Puck cried in his mother's arms, relieved that she still wanted him. Sarya smoothed back her son's short dark hair and placed a kiss on his forehead.

Sarya sensing his thoughts, whispered, "I would choose you, Puck, my sweetheart, my son. In every lifetime, in every scenario. I would always choose you, no matter what."

Lera came and stood beside them, tears welling up in her eyes. As she wiped them, she looked down to see Sarya reach up, grab her hand and pull her down into their hug.

Surprised, she quickly softened and rested her head on Sarya's shoulder. "You all are an intense bunch," she said, her voice muffled. Puck and Sarya laughed as they pulled apart.

Sarya cupped Lera's face, "You are welcome in our home as well, little wood elf." Lera blushed and looked at Puck, a question in her eyes. Puck looked back at her and nodded, pulling her to him as he kissed her.

Atmos started to walk across the room, a sincere apology forming on his lips. He intended to bow before Annika, to acknowledge the centuries of mistrust from Tenebris and begin to mend the fractured relationship between their realms, and to apologize for hiding his lineage to the Clans.

However, as he took a step, his foot connected with something that had fallen in the cracks of the stone floor during the fight. A sharp crack echoed through the room as his weight shattered the object.

He looked down in surprise, and then looked back up, his eyes meeting Taion's across the room. Taion's face paled, his eyes wide with a terror that mirrored Atmos' own. In that instant, a guttural scream erupted from beneath Atmos' foot, a sound that seemed to tear at the very fabric of reality.

A swirling vortex of darkness erupted from the shattered object, shards of glass raining down around them. "NO!" Taion yelled with a roar.

He dove forward, his wings unfolding in a blur of motion. He shoved Atmos out of the way, his body shielding him from the onslaught of pure, malevolent energy.

The Nightsinger screamed, a cacophony of evil cries, as she erupted from the broken vial, tendrils reaching out, seeking to consume everything in her path.

Atmos slid across the floor, out of the way of the tendrils. He watched in horror as it latched onto both Taion and Puck, dragging them towards its dark inky centre.

The swirling vortex of darkness erupted, its tendrils reaching out, seeking to consume everything in its path. Sarya and Lera screamed, their arms reaching for Puck as he struggled against the relentless pull of the darkness.

Lera's voice pierced the chaos, "You must not yield, Puck! For the love of the goddess, you do not yield! Don't let go!"

Taion, his eyes wide with a desperation, fought against the encroaching darkness, his body straining against the invisible force. But the Nightsinger was relentless, the power overwhelming. With a final, agonizing surge, he watched it consume Puck, his form vanishing into the swirling abyss.

Taion's eyes widened in horror as he watched his little brother disappear. He looked around at the group, their faces frozen in a tableau of terror and disbelief. Atmos struggled to his feet, his face contorted with grief and rage. Aria, her eyes wide with a mixture of horror and despair, a single tear tracing a path down her cheek as their eyes met. She knew what he was about to do.

With a heavy heart, Taion closed his eyes and stopped fighting. The darkness, sensing his surrender, enveloped him with a scream of glee, pulling him into its depths.

The silence was deafening as the remainder of the group looked around, wondering where Puck and Taion were taken.

Atmos sat down on the ground hard, his chest heaving as he pulled his knees up. He yelled as he grabbed his hair, rocking as tears streamed down his face. He had failed.

Annika carefully walked over to Atmos and sank down beside him, pulling him to her in a hug as she looked around at everyone.

"The worst is about to happen, you all need to prepare yourselves."

Chapter Thirty Three

Tenebris

The inky blackness seemed to erupt from the depths of the dungeon, spitting out the brothers as if they were mere playthings.

Puck and Taion each gasped for breath, their senses reeling from the disorienting experience. The Nightsinger, a swirling vortex of malevolent energy, seemed to writhe and twist around them, its tendrils reaching out like grasping hands.

"I can only take one soul at a time," a voice, cold and ancient, echoed through the chamber. "But which one to take? The strong one who has so much hatred in his heart, or the young one with so much to learn?" The darkness seemed to ponder, its attention shifting between the two brothers.

Puck looked at Taion, his eyes wide with horror as he saw the rage simmering underneath him. Taion, his face contorted in a mask of fury, stared back at the darkness, his hand instinctively reaching for the dagger at his hip.

"You took my father, you killed my mother," he growled, his voice a low, guttural growl, "if you think I'm going to let you take one more thing of mine, you can think again!"

With a swift, practiced motion, Taion dragged the dagger across his palm, a crimson stain blooming on his skin. The darkness hissed, its attention diverted by the sudden sweet smell his of blood, its tendrils reaching towards Taion with renewed vigor. Puck watched in horror as the darkness began to consume Taion, its tendrils wrapping around him like a suffocating embrace.

"Then I choose you!" it laughed as Taion roared, his voice echoing through the dungeon. With a desperate surge of power, he raised his hands, channeling his remaining energy into a desperate attempt to contain the darkness.

But it was too late. The darkness, sensing its prey within reach, surged forward, trailing down Taion's throat, consuming him from the inside.

Puck watched in horror as his brother was slowly consumed by the darkness, his body contorting and twisting as the malevolent energy took hold. With a desperate surge of speed, Puck scrambled up and turned, fleeing the dungeon, his feet pounding against the stone steps as he raced towards the surface, his wings pushing him forward.

He had to warn the others, to find a way to stop the darkness before it consumed everything in its path again.

As Puck ascended the stairs, the echoes of Taion's struggle faded behind him, replaced by a chilling silence. The Nightsinger had claimed another victim, its insatiable hunger growing with each passing moment.

His chest heaved as he ran through the second floor of the dungeon, reaching for the light at the end, gasping as he tried to fill his lungs. He scrambled up the final flight of stone steps and collapsed on the stone floor, his chest heaving as he tried to yell.

Aria glanced over at the movement and with a double take, cried out, running to Puck as Sarya and Lera followed on her heels. They reached him and Puck gasped out, "It took Taion. He's in the dungeon. The Nightsinger is coming for us. Run!"

Sarya felt a wave of nausea wash over her, the thought of Taion, his eyes gleaming with the darkness' predatory hunger, was enough to make her stomach churn. She spun around, her eyes connecting with Annika, her face frozen in a mask of shock.

Annika's gaze was fixed on the balcony, where Taion crouched, his grey wings spread wide, a dramatic display of power. His hand rested lightly on the stone railing, his iridescent eyes gleaming with an unsettling intensity. He was closer than they had realized, a predator assessing its prey. And they were all sitting ducks.

Annika shuddered, the memory of her previous abduction flashing through her mind. She couldn't endure that again, the fear, the helplessness, the violation. She stepped back slowly, her eyes wide with apprehension.

Taion tilted his head, observing her with an unsettling curiosity, almost as if he was tracking a particularly elusive prey. A feral smile spread across his lips. "Sweet Annika," he purred, his voice a low, seductive growl, "bedmate to Damien the strong. What fun I could have with you, your powers, he's not here to stop me now...."

He trailed off, his gaze lingering on her. Annika felt a shiver crawl down her spine, a primal fear awakening within her. She knew, with a chilling certainty, that they were all in grave danger.

She kept her eyes on Taion's as she slowly walked backwards, hoping to give the rest of the group enough time to run away.

"Taion, you know that my powers are the most sought after; you'll have to fight me for them, and I won't go willingly."

She would do everything in her power to keep the darkness from destroying Tir Siorghlas, from taking another soul, like it had taken her friend, Elara.

Taion responded, "I love a good fight, little brave queen."

As he stepped down from the railing, Taion's eyes slowly changed from inky black to his iridescent blue and purple. He gasped and looked at them all, struggling as he clawed at his body.

"You all need to leave, get out of here, before it's too late!" He howled as the darkness tried to pull him back in. He struggled again and clenched his jaw.

"I'm sorry I took the children, I was wrong. I will spend a lifetime trying to right that wrong." He groaned as the Nightsinger screeched, its claws digging into Taion's back. He cried out and arched his back, falling to his knees.

Aria cried out and started to run to him, but Saphielle grabbed her, pulling her back. "No, Aria, it's too dangerous! The darkness will make him kill you, just like what happened to his mother." She turned and looked at Saphielle, whose face was filled with sorrow.

They all ran. As Aria looked back, she saw Taion look at her, his face filled with regret as he struggled against the darkness that had claimed his father. With tears streaming down her face, she watched his eyes turn to inky black again.

They followed the path down through the tunnels and ended up in the eastern entrance again. Atmos grabbed Saphielle in a bridal hold and ran over the edge, soaring down as quickly as he could. As they touched the ground, he carefully placed her, ensuring she was ok, and shot back up into the air, the tears in his eyes making it hard for him to see.

Was the wish to have a family with his brothers that unrealistic? He had hoped that after all that time, after sharing those memories, that they would be able to bond, to create what he never had. He wiped the tears as he saw the eastern entrance coming up fast.

As he landed, he looked around, Puck was holding Lera and tilted his head over to the last one needing transport; Aria. She stood close to the cave wall, her arms wrapped around herself, tears falling down her face, the dark blue cloak wrapped around her.

Atmos walked up to her and gently placed his hands on her shoulders. "I'll figure out how to save him, Aria. I promise."

Aria, her eyes blazing with a fierce determination, shook her head. "What kind of people are we to leave him alone? To let him fight a darkness that has consumed countless other strong royals? How are we any better if we walk away? We are exactly what he said we were." she demanded, her voice rising with each word.

Atmos, at a loss for words, tried to pull her arm, intending to gently guide her back from the edge of the precipice. He had underestimated the force of her grief and anger. Without realizing it, he had opened himself up for her to shove him with all her might.

Losing his balance, Atmos stumbled backward, his wings catching the air momentarily before he plummeted towards the chasm below.

"Aria, no!" he yelled, the wind whipping through his hair as he desperately flapped his wings, trying to regain control and steer himself back towards the safety of the cave mouth.

With each flap of his wings, he counted the steps she would be taking back down the tunnel, back towards Taion and the darkness and he cursed realizing by the time he made it back, he'd be halfway down the tunnel, and she'd be at Taion's side.

Chapter Thirty Four

Tenebris

Aria ran. She didn't just run; she sprinted, her feet pounding against the hard floor, each step a desperate plea for time as she held her skirt in her one hand, her other holding up a ball of firelight. Adrenaline surged through her veins, fueling her flight. The image of Taion, consumed by the Nightsinger, haunted her, his eyes wide with a terror that mirrored her own.

She had to reach him, to stop the darkness, to somehow pull him back from the abyss. Desperation fueled her forward, her heart hammering against her ribs like a caged bird. She scrambled around the curve in the tunnel, her vision blurring with tears.

She was running towards the man who had kidnapped her, the man who had shattered her world. Yet, in that moment, all that mattered was reaching him, protecting him, even if it meant facing her own fears and confronting the impossible.

For in that terrifying encounter with the darkness, Aria had realized that her feelings for Taion, forbidden and dangerous as they were, ran deeper than she had ever imagined. They were a force of their own, a powerful current that pulled her towards him, despite the danger, despite the consequences.

She had to reach him. She had to save him.

Aria burst from the tunnel, her lungs burning, her heart pounding a frantic rhythm against her ribs. She ran up the stairs, her feet pounding against the cold, hard stone, her eyes frantically scanning. She had to find him, had to make sure he was alright.

Finally, she reached the main floor, her breath coming in ragged gasps. She stopped, her eyes scanning the hallway, searching for any sign of Taion. She slowed down, walking as she looked. Where was he? Was he hurt? Was he...

Her gaze fell upon the throne room, the doors standing wide open. She carefully walked towards it, her heart pounding in her chest.

As she entered the room, her breath caught in her throat. Sitting on the throne, his posture regal, a mischievous glint in his eyes, was Taion. He was leaning back, his grey wings tucked behind him, his one leg resting on his knee, seemingly lost in contemplation. He looked every inch the Tenebris Night King, a picture of effortless power and grace, shadows floating around him.

Aria stared at him, speechless. The fear, the desperation, the raw terror she had felt moments ago seemed to evaporate, replaced by a strange sense of calm. He was alive. He was here.

Taion, sensing her presence, turned his head, his eyes meeting hers. A slow feral smile spread across his face, a dark glint in his eyes. "Took you long enough," he murmured, his voice a low rumble.

Aria, still reeling from the shock of seeing him alive and well, could only stare at him, her mind struggling to comprehend what she was seeing.

"Taion, you're... you're ok." She whispered, her voice catching in her throat as she scanned his face.

"You shouldn't have worried," Taion said, his voice a playful tease. "The darkness... well, it decided it wants to play."

The moment the words left his lips, a chilling realization dawned upon Aria. The playful glint in his eyes, the predatory tilt of his head – it wasn't Taion speaking. The darkness, the entity that had consumed him, was using his voice, mocking her, toying with her.

Terror, cold and paralyzing, gripped her. She spun around, her instincts screaming at her to flee. Taion pounced. His movements were swift as his wings propelled him across the room. Aria, caught off guard, was thrown to the ground, the impact jarring her breath from her lungs.

The Nightsinger, sensing its opportunity, surged through Taion, its power amplified by her struggle. He pinned her down, his eyes burning with inky fire. "You should have known better," he hissed, his voice a guttural growl. "Interfering with the darkness... it always comes at a price, little pretty plaything."

Aria, trapped beneath him, felt a surge of fear. Desperation fueled her; she lashed out, her teeth sinking into his arm, drawing blood. The darkness within him shuddered, a low growl rumbling in his throat. It had not anticipated this, this unexpected resistance. The little plaything had some fire to her.

Taion, his eyes widening in surprise, roared in pain. The darkness, thrown off balance, recoiled, its hold on him loosening. He looked down at Aria, his face a mixture of rage and confusion.

Aria, seizing the opportunity, kicked out, her foot connecting with his crotch. He gasped, the force of the blow sending him reeling. The darkness, thrown off balance, struggled to keep its hold on Taion.

"No!" Taion snarled, his voice a guttural growl as he winced through the pain. He tried to regain control, to fight back against the darkness that was consuming him. But it was too strong, too insidious. The Nightsinger, sensing his weakening resistance, surged through him again, its icy tendrils wrapping around his mind and soul.

Taion stood to his feet, his eyes now completely black, devoid of any trace of the man Aria had come to learn. He walked towards her, his movements fluid and predatory, a chilling grace in his every step.

Aria, her heart pounding a frantic rhythm against her ribs, scrambled backwards, her eyes wide with terror. She tried to scramble to her feet, to escape, but her legs felt weak, her body trembling with fear.

Taion, his face contorted into a grotesque mask of pain and pleasure, lunged at her. Aria screamed, her voice a raw, desperate cry, as he landed on top of her, pinning her beneath his weight.

The Nightsinger, sensing its victory, surged through Taion, his body trembled as he tried to fight against it. He leaned down, his eyes fixed on her throat, a chilling gleam in their depths. With a low, guttural growl, he sank his fangs into her neck.

Aria's scream was cut short, replaced by a gurgle as the darkness, cold and consuming, entered her bloodstream, sucking her life from her. The world around her faded to black, the last image seared into her mind was a tear falling down Taion's cheek.

Atmos ran into the throne room, his chest heaving as he took in the scene in front of him. Taion was sitting on the floor, his legs stretched out, Aria's lifeless body cradled in his arms as he sobbed into her neck. He lifted his head to look at Atmos who was looking at him in horror.

"I..." Taion sobbed "I killed her, Atmos. Why did she come back? Why in the gods did you let her come back?" He pulled her body against his as he keened.

Atmos carefully walked up to Taion, assessing if the darkness was still lingering. Taion whispered, "It's gone. It left me once Aria's life force was taken."

Atmos looked around the room, concerned as he walked around. Taion glanced at him then back at Aria, tracing her face with his finger, realizing he would never see those golden eyes flash with anger or laughter again, or taste her lips on his. He would never get to tell her his secret, how he felt about her, or figure out how to break the marriage contract so he could grow old with her.

A chuckle in the corner of the room made both Atmos and Taion turn and look. The Nightsinger floated around them, spinning and turning. Atmos shuddered as he watched it. He despised the game that this creature played.

"I don't leave that easily, little Night King." The creature giggled. "I just wanted to watch you as you realized what you did. See, you really are just like your grandfather and your father." Taion lifted his head slowly and looked at the darkness.

"You took the one thing that I loved. I don't care what you do to me now." He pressed his forehead to Aria's and ignored the darkness.

It stopped, musing as it turned towards Atmos. "You. You have resisted since a wee lad. Don't you want to take a turn and feel the power that you could have with me inside you?" Atmos frowned, "I've been protected from you since birth, you pile of scum, you couldn't breach the barrier even if you tried."

The darkness chuckled, "It was worth a try." It slinked back over to Taion and stroked his face. "What a sad vessel to be in." It purred as it paced the room. "Such a waste," the Nightsinger sighed, its voice tinged with regret. "Such potential. But without the fire, without the rage, he was merely a vessel, a puppet without strings."

Atmos racked his brain, trying to remember if he knew any other way to trap the darkness or to save Aria. His eyes widened as he remembered Orin. He looked at Taion and whispered "Amodra"

He watched as if everything was in slow motion. Taion's eyes widened and he flung his hand up, a shout from his lips as a flash of light lit the room up, the Nightsinger screeching as it flung itself away from the light.

Taion stood up and cradled Aria, running as fast as he could, his wings propelling him across the room. Atmos turned and flung his arms out at the darkness, whispering a containment spell. The darkness screeched again as it smashed against the barrier.

Taion flew down the hallway and down the stairs of the dungeon. He ran towards Amodra's cell and collapsed in front of it, Aria's lifeless body cradled carefully in his arms. Amodra rushed over and sat down beside the bars, her hand reaching through as she stroked Aria's hair. Taion looked up at Amodra, his eyes searching hers, beseeching, "Please, can you please bring her back?"

Amodra paused, checking Aria's neck and shook her head, softly responding, "I'm too late." Taion slumped forward and closed his eyes. It was over.

"However, I am not, Night Eldatár." A hand gently touched his shoulder, and his eyes snapped open as he looked up beside him.

Standing beside him was Death, a soft smile on her face as her dark hair floated around her.

"I don't know what it is about the Tir Siorghlas Clans," she paused as she bent down to brush Aria's hair gently off her face, "But I have a soft spot for some of them." She gently leaned down and kissed Aria's forehead. "It's not her time yet, she has work to do."

A soft flush spread out from Death's kiss, and Aria's skin started to pink up. Taion looked at her body as she gasped a breath and he shouted with joy, pulling her to him as he openly wept. Aria pulled her arms around Taion and cried, her body shaking from the ordeal.

Amodra sat in the cell, tears falling down her cheeks as she looked over at death. "Hello, sister." She smiled through her tears.

Death bent down and leaned against the bars, "Hello to you too, sister. Are you ready to come home?"

Amodra sighed, "I wish I could stay a bit longer, if only to hug my son?"

Death looked at her sister and reached through the bars, "I think after the time you've spent here, a few more years on this realm outside this cage would do you good." She shrugged, "After all, I seem to be giving life back a bit freely these days."

She smiled as they looked over to see Taion kissing Aria frantically. Death cleared her throat and Taion and Aria stopped, looking at her as they realized who they owed a debt to. Aria stood up and bowed looking at Amodra through the cell.

"I am sorry that I did not realize who you were, Goddess Aine." She softly said Life's true name. She smiled as she turned to death, "and you, Goddess Macha. We owe you both a debt of a lifetime."

Taion stood behind her, his hand on her shoulder as he bowed to the goddesses as well.

"I too, owe you both a debt of a lifetime."

Death, also known as the Goddess Macha, scoffed and waved her hand, "Just lay some flowers down at my statue and we'll call it even. You caught me when I was soft- don't make a habit of it."

She turned to her sister, "Since your cover is now blown, Aine, do you still want to stay here for a while? Do you think King Osian will want to see you?"

Aine, her true name finally being said after so long, stepped through the bars of the cage, the spell finally lifted. Aria gasped. "That's what the spell was, someone had to remember who you were so that you could be freed!"

Amodra- or Aine- smiled and gently took Aria's hand. "Thank you for trying to release me from the prison when you could have left me behind like so many others did. For that, I wish to reward you with a gift. You will know what it is when it needs to be used."

She softly kissed Aria on her forehead, Aria closed her eyes as she felt the warmth from Aine's kiss flow through her body.

Aine stepped to Taion. "Your battle isn't over yet, Night Eldatár. You need to make a choice- will it be revenge or peace? Once you decide that, you may be surprised to see what happens."

She turned to her sister, "Come, Macha, I have a son that I want you to meet."

Death grinned and they disappeared from the dungeon.

Orin lay in the infirmary, his chest aching even though his wounds had healed. The healers were shocked as he slowly sat up on the bed.

"Sire, are you sure you are ok?" the healer whispered as they carefully touched Orin's shoulder. Orin looked over at them and ran his hands over his chest.

"I don't understand. I should have died from that." He whispered.

"You didn't die, Orin, son of the goddess Aine, because you yourself are a half god." Death stood in the doorway of the room. The healers gasped and stepped back, bowing as both Aine and Macha walked towards Orin, their bodies glowing as Aine bent down and kissed Orin on the forehead.

"It has been far too long since I've held you, my son. Could I?" she asked, her voice thick with emotion. Orin nodded mutely, and she gently gathered him into a warm embrace. He closed his eyes, inhaling deeply, the scent of her – a comforting blend of fresh meadows and distant memories – washing over him.

Pulling back, he looked into her eyes, a question burning within him. "Did Amil know? Did he know he had fallen in love with a goddess?"

Aine smiled, shaking her head. "I was a young, perhaps even reckless, goddess then. Macha and I were tasked with assessing the Clans, evaluating the heirs. But one look at your father, and all thoughts of duty vanished. I fell utterly, hopelessly in love."

She gently smoothed back his dark hair. "Looking at you, I see your father at your age. The same mischievous glint in your eyes." A wistful smile touched her lips.

Orin pulled back, "Why didn't you escape?"

She responded, "I couldn't return with Macha. I was carrying you."

Orin frowned, his gaze shifting between Aine and the stoic Macha. "Alright, then why didn't you do something, Aunt Macha?" he asked, trying to reconcile the reason why she was left in the dungeon for so long.

Macha crossed her arms, her expression grim. "Believe me, nephew, I tried everything." She sighed, "We goddesses are not omnipotent. Blood magick is a powerful thing. We needed someone pure of heart, someone who truly saw Aine for who she was. Aria... she was the key. We saw it written and knew it was time."

Orin stood up and grabbed his mother's hand. He looked at Macha and nodded, deciding he could forgive them, for the past was not where he wanted to dwell, not when he wanted to spend what time he may have with his mother before she left again.

"I am in no rush to take Aine back to our realm, Orin, relax." Macha chuckled. "I am quite looking forward to seeing the look on Osian's face when we appear."

She grabbed Aine's hand, then held out her hand for Orin to accept. He looked down and clasped his hands to her. With a soft gust of wind, they disappeared from Tenebris.

When Orin opened his eyes, they were inside Castle Elden. Osian was standing in the entrance of the castle, his mouth open in shock as he realized Orin was standing between the two goddesses.

Wordlessly, Osian bowed, still reeling from the unexpected sight of Aine standing beside Orin and the imposing figure of the Goddess of Death, slowly raised his head. His eyes, wide with disbelief, darted between Orin and Aine, then to Macha, who stood observing him with an amused glint in her eyes.

Aine, ever graceful, moved towards him, her hand outstretched. Osian, still in a daze, reached out hesitantly, his fingers trembling slightly as they met. The moment their hands connected, a jolt, like a burst of static electricity, surged through him. He looked into her eyes, searching for any sign of deception, but found only love – a love that transcended time and defied all expectations, just like it had been when they had first met.

Without another word, he pulled her close, burying his face in her white hair. Aine, in turn, wrapped her arms around him, her heart overflowing with joy. The years of separation, the agonizing loneliness, the torment of uncertainty – all of it seemed to melt away in the warmth of his embrace.

Macha watched the reunion with a satisfied smile. "Well," she declared, her voice echoing through the entrance hall, "seems like some things are meant to be, after all."

Orin, witnessing the tender embrace, felt a profound sense of peace wash over him. He had reunited his parents, and though he knew his time with his mother would be fleeting, this moment, this precious glimpse into the happiness that had been so cruelly denied them, was a treasure.

He turned to his aunt, pulling her into a tight hug. "Thank you," he whispered, his voice thick with emotion.

Macha stiffened initially, surprised by his sudden embrace. Then, her stern facade melted away, and she returned the hug, pulling him closer.

"You're welcome, nephew," she admitted, a rare softness in her voice. "These... these moments," she gestured towards his parents, "they're making even this old goddess a bit sappy. I'm going to lose my scary reputation if this continues."

Orin laughed as they pulled apart.

Chapter Thirty Five

Tenebris

Atmos stood at the throne room doors, his brow furrowed as he watched the darkness writhe and scream against the shimmering barrier. It was a ferocious struggle, the very foundations of the castle trembling with each impact.

He wasn't sure how much longer the barrier could hold, how much longer he could contain the monstrous entity within. He knew, with a chilling certainty, that if the darkness escaped, Taion would likely be consumed again, lost forever to them this time.

He heard footsteps behind him, the sound echoing through the silent hall. He glanced over his shoulder, expecting to see one of the guards, but instead, he saw Aria walking towards him, hand in hand with Taion.

The sight almost made Atmos' knees buckle. Taion, his face pale but resolute. Aria, her eyes sparkling with an unexpected joy, looked radiant. "It worked!" Atmos exclaimed, his voice thick with relief. "Oh, thank the goddesses that you're alive, Aria!"

Aria smiled, her eyes crinkling at the corners. "We did thank them,

Atmos." She looked up at Taion, who returned her gaze with a tender smile.

Atmos, still reeling from the shock, felt a wave of confusion wash over him. "I... I'd ask for an explanation," he stammered, "but that's going to have to wait. Taion..." He looked at his eldest brother, his eyes pleading. "I don't know what else to do. The barrier is weakening."

He watched as the darkness, sensing its impending freedom, unleashed a wave of energy, the barrier flickering dangerously.

Taion put his hand on Atmos' shoulder and looked at him. "I know what has to be done, brother. Take Aria, run and don't look back. When it's done, you'll know. I'll find you."

Aria looked at Taion, fury building over her as she realized he was sacrificing himself again. She lunged at him as Atmos grabbed her, her feet flying as she swung her fists, Atmos hauling her away.

"You bastard! You lying bastard! You don't win by sacrificing yourself to the evil that your godsdamned father unleashed!" she pummelled Atmos' shoulder, "Unhand me at once, Atmos! That's an order!"

Atmos kept walking fast down the hall, away from Taion who stood watching them go. "I'm afraid the Eldatár outweighs the Princess in commands right now. Sorry, Aria." He stepped into a jog as Aria helplessly bounced along, her eyes never leaving Taion's until they were out of sight into the tunnel again.

Taion waited another minute to make sure they were well and gone and then he turned back to the barrier and the darkness. He stepped forward and pressed his hand against the barrier and the darkness stopped, intrigued as it swirled in front of Taion's face.

"You should be scared, little Night King. I'm going to make you kill every single person you love, and I'll laugh while you drink their blood for me."

Taion glared at the darkness, his iridescent eyes swirling. "I forgot for a moment who I was, darkness, for I am also my mother's child. It's you who should be scared of me."

With a battle cry, Taion shattered the barrier and lunged at the darkness.

At the edge of the eastern entrance, Atmos paused, his gaze sweeping across the cold landscape. He took a deep breath, the wind whipping through his hair, carrying the scent of pine and something faintly metallic. He looked back towards the dark tunnel one more time, his eyes searching for Taion, any indication that he could turn around and help.

As he waited another 30 seconds, he sighed. With a grim determination, he pushed off the ledge. Aria, clinging to him with a desperate grip, cursed him with a torrent of fury.

"I hate you, Atmos!" she screamed, her voice raw with fear and anger. "You're a coward! A godsdamned jerk!"

Atmos flinched, her words cutting through the wind like shards of ice. He tried to ignore her, to focus on guiding them through the treacherous air currents, but the sting of her words lingered, a bitter taste in his mouth.

He knew she was angry, terrified, and understandably so. He tried to remember that, to remind himself that her harsh words were born from fear, not malice.

He had to focus. They were falling, the ground rushing towards them with terrifying speed. He spread his wings, the wind rushing beneath them, lifting them momentarily.

As they coasted over the landscape, he watched to find the rest of the Clans where they had converged and created a temporary stronghold. In the distance he could see the smoke from their fire and he flapped his wings, heading towards the old Willowgreen keep.

As he landed and gently put Aria on the ground, she turned and smacked him across his face. She stood her ground as Atmos reached up and touched the sting, his eyes never leaving hers. His eyes widened as he watched the emotion swirling in her golden eyes.

She was in love with Taion; how could he have missed that? Atmos swallowed hard as his eyes looked over Aria's head, a soft nod to Aria to let her know to hide her feelings. She turned around to see Theo walking through the encampment, a bright smile on his face.

"Aria! There you are! I was just coming to rescue you myself." He patted her on the shoulder and kissed her, his eyes darkening as he looked Atmos over.

"I guess I have you to thank for bringing back my wife to me.

Theo smiled and offered his hand. Atmos looked at it and scoffed, walking away before he decided to plant a fist in Theo's face.

He stormed through the encampment, leaving Aria and Theo behind. He was looking for where they would have set up the alcohol. After that adventure, he needed a drink and a nap; in what order, he didn't care. All of the work that he had done to try and ensure the darkness didn't take another, gone. He had failed.

Atmos rubbed the back of his neck as he stood at the makeshift bar. He lifted his finger, and the barmaid placed a flagon of ale in front of him. "You look like you could use it," she said, her smile tinged with a sadness that mirrored his own.

He grunted in acknowledgment, bringing the large vessel to his lips. He took a long sip, the ale burning a welcome warmth in his throat. But as he swallowed, a hand clamped down on his shoulder, causing him to cough violently, the ale spraying across his face.

Spluttering, he turned around to meet his mate's eyes. Ephyra, looked back at him, her expression unreadable.

He coughed again, wiping the beer off his face with the back of his sleeve. He looked at her, his gaze searching hers for any sign of judgment, of the lingering fear that had haunted their relationship since the Nightsinger had reared its head again.

She looked him up and down, her gaze lingering on his face. Then, with a gentle hand, she pulled him into a hug. He embraced her, burying his face in her hair, the scent of rain and woodsmoke filling his senses. He sighed, a heavy sigh that seemed to shake him to his very core.

"I'm sorry, my love," he confessed, his voice rough with emotion. "For everything."

She pulled back, her eyes searching his. "I know, Atmos. I know." She gave him a light tap on the chest, her touch a comfort, a reassurance. "But we're here, we will figure it out."

"The Eldatárs and Elentáris would like to debrief," she said, nodding her head towards the large tent in the middle of the encampment.

Atmos sighed, rolling his shoulders in an attempt to ease the tension that had settled deep within his muscles.

They made their way through the encampment, Atmos sniffing himself and groaning as he realized he smelled all sorts of awful. He would have a bath after the debrief; a couple of hours of solitude and he'd start to figure out a new plan.

As they stepped into the large tent, the Kings and Queens were all huddled over a long table- pointing and discussing quietly. Atmos walked into the room, and they all stopped talking to look at him.

Damien stood up and walked around the table, approaching Atmos. He smiled and gently bowed. "We had no idea, Atmos."

Atmos flushed and a wave of self-consciousness coursed through him, "Please, don't bow. I don't deserve…"

Carwyn stopped him, holding his hand up as he walked up to Atmos, "You deserve that and more. You saved our children, Atmos. For that alone, we are all in your debt."

Atmos watched as they all bowed to him. He swallowed thickly as he nodded his head back to them all. Carwyn stepped forward and pulled Atmos into an embrace. As he pulled back, they pressed their foreheads together and Carwyn whispered, "For helping Puck find himself, I owe you another debt."

Atmos closed his eyes and nodded as they pulled apart. Carwyn smacked Atmos on the shoulder and walked back to the table, beckoning him to follow. As they stepped up to the table, Atmos could see the layout of the mountain and the city of Tenebris.

Annika and Sarya were discussing some of the rooms that they had seen in the castle and Saphielle was standing off in the tent, Hagen softly rubbing her arms as she looked up at him, their discussion quiet.

Atmos quietly glanced at them, wondering if Saphielle had figured out the same thing he had; that Hagen's sister was skirting a dangerous line. She was married and in love with another.

Theo and Aria walked into the tent and Saphielle and Hagen turned to look at them. Atmos watched as Hagen's face became unreadable as he pulled away from Saphielle. She tried to grab his arm as he walked towards Aria and Theo.

Theo grinned and reached his arm out to offer his hand to Hagen and Hagen looked down at it then back at Theo. Without warning, he pulled back and punched Theo. They all gasped as they watched Theo's feet lift and he fell a few feet away from where he had been standing.

Blood gushed from Theo's nose as he sputtered, his hand instinctively reaching to touch his face. "What the hells, Hagen!" he roared, his voice a guttural growl. "You broke my nose, you bastard!"

He spat into the dirt, his face contorted with a mixture of pain and confusion. Hagen, his golden eyes flashing with a dangerous light, took a step towards him, his fists clenched.

But before he could take another step, Atmos and Carwyn intervened, their combined strength restraining him. Hagen, his eyes still burning with rage, glared at Theo, his face contorted with a venomous scowl. "You're the bastard, you woman beater." he spat, his voice dripping with contempt.

Theo's face fell, the confusion in his eyes vanishing completely. He scrambled to his feet, his movements surprisingly agile for a man of his size. Aria, rooted to the spot, watched the scene with a mixture of fear and disbelief. Her eyes darted between Theo and Atmos, her mind reeling.

Atmos, sensing her distress, subtly shook his head, a warning glint in his eyes. Aria, understanding the unspoken message, remained where she stood, her body trembling slightly.

Saphielle, her face a mask of fury, crossed her arms over her chest and walked towards Theo. "Release him," she commanded, her voice a low growl. "Now."

Theo smirked, a chilling display of arrogance. "You think you're all tough, all these mighty Eldatárs," he sneered, his gaze sweeping across the assembled monarchs. "But you let your women tell you what to do, just like that. Pathetic."

Carwyn, his face a mask of thunder, chuckled, a low, dangerous sound. "You've really done it good, you idiot," he growled, his voice a low rumble. "The women are our equals. You'd have figured that out if you had spent any time with us. We are only as strong as the women who stand beside us."

Saphielle stepped towards Theo, her eyes burning with a cold fury.

Hagen, sensing the rising tension, tensed, his golden eyes narrowing, molten with the rage that simmered beneath the surface.

"We won't finish you," Saphielle said, her voice a silken whisper that held the promise of unimaginable pain. "You'll spend time waiting to see when judgment will be passed, Theo. You'll look over your shoulder every day, wondering when the time will come that your depraved deeds will be called to account."

She looked him up and down, her gaze contemptuous. "Aria deserves better," she declared. "She always did."

With a final, chilling glance at Theo, Saphielle turned and walked towards Aria, pulling her close. Aria, still shaken but finding strength in her sister in law's presence, leaned into her embrace as she looked back at Theo. They walked back towards the table, leaving Theo standing alone in the center of the room.

Theo laughed, "Aria is my wife, she belongs to me. No marriage contract has ever been broken before in Tir Siorghlas. I'd like to see you do it now."

Saphielle responded without turning her back, "I'm certain Aria can make that decision if she so wishes it." She rubbed Aria's arm and quietly started to talk to Alyndria, Annika and Sarya. Aria looked over at Theo again, her teeth worrying her bottom lip.

Theo stood by the door, his hands clenched at his sides. "Aria," he commanded, his voice a low growl, "you are to come with me now. We're going home."

Hagen, standing beside his sister, frowned. He shook his head, a silent warning to Aria. Aria looked at Hagen, her eyes wide with apprehension. Their sibling bond, a powerful connection forged over years of shared experiences, twinged painfully. She could feel the pull towards Theo, a strange, unsettling urge to obey his command, tightening around her chest uncomfortably.

With a heavy sigh, she hung her head and began to walk towards him. Theo, sensing her hesitation, grabbed her arm, his grip surprisingly strong. He glared at the assembled monarchs, daring them to intervene.

Alyndria, her face a mask of fury, stepped forward. "Now is not the time, little nymph," Silvan whispered, his voice low and dangerous. He placed a restraining hand on Alyndria's shoulder, holding her back. "We will need to make a plan to rescue her, so that she is safe."

Theo, a triumphant smirk playing on his lips, roughly pulled Aria out of the tent, dragging her behind him as he strode away. He disappeared with her into the encampment, leaving the assembled monarchs in stunned silence. The air crackled with tension, the men shifting on their feet as they pondered the situation.

Aria, trapped in Theo's iron grip, felt a wave of despair wash over her. She had been captured, not once, but twice. And this time, she feared, the consequences would be far more devastating now that they all knew what Theo was doing to her behind closed doors.

Chapter Thirty Six

Willowgreen Lands

Alyndria waited patiently, her brilliant green eyes drawn to Osian as he engaged in a quiet conversation with Damien. Approaching him, she gently placed her hand on his arm. "Osian, can we speak privately?"

He paused, his eyes searching hers for any unspoken clues. "Of course," he replied, turning to Damien with a brief nod. "Be back in a moment."

Damien, left to his own devices, turned to Silvan. "How is she adjusting to your limitations, friend?" he inquired, gesturing towards Alyndria and Osian, who were now conversing in hushed tones, her hands gesturing animatedly as Osian gently placed a comforting hand on her shoulder.

Silvan sighed, a melancholic expression gracing his features. "I'm not sure, Damien. I don't regret the bargain I struck with Death, it saved her life. Alyndria is a strong leader, and I know she will rule the Clan wisely when the time comes. But she's been quiet since she witnessed my... mortality."

"I can't say I fully understand how either of you are coping," Damien admitted, his voice laced with genuine concern.

Alyndria returned, a soft smile gracing her lips. She gently pulled Silvan towards her, their fingers intertwining. "All is well, my love," he murmured, his gaze following Osian as he exited the tent. "How is Osian truly faring since his encounter with the Baobhan Sith?"

Alyndria looked up at him, a thoughtful expression on her face. "Surprisingly upbeat," she mused. "It seems little can truly dampen his spirits."

She leaned up and kissed Silvan on the cheek, pulling away from him. She followed the path of Osian, walking out of the tent alone. Silvan, Damien and Hagen watched.

"What are those two scheming, do you think?" Hagen pondered.

"Who knows," Silvan chuckled. He walked over to a chair and sat down, taking the weight off of his back. The aches and pains that came with the mortal body were shocking. No longer could he ride his horse for as long as he used to or run as fast. It was both humbling and embarrassing trying to keep up with his friends.

Alyndria stood outside of the tent beside Osian. He whispered a request to the goddesses and suddenly in front of them stood Aine.

She smiled and ran to Osian, wrapping her arms around his neck as they kissed. Alyndria smiled, this was why he was ok. He'd found himself a new woman already.

As if reading her mind, Aine turned to Alyndria, "I'm not new, Alyndria, Queen of the water, I am older than the cosmos. I am the air you breathe into your lungs. And, I'm also Osian's first love and Orin's mother."

Alyndria's eyes widened. "I meant no disrespect. Truly." She bowed to Aine.

"Osian tells me that you have a request, Alyndria?" Aine inquired. Alyndria nodded and swallowed hard.

Osian cleared his throat and walked away, "I'll be in the tent if you need me."

Alyndria watched him walk away and then she faced Aine again. "As you are aware, Death made a bargain with Silvan, my husband, to save my life. Had I been alive, I would have told him to not bargain what he did."

Aine nodded thoughtfully, "Yes, he gave his powers up to Death as payment for not taking your life."

Alyndria nodded, "I would like for his immortal life to be restored, Goddess. What do I have to do or give for that?"

Aine mused, stroking her chin thoughtfully, "That is quite a heavy ask, I'd have to pull his immortal life from my sister." She paused.

"I can sense what you desire so strongly. It's a sweet taste on my lips. Would you be willing to sacrifice that desire for the return of his immortal life? I think that would be a sufficient trade."

Alyndria, her face pale but resolute, nodded wordlessly. Aine stepped closer, "May I?" Alyndria nodded again. Closing her eyes, Alyndria felt Aine's palm press gently against her belly. A sharp pain, a wrenching sensation, erupted low in her pelvis, forcing a gasp from her lips.

Aine stepped back, her eyes drawn to the commotion inside the tent. Shouts and cries echoed from beyond. Alyndria opened her eyes, her hand instinctively moving to cradle her aching belly. She bowed her head, a silent tribute. "I wish I had more to offer, Goddess. Thank you."

She rushed into the tent, her heart pounding. Silvan stood tall, the grey hair at his temples vanished, replaced by a vibrant auburn. Magick shimmered around him as he flexed his fingers, a newfound strength radiating from him.

He frowned as he walked up to her, his gaze fixed on her face, his hands gently shaking her arms. "What did you barter, nymph?"

She smiled, tears welling up in her eyes. "We will be barren, but we will have each other," she whispered, her voice thick with emotion.

Silvan's eyes welled up with tears. He pulled her close, holding her tightly, his heart overflowing with gratitude and a profound sense of loss.

Their friends watched, a hush falling over the tent. They all stood in stunned silence, witnessing the depth of Alyndria and Silvan's love for each other.

Chapter Thirty Seven

3 months later in Oblor

Aria stood looking out through the tall windows of their residence, her eyes drawn to the bustling activity in the streets below. Theo had moved them closer to the city center and further away from the watchful eyes of the castle. She looked up, her gaze drawn to the distant silhouette of the castle, a pang of longing twisting in her chest.

It had been months since she'd seen any of them, months of suffocating isolation. News from Tenebris had gone cold; no updates, no messages, as if a shield had been erected around the mountain, cutting the night realm off from the rest of Tir Siorghlas.

Since they came back, Theo had been acting strangely, a shadow of the man she had fallen in love with. He was possessive, his moods shifting erratically, his words laced with a chilling possessiveness. He would often pace the room, muttering to himself, his eyes gleaming with an unsettling intensity.

Each time his hand connected with her, a possessive touch that would quickly escalate into something more, Aria closed her eyes and dreamt of dancing under the fairy lights, Taion's arms around her, his smile lighting up his face as they twirled.

But those were just dreams, fleeting moments of happiness in a life that had become a gilded cage. She turned away from the window, the last image she had of Taion haunting her. She had to find a way to break free.

Every night she would desperately pray to the goddesses to help her, but her pleas were unanswered. She had all but given up at that point, resigning herself to the abuse.

Theo had been right- not a single marriage contract had ever been nullified before in Tir Siorghlas between the Royals. Their contract was sealed and witnessed; she couldn't break it.

She felt him walk into the room and stiffened as she felt the presence of him behind her, preparing herself for his hand to connect with her. She wrapped her arms around herself, waiting, wondering what was taking him so long until she heard him speak.

"Why are you flinching like that, little firecracker?" her eyes flew open as the deep voice softly asked. She whirled around and standing in front of her was Taion, his grey wings tucked behind him, wearing a white tunic and dark pants, his long black hair pulled back in braids. He was wearing a couple of rings on his right hand and an iron bracelet. A vial was tied around his neck.

His iridescent eyes flashed as he looked her over, taking in the bruises on her arms and neck. He stepped forward and gently traced the outline of one that splashed across her collarbone, and she heard him growl.

"Who did that?" The undercurrent was ice cold. The rage flooded through Taion as his eyes connected with Aria's. She looked at him, her golden eyes wide with worry as she whispered, "Please, Taion." She whimpered as she looked over to the open door, praying Theo wouldn't step through.

Taion stepped back, his face a mask of murderous rage as he followed her line of sight, the empty doorway. He turned back and asked, "Your husband did that to you?" and he frowned as she slowly nodded.

His vision blurred red with rage. Before he knew what he was doing, he stormed across the room, his voice booming through the small chateau, "Theo, show your face, you coward!" He wasn't waiting for Theo to show himself, he'd find the bastard and leave pieces of him spread through Tir Siorghlas at this point. "I'll kill him."

Aria ran after Taion, "He's not here! He's... I don't know where he is." Taion swung around and Aria fell into his arms. He couldn't stop himself; he gently pulled her to him and stroked her red hair as she rested her cheek on his chest, her hands pressed together against them. She shut her eyes and breathed in deeply; he smelled of the mountains and trees, fresh outdoors and grass... She sighed and melted into him as he gently placed a kiss on the top of her head.

"We have a lot to discuss, but I'm not doing that until this matter is settled." He gently pulled her away, his gaze intense. "You," he said, his voice low and urgent, "you need to head to your brother's castle, and now. Do not look back, do not stop until you are there. They are waiting for you."

Aria frowned, confused. "What do you mean, Taion?" she asked, her brows knit together.

Taion gently guided her towards the door, his touch surprisingly gentle. With a wave of his hand, the shimmering barrier that had encased the room began to waver and then, with a snap disappeared.

Shocked, Aria watched as the last ripples of magick dissolved into the air. "They couldn't find you, Aria," he explained, his voice a low murmur. "Theo used a witch to put up a powerful barrier around the chateau, effectively isolating you from the rest of the world."

"But how did you find me then?" she asked, her heart pounding in her chest, hoping he felt the same way about her as she did him.

He smiled, a rueful smile that reached his eyes as they swirled with love. "Because we are bound, little firecracker," he said, his voice a low growl.

With a final, lingering look, he snapped his fingers, and a surge of power transported her a short distance from the castle gates. She stumbled as her feet touched the cobblestones, disoriented by the sudden displacement. But then, she saw it – the familiar silhouette of Castle Leyebourne.

A cry escaped her lips as she scrambled to her feet, her heart pounding with relief. She lifted her dress and ran towards the castle gates, her footsteps echoing through the fading light.

The guards, startled by her sudden appearance, pushed the heavy doors open with a shout. Hagen, Saphielle, and her parents came rushing towards her, their faces etched with worry.

Aria, tears streaming down her face, ran into their embrace. She was home.

The setting sun started to cast long shadows across the sitting room, painting the velvet curtains in hues of crimson and gold. Taion sat in the front room of the chateau, the silence broken only by the ticking of a clock and the rhythmic clinking of ice against glass. His leg was resting on his knee, a forgotten battle wound throbbing a dull ache.

He had helped himself to the finest alcohol in the house, the cabinet door now hanging precariously from a single hinge, a testament to his earlier frustration. He swirled the amber liquid in the crystal glass, the ice cubes clinking melodically, and took a long drink, the fiery liquor burning a welcome warmth in his throat.

He rested the glass on the arm of the chair, his other hand tapping a restless rhythm against the polished wood, counting the minutes that seemed to crawl by with agonizing slowness.

He heard footsteps, a soft thud against the thick rug, but didn't move. He knew who it was. Atmos cleared his throat, the sound breaking the heavy silence. "Taion," he said, his voice low and cautious.

Atmos walked in, his gaze sweeping the room, his posture alert. He bowed slightly, his wings flexing slightly behind him, a silent display of respect and a subtle reminder of his brother's power. He pulled a chair up beside Taion, flipping it around and resting his arms on the back, relaxing as he looked at him. Taion nodded and took another sip of the alcohol.

"Do we have much longer to wait?" Atmos inquired as he looked at the doorway.

Taion shrugged, "I'll wait a lifetime if that's what it takes."

Atmos nodded and clicked his tongue.

More footsteps fell across the landing and Puck sauntered into the room, his hair dishevelled, a mischievous grin on his face. He bowed slightly at Taion who returned a smile at his little brother. Puck walked over and sat down to the right of him, tucking his wings in as he leaned on the settee.

"Everything has been done, Puck?" Taion asked as he looked at him.

Puck smiled, "All done, tied up in a neat bow, Night Eldatár."

Taion chuckled, "Brother. Don't be starting that now."

Puck smiled and crossed his arms behind his head and relaxed on the settee.

"We might be here for a while, Theo was busy at the tavern from the last spy report." Puck responded.

Taion grunted, "We can wait."

The sun continued to set, and the men stayed, unmoving as the room slowly descended into darkness.

Just as Puck started to feel restless, they heard the front door open and then close. Footsteps echoed through the chateau; up the stairs where they could hear Theo curse, then back down the stairs as he rushed into the dark room. As he lit the lanterns in the room, his eyes landed on the three winged men sitting in the centre of the room.

He stopped moving and he sneered, "What are you doing trespassing in my house, Nephilim." He spat and curled his lip at the word.

Puck went to stand up and Taion lifted his left hand, stopping Puck. Puck sat back down and watched his brother.

"You'll address me as the Night Eldatár." Taion quietly responded, his iridescent eyes calculating as Theo stood in the doorway.

Theo scoffed, "Am I supposed to be scared of you three? You're nothing but a virus on Tir Siorghlas..." he paused, "Why are you here? I have no quarrel with you."

Taion licked his lips and narrowed his eyes as he willed himself to stay calm, "I have a quarrel with you, Theo. When you decided to lay your hands on the woman I'm bound to, I became your problem."

Theo stepped back, his eyebrows raising as he started to laugh, "Who are you bound to, Nephilim, why it wouldn't be my wife would it? What's the irony in that? Bound to something you'll never have." He sneered as the last part left his mouth.

Taion stood up and flexed his wings as he slowly walked towards Theo. Theo swallowed hard and stepped back as Taion got closer. Theo's back hit the wall and Taion stopped, bending down slightly so he could look directly into Theo's brown eyes.

"You cannot expect her to love you, to want to be with you, when you keep her in a cage, clip her wings and lay your hands on her. She will be free, she will find the sky again." He paused.

"You will never lay another finger on her again, Theo. I promise you that. As a matter of fact, killing you isn't out of the question." He raised his hand and watched as Theo flinched, scrunching his eyes closed as he waited for Taion to hit him.

"Lucky for you," Taion muttered, "We don't hurt defenceless creatures."

Theo waited for the pain and when he realized he wasn't going to get punched he opened his eyes and straightened up, looking around at an empty room.

Taion, Atmos and Puck soared over Oblor, their wings gently coasting over the breeze from the mountains. Puck chortled with laughter as he recounted watching Theo freeze and scrunch up.

"I'm almost sure he peed himself, Taion! Did you see that Atmos?" Puck barrel rolled in the sky, his laughter echoing through the air.

Atmos shook his head and looked over at his brother, "Taion, what's going through your mind?"

Taion flapped his wings, silently thinking about the next steps that had to happen in order for Aria to be free. Spy reports to the Night King had revealed a disturbing truth: Theo, fueled by jealousy and a lust for power, had been amassing an army outside the city limits, plotting to overthrow Hagen and Saphielle.

His first mate, Frig, and the crew had posed as mercenaries, ready and willing to help take down a monarchy. Theo, blinded by ambition and a thirst for power, had eagerly embraced the offer, detailing his plans with chilling clarity. He was relying on elves and witches with power to do his bidding, unaware that he was playing into their hands.

For it had been revealed that Theo possessed no powers of his own. He had merely posed as a distant royal, a charismatic and charming facade concealing his true nature: a cunning opportunist who had married Aria for power and influence.

As they landed near the forest of Oblor, Taion whistled and out of the darkness, Frig and the crew materialized. They approached Taion, grinning and bowing theatrically as they teased Taion. Atmos and Puck watched as Taion laughed with the crew and playfully shoved some of them. There was a long history with the crew, and it showed.

Puck smiled and nudged Atmos, "It's nice to see him smile, you know."

Atmos nodded and crossed his arms, keeping his eyes peeled for anyone approaching.

"Theo sent a missive today, the attack is supposed to happen tomorrow, in broad daylight of all times. The man is crazy." Frig shook his head. "He wants it public so that it's obvious that he wasn't involved, which, I give credit, is smart."

One of the crew members stepped forward, "Do we get to gut the bastard when it's time?" he growled, his dagger shining in the moonlight.

Taion grinned, "We'll make sure he winds up where he belongs, Jep."

The crew cheered and Taion chuckled. As he turned to look back at his brothers he smiled at them, a genuine smile.

Puck and Atmos blinked in shock. "Do you think he loves us?" Puck whispered out of the side of his mouth at Atmos. "That looked like a 'I love my brother' smile." Atmos groaned and rolled his eyes, shoving Puck as Puck chortled.

Since Puck had grown into his new identity, the shy young man had morphed into a self-assured, sometimes pain in the ass, but happy young half Nephilim half mage. Atmos was proud to see his young brother standing strong and confident.

He looked over as Taion walked towards them, the crew fading back into the forest again to wait for Theo's signal. "We wait now, brothers." Taion said as he clapped them both on the backs, gathering them to his side as they walked together.

Atmos felt his heart clench; maybe after all this was done, they'd be able to sit down and discuss being a family. It was almost within reach.

Taion turned around and laid out the instructions one more time, "Puck, you're going to have the advantage, Theo doesn't know exactly who you are, so he won't realize that you're from Clan Basalt until it's too late. Use your powers wisely, use Atlas if you need to as well, but make sure that you transport the royal family out of the castle at the right time to avoid arousing suspicion. Carwyn and Sarya will be waiting for them at your home."

Puck nodded. "I've got this, brother."

Taion turned to Atmos, "You need to ensure that there are no innocent people in the way of Theo's wrath once he finds out he's been duped. I don't want someone in his line of fire. We don't know what tricks he has up his sleeve. He's now a desperate man."

Atmos nodded back at him, "Yes, Taion. We've got this."

Taion nodded, rubbing the back of his neck, almost as if he was trying to reassure himself. This was the first time he had planned a mission on his own, the first time someone he truly loved was in the line of danger. He couldn't afford to falter now.

"Our plan is to capture him, not kill him. Hagen and Saphielle will be the ones to determine his punishment."

Atmos mused as he watched Taion. They all knew what needed to be done to break the marriage bond, yet Taion was still focussed on protecting everyone, not moving forward to kill Theo to gain access to Aria. It was admirable.

All three of them stepped out of the forest together and took flight.

Chapter Thirty Eight

Oblor

The first rays of dawn peeked through the curtains and Aria stirred, blinking against the sudden intrusion of light. She stretched, her muscles protesting from her deep sleep, the scent of lavender and sunshine filling her nostrils.

Sitting up, she remembered she was in her old room, the stuffed animals haphazardly strewn across the floor that her mother had refused to get rid of when she left. A wave of relief washed over her. She had escaped the nightmare, hopefully forever.

She crawled out of bed, her bare feet touching the cool stone floor. A shiver ran down her spine, a lingering echo of the fear and cold that had clung to her for so long.

She walked towards the bathing room: her gaze lingering on the familiar objects – her perfumes scattered along the counter, the faded floral rug, the embroidered slippers left by the door. It felt surreal, like stepping back into a forgotten dream, it felt safe.

She reached the in-floor tub and waved her hand over it, a silent command activating the magick that filled the room with warm, fragrant water. As she slipped into the soothing embrace of the bath, she winced as the hot water touched some of the newer bruises that marred her skin, grim reminders of her captivity.

But even through the pain, a sense of peace settled in her. She was home. Safe. Free.

And for the first time in what felt like an eternity, hope, a fragile but persistent spark, began to flicker within her. She closed her eyes and leaned her head back with a happy sigh. Maybe she would be able to see Taion again.

Hands threaded through her hair and she stopped cold. "You look like you did back when we first started courting." Theo mused as he carefully massaged Aria's scalp. Aria's hands clenched around the tub as she tried to hold back a sob in the back of her throat.

"Funny, I was just thinking about our wedding night. It's been a while since we've had that much fun. What do you think, Aria? Or are you now just a whore for the Nephilim army?"

With a growl, he pulled Aria up by her hair. Aria cried out as she tried to grab Theo's arm to release her. He dragged her across the stone floor, her delicate skin scraping across the floor as she grabbed her hair to release some of the pain of him pulling her.

"Theo, you're hurting me! Please!" she begged. She realized that she was at the point of no return.

She blindly swung out, trying to find something to hit Theo with. She knew that this time, she wouldn't come out of it alive. Theo's face was contorted in murderous rage as he bent down and looked at Aria, his eyes small pinpoints of darkness.

"You slut. You opened your mouth and now look what happened." He stood and kicked her in the ribs. Aria cried out, curling into a ball from the pain. "Our little happy ending, ruined, all because of you. I hope losing your family was worth spreading your legs for that filth." He spit beside her as he swung again, connecting with Aira's head.

She recoiled from the contact and her eyes lost focus as they faded to black.

Theo's chest heaved with the exertion of dragging Aria into the bedroom. He sneered as he looked at her, passed out on the floor. A thought crossed his mind, but he shook his head and wiped his face with the back of his arm before he stormed out of the room. She was tainted goods now.

As he walked down the hallway, he looked into the bedroom to confirm that Aria's parents, Cohnal and Salihn were still laying where he had killed them. With a grin he nodded as he confirmed the lifeless stares from their bodies. Two down, two more...well, three to go. Then he'd have to hurt himself somehow and let the guards know that there had been an assassination attempt by the Night King to kill the entire Emberlin family. Only Aria and he would survive. He'd have to figure out a way to bind Aria's tongue after this though, it would do no good to have her talking.

He walked further down the hallway, trying to remember which rooms Hagen and Saphielle had taken now that they were the crowned King and Queen for Clan Bayle. As he pushed the doors opened to the last room, he grinned as Saphielle swung around, her eyes wide as she realized Theo was in the castle.

"What do you think you're doing, entering the private chambers of the Eldatár and Elentári unannounced, Theo? Guards!" Saphielle called. Theo slowly walked towards her, his fists clenching and unclenching as he thought about what he'd do to the royal bitch once he had his hands on her.

As he lunged, Saphielle threw her hands up, lightning flashing down as it connected with Theo, throwing him across the room. He rolled until he hit the wall and Saphielle gathered her skirts, running through the doors and down the hallway, screaming for the guards.

As she ran, she saw two guards, unconscious on the ground outside Aria's room. She gasped and pushed the door open, falling and crawling to the floor, sobbing, as she found Aria naked and bleeding on the floor beside her bed.

"Oh, melethel," Saphielle cried as she carefully touched Aria's face, checking to see if she was still breathing. When Aria's breath warmed

Saphielle's palm, she breathed a sigh of relief and pulled her to her body, shifting to slide under the bed as she heard footprints coming closer.

Just as her foot disappeared under the bed, Theo's voice echoed through the room.

"Where did the two royal bitches end up disappearing to?" He mused as he walked around. Saphielle closed her eyes and prayed frantically to the goddesses to protect them. As she mouthed every prayer she could think of, the room went silent, and she could hear Theo's breathing.

He suddenly walked out of the bedroom and started to talk to someone. Saphielle wished with all of her being that Hagen hadn't been called to council in Oblor, that he was home. She pulled Aria tighter to her and waited under the bed.

Puck was out of breath as he flew as hard as he could to the checkpoint, Atlas hot on his heels. The plan was failing before his eyes and he had to let Atmos and Taion know that Theo was in the castle, alone and the family was still there. He called out as he saw Taion standing in the field beside Atmos.

"Taion! Atmos! Help!"

As he swung low and tried to land, he slammed into Atmos and Taion, knocking them off their feet. As Puck landed in a heap, he was trying to breathe out what was happening to Atmos and Taion as they hauled him up.

"Theo... he changed the plans! He's in the castle now! I found Hagen and told him. Hagen is heading back but it might be too late!" Puck deeply breathed and started to run back towards Oblor.

Taion's eyes widened in surprise, a jolt of adrenaline coursing through him. He rushed forward, his wings a blur of motion as he soared past Puck, the wind whistling in his ears. Atmos, a blur of black feathers and fury, followed close behind.

Taion flew like a man possessed, his mind a whirlwind of fear and determination. As the castle came into view, he dove down, the wind screaming past him as he narrowly missed the towering stone walls, landing with a thud in the courtyard. Dust rose around him as he scrambled to his feet, his heart pounding a frantic rhythm against his ribs.

He burst through the oak doors, the heavy wood splintering under the force of his assault. Guards, scattered and disoriented, stared at him in stunned disbelief, some of them groggy, some still unconscious. How had a single elf, a weak courtesan, manage to cause this much damage in such a short amount of time?

Taion ignored them, his eyes scanning the room, searching for any sign of Aria. He sprinted up the grand staircase, his boots pounding against the stone steps, each step bringing him closer to his destination.

As he reached the landing, his eyes met Theo's. Theo, his face pale but defiant, grinned, a chilling predator's grin. He crooked his finger at Taion, a silent invitation to approach.

Taion, his blood pounding in his veins, took the bait. He lunged forward, a whirlwind of motion, his claws extended, ready to strike.

Chapter Thirty Nine

Oblor

What happened next took everyone by surprise. Taion lunged at Theo who flung his hands up and a dark current shot out of his palms, connecting with Taion.

It flung Taion back as he yelled in pain, twin burn marks on his shoulders. He looked up, shock etched on his face as he realized that Theo had made a bargain with some dark entity to gain that kind of magick.

Theo gleefully laughed as he walked towards Taion, taunting, "You're not so tough now, are you, Night 'King'." He kicked Taion who rolled with momentum and got up off the ground, wincing at the pain shooting through his shoulders.

Atmos and Puck burst through the castle doors, Hagen hot on their heels. Theo, a cruel smile playing on his lips, watched Taion approach with a chilling indifference. He raised his hand, a gesture of mocking defiance, as if daring Taion to stop him.

Taion, a whirlwind of motion, soared through the air, his eyes locked on Theo. He dove, a feathered missile, intent on killing the man, fire, like lava, pouring out of his hands towards Theo.

The air around them crackled with energy, the clash of their wills palpable. Theo raised his hands, a dark energy coalescing around him. A wave of pure, malevolent power erupted from his hands, colliding with Taion's assault.

The impact was devastating. The room shook, shattering the windows and sending furniture crashing to the floor. The air itself seemed to crackle and split, the very fabric of reality tearing at the seams from the unrestrained use of magick in a smaller space.

Taion, undeterred, fought back, his own power a raging storm. Lightning crackled between them, their clash a symphony of destruction.

Below, Atmos and Puck watched the battle unfold, their faces grim as Hagen looked around for a way to stop them before they brought the castle down around them.

Just as Hagen reached the epicentre of the fight, Taion, distracted by Hagen's shout turned, surprise on his face as he registered Hagen was back.

"Hagen! Find the women! We need to make sure they're ok!" As he turned back towards Theo, he grunted and his jaw clenched. Taion's eyes widened in disbelief as he looked down.

Blood, a crimson stain against the white of his tunic, was blossoming around the sword protruding from his chest. Theo stood in front of him, the sword still embedded in Taion's flesh, his face a mask of satisfaction.

A strangled gasp escaped Taion's lips as he stumbled back, his knees buckling beneath him. He clutched at the sword hilt, his fingers trembling. The world tilted, the colors swirling around him. He tried to fight it, to stay upright, but the pain was searing, consuming. He flung his hand towards Theo, his fire magick fizzling from his fingertips. He couldn't feel anything.

He slumped, his vision blurring. The world tilted, the colors swirling into an abyss. He tried to reach out, to call out to Aria, but the sound died in his throat. Darkness, a welcome oblivion, was already creeping in at the edges of his vision. He saw Atmos fling his arms up towards Theo, dimly registering that Theo's body shuddered and contorted, as if his life force was being sucked out of him. Taion closed his eyes slowly, he was so tired and cold.

He could hear shouts as he felt someone grab his body, strong arms pulling him as he felt the breeze dance across his face. Everything was happening in slow motion as Puck and Atmos laid him down on the grass in the castle courtyard, Atmos running back to the castle, guards on his heels.

Hagen yelled for the healers as he ran through the castle instructing the guards to man the front gates and find his wife. He stormed up the stairs and ran down the hallway, calling for Saphielle, praying she was ok, that their babe was ok.

Saphielle heard Hagen's voice and sobbed with relief. She crawled out from under the bed, carefully pulling a sobbing Aria out. She crawled over to the armoire and pulled down a loose dressing gown, carefully pulling it over Aria's head to cover her. She pressed her lips against Aria's forehead as she pulled her to her, waiting for Hagen to find them.

Hagen entered the doorway, his eyes heavy with sorrow as he walked over and sat beside them, registering the bruises on his little sister, his wife's tear-streaked face. He gathered the women to him, cursing under his breath.

The air in the castle hung heavy with the metallic tang of blood and the cloying sweetness of fear. Dust motes danced in the single shaft of light piercing the gloom, illuminating the grisly scene before Atmos on the second floor.

Theo lay sprawled on the cold stone floor, his limbs twisted at unnatural angles. His eyes, once radiating with anger and hatred, now stared vacantly at the rough-hewn ceiling.

Atmos, his obsidian armor gleaming in the castle light, surveyed the scene with a grim satisfaction. Theo, the charlatan, the wife beater, was nothing more than a discarded shell, his life force extinguished with efficiency.

Atmos bent down and pulled out his blade. He pulled Theo's hair up and severed his head from his body with one swipe. It was a safety precaution to ensure that any lingering magick, any desperate attempt at a spectral return, would be utterly thwarted.

The air grew thick with the stench of decay almost instantly. Atmos, however, remained unfazed; he had faced death countless times, and he had always emerged victorious. He knelt beside the lifeless body, his gaze drawn to Theo's severed head, a grotesque mask of death frozen on his pale features.

A cruel smile touched his lips. He'd kill him all over again for touching his brothers. He'd destroy anyone who decided that they'd attempt to take them from him. He walked away, jogging down the stairs, running through the foyer and outside to where they were gathered on the grass.

Taion smiled as he saw Puck peer down at him, tears streaming down his face. Then Puck's face morphed into Aria's, her eyes taking him in, tears streaming down her face. Taion looked at her with wonder.

"Am I dreaming?" he whispered as he coughed, blood splattering his face as he tried to reach up to touch the red hair that he was so fond of. Aria sobbed, holding his hand to her face as she watched his eyes flutter closed, and his arm go limp.

Aria flung herself over his body and sobbed, her already broken heart shattering into pieces.

"No... no, no, no. Don't... don't leave me. Please, don't." Aria sobbed, "You can't... you just *can't*. You promised. You promised me that you were the right one. Remember? You promised forever. And... and this isn't forever. This isn't..." she shook her head, reaching out a trembling hand to touch his face, "You're cold. So cold. You're not supposed to be cold." she murmured as she stroked his face, trying to wipe off the blood, willing his beautiful iridescent eyes to open again.

"You're supposed to be... warm. Like... like our fire magick. Remember how you used to say that? That I was your firecracker?" she choked out a sob, "Well, the flames... my flames can't burn without you. They just... they just can't."

Aria reached over and rested her forehead against Taion. "Remember that day? The market? You thought of me and gave me that necklace... and you showed me what kindness was. And I forgot about everything else. Just for that moment. And I... I knew then. I knew that you were... you were the one. The only one, my heart bond. And I was so... so afraid to tell you. Afraid that I couldn't give you what you deserved. And now... now it's too late. It's too late."

She stroked his hair, her voice barely a whisper, "Come back, Taion. Please, come back to me. I'll... I'll do anything. Anything, I'll give up my immortal life. Just... just open your eyes. Just... just look at me. Tell me... tell me you love me too. Please."

She sobbed uncontrollably. "Don't... don't leave me alone. Don't leave me. I... I need you. I love you. Please..." Her voice trailed off into broken sobs as she clung to his body.

Saphielle stood nearby in Hagen's embrace, tears streaming down her face as she watched Aria and Taion, her heart breaking as she witnessed them, her hands clutched to her heart as Hagen stood watching, unable to do anything to pull the pain he could feel radiating off of his little sister.

Puck sat back, his legs splayed out on the ground as his shoulders slumped, Taion's lifeblood on his hands. He started to shake as tears rolled down his face. Atmos fell to his knees beside Taion and looked wordlessly as he tried to figure out where everything went so wrong. The clearing went silent, as if the earth was holding her breath.

"Aria, sweet child, I would have thought you would have figured out the gift that was bestowed on you or you wouldn't be crying over your true soul bond like this." Death tsked as she walked from across the courtyard, her black dress swirling around her, her eyes assessing the damage in the clearing.

Aria's head snapped up and she looked at Macha, the goddess of Death. She frowned as she sniffled and wiped the tears off of her face. She placed her hand over Taion's heart and looked at Macha.

"You never came. All that time I prayed for you, and you never came. Now you come? To take him?" her voice shook. "You won't take him. You can't." her sobs wracked her body as she gathered Taion's tunic in her fist. "He saved me. He was the only one who saw me, who saw my pain, and saved me."

Death sighed as she bent down beside Aria. "We can't answer every prayer, child. If we did, the world would be a very different place. It's bad enough that I keep finding myself being overly lenient and letting souls go back when their life has been stopped."

She gently touched Taion's forehead with the back of her fingers as she continued, "However, Aria, dear child, Aine gave you a gift. You may want to use it before it's too late and I am forced to take his soul with me."

Aria blinked rapidly as she looked at Death, stunned. "You mean, the gift was..."

Death nodded and softly smiled, "A life for a life. You saved the goddess, and she felt you were worth it. She saw you for who you are."

Aria gasped and she ran her hands over Taion's chest. "But how do I do it? Please tell me, Goddess. I can't lose him now." She looked up, her eyes begging Death to help.

Death gathered Aria's hands in hers and whispered, "Use your heart, child." And faded away.

Aria sobbed and she gently leaned over Taion's body, her lips gently pressing against his forehead, the same spot that Death had gently touched. As her lips touched his skin, a flush appeared and slowly spread down his face and through his body, the wound that the sword caused knitted up and left a small star shaped scar.

Taion felt his soul slam back into his body and his took a deep breath as Aria quickly sat back, surprise on her face as he opened his eyes and looked around.

"Taion! Oh my gods!" she screamed. Saphielle and Hagen stood, speechless as they had watched the interaction. They were now grinning, Saphielle covering her mouth as she sobbed tears of joy.

Puck and Atmos grabbed each other and waited as Taion turned over to look at all of them. They all watched as his eyes took Aria in, their iridescent blues and purples clouding over with tears as he pulled her to him, crushing his mouth to hers.

Puck scrunched his face up and looked at Atmos, "I think we might want to give them a bit of privacy. I like being close to my brother but not that close."

He scrambled up and walked into the castle, Atmos, chuckling as he followed behind. Saphielle, realizing that Taion and Aria had blocked everyone else out, pulled her husband to her and they followed into the castle as well.

"I want the healers to check you and the babe over, little fox," Hagen instructed as he guided her down the corridor towards the healers wing. Saphielle nodded, "I feel fine, but it wouldn't hurt to look. Hagen," she stopped walking, "what we witnessed... I've never seen anything like it."

Hagen nodded and placed his hand on the small of her back, gently guiding her to walk again.

"I imagine we may see more of Aine and Macha in the next while." Hagen chuckled and then stopped, realizing he had some work ahead of him. His parents needed to be buried, they needed to clean up the mess in the castle, fix some of the walls that had cracked from the magick battle on the second floor.

He brought Saphielle to the healers, nodding as they took her into the room.

"I'll be back shortly, little fox. I just need to do some cleaning."

Saphielle looked at him, sadness on her face, "I am truly sorry that I couldn't save your amil and amille, my love."

Hagen cleared his throat and softly smiled, "That was not for you to take on, Saphielle. You're safe. The babe is safe. That's what they would have wanted, if it meant them giving their lives up."

He walked back down the corridor, his mind swirling. As he turned towards the stairs, he sighed heavily. This would be the hardest thing he had ever had to do. Four guards followed him as they reached his parents' living quarters.

A healer stepped into the room, having silently followed. She bent down and checked Cohnal and Salihn, shaking her head to confirm their souls had left.

The guards carefully carried their bodies down the stairs, towards the rooms saved for moments like this. Their bodies would be prepared for a traditional funeral- a pyre lit with fire magick from their children to send them off to their next journey.

Hagen looked around as he walked down the stairs, the servants and guards bowing as he stepped onto the landing.

"Gods and goddesses, all hail the King of Clan Bayle."

As Taion pulled Aria back, he quickly checked her over, his hands checking for broken bones and bruises. Aria winced as he touched her, the damage from Theo evident on her body.

He frowned as he locked eyes with her, his hand carefully holding her chin as he fiercely whispered.

"He will NEVER be able to touch you again, a rúnsearc, my firecracker. No man will ever hurt you and live. I swear that to you."

Aria softly laughed and grabbed his hands, kissing them as she looked at him.

"I love you too, Taion." She whispered.

Taion chuckled and stood up carefully, pulling Aria with him. He realized that whatever she had done had left him feeling stronger than he had before. He mentally reminded himself to lay down some flowers and honey at their statues when he went back to Tenebris.

He scooped Aria into his arms as he walked around the castle, flexing his wings to ensure they would work and he grinned, taking flight. Aria squealed with delight as she clung to him.

He wanted to get her away for just a moment, to breathe, before they had to come back to reality and deal with what waited for her. The next while would not be easy, for any of them, as they picked up the pieces left behind.

Aine and Macha watched as Taion and Aria headed north away from the castle. Their eyes followed until they could no longer, and Macha turned to Aine, threading her arm through her sister's as they walked away from the castle.

"They always were my favourite," she giggled as they disappeared.

Chapter Forty

Two months previously—
Tenebris

Taion watched as Atmos ran with Aria in his arms, her cries as she realized what he was going to do echoing through the hallway as they entered the tunnel.

He turned back around, his eyes taking in the darkness as it shrieked and slammed itself against the magickal barrier. Taion counted another 60 seconds to ensure that Atmos and Aria were far enough away and then he dropped the barrier.

The air crackled with a malevolent energy, the Nightsinger surging towards Taion, its tendrils reaching out like grasping claws. Taion, his eyes narrowed, braced himself for the onslaught. This was it. This was the end.

But instead of fighting, instead of resisting, he did the unexpected. He dropped to his knees and opened his arms up. The Nightsinger, momentarily stunned by his unexpected acceptance, recoiled. Then, with a deafening roar, it surged forward, engulfing Taion in a suffocating embrace.

Taion, his eyes closed, awaited the inevitable. But instead of the expected pain, a strange calm descended upon him. He felt a sense of acceptance, a quiet resignation. Visions of his mother, her soft smile as she cuddled Taion in her arms, embraced in his father's arms. A family, full of love, full of light.

"I forgive you," he whispered, his voice barely a whisper against the howling wind of the Nightsinger.

The darkness, taken aback by his unexpected response, recoiled. It shrieked, a sound that almost split Taion's eardrums. Then, in the heart of the darkness, a blinding light began to form, a tiny spark that grew brighter, more intense with each passing second.

The Nightsinger struggled against the encroaching light, its tendrils lashing out in a desperate attempt to extinguish it. But the light grew stronger, expanding until it filled the entire room, pushing back the Nightsinger, consuming it.

Unable to withstand the onslaught of pure light, it began to dissipate, its power waning, its hold on Taion weakening. Finally, with a final, desperate shriek, it vanished, leaving behind only a faint, lingering scent of sulfur.

Taion, weakened but alive, opened his eyes. The room was bathed in a soft, ethereal light as the remnants of the evil that had consumed so many fell to the ground like stardust, the darkness completely vanquished.

He scooped some of the ashes and got up, walking down the hallway to the apothecary. He looked around and found a small vial that he carefully poured the ashes into.

He capped the vial and wrapped cordage around the top, making a necklace that he slipped over his head; a reminder to never let the darkness take over again.

Chapter Forty One

Clan Tempestus;
Castle Dewmire – 5 months later

The air was ripe with anticipation as Aria stood at the castle doors of Dewmire, the massive white stone structure casting long shadows across the manicured lawn. She was dressed in a beautiful gown of dark blue, the skirt overlaid with sparkles that caught the sunlight. A dark cloak with a fur trimmed hood hung on her shoulders, keeping the cool air at bay.

Beside her, Hagen stood tall and imposing with the crown of Clan Bayle on his head, a slight frown creasing his brow. Aria, however, could barely contain her excitement as she danced on the balls of her feet. The bruises that had marred her skin after her escape from Theo had vanished, leaving only mental scars behind.

Unbridled joy danced in her eyes as three figures descended from the sky, their wings, a magnificent display of grey and black, folding as they landed gracefully on the emerald green grass of the castle's front lawn.

"Taion!" Aria squealed, unable to hold back her excitement. With a burst of unrestrained energy, she broke free from Hagen's hand and sprinted towards the tallest of the three, her laughter ringing out as she reached him.

He caught her in a whirlwind embrace, his own laughter echoing hers. They spun in a dizzying waltz, his lips finding hers in a passionate kiss that stole her breath away. His crown fell to the ground, her cloak accompanying it and they laughed as Aria picked it up, placing it back on Taion's dark head. He bent down and carefully slid the cloak around her shoulders, fastening it securely. He gave her a quick kiss again, under the frown of Hagen.

Puck and Atmos, the other two winged figures, exchanged mirthful glances at the scene. They continued their walk towards the castle, their expressions a picture of brotherly amusement.

Inside, Ephyra, her elegant figure draped in a black gown, her purple hair left loose except for a side braid, a small circlet on her head, emerged from the depths of the castle.

She walked up to Atmos and linked her arm through his. She looked up at him and smiled as he uncomfortably shifted in the royal clothing, a small crown on his head.

"I can't believe I let my brother persuade me into wearing this getup." He muttered as he rolled his shoulders against the fabric of the shirt. Ephyra laughed, "But you do look quite delicious, all dressed up..." she ran her other hand down his arm, and he grinned at her.

Together, they strolled down the grand hallway towards the throne room, where the Clan Kings and Queens awaited their arrival.

Puck, ever the whirlwind, raced ahead, pushing the small crown back on his head as it slid, his eyes searching the gathering for his family. He spotted his parents, Sarya and Carwyn, amidst the throng.

Sarya, her face radiating a soft glow of maternal contentment, cradled his half brother in her arms, Carwyn's arm around them. Puck moved towards them, and his eyes landed on Lera standing beside them.

She had acclimated to life by the coast and had started wearing gowns that accentuated her curvaceous beauty. She still kept the feathers and crystals in her hair, a silent expression of her heritage. He leaned down and kissed the top of Lera's head and a whisper in her ear of his love for her.

Orin walked up to them, a smile on his face as his father, Osian, followed. Their relationship had strengthened considerably, and his mother promised to visit as much as she could from the god realm. The past with the Baobhan Sith was finally behind them, a distant memory as the last one had been hunted down by their general, Solana.

Puck and Orin embraced warmly, and Puck couldn't resist asking, "So, how does it feel knowing you're half a god?" Orin grinned, a mischievous glint in his eye. "Just don't try and die anytime soon," he replied, a playful warning laced with affection.

His eyes scanned the room as he watched all of the people he loved, laughing and celebrating. Osian smiled at his son as he threw an arm over his shoulder, pulling him closer.

Osian, noticing his son's gaze lingering on Lera's friend, chuckled warmly. "You're welcome to explore Tir Siorghlas and the realms, son. See what adventures await you, it's a rite of passage for a young elf such as yourself." His words were a gentle nudge, but Orin needed no further encouragement. His eyes had landed again on Lera's friend, Aurae, and quite frankly, nothing else mattered.

She shyly smiled under her lashes, a flush creeping up her cheeks as she was caught staring. Orin, captivated, drank her in – her olive skin, dark green eyes, and flowing brown hair, her figure both graceful and curvaceous. He swallowed hard, his heart pounding a frantic rhythm against his ribs. With a playful laugh, Osian gently pushed him towards her. "Go on, enjoy yourself."

Osian, leaving his son to his fate as he watched him cross the room, walked over to Damien. He crossed his arms, a contented smile gracing his lips. "No matter what has been thrown at us, Damien," he mused, "life... it's still beautiful, isn't it?" Damien smiled and nodded wordlessly as he looked across the room, surveying his friends, his family and his people.

Nearby, Alyndria and Silvan stood with little Erawyn, her blue eyes wide with wonder as she surveyed the opulent surroundings of Dewmire Castle. Alyndria, her voice gentle, soothed the baby in her arms.

Their lives had taken an unexpected turn after the sudden disappearance of their mother in the middle of the night. She had left a note, declaring that she had to go find her mate and couldn't bear to look at the children anymore; their faces were a constant reminder of his abandonment.

Alyndria and Silvan, touched by the children's plight, had stepped in, offering Erawyn and her sister, now named Neia after Silvan's sister, the love and security of a home. Their adoption had just been finalized. Their birth mother and father had never come back. They still had a mystery of finding out about their royal blood and were working with Sarya to detect it.

Silvan looked down at Erawyn who squealed with joy as he lifted her up in his arms. She squeezed his neck and declared, "I love you, amil and amille." Alyndria felt tears shimmer in her eyes as she cupped Erawyn's cheek, "We love you too, little Erawyn, always and forever." Silvan smiled at his new family with so much love. He gently caressed baby Neia's cheek who was sleeping soundly in Alyndria's arms.

Kilyn walked up and gruffly asked Alyndria, "Hand over my niece please. Uncle Kilyn needs some cuddle time." Alyndria laughed as she passed Neia over to him. Kilyn smiled as he looked at her sleeping form, a sigh escaping her little pursed mouth. Nyana walked over from talking with Ilyana and Annika across the room. She cooed as she softly touched Neia's auburn curls. "She's so sweet, Kilyn! Oh, I can't wait."

Kilyn grinned, a slow, contented smile that crinkled the corners of his eyes. He looked at Nyana, his wife and his soul bond, her face glowing with a soft inner light that seemed to have intensified since their hand-fasting. His secret was well and truly out now: Osian and Puck having been beyond shocked when he told them.

She was just beginning to show, the precious life within her a gentle swell beneath the flowing Locryan gown. These island dresses, with their loose, graceful lines, were designed for movement and comfort, and Nyana, ever the dancer, moved with an effortless grace that belied the growing weight beneath her robes.

He remembered the negotiations with her father, a formidable man who had initially been reluctant to give his daughter's hand to a 'pirate from Tir un Uisce'. Kilyn had paid handsomely, of course, for taking her without his permission, but more importantly, he had insisted on a proper hand-fasting ceremony, a union that honored both their traditions. Her father, despite his initial reservations, had eventually relented, witnessing the deep love that bound them.

Now, as he watched Nyana, his heart swelled with a mixture of awe and anticipation. He wondered what their child would look like – would they inherit his dark, windswept hair and the deep emerald hue of his eyes, or would they favor Nyana's delicate features and the sun-kissed sea foam hue of her hair? The possibilities, both exciting and terrifying, danced before him.

The atmosphere in the throne room was a vibrant tapestry of emotions. Laughter mingled with hushed conversations as they watched the children of the Clans – a boisterous, energetic bunch; Gabriel and Ilyana running as Ward, Emery, Aywin and Rina followed – chasing each other through the grand hall, their joyous shrieks echoing through the ancient stone walls. Damien and Annika, their faces creased with smiles, watched the playful scene unfold from their seats by the crackling fireplace.

The entrance of Hagen, accompanied by Taion and the radiant Aria, brought a hush to the room. All eyes turned towards the newcomers as a very pregnant Saphielle walked over to Hagen, threading her arm into his. He looked down at his wife and smiled at her softly as she beamed up at him. They were due any moment and both were eager to welcome their first child.

Saphielle looked over at Aria and Taion, smiling as she took them in, "Who would have known that the journey would have found us here, nésa. You deserve all the happiness that this life and the next can offer."

Aria smiled back and felt tears welling in her eyes. The past was done, it was behind her, and she was free. Free to discover, to explore, to dance, to feel the wind on her face and the grass under her feet... and to love.

She looked up at Taion, his eyes already on her, the iridescent colours dancing as he drank her in.

Taion lifted his head and looked around. Now was as good a time as any. He swallowed hard and readied himself. A wave of anticipation washing over the assembled guests as Taion raised his hand over the crowd, the quiet lending an air of something important to come.

Taion, his gaze fixed on Hagen, cleared his throat, a hint of nervousness in his voice as he looked around the room, noting everyone who was there to witness.

"Hagen," he began as he turned to him and Saphielle, his voice firm yet tinged with emotion as the crowed quieted, "I stand before you today with a request that will forever shape my destiny." He paused, taking a deep breath. "I ask for your blessing, your approval, to make Aria, your sister, my wife and soul bonded partner for the rest of my immortal life."

A collective gasp, followed by a wave of excited murmurs, rippled through the crowd. The children, momentarily distracted from their game of tag, paused, their eyes wide with curiosity.

Hagen, his expression a mixture of pride and amusement, regarded his sister and her chosen mate. He already knew, it was written all over them, their souls glowing when they wear near each other. He looked down at his own soul bond and remembered the first time he had realised that Saphielle was his.

He looked back over at Taion and Aria who were holding hands, expectantly looking at Hagen to speak. Saphielle cleared her throat and bumped her hip to his, "Well, don't make them stand there waitin' too long, my love." She chuckled warmly. Hagen smiled: she was right, he had drawn the moment out long enough.

"Aria," he began, his voice low and resonant, "has always been a whirlwind, a firebrand, a force of nature. But in Taion, she has found her equal, a man who can match her spirit, who can cherish her wild heart, who will protect her with the last breath in his body, which many of us witnessed once already." He turned to Taion, his gaze unwavering. "I give you my blessing, my brother-in-law. May your lives together be filled with joy, laughter, and an enduring love."

The room erupted in cheers. The children, their faces beaming, resumed their playful chase, their laughter mingling with the joyous clamor of the assembled guests. Taion carefully took Aria's hand and slipped on a beautiful ring, the swirls of the gold coming together to gently hold a stunning fiery crystal.

"It reminds me of your eyes, little firecracker." Taion murmured as he leaned down to softly kiss her. She sighed as she felt her heart soar.

Damien, his face alight with a warm smile, stepped forward, extending a hand to Taion.

"Welcome to the fold, Taion," he declared, his voice booming across the room. "The Clans of Tir Siorghlas will always stand beside you, ensuring that trade flows freely between Tenebris and our Clans. Together, we shall forge a future of peace and prosperity. I am sorry it wasn't always that way and I apologize for the hand our ancestors had in that."

Taion swallowed and bowed his head, "Damien, I am sorry that I caused you all upset when I stole the children. I should have realized that you all would have done something had you known. I hope you all will forgive me."

Daimen clasped Taion's hand, their foreheads touching in a gesture of respect and unity. Aria, her eyes sparkling with happiness, watched the exchange, her heart overflowing with love and gratitude.

A servant cleared their throat, and they all turned to look as he bowed and handed Hagen a small wooden box. Hagen nodded and turned to Taion, holding out the box to him as he explained.

"This box has been kept in our castle for, oh, centuries possibly. Since the darkness took over Tenebris. Your mother smuggled it out and gave it to Constance for safekeeping for you. She then handed it to our Clan- being that our power lies in fire. It's time for it to return home."

Taion carefully stepped forward to take the box: his breathing quickening, his heart thudding in his ears as he slowly opened the box. Nestled inside was the dragon egg from his childhood; its blue and purple scales capturing the light in the room.

He looked up quickly at Hagen and Damien, trying to formulate the words that were swirling in his head. He pulled the dragon egg from the box and gently put the box down before standing up, the egg cradled in his arms.

Tears welled in his eyes as he remembered being cradled in his fathers arms, his mother flipping the pages of his beloved childhood book, their laughter as they followed the adventures of the little dragon.

He swallowed thickly and hoarsely whispered, "Thank you. For returning something to me that was so precious to us. Thank you."

Aria rested her hand on Taion's arm, her eyes swimming with tears as she watched his emotional turmoil.

As Taion turned to her, his gaze filled with an intensity that stole her breath away, she knew that this was just the beginning of their extraordinary journey together.

Taion landed softly at the southern entrance of the underground city of Tenebris, carefully putting Aria down, adjusting her cape to ensure she wasn't cold. She laughed and looked up at him from under her lashes. She turned around and held her hand out as they walked together towards the castle.

Their footsteps echoed as they walked through the tunnel into the castle hallway, the packed ground turning to cobblestone. The servants, hearing their arrival excitedly ran to help their Night King and his newly betrothed, who he begrudgingly handed off to them.

Aria waved to him as the servants took her to her new rooms, Taion walked to his, his eyes still on Aria as his footman hovering around him, "Sire, are you ok?" he exclaimed as Taion bumped into the wall. Taion smiled as he watched Aria, answering with only, "She saved me."

What Aria didn't know was that she had saved Taion more than once. Thanks to her outburst Taion had realized the key to fighting and winning over the darkness. He carefully felt the vial under his shirt; he swore to wear it as a constant reminder of that lesson.

As he pulled off his shirt, he flicked his hand as he walked into the grand bathing room, checking the water as he slid into the tub. The ache of the flight disappeared as he dunked his head under the water. He came up and shook his wings off. He'd have to get used to carrying additional weight as they made their visits to the Clans.

Dragging a bar of soap across his body, he touched the spot where the sword had gone through him, tracing the star shape and mused about what the alternative could have been.

As he cleaned himself up, he quickly dressed and exited his room. He walked down the corridor, his footsteps echoing in the hushed silence of the castle. He reached Aria's chambers, his heart pounding a frantic rhythm against his ribs.

Taion smoothed down his tunic, his fingers lingering a moment longer than necessary on the material, a strange sense of anticipation coursing through him. He knocked on the door, his voice a low, husky growl as he said her name.

The door creaked open, revealing Aria standing in the doorway. His breath caught in his throat. Her hair, damp from her bath, clung to her shoulders, framing her face in a halo of moisture. Her dark green gown, thin and clinging, offered little in the way of concealment, revealing the curves of her body in tantalizing detail. He felt a primal urge stir within him, a hunger that had been teasing him since he first set eyes on her.

Aria, her eyes wide with surprise, stared at him, her lips parted slightly. A blush crept up her neck, staining her skin a delicate shade of pink.

For a long moment, they simply stood there, their gazes locked, the air between them thick with unspoken emotions. Finally, Taion cleared his throat, his voice rough with suppressed desire. "Are you... alright? You've settled in ok?" he asked, his voice barely a whisper.

Aria, her voice trembling slightly, nodded. "I am, the room is lovely," she replied, her gaze lingering on his face, on the lingering traces of the battle, the exhaustion etched on his features.

He took a step closer, his eyes drawn to the delicate curve of her neck, the way the light caught the damp strands of her hair. He wanted to touch her, to feel the warmth of her skin beneath his fingertips again.

Aria, sensing the shift in the atmosphere, took a step back, encouraging him to step into the room. The air between them crackled with a potent energy, a mixture of longing and apprehension.

Taion, unable to resist the pull of her gaze, took another step towards her. "Aria," he whispered, his voice husky with desire, "you are more beautiful than any sunrise I have ever witnessed."

Aria, her heart pounding in her chest, felt a shiver run down her spine.

Taion, his eyes darkening with desire, reached out and gently brushed a stray strand of hair from her cheek. His touch sent a jolt of electricity through her, igniting a fire deep within her.

"You have carved your name into my soul, where every breath whispers your name, every heartbeat hums your presence," he continued, his voice a low growl. "I want all of you, your tears, your joy, your fire, your passion. I want to kneel at your feet, worship at your shrine. I will for your entire immortal life, and into the next life as the goddess blesses us. I will follow you, little firecracker."

Aria, her breath catching in her throat, could only nod, her eyes fixed on his. The air between them crackled with unspoken desires, threatening to ignite them both.

With a soft whisper she responded, "I'll never leave you, stargazer."

His eyes widened in surprise at the name, and he took another step closer, the distance between them shrinking. His gaze, intense and searching, roamed over her face, lingering on her lips. Aria, her senses heightened, softly moaned.

Taion leaned closer, his breath fanning against her cheek. "I missed you," he whispered, his voice hoarse with emotion.

Aria, her voice barely a whisper, echoed his words, "I missed you too."

Their gazes met, and they paused, drinking each other's faces in. Finally, he leaned in, his lips brushing against hers in a soft, tentative kiss. Aria, her heart pounding a frantic rhythm against her ribs, responded, her arms instinctively wrapping around his neck.

The kiss deepened as Taion crushed his lips to hers, a passionate dance of lips and tongues, a desperate hunger fueling their embrace. They clung to each other, their bodies pressed together, their souls yearning for the intimacy they had been denied for far too long. In that moment, all their fears, all their doubts, seemed to fade away. There was only him, and her.

Aria felt a surge of warmth spread through her, a feeling she hadn't experienced in what felt like an eternity. Taion tasted of victory, of triumph, of the life they had almost lost. He pulled back slightly, his eyes searching hers, a mixture of longing and possessiveness burning within them.

"You are mine," he whispered, his voice rough with passion.

Aria, her breath catching in her throat, leaned into him, her hands tracing the contours of his face. "And you are mine," she replied, her voice barely a whisper.

He pulled her to him again, his body pressed against hers, a symphony of sensations igniting between them. Their hands moved over each other, exploring, discovering as Taion shut the door behind them, leaving the world behind.

He picked her up and carried her to the bed, gently placing her down as he crawled in with her. He pulled her into his arms as he caressed her hip, trailing his hand down her thigh, pulling her leg over his hip so he could access her.

His hand trailed between her legs and he gently stroked, finding her clit as she arched against him, the sensation sending sparks through her body. She gasped and wrapped her arm around his neck as her eyes fluttered closed, savouring the delicious feeling as his fingers swept against her. He dipped his head down and kissed her neck, trailing his lips down until he reached the swell of her breasts.

He pulled his hand up as she whimpered from the loss of contact and quickly ripped her gown off of her, bending his head down to capture her nipple in his mouth. Aria moaned and pulled his head closer to her, grinding against his hard length in his pants.

He licked her nipple and teased it with his teeth, grazing gently as she whimpered against him. He ran his hand down again, teasing her clit with his fingers, and as he pressed between her folds, she gasped, his fingers slowly sliding into her wetness.

"You have too many clothes on." She gasped as she reached down to press her palm against his length straining against his pants. He chuckled and continued to slide his fingers in and out of her, his mouth trailing back up her neck as he captured her lips with his again.

He kissed her like she was the last breath of air before drowning, desperate and all-consuming, the missing piece of his soul, finally finding its rightful home. He carefully pulled his fingers out and pulled his pants off, tossing them to the floor as he pulled her hips towards him again.

As his length pressed against Aria, she broke the kiss and looked down. A smile crossed her face as she reached down, circling her hand around his cock. She slowly stroked and felt him tense against her.

He groaned as he closed his eyes, the feeling of her small hand around his cock, stroking, squeezing, was enough to make him want to bend her over and take her. But he would do it slow, let her set the pace.

Her eyes watched his face as he opened his and looked at her. His iridescent eyes swirled, the blues and purples coalescing as she stroked him. Carefully, reverently, he pushed back her hair from her face with his finger, trailing it down her neck as her eyes fluttered closed.

He bent down again, his lips against hers as he gently pulled her hand away from him. He held his cock and carefully pressed it against her entrance, watching her face as he slowly thrust into her. Aria moaned against his lips, her body tightening around him as he filled her.

They lay together for a moment, Taion not moving as he kissed Aria, their tongues clashing as she dragged her nails down his chest. He chuckled lowly as he felt her hips starting to move against him, mewling from the feeling of fullness from him.

He started to thrust slowly again, and their kissing intensified as Aria ran her hands into his hair, finding his scalp. She grabbed tightly as he ran his hand up her back, holding her close to him as he continued his slow movements, his cock sliding in and out of her in a delicious pace that had Taion clenching his jaw. She felt so good.

Aria suddenly pulled away and looked at Taion, her pupils blown, her golden eyes reaching a hue of orange that made her look like a fire goddess.

"Taion, please, take me. Make me yours." She pleaded. Taion smiled and whispered, "As you command." He rolled over and loomed over Aria as she looked up at him. His wings flared out as he thrust into her, over and over again. She cried out, her hands holding onto his hips as he drove into her. She wrapped her legs around his hips, and he bent down to whisper,

"I want to hear you say my name as you come around my cock, little firecracker."

Aria came undone. She arched her back as the wave of her orgasm slammed into her. He continued to thrust into her, his lips on her neck, her breasts, his hands teasing her while he stroked her. She felt herself tightening all over again as she gasped, "Taion, my gods."

Her nails dug into his shoulders as another wave crashed into her. He couldn't take it any longer, his thrusts erratic as he felt a wave crash into him, pulling them both under.

They fell asleep in each other's arms, Aria cradled against his large frame, his wing covering her. She was where she belonged. The moonlight filtering through the bedroom window cast a silvery glow on Aria's face, her brow furrowed slightly in sleep.

Taion, his gaze fixed on her, felt a wave of protectiveness wash over him, so profound it took his breath away. He traced the delicate lines of her jaw, the curve of her cheek, each touch sending a jolt of tenderness through him.

He would do anything for her.

The thought filled him with peace. He would face any danger, conquer any obstacle, shatter any enemy that dared to threaten her. He would bathe in the blood of her enemies, be her protector, her unwavering anchor in the storms of their life together.

He leaned down, his lips brushing against her hair, inhaling the sweet scent of cedarwood that clung to her. In that moment, a vow was made, silent yet unbreakable. He would love her, cherish her, and protect her with every fiber of his being, forever.

Taion walked into the throne room, cleaned up with his hair tied back and his wings tucked behind him. On his head sat the crown that his father had worn. The court bowed as he walked through them and turned to sit on the throne.

He stood however as Aria entered the room. His eyes lit up as their eyes connected and she bowed slightly towards him. The court parted, their eyes on the new woman walking towards their King. Her gown shimmered in the torch light, sparkling against the soft purple fabric she had chosen. On her head, sat the dark crown that his mother had worn. The crystals shimmered like pure starlight as they caught the light. Nestled in the dark metal they were the perfect balance.

Taion took her hand and turned her to his court.

"Please bow to Princess Aria, my betrothed and soul bond." The court broke out in cheers and applause; Taion and Aria smiling at each other, love brimming in both of their eyes. Tenebris would indeed be ushered into a shining new era.

The dragon egg sat between the two thrones, its blue-purple scales glimmering in the torchlight, back in its rightful place.

Macha and Aine stood in the crowd, disguised as part of the court of Tenebris. Aine jumped with joy, her eyes alight with happiness as she clapped with the crowd. Macha grinned and pulled her sister down, "Shush, we're supposed to blend in!" Aine leaned over and kissed her sister on the cheek and Macha scoffed.

"I knew they were your favourite too."

CLAN AETHER (STARS)

Towering above all other Clans in both stature and power, this Clan stands as the guardians of harmony. These High Elves, with their flowing hair and eyes that mirror their powers, possess an unmatched connection to all four elements - fire, water, earth, and air.

Their magick flows with the currents of nature, allowing them to wield devastating attacks or nurture life with equal ease. Each Clan Elf harnesses an element, and their features allude to their power. This Clan resides to the east of Tir Siorghlas where the sun meets the horizon.

Osian, being the eldest of the children, claimed the throne after his parents stepped down. His brother, Damien, had left the Clan centuries ago to be placed on the throne of Clan Tempestus.

Osian's love of all beasts in Tir Siorghlas shows with his beautiful large heard of unicorns that roam free across the Clan lands.

His kind and caring nature pushed him to agree to a truce with the Baobhan Sith when they arrived back to Tir Siorghlas, giving them a section of the dark woods as a sanctuary. Amodra, one of the Baobhan Sith, and Osian's wife, negotiated the treaty to keep her mates safe.

CLAN TEMPESTUS (WATER)

Located centrally in Tir Siorghlas, they are the weavers of spells, the protectors who rely on intricate enchantments and wards to safeguard their people and their realm. Their power stems from the deep connection they share with the spirits of the forest and the rivers, drawing upon ancient pacts and whispered secrets passed down through generations of powerful elders.

Elder elves that live in Asthemar, the Clan's capital city, possess an unparalleled understanding of ancient Elven magick, crafting spells that could heal the wounded, bind malevolent forces, or create intricate illusions.

King Damien claimed the throne at a young age, coming from Clan Aether. His betrothed, Annika, having been taken away from the realm to keep her magick safe from the clutches of Blackwood, left a throne empty.

Annika reappeared through a memory portal once she was old enough that she could enter the fight against Blackwood. It also enabled her to harness her unique, amazing power, the nightingale song, a gift from her parents ancestors: an elven king with wind magic and a powerful witch queen from the circle of Mystics.

Annika claimed her ancestral throne with her husband by her side once she regained her magick and her memories. Together they destroyed the darkness that Blackwood worshipped, removing him and the blight from Tir Siorghlas, and saving her brother, Callum, at the same time.

Callum recovered and under the care of Morena, a witch from the Silverbark Coven, was able to move forward and create a life once the evil was removed from his soul. They moved to Riverstone, accepting the lands' offering to be stewards, protecting everything inside their borders.

CLAN BASALT (EARTH)

Rooted on the shores in the west of Tir Siorghlas, these stoic warriors' very essence is intertwined with the earth itself. These elves, their skin the color of sun-baked clay and eyes smoldering like molten golden rock, possess an unparalleled mastery over the earth element.

With a flick of their wrists, they can summon tremors that crack the very ground, erupt towering walls of stone to shield their allies, or unleash devastating avalanches to crush their foes. This Clan is a force of raw, unyielding power. Their warriors are renowned for their impenetrable defenses and earth-shaking strikes, forming an immovable bulwark against any who threaten their domain.

The King and Queen of Clan Basalt had two children-twins-however, Carwyn had no idea that he had an older sibling until the secret was discovered by his wife, Sarya, and her son, Puck. Centuries of hiding away their eldest twin son, Gaeleath, resulted in their deaths and almost tore apart the royal family. Gaeleath chose to end the blood pact against his own child that his father had agreed to.

Having no interest in claiming the throne, he passed it over to Carwyn. Gaeleath lives in the Silver Lands with the circle of Mystics with his wife and daughter.

CLAN EMPEREAL (AIR)

Located in the high north-west of Tir Siorghlas, this Clan carves their legacy amongst the swirling clouds and mountains. These elves, tanned with eyes the color of a summer sky and feathers woven into their auburn braids, possess an unmatched dominion over the very air itself.

With a mere thought, they can summon powerful gusts that send enemies reeling, create invisible currents to propel themselves across vast distances, or whip up tornadoes that tear through the battlefield. Their mastery of the air extends beyond mere manipulation; they share an unparalleled bond with winged creatures.

Falconry is not just a hobby for the Clan, but an extension of themselves. Their trained falcons, swift and deadly, serve as their scouts, messengers, and even aerial warriors. Additionally, they are unmatched archers, their arrows tipped with enchanted fletching that sing through the air, guided by the very winds they command. Their prowess in the sky and with the bow makes them a formidable aerial force, unmatched in their swiftness and lethality.

Silvan, having taken the throne from his parents, was gifted not only the ability to control air but also water, an ancestral tie from his mother's family, distantly related to Clan Tempestus.

His love of his Clan is shown with his kindness, his determination to protect all innocent life at all costs. This was a downfall for him at one point when his old love, Elara, appeared back into his life.

A struggle with his morals and values lead him to realize that he could answer the heart bond call from Elara; however, it was too late. Elara was taken by the Nightsinger and the darkness and used as a vessel to attack Tir Siorghlas.

Silvan had to walk away from Elara, leaving her with her bonded dragon in the Night Realm, binding her soul to the mountains, forever captive.

Years later, Silvan encountered a fierce woman demanding he release his claim to Riverstone lands; the lands that belonged to his sister who had passed. He fell in love and married Alyndria, claiming her as the Queen of Clan Empereal, ruling fairly and justly beside him.

CLAN BAYLE (FIRE)

Located in the south of Tir Siorghlas, the Clan pulses with a vibrancy that mirrors their fiery magick. These elves, their hair the color of embers and eyes that shimmer like molten gold, possess an innate connection to the element of fire.

They move with a dancer's agility, their bodies as limber and quick as flames. Their magick crackles at their fingertips, allowing them to forge searing blades of pure fire, unleash waves of heat that could melt stone, or cloak themselves in a protective inferno that deterred even the most determined attacker.

Clan Bayle elves wield fire with finesse and precision. They are masters of both devastation and creation, using their flames to forge weapons and armor, illuminate the darkest night, or even perform intricate rituals that soothe the savage heart of a wildfire.

Hagen and Aria are the two children of the loving King Cohnal and Queen Salihn. The siblings are on opposite sides of their views on love, Hagen avoiding his mother and her wish for him to marry, Aria having hearts in her eyes when any elven males approached her.

Hagen had committed that he would never marry; that was until he locked eyes with Saphielle, a feisty and stubborn female from Efrana, in Bloodrose lands. He had tried to ignore the soul bond that had hit him, reminding himself that they hated each other. Now, years later, she is his sun and moon, his reason for living and he would destroy anyone who dared look at her wrong.

Aria, a young elven woman, was swept off her feet during her debutante year and fell in love with Theo, a royal elf from a distant island that she had never heard of. Even though her parents cautioned her against moving too quickly, she chose to marry Theo without the proper protocols of researching his family line. Theo successfully achieved his wish of becoming a prince of the Clan and ensured that Aria was a slave to him, muting her fire magick and her spirit.

Marriage contracts are not breakable in this realm; the only way to get out of them is death.

HOUSE BLOODROSE

Secluded in the east, House Bloodrose rules their domain with a focus on knowledge and diplomacy. Lord Thelian, short and stout, was known for his battle knowledge and hunger for power. Thelian defected to support Blackwood during a period due to arguments with Tir Siorghlas' rulers, capturing Lady Elara as his indentured and bound servant to try and pull her magick to use with Blackwood. When his plan failed, he retreated further into his mansion, defeated.

While he disappeared from his lands, the city of Efrana bustled, creating a seedy underbelly of slave trading. Saphielle was one such slave, unsure of her past and who she was. One day she decided she had enough and bought her freedom, running away from Efrana, determined to find out who she belonged to. As she stepped into the city of Oblor, she bumped into Prince Hagen.

HOUSE BLACKWOOD

Located in the west, Lord Blackwood hungered for power with an insatiable greed. Fueled by whispers of ancient prophecies and dark magick, he and his brother Corvus, a shadow sorcerer with a repertoire of forbidden spells, had tasted a sliver of this power years ago. It was then their ambition turned into an obsession centered on the Elven and Witch bloodline in Clan Tempestus and the obsession to control a legendary power that the legends had spoken of: the nightingale's song.

After an epic battle against Queen Annika and King Damien, Lord Blackwood and his brother were both destroyed. The Blackwood lands have been left untouched since then.

HOUSE STONECASTLE- RIVERSTONE

Located in the southernmost tip of Tir Siorghlas, Riverstone is veiled by a perpetual mist that clings to the verdant valleys. Steeped in a sad history, the imposing fortress had once stood shrouded in an unsettling silence. Banners laid in tatters, and the very stones seemed to weep with a sorrow that hung heavy in the air. Lord Ryul and Lady Neia, respected leaders, had vanished from sight, their laughter and music replaced by an eerie silence. Whispers had claimed their withdrawal was a consequence of the tragedy that befell them - the abduction of their newborn daughter, at the hands of House Blackwood. Unable to bear the pain, they retreated into the deepest recesses of their domain, their fate a mystery.

Years later, their daughter, Saphielle, was found by Prince Hagen. Once their daughter was safe, Lady Neia disappeared into the night and Ryul was beheaded for his infractions against the crown for siding with the darkness to sell his daughter off to fulfill a prophecy.

Alyndria of Clan Nibi stepped forward to claim the title of Lady of Riverstone- if only for a short while. The land once again was covered in darkness in the way of shapeshifters, determined to take over Tir Siorgh-las. It was only through Alyndria sacrificing herself that the land was taken back. Alyndria realized that the land truly never belonged to her, and she gave it willingly to Prince Callum and Lady Morena.

HOUSE WILLOWGREEN

Located in the Silver Lands, Willowgreen is a manor imbued with both magick and a touch of defiance. Lord Lucius and Lady Starla, formidable witches, resided there.

Their loyalty lay not with the Clans or the Witches, but with their own brand of magick and the secrets it held. House Willowgreen fell years past due to Lucius' obsession with gaining Queen Annika's magic after Blackwood had failed.

The battle was brutal and swift, many fatalities were tallied, and the land was left to heal itself with no lord looking over it, both Lucius and Starla dead.

CIRCLE OF MYSTICS

Hidden in the north of The Silver Lands, steeped in forgotten lore and wielders of magick that predated even the Elven Clans, lives the Circle of Mystics.

Their power was woven from the very fabric of reality; they could manipulate time itself, slowing its relentless march or even peering into the future's swirling mists. Their connection to the spirit world runs deep, allowing them to commune with ancient entities and harness otherworldly energies.

They are the keepers of balance, the guardians of arcane secrets, and a legacy whispered with reverence and a hint of fear throughout the lands.

Annika's mother, Queen Aurora, hailed from the Circle of Mystics, as did Constance.

Gaeleath found his way back to his wife and daughter, witches of the circle of Mystics when the blood pact his father had created was removed; this secured the safety of his daughter- the firstborn grand-child of the Solterra line.

THE SILVERBARK COVEN

A beautiful space within the Whisperwoods was home to the Silverbark Coven, a medium group of witches with varying talents. They worked closely with Clan Tenebris in creating spells for portals and the likes.

Constance, the matron of the coven was a witch with ties to the Clan of Mystics, having come down from the Silver Lands to follow her Queen, Aurora who married King Alwyn of Clan Tempestus. She was instru-mental in saving young Annika from the clutches of Blackwood, ensuring that she was sent away to the earth realm, her powers spell-bound and her memory shuttered.

Constance also was Tir Siorghlas' most fierce protector, ensuring the balance of light and dark. However, that protective work caused her to be taken by the grey death.

Constance had one daughter- Sarya- the light of her life. Sarya grew up following her mother's footsteps, destined to one day take the title of coven matron.

Sarya's son, Puck, was born after she had been held captive by Blackwood and his soldiers. Being saved by Carwyn let her believe in love again.

Destroyed by the evil darkness that consumed Elara, the Silverbark Coven perished under horrific circumstances; their witches were murdered in cold blood as Sarya escaped with her son and Morena. The Whisperwoods never recovered from the carnage that occurred in the heart of the forest; a lone Stikini was left to guard the entrance for the prophecy to be.

THE NIGHT REALM

An eternal twilight shrouds the Night Realm, an inky canvas painted with the faintest whisper of stars even though it is tucked under the Craggy Mountains. Jagged obsidian mountains pierce the gloom, their peaks clawed by storm clouds.

Here, in soaring fortresses carved from the very rock, reside Nephilim warriors cloaked in midnight armor and blessed with raven wings that unfurl like living shadows. They patrol the skies with unwavering vigilance, ever watchful for any who dare attempt to breach their borders.

The city, known as Tenebris, was ruled by a kind and fair Night Prince and Princess, until the evil darkness took over, destroying everything they held dear and setting its sights on Tir Siorghlas and her Clans.

As a final hope to fight the darkness back one day, the Princess gave her son, their heir, to the Silverbark coven along with the last dragon egg, to keep safe until the time would come again for the child to take the throne back.

However, those were ages past, a dark age shattered by the Kings who toppled the Night Prince's reign, leaving the throne empty. Now, Tenebris waits, watching for the rightful heir of the throne to return.

CLAN NIBI

Located in Tir an Uisce, Clan Nibi are a Clan of seafaring elves, their skin a rich bronze hue beneath the sun and moon. Their eyes, a vibrant emerald green, hold the mysteries of the ocean depths. Masters of harnessing the power of water, they weave the water into intricate patterns, calming the tempest or raising tidal waves and use it as their magick.

Their ships, sleek and swift, are as much a part of them as their own limbs. They chart the uncharted, mapping the hidden currents and secret coves. In the harsh winter months, they return to their coastal haven, using the treasures of the sea - pearls, coral, seaweed - to craft tools and enchantments.

Their bond with the ocean is profound, and their magick, born from this connection, is both awe-inspiring and formidable.

Alyndria's family are distant relatives to Lord Ryul; when he fell, the title of Lady of Riverstone fell to her. After a battle against the shapeshifters and darkness, Alyndria lost her life battling to save the land. Silvan bartered with Death to bring her back, ensuring that he would not lose his soul bonded mate.

After speaking with the land, Alyndria realized that she was only needed to help save it from the evil; the land was calling for another couple to be the stewards: Callum and Morena.

She gave her claim up and moved to Clan Empereal with her love, Silvan, to rule together.

Kilyn, the youngest child of the two, moved quickly as a sailor, buying his own ship and crew, giving him the title of captain at an age where most elven males were still under their parents' thumb. Kilyn sailed the oceans, procuring riches and trading where he could. His water magick giving him unparalleled success against the weather.

LOCRYA

East of Tir Siorghlas, the island Locrya sprawls like a jewel-encrusted tapestry, its vibrant hues a siren's call to those seeking fortune and fame.

Here, amidst the forests and beautiful coast, dwell a diverse array of elves and beings, each drawn by the promise of riches and fame. Locrya has become one of the grandest hubs of trade in the known realms thanks to a few merchant pirate ships, Frig's and Kilyn's being two of them.

The city of Mistshore, nestled on the coast, serves as the heart of Locrya; wares are traded daily as ships come and go. Its markets, a kaleidoscope of sights and sounds, overflow with treasures from every corner of the world. Silks from the far East shimmer beside dwarven steel, while exotic spices perfume the air with their heady aroma, sold by shrewd-eyed half-merfolk.

Mistshore's streets, paved with smoothed river rock, wind through districts that cater to every taste and desire. The Merchant's Quarter, a labyrinth of stalls and shops, echo with the haggling of traders and the clink of Locryan coins. The Pleasure District, a riot of color and music, beckons with promises of indulgence and escape.

Mistshore is home to many wealthy merchants; their lineage matters not here.

This is the history of Réimse an Tsolas
as it has been written and remembered.

ACKNOWLEDGMENTS

Now onto the important parts:

Thank you, Taanishi!

My soulmate, my heart bond, my MMC cinnamon roll. I love you. More than I can sometimes explain in words. Our journey has somehow made its way into my books and I am so blessed that my soul found yours.

My children and family; I am so blessed to have you all. I hope that you look up and realize that magic is all around you, not just in the stories that are written.

My besties: Katie & Pam. You ladies mean so much to me. Thank you for being always so excited for my books, for gabbing with me as I hyper fixated and for just being the amazing strong women you are. I am blessed to have you in my circle.

To all of my kind and helpful beta readers: Katie, Marci, Bobbi, Ellie, Saga, Lauren, Amanda. Without you all, I don't think this book would have become as amazing as it did. Thank you to your suggestions and all of the comments! I enjoyed kicking my heels with joy each time you all came to a part in the story that had you screaming.

To my ARC team: I adore you all. What a wonderful group of humans I have been fortunate to find in this journey.

Michelle: for the amazing formatting. I am in love with the work that you do to make these books so beautiful.

Gabriela: your images of Taion, Aria & the winged warriors absolutely blew me away and elevated how special this book was to me. Thank you.

To everyone on social media that I have ever crossed paths with in writing my books: thank you. For the help, inspiration, and cheerleading you did. It means more than you'll ever know!

To my following author friends who I have had the absolute pleasure to get to know on this journey:

B. Mackenzie
David White
C.F. Folan
A.H. King
L.R. Powell

To my readers: I absolutely wish I could hug each and every one of you- to thank you for taking a leap of faith in an indie author, for supporting my journey and for coming along for the ride.

I want to also, lastly take a moment to say a small blessing for those who I had the honour of loving who have left for their next journey. Dad, Madeline (Doodah) You both blessed me with love and support. Your teachings and encouragement meant so much, and we miss you both. How blessed were we to have known your love.

Maarsii